# BLACK LIGHT: RESCUED

## LIVIA GRANT

e-Book ISBN: 978-1-947559-91-2

Print ISBN: 978-1-947559-98-1

❀ Created with Vellum

# BLACK LIGHT: RESCUED

By

Livia Grant

# PROLOGUE

*Valentine's Day – Washington, D.C. – Black Light Club*

KHLOE FELL onto her knees to steady herself before lunging forward to suck his wet cock into her mouth. For the first time in a long time, Ryder was truly caught off guard. He was no longer in control, and it rocked his world. The submissive in front of him got bolder, reaching around to grab his ass with both hands to help leverage her rocking up and down on his rod.

With each thrust, she took him deeper until she was gagging on almost every insertion. Still, she didn't back down. It was when she returned her gaze to his from her knees, pausing with his manhood obscenely filling her wide mouth and throat that he had to reach out and steady himself with the tiled wall. He could swear the naughty submissive at his feet had tried to smile around his cock as she'd recognized her effect on him.

"Christ, Khloe, baby. You feel so warm and wet." When he was close to spurting, he knew he needed to take back control. Ryder released the wall, wrapping his fingers through her wet mane to grab her in a headlock. He held her stationary and took over, thrusting his erection down her throat again and again until she sputtered. He watched her eyes carefully, knowing when she was panicking and needing air. He gave her a hit of oxygen, enough to take the edge off and then resumed his face-fucking of the gorgeous woman at his feet.

He squirted the first shot of cum down her throat, holding them together until the second spurt filled her mouth and then finally pulling out to let her gasp while he deposited the rest of his load onto her chest. Each of them took deep breaths after their impromptu exertion. He could see the exhaustion returning to Khloe as she came down from the high their scene had given her.

Ryder held out his hand and helped her to her feet. He pushed down the regret of their night coming to an end.

Only after she was on her feet, she pulled her hand from his and took a step back, defiance in her eyes once more.

"You know everything about me, but I know nothing about you except your name. It's not fair."

He couldn't help but smile at her petulant tantrum. "Careful, Princess. I'd hate to end the night with you over my knee for your sass."

She took it as a dare. "Fuck you. I'm not leaving until you tell me something. And not some bullshit. Something real." She folded her arms across her chest for good measure.

"Baby, every minute of tonight, you had the real me."

She didn't back down. "At least tell me where you live. What you do for a living."

"Why, so you can schedule a visit? It doesn't work like that with me, Princess."

"So how does it work? You fuck strangers, spend the night doing all kinds of intimate things with them and then you walk away, never to see each other again?" Tears floated in her eyes.

He saw her struggle with her feelings. "Khloe, you've had an emotional night. You need a good night's rest."

"Bullshit. I need you to level with me. Was tonight just a game? Something you do with a different woman every week?"

Her inquisition pissed him off. This, right here, was why the Moscow subs were perfect for him. Not one of them expected anything emotional from him. He didn't have room for emotional attachments in his life. The worst part was that tonight he was already having to push down his own crazy inclination to drive her back to her hotel, and spend the next three days holed up, fucking like rabbits. He didn't need her tempting him further.

He hardened his heart, knowing tonight was all they were meant to have. She had her glamorous, very public life to return to–and Ryder, well he had to stay in the shadows. He couldn't afford to be splashed all over newspapers and social media as the mysterious man in Khloe Monroe's life. He took a deep breath and said the words he needed to say, "Tonight was a game, Khloe. A game called Valentine Roulette. I'm sorry if you thought it was something more than that. Don't get me wrong. I had an amazing time, and I'll admit I hate to say goodbye too, but we each need to go our own way, baby. I don't have the kind of life you would fit into."

His words hurt her. For once, the sadist in him hated to see the pain cross her face. He wanted to reach out and hold her to him and take back his harsh words, but he was too disciplined for that. He allowed himself one weakness. He leaned down, capturing her lips in a farewell kiss. He still felt the incredible electricity coursing between them. He luxuriated in sliding his tongue into her mouth, tasting the toothpaste she'd used minutes before as they'd cleaned up together.

In the end, Khloe was stronger than him. He felt her hands on his chest before she yanked back, pushing him away so hard he almost fell backwards.

Christ, she was amazing. Not a stitch of makeup. Her hair still wet, hanging down the back of the oversized robe. Yet she was the most beautiful woman he'd ever seen. She reached up to touch her swollen lips as a tear spilled down her cheek. When he reached out to swipe it away, she flinched away from him.

She fought for control of her voice, quietly whispering, "Good-bye, Ryder."

# CHAPTER 1

*F*uck it was cold for April. Ryder pulled the wool collar of his coat up around his neck in an attempt to block out the frigid Moscow night. It didn't help that his ride was thirty minutes late.

*I hate waiting.*

The extra time spent milling about in the parking lot of the all-night sex club only jacked up his already frayed nerves. If he thought it would help relieve his stress, he'd head inside to warm up with a double shot followed by a hard ride on a nameless whore who wouldn't mind him banging out his frustrations on her already bruised body.

Unfortunately, the booze would dull his reactions and he needed to stay sharp if he had a hope of getting out of his next meeting alive. Ryder Helms was not an alarmist. He'd honed his nerves of steel in dozens of close calls over the years. The fact that he was nervous was a sign of how fucked up his current mission had turned. If it weren't for the fact that he'd spent years building his badass reputation with the Volkov Bratva, he'd pull out of tonight's meeting. But when Viktor Volkov wants to do business, you show up to the meet or you have a hit on your head the next day.

A drunk couple ambled out the side door of the club. They barely stayed on their feet as they slipped on the perpetual sheet of ice that might melt by June if the weather held. He allowed himself to be distracted by the perfect curves of the woman in the skin-tight dress. Her waist-length sandy-blonde hair was pulled up in a high ponytail and from the back, she reminded him of...

*Fuck. Get the hell out of my head. I'm on the job.*

The flashbacks were coming more frequently now, and he seriously needed to get them under control before he got himself dead. There was no room in his life for softness. Life was too hard for that. Memories of a princess who'd been his for three short hours pierced his thoughts when he least wanted them. If he thought it would rid himself of the memories, he would gladly bang every woman in the city to work Khloe Monroe out of his system, but he'd already tried that tactic and knew it wasn't going to work like that—at least not this time.

As much as he dreaded the upcoming meeting, he was relieved when he saw the high-end Ferrari with the neon racing lights on the undercarriage rounding the corner at too high of a speed. It screeched to a halt in front of Ryder.

Everyone drove like shit in Moscow, but it was always a toss up if the Bratva's henchmen or Alexi Ivanov's driving would kill him first. Hoping this wouldn't be his last ride, Ryder opened the door and slid into the heated leather seat. He hadn't even got the door closed yet when Alexi floored it, slipping on a patch of ice in the street, ass end of the sports car slip-sliding several dozen feet before he got it under control. Alexi managed to flick the ashes of his almost spent cigarette into the too-full ashtray even while wrangling the vehicle.

"You're a fucking lunatic, the way you drive, you know that?" Ryder accused.

Alexi grinned, obviously proud that he could get a rise out of the normally unflappable man sitting in the passenger seat. To Alexi, he was Nicolai Romanovski, arms dealer and all-round bad-ass who'd somehow managed to break into the inner circle of one of the world's most sophisticated crime families. He didn't want to think about the fucked up tests he'd had to pass to prove his loyalty to the family.

He needed to get his head in the game. Slipping into his deep-cover persona, Ryder conversed with the closest thing he had to a friend in Moscow in his flawless Russian, accent and all.

"You're late," he accused in Russian.

"Sasha came home drunk after work." Alexi grinned before adding a sly, "I needed to take care of her."

Ryder grunted, "Yeah, I bet you did."

Alexi took another drag on his cancer stick before flipping the butt out the cracked window. "You're just jealous. You haven't had a nice piece of ass like Sasha in months."

Ryder had met Sasha and didn't know what was more surprising. That she was Alexi's gold-standard in women or that a few months ago, he might have agreed with him. The scale of which every woman he'd ever meet for the rest of his life would be measured and forever be skewed by one A-list actress named Khloe Monroe.

She'd ruined him.

When he didn't rise to Alexi's bait, the driver added, "And anyway, I'll make up time on the drive out to Barvikha."

Yet another reason for Ryder to be on edge. The meeting location had changed, and he didn't like it. He had access to additional friendly assets in the city if he ran into trouble. He also had hidden weapons and ammo in the Bratva's compound in town.

He lost access to all of those benefits with the location change of tonight's meeting. He'd been to the luxurious estate in the upscale suburb several times, but had never been able to fortify his position on his visits. He was going in cold. No wire. No backup. Not even a real grasp of why the family had called the last minute emergency meeting.

He needed information.

"So what's this get-together about anyway?" he prodded, hoping to get Alexi talking.

Alexi was already lighting his next cigarette, filling the small interior with stagnant puffs of smoke before answering. "I'm not sure."

Ryder knew him well. He was lying.

*Interrogation time.*

"Viktor better not pressure me for another load of SVK semi-automatics. I told him I won't be able to get another batch for at least six weeks." Ryder left out the critical information that it would take his CIA handlers that long to locate the weapons and put the undetectable tracers inside them so the US could keep track of them wherever they ended up around the globe. The last load had already led Navy SEALS to two previously unknown terrorist hideouts. Remembering the good that came out of his sanctioned crime was the only thing that helped him sleep at night.

Alexi waited until he'd navigated a tight turn in the road to answer. "Naw, I think he has a favor to ask of you."

"A favor? Fuck." The last favor Viktor had asked of him had ended with him getting shot.

"Da. Artel called me himself."

*Double fuck.*

The aging Viktor might be the head of the family, but his oldest son, Artel, was one ruthless sonofabitch. If he was involved, the favor would be costly for Ryder. Not financially, but to his soul. He'd already done unspeakable crimes against humanity in the name of the greater good, but the tests were getting harder–taking a bigger toll on his body and his character.

Maybe his boss, Webster, had been right. Maybe it was time for him to retire before he got himself dead.

*And maybe you should get your head out of your ass and into the game, Helms.*

He was surprised when Alexi offered up more information. "He told me the family had made their move." At Ryder's sideways glance in his direction, the Russian added, "Something about going on offense."

Ryder nodded a stiff acknowledgment of the comment as Alexi reached out to turn on the radio, filling the car with a pulsating song that sufficiently covered the thump of Ryder's pounding heart. He'd had a bad feeling about the meeting before, but now every ounce of his fiber knew he was walking into a trap. He hadn't been a deep cover CIA agent for over thirteen years by ignoring his gut. Sometimes his gut was the only thing that got him home at the end of the day.

Maybe he should go on a little offense himself.

As the ass-end of the car spun out of control banking around a pin-turn corner in the dark road, he spoke louder to be heard over the loud song. "Remind me again why I couldn't just drive myself to the meet? You're gonna kill me before I even get to the compound."

Alexi grinned, openly showing his pleasure that his driving was bothering his passenger.

"They limit access in and out. That piece of shit you drive isn't authorized for entrance."

Ryder scoffed at having his high-end Mercedes-Benz referred to as a piece of shit. It was one of his favorite perks of his job.

"I get the need for security, but shouldn't they trust me by now?"

He was fishing. Alexi was a bad actor. If the family suspected Nicolai was anything but what he portrayed of himself, Alexi wouldn't be able to keep that to himself. His lack of concern was comforting.

"What's your last name again?" his friend inquired. When

Ryder sat silently, he added, "Unless it's Volkov, you aren't part of the family."

He pushed on that point for a bit. "That's bullshit. You've been in the family your whole life."

"My mother was a Volkov but she married outside of the Bratva. That makes me a second-class member. I'll know I'm really in when they ask me to change my name to Volkov."

Ryder didn't argue because he knew his friend was right.

Alexi was just slowing down as they approached the outskirts of the upscale suburb when the song on the radio abruptly ended. A radio announcer broke in to the programming with a breaking story.

Ryder only believed about half of what he heard coming out of the government controlled public broadcasting station, but his ears pricked just the same. A big part of his job on the ground in Moscow was relaying news being reported locally to his handlers back in Langley, whether it was true or not.

"The prominent businessman's family was kidnapped outside of the ballet studio as they exited. Dead on the scene was one armed guard they'd hired as protection while in Russia. Mr. Marshall is offering the generous reward of three million rubles for information that leads to the safe return of his family. Anyone with information is asked to contact 112."

Marshall. That name sounded familiar. An American?

He didn't have time to worry about that poor bastard's problems. He had his own to worry about. He needed to pay attention as they wound through the labyrinth of streets, always plotting out an escape route.

As they approached the fortified iron driveway gates of the Volkov estate, Ryder fought the urge to open the car door and disappear into the night. Every alarm bell he'd honed in his years of active duty was sounding, but he pushed the snooze button, silencing them. No way, he couldn't wimp out. He'd invested too many years in his cover to walk away now.

He pushed his apprehension down to greet the approaching armed guard, pressing the button to lower the window. The music had returned and was playing loud enough that it made it hard to hear.

"Nicolai, you here to try to win back some of the money you lost last time?" The burly guard's fierce appearance softened as he cracked a sly smile.

Ryder relaxed slightly. In his recent paranoia, he'd halfway been expecting to be treated like the spy he was when he arrived. That the guards were so casual helped him take a deep breath. "Don't forget I've come out ahead every other time we've played. I just felt sorry for your ass last time. It won't happen again," he countered.

The guard, Ivan, barked a laugh, the semi-automatic rifle he had slung over his shoulder coming into view to remind Ryder this was not a friend. Ivan remembered as well, getting serious and delivering his instructions. "No weapons allowed in the house tonight. I won't insult you by disarming you now, but I warn you. Leave your weapons in this piece of shit car Alexi insists on driving before going inside."

Alexi leaned over to shout out the window, "Jealous?"

While the two men exchanged barbs, Ryder thought through the odds of being caught carrying in his hidden stash of weapons. There was no way he was going in completely unarmed, but he just didn't know how much risk he should take.

Mature trees, bare from the hard winter, lined the long driveway leading to the main house of the estate. Old-fashioned lamp posts were spread out every twenty-five feet, lending light to the dark night. To an uneducated tourist, the property looked like the upscale mansion of a reputable businessman, but locals called the property очистительный which loosely translated to *purgatory*; the place people came to be judged. Only it wasn't God who did the judging here. It was Viktor Volkov or one of his three sons who decided who lived and who disappeared forever.

Alexi drove around the mammoth circle drive, pulling into a parking spot to the right of the grand steps leading to the double front doors. Silence greeted them as he turned off the roaring engine. A dusting of snow fell from the sky, blanketing the ground. For a brief moment, all was peaceful, but Ryder reminded himself this was just the calm before the storm.

Making a show of removing the Glock weapon he wore in his shoulder holster, Ryder leaned down to place it on the floor near his feet. He knew from experience they were already on surveillance cameras. Every inch of the property, save the Volkov personal bedrooms, was taped at all times. If security didn't see your actions in real time, they could go back and review any footage later. It was just one of the reasons Ryder hated meetings here.

He was already on the stage. Not for the first time he thought about how ironic it was that some of the world's best actors never got recognition for their talent. Unlike Khloe Monroe, his only reward for a job well done was living to see another day.

It was a hell of an incentive.

The massive door opened just as their shoes hit the top step. The regal doorman, Yurdin, had greeted him each time he'd visited, no matter what the time of day.

"Mr. Ivanov. Mr. Romanovski. We've been expecting you. Please follow me." The butler bowed slightly, letting them stomp the excess snow from their shoes before closing the door and moving in the direction of the grand staircase.

Ryder wasn't surprised they were heading down to the base-ment conclave. It was a mammoth man cave on steroids. If it wasn't for the fact that he'd personally witnessed two murders there in his limited visits, it was the kind of room he could get down with spending quality time in.

The only women allowed were whores there for eye candy and sexual favors when the men wanted to take a break from their world domination planning. It wasn't that he was opposed to working off a few calories banging a submissive who liked it rough. What bothered him was that not once had he seen the same woman there twice. His sixth sense told him women were brought there to serve until they wore out their welcome. That was when they'd be carried out in a body bag and the next shift would arrive.

Dead bodies couldn't testify in court.

His foot had just hit the first step down when he heard his name being called from the stairs above him.

"Nicolai! I've been waiting for you, darling."

Ryder hesitated long enough that Alexi crashed into his back from behind. His friend spoke softly, "Keep going. You're just asking for trouble if you let her catch up to you."

He couldn't agree more. He resumed his walk to the basement, but Yurdin kept his stately speed allowing one of the ladies of the house to catch up to them just as they hit the landing at the bottom of the steps.

Irena Volkov was as beautiful as she was tragic. Ryder knew the second they'd met she was trouble. Ignored by her powerful husband, Vladimir, she made it a point to flirt with every man who crossed paths with her. At first he'd thought it was because she was lonely, but having watched more than one man be beaten for looking at Vlad's wife the wrong way, Ryder had come to realize her flirting was her sick way of goading her neglectful husband into proving he still cared about her in his own sick way.

She'd flung her arms around Ryder's neck and was leaning in for a kiss by the time he reacted, grabbing her forearms and pushing her away from him just as the steel doors on the other side of the basement foyer opened. Vladimir Volkov himself stood in the doorway, watching his wife as she pouted at Nicolai's fast rebuff. Her husband was at her back, so she had no idea that he was watching as she lunged forward again, grabbing onto Ryder harder than before.

The men's eyes met, and for several seconds, Ryder wondered

if he'd even make it past the foyer tonight, especially when Irena started kissing his neck. "I've waited for you to return, Nicolai."

He saw a split-second of pain in the Russian's eyes just before it was replaced with slow-burning anger. To his relief, it was the arms dealer's wife who received the furious look from her husband.

Ryder pulled her arms away again, and this time as he pushed her away from him, she fell against the hard chest of her husband, who caught and squeezed her until it looked like he'd cut off her ability to breathe. Vlad leaned down to speak softly into his wife's ear. Ryder, being only feet away, heard his threat.

"I see you're bothering another one of our guests, *malysh*. I believe I was very clear the last time we *discussed* this, was I not?" Ryder watched as the powerful man crushed his wife in a bear hug. Only when she'd started to turn pale did he release her, shoving her hard and fast, her knees crashing into the marble tile beneath their feet. As she fell forward on all-fours gasping for air, Vlad yanked her head up by her flowing black hair, and as soon as her beautiful, tear-stained face was visible, he backhanded her across her cheek with such force that her neck made a cracking noise as she was tossed across the foyer, slamming into the far wall.

All four men in the foyer stood silently, listening to the woman's pitiful cries for several long seconds. Regardless that he'd done nothing to encourage Irena's attention, Ryder half expected Vlad's fists to seek him out next. He prepared for a fight. After all, that was how things worked with the family. He was surprised when Vlad smiled apologetically.

"Seems I have a bit more training to do with that one. It's a good thing she's beautiful and a good fuck or she'd be too much trouble."

Ryder played it cool. "Yeah, well, I'm guessing her training will be fun. There's nothing quite like delivering a well deserved punishment."

14

He played to his host's known proclivities with his comment, knowing they both enjoyed playing at the darker end of the sexual continuum. Still, as he glanced back at the crying woman who was trying to get her nose to stop bleeding, Ryder conceded Vlad wasn't a dominant. He was an abuser.

"You gentlemen head on in. Father is sitting down to a late dinner. He asked that you join him. I'll finish dealing with my errant wife and then I'll join you."

Ryder avoided looking back at the broken woman huddled on the floor. There was nothing he could do to help her, even if he'd wanted to. She'd chosen to marry into the Volkov family two years before. There was no way she hadn't known what she'd signed up for before walking down the aisle with the youngest, most handsome son of Viktor Volkov.

Irena's scream was the last thing he heard before the heavy steel doors slammed closed behind them.

"Shit, that was close. I expected Vlad to castrate you back there."

Alexi patted him on his back in a universal 'atta boy sign. Ryder didn't waste time celebrating the small win. He was too busy planning his escape route should their meeting go south to comment.

Six. That was how many of Volkov's armed henchmen were in the conclave, although four of them were busy being entertained by the whores of the week. As he cased the joint, Ryder found he was surrounded by debauchery. One blowjob, well closer to a fast face fuck, was in progress on the pool table. The restrained, naked woman's head fell over the edge of the table at dick level. The guard's cock choked her as he thrust balls deep over and over until she passed out.

Alexi pulled him to a stop to admire the naked submissive spread out like a smorgasbord for the taking in the middle of the room. She was strapped to a leather spanking bench, situated with her ass high in the air. She wore a spreader gag, holding her mouth open wide for use. It was easy to see both of her other holes had recently been ridden hard as she was still stretched wide, jets of white cum across the welts on her bare back and legs.

The fact that his own cock rose to the occasion reminded Ryder he wasn't that different from the aggressive men in the room. Only a thin line of veiled consent separated his submissives from the unfortunate women who'd found themselves as the main course at their last sex party. He pushed women hard, too. To the edge. It was a rare woman who could handle his unleashed libido.

Yet Khloe Monroe had handled it perfectly.

Ryder physically shook his head to chase the unwanted memories out of his system. He didn't want to think about how perfect she'd been on a good day, let alone here tonight when he needed to stay focused on the job. Her frequent appearances in his thoughts were pissing him off. He was nothing if not disciplined, and quite frankly, the fact that the remarkable actress popped into his head so frequently, shook him to his core. He needed to get a handle on himself before he fucked up years of work.

"I could sure use a drink before we meet with Viktor," he suggested, heading in the direction of the fully stocked bar not far from the pool table. Alexi didn't complain about the detour.

A scantily clad woman greeted them with a nod as he approached. She was gagged, unable to speak. As he sat on a high barstool, he could see she was tethered to the bar with only enough length of chain to allow her to get to the supplies she needed to make his martini. As she turned to grab the vodka, the jeweled end of her butt-plug peeked out from between her raw ass cheeks. Lines of fresh welts crisscrossed with older bruises, revealed she'd been serving the Volkovs at least long enough to acquire layers of punishment marks.

Knowing they couldn't delay, both Alexi and Ryder downed their drinks in a gulp before pushing away from the bar to head in the direction of the double-doors at the far end of the room. As he walked, he let the hot liquid snake through his veins, helping to take off the nervous edge that would get him killed. A tattooed goon who looked like he could start on the defensive line of a professional football team stood guard; his semi-automatic Uzi prominently displayed as they approached.

*Another layer between me and a fast exit.*

The men halted, unable to pass when the guard made no motion to step aside.

"No weapons allowed into the dining room." He met Ryder's cool gaze. "That includes your hidden knife, Mr. Romanovski."

Ryder kept his face a blank expression as he quickly assessed his options; admit he had brought a weapon in against the original instructions or deny packing and risk a pat down that would have the guard finding not one but all three of his secreted threats.

He went with his gut, reaching down to his left pants leg, lifting the fabric to reveal the hunting knife strapped to his shin. He handed it over to the guard without apology, ignoring the smirk on the man's face at thinking he'd outsmarted the guest to the estate. Little did the asshole know, Ryder still had a Ruger .38 Special and syringe full of poison hidden away.

He normally would have been asked to forfeit his cell phone to avoid allowing recording devices into the heart of the conclave, but Ryder knew from past visits that the room he was about to enter had thick walls and electronic blocking equipment ensuring no recordings could be made of the events occurring inside. The Bratva conducted the most secretive business between the four medieval inspired walls of the *krepost* or fortress.

A mammoth table took up the center of the immense room. With seating for twenty, it was the perfect location for doing the dirtiest of deals. Chairs for support personnel lined the wall closest to the door while the shorter walls at the ends of the long table held counters full of expensive food and drink to be served to the family and their guests. Still, there was room left to fit additional tables in the room should the occasion call for it.

It was the far wall that was difficult to ignore for any warm-blooded dominant. Punishment and torture devices hung from dozens of hooks, leaving room for the small platform in the center of the wall where a whipping post and stockade stood prominently. The platform had been empty the last two times he'd visited, but today an unfortunate submissive hung limply from the hook high above her outstretched arms. It was easy to see the unyielding whipping post she was attached to had done its job well as the entire back of her body, from shoulders to calves, was a crisscross pattern of raised welts left from what looked like a heavy duty bullwhip. Droplets of blood pooled in about a half-dozen spots where the whip had dug too deep.

This was no playful BDSM scene. The moaning young woman had been whipped brutally and then left on display for the dominant men as if she were a decorative table centerpiece. Ryder wasn't playing with any typical crime family. The Volkov Bratva had worked hard to earn the ruthless reputation they now enjoyed, reminding him he had to be half-crazy to keep coming back for more after all of the shit he'd already been through for this assignment.

"Nicolai, welcome! It's good to see you back in town after your trip away." The family patriarch himself stood to greet him, approaching as Ryder had stood frozen near the door to observe the unfortunate woman on display.

Ryder turned in time to greet the elderly man with the customary welcome of affection reserved only for his inner circle, double-kisses on the cheeks. It had always felt odd that a man of such violence still chose to observe the old-European tradition.

Viktor turned his attention to the cries of the bleeding victim in the room, tsking his disapproval. "Such a shame to have to mark such beauty. I'm sorry you missed observing her lesson, but her discipline session couldn't wait." He continued on, answering Ryder's unspoken question. "The little bitch is a spy for the Linenkos. Artel found out she's Ivan's illegitimate daughter."

The dangerous Moscow families were the equivalent of the Hatfields and McCoys in America. If it were true, it had been a suicide mission for her to try to gain access to the enemy's lair. Despite her still being alive, Ryder suspected the Volkovs would be sending her back to her father in a body bag as a nice 'fuck you' message.

"Not very smart, are they?" Ryder quipped.

Viktor barked a laugh. "Never have been. They'll learn eventually."

"Yes, sir. I bet they will," he agreed with his host.

"Sit. Eat. The lobster is fabulous. We had it flown in, of course."

Ryder and Alexi each took an empty seat a few chairs down from the host, careful to leave room for the two missing Volkov brothers to sit next to their father. The middle son, Oleg, was already seated on the other side of the table, enjoying his meal. He didn't bother standing to greet the newest arrivals, making it clear he didn't feel they were worthy of the effort.

Oleg was the brother Ryder had the least interaction with. Each of Viktor's sons was the brigadier or head of a different family specialty. Nicolai worked with the youngest, Vladimir, most often as he was the head of the arms and weapons wing of the family. Oleg led the trafficking of all types of illegal drugs.

But it was Artel who was the most dangerous of the three men. The eldest Volkov, who would one day inherit the helm of the family when his father died, was the most ruthless of all the rest combined. Dealing in human trafficking, slavery, prostitution and assassinations, Artel was responsible for the disappearance or death of more people annually than ISIS and Al-Qaeda combined. The only thing that kept the western world from knocking at the front door of the mansion was that the majority of those impacted happened to also be enemies of the USA and her allies. Instead of bombs or tanks, the US instead sent in men like Ryder to keep tabs on the family's dealings. He was only authorized to intervene when absolutely required.

Once he was seated, he realized he had an unfortunately unobstructed view of the suffering woman. She would most likely be dead before he left the mansion. Not for the first time, his gut clenched at the thought of walking out of a meeting like this, unable to help some unfortunate victim who had inadvertently been stupid enough to get caught up in the danger of associating with the crime family. Unfortunately for her, his mission had a higher purpose and would protect hundreds if not thousands of innocent people with the intel he gathered from the inner sanctuary of the Bratva.

At Viktor's nod, a previously unseen serving girl dressed only in a jeweled waist chain with matching nipple rings, pushed from her knees to her feet in the far corner of the room, crossing to the buffet. She filled two plates with the gourmet food and then turned to deliver them to the two newest guests at the table. She returned minutes later with a bottle of the expensive champagne the family drank like water.

Only once she had returned to her kneeling position, head down and palms up on her spread thighs, did the elder Volkov speak between bites.

"I'm pleased you've joined us tonight, Nicolai. I was bothered by news of your injury a few months ago while doing business for the family." The elder man hesitated as if he were choosing his words carefully. "I sent Artel to make sure you were receiving only the best medical care, but he found you'd left the hospital without warning. No one knew where you'd gone." At this pause he stared at Nicolai with an unreadable expression that had Ryder's pulse spiking. "It was a bit alarming when we couldn't find a trace of you for several weeks. We're..." he smiled indulgently before finishing his thought. "We're relieved to see you return to us alive and well after your mysterious disappearance."

Ryder controlled his breathing, staying calm through sheer will. He'd expected the question and was ready. "I'm sorry if my convalescence caused you any concern, *Pakhan*." He was careful to use the proper term of respect for the head of the family. "As soon as I was well enough to travel, I called in a favor from an old friend in Poland. He was able to transport me to a trusted hideout I've used when such unwelcome *accidents* occur. I appreciate your consideration, but as you can see, I was well cared for." He took a casual bite of the lobster dripping in butter and then cut into the thick steak on his plate.

"Vladimir was especially glad you returned and with the double order of the always welcome SVKs. Still... your absence is concerning."

Oleg finally looked in his direction from across the table. Ryder felt the weight of their combined mistrust and knew he was at a dangerous juncture. "My apologies for not checking in once I'd recovered sufficiently, but in order to keep the family safe, I had installed an auto-destroy feature on my cell phone so no unwanted attention could come your way should someone find it if I was incapacitated. Without your private numbers, I didn't know of a safe way to contact you without drawing possible attention to the family by whomever it was who had tried to kill me."

Ryder held the gaze of the older man, refusing to be intimidated, as most men would be when lying through their teeth to the devil. Thirty seconds later, Viktor Volkov broke into a broad grin, apparently satisfied with his explanation.

"Very wise, Nicolai. I only wish all of our *shestyorka* showed the same resourcefulness in adversity." The elder man took another bite before he continued on. "It makes me pleased that Artel chose you to handle one of the family's most important missions we've had in a long time."

Ryder had been expecting them to ask a favor since Alexi's hint on the drive. Still, his heart rate spiked higher knowing any important task the family asked him to complete would be dangerous, not to mention it was most likely a renewed test of his loyalty after his unexplained disappearance and sudden reappearance.

"I'm honored to receive your trust, *Pakhan*. I look forward to being of service to the family again," he replied respectfully.

"There are few I would trust with this task. I warn you. It's not without danger, but we can no longer allow the westerners to steal from us and from right in our own homeland. Every year they grow bolder and gain more influence. We've tried to solve the problem through negotiations, but the time for talk is over."

Ryder's curiosity was piqued at the word 'westerners'. The delicious food he'd eaten was settling in his gut like a heavy rock. He tried not to let his imagination run away from him before he got facts, yet his sixth sense told him his night was about to go to shit.

He didn't have long to wait. It wasn't the sound of the door opening behind his back, but rather the smothered screams of women that announced the arrival of additional *guests*. The thought of watching another innocent woman being whipped while he munched on caviar as if he hadn't a care in the world turned his stomach.

Yet the look of hatred mingled with joyous revenge in his host's eyes was the first clue they'd been joined by someone more important than another prostitute brought in for their perverted entertainment. With dread, Ryder pushed back from the table, turning his body until he could look behind him to the group now standing between the table and door.

Only years of experience kept him from blowing his cover in those first critical seconds. He felt the glare of the Volkov men on him, rather than the spectacle Artel and Vladimir had dragged into the room. If this was another sick test of his loyalty, Ryder had to admit, it was ingenious. His face may have frozen with feigned indifference, but his brain was racing to compile all viable options at his disposal, weighing the odds of getting out of the house alive and with his soul intact.

*I'm fucked. I should have stayed in D.C.*

Even as he thought it, he knew he didn't mean it. He was needed here. *Now.*

Viktor Volkov threw his cloth napkin on the table next to his now empty plate, pushing back from the table far enough that he could cross his right leg over his left, casually relaxing as he observed the newest arrivals.

He grinned victoriously as he switched to heavily accented English. "Welcome to my home, Mrs. Marshall. I've been awaiting the arrival of you and your daughters with great anticipation."

In a moment of clarity, Ryder recognized that the makings of the next World War stood in the room. Kidnapping the wife of a wealthy foreign businessman was risky, even for the most powerful Bratva in the country. That she was clearly American only made it worse.

But it was the frightened young daughters–*children*–that would find the Bratva condemned and hunted for their foolish risk should their involvement ever be traced back to them. The girls couldn't be more than ten and twelve. Clearly underage and clearly off-limits in any ethics manual, including that of crime families. Kidnapping or hurting children was a declaration of war and put the Volkovs squarely in Ryder's crosshairs.

Artel had hold of the youngest girl, but her sobbing clearly annoyed him. He thrust the frightened child into the arms of one of his henchmen just before barking his twisted orders.

"It's time to take a few farewell photos to send off to Daddy." As if the kids and their mother weren't scared enough, he taunted them. "I'm going to make sure he'll have nightmares of watching his family slaughtered each time he closes his eyes for the rest of his life."

Ryder was relieved at the order. It solidified his decision.

*I'm so fucked.*

# CHAPTER 2

"*I* need a few minutes. You go ahead. I'll meet you at the limo." Khloe turned her back on the room full of anxious people waiting on her. She carefully took a sip of her chamomile tea, praying not to spill it down the front of her Versace gown.

Her agent, Bernie Kaplan, complained for the umpteenth time. "We don't have a few minutes, Khloe. We should already be pulling up in front of the theater."

She was well aware of that. She didn't need anyone telling her the importance of tonight's event. It was a day she'd dreamed of since she was a little girl growing up in the Bronx, not more than thirty minutes away from her Time's Square hotel.

She caught a glimpse of herself in the full-length mirror. A small chuckle escaped as she compared her reflection to Cinderella. Despite working her ass off for years, self-doubt nipped at her, leaving her feeling like a fraud. A nobody, all dressed up, pretending to be someone important. The worst part was she had to fight down the panic that, like the Disney heroine, the clock would strike at midnight and everything she'd worked so hard for would be taken away. The more success she achieved, the more she lived in fear she'd wake up one morning and realize it had all been an elusive dream.

No, she wasn't ready to leave yet. It was either give the calming tea time to settle her upset tummy or risk losing the small snack of crackers she'd choked down when she got on the red carpet in front of dozens of reporters and paparazzi.

Khloe was used to being hungry, but even she suspected she'd been taking her starvation routine too far the last few months.

The clapping of Ricky's hands startled her. "Alright, everyone. Time to head down to the carport. We have two limos there waiting to take us all over to the theater. Everyone go ahead. Ms. Monroe and I will be right behind you."

She welcomed the mild chaos her personal assistant's announcement caused. The commotion was better than having a room full of people awkwardly standing around waiting for her to puke.

Luckily, the majority of the crew mingling in her seven-thousand-dollar-a-night suite at The Plaza were more than ready to head over to the grand theater in Lincoln Park to get the release party started. Khloe watched her makeup artist, hairdresser, personal shopper, and the assistant the studio had sent over shuffle out the door without a backward glance. Unfortunately, they weren't the people she was hoping would leave first.

Bernie and Natalie Kaplan, her agent and publicist, otherwise known as the dynamic duo of the entertainment industry, stood grounded, arms crossed, permanent scowls on their faces. In their fifties, they had helped launch many A-lister's careers during their illustrious time in Hollywood. They were amazing at their jobs. The problem was they knew it. As much as a pain in her ass as they were, Khloe knew they had helped her land the lead in *Dirty Business* and for that she was grateful.

Ricky, her diligent personal assistant, did his best to try to encourage the Kaplans to leave, but she knew it was futile.

"It's okay, Ricky. We can head out now. I'm feeling better."

*Liar.*

Her personal bodyguard, Trevor, approached, a faux fur wrap across his tree-trunk-like forearm, hidden under his stylish tuxedo. "You'll need this. The temp has dropped by at least ten degrees since we got here a few hours ago." He helped drape the garment around her shoulders in time to hide her shiver. She wasn't even outside yet.

As her entourage made their way to the elevator that would take them to the grand lobby, Khloe gave herself a pep talk.

Today should be one of the best days of her life. She'd reached a major milestone in her career. Tonight the world would celebrate the long awaited film—her first lead in a major box-office film. The fact that critics were raving about the film, and it hadn't even opened yet, was a real coup. The studio was spending millions on marketing. Tonight was the first of four red-carpet release parties scheduled over the next three weeks across the globe. Next up would be Hollywood, Washington D.C., and finally London.

The ding of the elevator had her putting on her final accessory for her outfit. Her public smile.

"Khloe!" The screams of her name came from several directions the second she stepped into the lobby. She was grateful for Trevor's steadying hand on her elbow as he stayed close enough to help clear a path through the throng of fans that had somehow discovered what hotel she was staying at. The flash of cameras was blinding. She felt hands daring to grope her. While her brain knew they didn't mean any harm, it always unnerved her.

She had never been the beauty queen in the parade, but she'd perfected her public wave nonetheless. A small part of her reveled in the attention. She'd been chasing fame for years after all, so it felt wrong to reject the outcome now after working so hard to get here, yet she couldn't shake the feeling as they finally pushed through the revolving door, Trevor jammed into the same small wedge as her, that there had to be more to fame than this.

A hotel doorman greeted them with an umbrella as they were spit out of the revolving door into the carport where her limo waited. The hotel had put up stanchions to hold the fans back. It didn't stop several teenage men from hopping the red-velvet rope to get closer to their wet-dream.

"Stand back, boys," Trevor admonished, keeping himself between her and the aggressive fans.

"We love you, Khloe! Give us one picture! Please!" The tallest of the three begged.

She wasn't sure why she stopped, but she did. She patted Trevor's arm as if to say 'it's okay' and stepped around him to approach her brave fans. Pimpled faces broke into lopsided grins as she greeted them.

"Hi, boys. I have time for a quick photo."

The shortest of the three looked like he might faint while the one closest to her held out a selfie-stick. She stepped closer to sandwich in for the photo she knew would be on Facebook and Instagram in thirty seconds, trying to ignore the grope against her lower back as the flash went off.

It took another minute to close the last few feet to the waiting car as she stopped to sign autographs for more fans lining the path until she finally arrived at the door being held for her by yet another doorman.

Only when the door closed and she was alone—or as alone as a celebrity got with her entourage along—did she let her public smile slip away.

"What the fuck was that, Khloe? I thought we agreed no mingling with unvetted crowds," Trevor admonished her.

Her publicist answered for her. "Hey, if you can't handle a little mingling with the public, you're in the wrong job. Her fans love her. She needs to be open to them and accessible to remain likable."

Her brand. Natalie was talking about her brand.

Trevor didn't back down. "That's your job. Mine is keeping her safe. Need I remind you all that she got another threatening email less than twenty-four hours ago?"

Khloe's stomach lurched at his reminder, although in truth, she never really forgot about the threats.

Bernie defended his wife, not his client. "Oh, come on. Every celebrity worth anything gets threats like that. Being in the public eye brings out the kooks. She wouldn't be succeeding if she didn't get threats. Most of them are harmless."

"Which implies a few of them aren't," Trevor shouted back.

"Guys, stop," Khloe interjected with as much force as she could muster with her tight gown cutting off her circulation. "I have enough shit on my mind right now. I don't need to add you two arguing to it."

The inside of the luxury car fell silent as her driver, Johnson, wove through the heavy Thursday evening traffic on the way down Broadway to the theater. She used the time to take calming breaths while looking at the crowds of mostly tourists. She needed to get into the right frame of mind for the eight interviews they had lined up waiting for her and for the photo shoot on the red carpet with her co-stars from the film, most whom she hadn't seen in the many months since the filming had completed.

She'd had to call in a few favors, but she'd insisted that her leading man be excluded from tonight's gala event. She wouldn't be as lucky the next week in Hollywood, but at least she'd have one night without having to pretend. No, she'd have to lie.

*Good thing I'm an actress. That's the only way I'll get through the next few weeks.*

She'd, of course, been to many movie release screenings in her career, but a zing of excitement coursed through her when, in spite of the rain, she saw the huge throng of fans filling the sidewalk in front of the Lincoln Square theater. Only then did she realize an insecure sliver inside of her had been worried. Like the kid who threw the birthday party that no one showed up to, she'd worried she would arrive to an empty theater. She let relief course through her.

Her relief was short lived.

Trevor got out first, and she waited for him to turn and offer his assistance. Only after a ten second delay, a different hand waved in front of her. A hand she recognized. The Piaget watch he loved giving him away.

Khloe shrunk back, refusing to take the upturned palm as she turned to question the Kaplans. "What is he doing here? We agreed he'd skip New York, but we'd both open Hollywood."

Natalie's reply was unwavering. "Mr. Reynold's manager and I agreed it would be a missed opportunity to have him skip tonight's grand opening."

"A missed opportunity!" Her voice was almost a shout. "For who? You? Don't forget who you work for, Natalie." The older woman's eyes widened. Her shock with Khloe's uncharacteristic anger registering.

Bernie showed where his loyalty lay. "And don't forget who the experts are at turning wannabes into superstars. You need to learn to trust us and say thank you." His threat was clear. She either put up with their heavy-handed shit or they'd cut her loose as a client.

*FML*

"Hi there, sweetheart. I'm getting wet out here. You ready to hit the carpet?"

Her cheating ex-boyfriend, Dean Reynolds, had dared to lean into the back of the limo. His handsome face was mere inches from Khloe. Her right palm itched to slap the arrogant smile off his mug.

"Don't you dare call me sweetheart."

His smile never wavered as he countered, "For the next few weeks, I'll call you whatever I need to to keep our adoring public thinking we're still a hot item. The producers demanded we hold off announcing our breakup until after the movie is out, so that's what we'll do."

Khloe hated the helpless feeling that washed over her. She was Khloe Fucking Monroe. She was supposed to have power now, yet she seemed to surround herself with people determined to ignore her wishes. She felt trapped.

She *was* trapped.

Fans screamed her name not far away. Flashes of cameras reminded her they were already on stage. It didn't matter that Dean had blindsided her with his appearance. For a moment, she remembered how he'd looked the last time she'd seen him. Naked. His cock pounding the married pussy of their good friend, Gloria Mining, as the older woman hung suspended from a hook in Khloe's own bedroom.

That she had to reach and place her small hand into his and let him help her out of the limo like the gentleman he pretended to be, galled her. That she had to plaster on her public smile as he placed his hand intimately–possessively–at the small of her back as they moved down the red carpet, infuriated her. But when he pulled her close to plant a wet kiss on her for the line of reporters waiting like vultures, she wanted to throw up.

But she didn't.

She smiled. She waved. She put on her celebrity-diva-smile and tried not to let Dean's presence ruin this special night for her. Like the actors they were, they each played their newest role. Star-crossed lovers.

And they did it well.

They moved from one media booth to the next in the grand lobby of the theater, answering interview questions. Posing for pictures. Flirting and kissing like the lovers they no longer were. By the time they made their way to the VIP seats inside the theater, even she'd begun to forget they'd broken up. That's why the sudden appearance of Gloria Mining and her husband sitting in the seats directly next to theirs figuratively knocked her on her ass.

Khloe stood grounded as their friends stood to greet them.

Daniel Mining hugged her, placing small kisses on both of her cheeks. "You look ravishing, Khloe. It's so good to see you again. I hated that you got called out of town and missed the opening of the play on Broadway in February."

She almost missed his words, too distracted by watching Gloria and Dean embracing intimately right behind him. Their bold display nauseated her. It was a slap in the face to both her and Daniel. Righteous anger consumed her at their audacity of flaunting their affair in front of hundreds of fans, the media and even Gloria's spouse. As Khloe looked up at Gloria's director husband, ready to fill him in on all he'd been missing, she knew immediately she was the one out of the loop. The raw sexual hunger on his face as he leaned down to whisper in her ear had her wobbly on her feet.

"Gloria and I are hoping to celebrate your and Dean's success a bit more privately tonight. The three of us are already checked into the suite down the hall from yours at The Plaza. We had a key made for you. Be sure to go to the ladies' room to powder your nose with Gloria. She'll fill you in."

Khloe would have toppled over if he hadn't hugged her closer. The price for his chivalry was feeling his erection poking her tummy. Their eyes met again. This time she saw amusement. Her shock was funny to him. It made her want to lift her leg to knee him in the balls.

That would knock the fucking smile off his face.

The next two hours moved by in a blur. It was surreal watching the movie she'd worked so hard on over the previous two years play on the big screen. The finished product was even better than she could have ever dreamed. Normally critical of her own performances, she lost herself in the drama. When the final credits rolled and the theater lights came up, for the first time in her career, she felt like she deserved the standing ovation she was receiving.

All eyes in the theater were on her and Dean. He was terrible boyfriend material, but he was a very talented artist, and like it or not, they would forever be linked by their partnership on this film. She hated to admit it, but the producers had been right. He deserved to be here as much as she did.

The party was really starting as they returned to the grand foyer. She excused herself from Dean, anxious to be away from him, if only for a bit.

Tables of food and drinks lined the walls. Her stomach growled loudly as the heavenly aromas of the room reached her. She'd barely eaten in days, yet as much as she'd love to splurge tonight, the thought of having to squeeze into the already fitted gowns for the next three release parties kept her from partaking in the heavy filet mignon being carved closest to her. She instead made her way to the dessert table to grab a plate of small pastries.

She'd splurge.

"Khloe! I've been waiting for you. I brought a chocolate éclair just for you. I know you don't like the calories, but since it's your favorite dessert in the whole wide world, I knew you'd want one."

Several seconds ticked by while her brain tried to comprehend why the man dressed in a waiter's outfit looked familiar. "Peter? What are you doing here?"

The gangly young man with unfortunate pockmarks and an active patch of acne on his receding forehead beamed that she'd remembered him. "I wouldn't miss tonight. The studio hired me to help serve refreshments."

It seemed odd they would spend money flying a coffee runner across the country for a one-night event, but he'd told her once he was the nephew of a studio bigwig. She suspected he had a learning disability based on his awkward social skills, but he was a nice enough guy who kept her flush in hot coffee while on set.

"Thanks so much. That's very thoughtful." Khloe reached out to take the offered dessert that had more calories than an entire day's allotment. "Everyone will be jealous that I'm the only one who will get one."

Several fans pressed into her personal space, wanting their time with a celebrity. She could see disappointment in his eyes at being pushed aside so quickly. She sent him an apologetic look. "See you later, Peter."

Within minutes, dozens of well-wishers surrounded her, anxious to take her picture with them or get her autograph. By the time the crowd was starting to thin out, she was exhausted. Only then did she look down at the small plate of desserts and realize she'd only taken a few bites. Guilt gnawed at her. Yet the hunger had begun to feel like her old, dark friend, seducing her back into an almost anorexic existence. She was skating close to the edge of her safe zone, flirting with a darkness she'd thought she'd kicked years ago.

Strong arms enveloped her from behind, hugging her back tight against a masculine, hard chest. "I've missed you, baby. You almost ready to head back to the hotel?"

Dean made sure to grind his hips forward enough to demonstrate that his appendage had indeed missed her. Instead of turning her on, Khloe fought the urge to laugh. So much had changed since the last time she'd slept with Dean. They'd never been in love, but they'd had an amicable romance. But that had been before his cheating with Gloria. And before...

Christ, memories of the most sexual night of her life slammed into her, drawing a full body tremble that a conceited Dean took as a green-light from her to slip a hand higher, brushing her breast in a brave display in the middle of the grand foyer. Of course he had no way of knowing that the woman he held in his arms had slipped into her favorite pastime–dreaming of a sex-god named Ryder Helms.

Ryder had begun to feel like a mirage to her. A figment of her imagination. Or maybe an actor who'd had too small of a role in her life before being written out of the script. That a man she'd only known for three hours of her life could consume her thoughts at a moment's notice frankly had begun to piss her off.

Khloe used her confusing anger to wrench herself out of Dean's arms. She turned on him, prepared to tell him exactly what she thought about his offer when she caught sight of cameras pointed in their direction. Instead, she leaned in close, giving the illusion of intimacy as she replied, "Tonight changes nothing, Dean. We're done. I'll play my part in front of the cameras, but you're nuts if you think I'm going back to the hotel with you."

He didn't seem surprised. "Oh, come on. I'm only talking about having a little fun. Don't be such a prude. Gloria and Daniel are coming over. You'll have a good time. I promise."

Considering she hadn't had sex since Valentine's Day, she had to admit she was briefly tempted, but in the end, she knew she'd just end up disappointed with Dean's watered down version of intimacy. She'd caught a glimpse of the real thing with Ryder, and she was certain Dean Reynolds would be a poor substitute. The problem was, Ryder was a figment of her imagination and she didn't have the first damn clue how to go about finding him or even another man like him. Unexpected tears pricked her eyes at the reminder of her loss.

The room was suddenly too warm. Too closed in. She needed to get out of there. She'd stayed long enough.

Khloe yanked herself out of Dean's clutches, searching the room frantically for Trevor. Or Ricky. Hell, she'd even take the Kaplans, but she couldn't spy any of them. She reached for her small purse and pulled out her phone, texting Johnson and asking him to bring her car around before shooting off a text to Trevor to meet her at the door with her fur shawl.

Dean shouted after her as she turned to leave. He pulled her to a stop long enough to thrust a magnetic keycard into her hand before leaning in to whisper in her ear, "Don't be like this, Khloe. I promise. I'll make it good for you. Room 1232. We'll be waiting for you, baby."

Their eyes met long enough for her to see his smug confidence. It didn't dawn on him that she'd refuse their offer for a debauched night of swinging. Memories of another debauched night in her life were crowding in fast. She needed to be alone. She could feel a familiar tug of temptation. Of loneliness.

She was relieved to see Trevor waiting for her near the door. She was stopped a few times by well-wishers, but finally reached him just as she looked out the glass doors to see Johnson pulling up in front of the theater. It was raining harder now and he exited the driver's seat to hold open the back door, an umbrella held high meant to protect her and her gown from getting drenched.

She and Trevor made a dash from under the awning of the theater, diving into the back seat as quickly as possible. She didn't truly relax until the limo was in motion. Khloe collapsed against the rich leather seat, exhausted. Keeping up her public facade was work on a normal day. Dealing with being the center of attention and Dean's unexpected appearance had taken every ounce of her mental tenacity. She was grateful that both Trevor and Johnson had been with her long enough to understand she needed the silence of the car in that moment more than anything else.

She was starting to feel more like herself as they pulled up into the carport of The Plaza. When the doorman opened the door next to her, she froze.

"Come on, Khloe. Let's get you upstairs."

"No," she countered. "I want to go home."

Trevor tried to reason with her. "We've already paid for the suite through tomorrow, you know. And all of your stuff is still upstairs."

"I don't care. I want to sleep in my own bed tonight. You can come back over and pick up my stuff tomorrow."

She kept her face as passive as possible. She didn't want to share her main reason for wanting to go home was because she didn't trust herself not to use the electronic keycard still clutched in her palm. She knew she would hate herself if she let her loneliness and hunger for intimacy drive her to suite 1232. She'd never find those things there. She'd only find a shallow replica, and she wasn't willing to put herself through that disappointment.

Trevor had waited, hoping she'd change her mind. When he accepted she wouldn't, he pulled the door closed and Johnson took off, pointing the limo in the direction of her apartment in Chelsea, less than fifteen minutes away.

Raindrops streaked down the window, taunting her. Tonight was supposed to be one of the best nights of her life, and in some ways, it had been. So why was it getting harder to repress her tears. She swallowed often, hoping to hold it together until she was alone.

She was relieved when they pulled up in front of her apartment building and the night doorman met them, holding open her door. Trevor got out first, taking the large umbrella and helping Khloe out next. She lifted her long gown, trying to avoid the hem from getting too wet as they dashed into the lobby.

"Thanks, Trevor. I'll talk to you tomorrow." For some unknown reason, she felt an overwhelming urge to be alone, even from her friend and bodyguard.

He grinned. "Aren't you forgetting something?" When she didn't answer, he reached into his pocket and pulled out a key ring. "You don't have your set of keys with you. You might want to sleep in your apartment instead of on the couch here in the lobby."

That made her smile and eased her tension while he escorted her to the door of her 23rd floor luxury apartment. He unlocked her door and swept inside first, taking the time to turn on several lights and look around the main living space, making sure everything was in order. Not for the first time, Khloe was grateful to have Trevor in her inner circle, protecting her from the crazies.

He started to head down the hall towards her bedroom, but she stopped him. "It's okay. I wasn't even supposed to be here tonight so I'm sure no one is lurking in the off chance I'd drop by."

Trevor hesitated, looking less sure about aborting his inspection of her apartment, but finally turning back to her.

"You want me to sleep on the couch?" he offered. He'd done that before when he'd escorted her to events in NYC. He didn't have an apartment here like he did in California.

"Naw. You go back and take advantage of the huge suite we are paying seven grand for. It's early enough, you might be able to find some sweet thing to enjoy it with."

She knew her racy comment would make him blush, yet she also noted he didn't dispute her idea.

"If you're sure, I guess I'll head back. Call me when you get up. I'll come back with all your stuff. Don't forget, you have dinner reservations tomorrow night at eight."

Oh she hadn't forgotten. She'd been dreading seeing her parents. Just one more stress in her life.

"Okay, will do."

As soon as Trevor left, Khloe made sure to lock the front door, sliding the deadbolt into place. The click of the lock comforted her. Not only because it kept her safe, but told her she was finally alone. Finally off the public stage. It happened so rarely these days.

Khloe turned to take in the space she'd called home for the last four years, although in reality, she'd spent more time on the west coast than in NYC the last two years. Kicking off her too-tall high-heels that were killing her feet, she enjoyed the feel of luxurious carpet between her toes. The kitchen tile was cold in contrast and she opened the refrigerator, pulling a cold sparkling water out. She may not eat right, but she knew enough to at least stay hydrated.

Tension fell from her with each step she took down the hallway towards the sanctuary of her bedroom suite. As she flicked the switch to bathe the room in a soft glow, Khloe spotted her king-sized bed and couldn't wait to fall into it.

Only then did she regret not having Trevor help her with her zipper. She spent a few minutes struggling until she was able to get the zipper lowered enough to slip the gown off her shoulders, letting it pool at her feet.

The reflection of the woman in the nearby mirror jarred her. The mind was a funny thing. In the briefest of seconds before she'd registered that it was her in the mirror, she'd been horrified at the thin skeleton of a woman staring back at her. Yet, within seconds, recognition of her own body brought self-recrimination.

*I'm not thin enough. Pretty enough. Famous enough. Talented enough.*

The tears she'd repressed earlier were threatening, and she hated it. She took a final minute to step out of her tiny panties and flick her bra off before crawling into her bed, pulling the covers up around her. Only then did she give herself permission to lose it.

The invisible wall she often constructed to keep the world at bay crumbled like a dam that had been breached by swelling floodwater. Waves of emotions, good and bad, crashed over the dam, hitting her squarely until her chest hurt from the weight of it all.

For months she'd been the perfect soldier, marching through the daily crush of responsibility. She'd stayed focused on the work because it was easier that way. It had been safer to keep working until she'd fall into bed, exhausted, each night. The alternative was obsessing on every sordid detail of her soap opera life.

Tonight she'd finally face it all. Everything she'd been refusing to let get close enough to hurt her for months. It was the only way she could purge the negativity out of her system and start fresh again tomorrow.

She cried for her strained relationship with her parents. They'd been only thirty minutes away tonight, yet they might as well have been halfway around the world. Just once, she wished they could be proud of her and her success. Just once, not compare Khloe to her perfect brother, Milek, who'd had the audacity to die in a fiery car crash. She'd give anything if Milek could have been there with her tonight to celebrate her success with her.

Khloe cried harder remembering it had been her first release party without her best friend–strike that–*ex*-best friend, Monica, there beside her. The Kaplans had warned her that betrayal was often the price of success. Being sold out by the half-dozen other friends she'd started acting with had hurt, but never in a million years had she thought Monica, her best friend since high school, the woman she'd trusted with every secret, would betray her by giving an expose on Khloe's inner circle to *Rolling Stone* magazine. The irony was there hadn't been that much to reveal. She lived a rather boring life for a celebrity. Still, it hurt to know her friendship was apparently not as important as the fifty grand the magazine had paid to find out that Khloe slept in the nude and struggled with the remnants of an eating disorder, like fifty percent of the women in Hollywood.

But more than anything, she sobbed for a man she barely knew. Even as she bawled, she knew it sounded melodramatic, and maybe it was, but regardless, Ryder Helms had ruined her. She'd known it the minute she'd gotten in the limo that night in February and had been driving away from him. There would never be another man in her life who could push her buttons, literally, the way Ryder had.

In a moment of weakness, Khloe got up and shuffled to the dresser across the room. She pulled open the top drawer, reaching to the very back corner and pulling out a sealed baggie before rushing back to the cocoon of her heaped blankets, burrowing in. Her hands trembled as she opened the zipped top of the small plastic bag and pulled out a crumpled man's hankie along with a pair of purple thong panties. A dangerous cocktail of regret, anger, and sexual heat flooded her as her core contracted with an empty longing for something she couldn't have.

Like a junkie sniffing a line of white powder, she held the fabric close to her face and took a long drag. Memories of the most intense night of her life came to life. Her time with Ryder had been so brief, there were times she worried she'd dreamed the whole thing. Playing with him at Black Light, the hottest BDSM club on the east coast, had been life changing and, at times, felt more like a plot of a movie. The masculine smell of his cum on her panties and his cologne on the handkerchief were the conclusive proof she needed to keep her sane. To remind her he really had been her Master for three short hours.

Closing her eyes, she took another drag, letting the faint scent of his masculine cologne take her back to Valentine's Day. Her body shuddered, remembering how he had mastered her–missing his dominance more than ever. She'd gone to Black Light feeling completely out of control, not unlike tonight. She still didn't understand it, but Ryder had seen through all of her layers of protection. Her public persona. Her celebrity shield she wore to protect her from anyone getting too close. He had torn through every layer and stripped her bare. Both physically and emotionally. His desertion at the end of the night had cut her to the core.

Memories of his dominant control of her body heated her from the inside. She flung back the covers, suddenly burning up. She laid the hankie on the pillow, close enough that she could smell him and then let her hands roam her body, pretending it was his touch squeezing her left breast so hard it hurt. Ryder's probing fingers sliding down her tummy to graze her wet clit. A full-body shudder consumed her as she let her legs fall open obscenely wide, exactly as that night when she'd been restrained to the medical examination table.

As an actress, she enjoyed getting deep into her character and tonight, she was playing the role of Ryder Helms's sex slave. Her fingers pinched her tit, as she remembered he had done. Her hand slid through her dripping folds, faster and faster until she felt the desperation of emptiness. How she longed to have his cock thrust into her. Her own fingers were a sorry substitute as she started finger-fucking herself as she moved her left hand from her breast to her clit, pressing and rubbing it harder and faster, matching the quick insertions of her three fingers inside her neglected cunt.

How sad that it took less than two minutes to bring herself off with a weak climax. It was a poor substitute for the real thing, but it was all she had left of a man she'd never see again.

Post orgasm exhaustion closed in and she welcomed it. Suddenly chilled, she snuggled back under the covers, but then regretted not peeing before she'd gotten into bed. She'd regret it in the morning if she didn't take off her layers of makeup and replace them with layers of the high-priced anti-aging creams she lathered her body in nightly, hoping to fend off the wrinkles she knew would end her career. Eventually, the pressure on her bladder insisted that she'd have to brave the chill of the room at least long enough to dash to the toilet if she hoped to sleep.

Swishing back the heavy comforter again, she dashed for the door to the bathroom across the room, flicking on the light as she sped into the room.

Too late she registered the danger.

Too late she tried to shrink back, but momentum propelled her into the center of the room before she lost her balance, falling to her knees. She was surrounded by a shrine of pictures of herself, taped to the mirror, the walls, hell even the glass slider to the shower. Photos cut from magazines. Grainy printouts of images she recognized from being posted online.

The ones that scared her the most were the candid shots. Someone had gotten close enough to her to snap her ordering a drink at Starbucks. Another picture caught her jogging in Malibu, close enough to see the damp perspiration soaking her tank top. One photo showed her conferring with the director on the closed set of her current film project, a place no one unauthorized should have been able to access.

But it was the word MINE written in what looked like her own red lipstick above the bathroom sink that finally filled the room with her scream. Some pervert had been in her home. In her private bathroom. Only then did she think to scan the room, frantically praying she was alone. Self-preservation kicked in as she pushed to her feet and dashed back towards the bedroom. She grabbed the thick white robe from the back of the door struggling to wrestle it on as she full-out ran back through her bedroom, down the long hall and towards her front door, praying an intruder didn't tackle her before she escaped.

Khloe didn't stop running until she arrived at the elevator. Tears made the down button she was pressing frantically swim before her eyes. Her heart thumped in her chest as she dared a glimpse back over her left shoulder, praying the boogieman wouldn't be chasing after her and grateful when the hall was empty.

She rushed inside the small lift the second it arrived, pressing L for lobby over and over until the doors slid closed. With each floor she descended, awareness of the gravity of what had happened grew in the pit of her empty stomach. This was no crazy email threat or innocent message from an avid fan on her Facebook profile. Someone, presumably a man, had been stalking her. Photographing her. That man had been in her apartment. Her home. Her *bedroom*.

Only when the doors opened on the first floor did she realize she had no idea where she was going or how she would get there. Hell, she didn't even have on shoes.

Patrick, the doorman, stood behind the front reception desk. He looked up, smiling at first, until he realized something was very wrong. Her logical brain knew Patrick was safe, but in that moment, her body reacted to a large man rushing towards her by shrinking back until she slammed into the now closed elevator doors, screaming at the top of her lungs. She saw his mouth moving as he got near, but a loud ringing in her ears blocked out his voice. White spots blurred her vision as she began to feel lightheaded. In a last ditch effort to protect herself, Khloe swatted his hands away from her as he reached out, not recognizing he was only trying to stop her from falling as she felt herself teetering.

The last thing she remembered before feeling his arms wrapping around her to break her fall was wishing it were Ryder there catching her instead.

# CHAPTER 3

Twenty-six security cameras. Twelve armed Bratva soldiers. Four Volkovs. Two locked doors.

When Ryder added up all of the obstacles that stood between him and escape, he had to face reality. Rescuing the Marshall family was a suicide mission... for him and them.

He sat idly by, trying to look interested and not horrified by Artel's lecherous action plan. The naked servant girl kneeling in the corner had been summoned by Viktor to distribute fat cigars and fingers of liqueur to the seated men as if they were about to enjoy an after-dinner entertainment. As Ryder lit his cigar, he glanced to his left to find Alexi looking as uncomfortable as he secretly felt.

Mrs. Marshall fought like a madwoman to get to her daughters, but her bravery only earned her a backhand so hard that she collapsed to the floor in a dazed heap. Her face, already puffy and sporting multiple bruises, attested to the fact this blow had not been the first. She was bleeding from her nose hard enough that streaks of bright red dripped down her chin and onto her ripped dress. The young girls cowered, clinging to each other while

Artel's henchmen easily lifted them, throwing each of them to the floor near their mother where they scrambled into her arms.

The scene was surreal. The only sound in the room were the whimpers of the women and children along with the click of the camera as a Bratva goon took dozens of photos of the unfortunate family now huddled on the floor.

Only now did Ryder recognize a white curtain had been pulled across a drapery rod. It conveniently hid the distinctive carved mahogany paneled walls. Anger flared hot as he realized they did this sort of despicable thing often enough that they'd permanently installed camouflage to disguise their sickest of crimes.

The gunman turned photographer stopped snapping shots to force their faces up so the camera could accurately capture their terror. Each tear that fell turned Ryder's stomach more than the one before until he felt like he was about to throw up his lobster dinner. He'd been party to a lot of fucked up shit in his deep undercover career, nearing his ethical limit more times than he wanted to remember. He'd dreaded the day he'd come face to face with the limit to his immorality.

With a calm certainty, he knew that day was today.

As the minutes ticked forward, Artel's and the guards' behavior grew increasingly aggressive towards the innocent family—slapping the youngest girl who refused to stop sobbing and ripping the mother's bodice to expose her blood-stained bra. It helped Ryder press forward with his decided plan.

He forced a practiced ruthlessness into his voice as he spoke. "If you don't mind my asking, *Pakhan,* how much do you plan to ransom them for? I'm sure they are worth a great deal."

Viktor didn't take his eyes off the spectacle playing out in front of him as he answered. "No ransom. The bastard doesn't deserve the courtesy."

Based on Artel's earlier comments, Ryder wasn't surprised by the information, yet he suspected the American businessman wouldn't see anything about the abduction and terrorization of his family before they were murdered as a courtesy.

"Of course, sir. But surely it's too dangerous to hold such valuable assets here at your home."

Finally, the elder Volkov glanced his way. "I'm glad you're on our side, Nicolai. It is also why I've chosen to trust you with our most valuable task."

"I'm honored to be of service to the family," he replied with trained sincerity. "How may I be of assistance?"

He'd asked Viktor, but it was Artel standing behind him who answered his question.

"You've been chosen to deliver our very strong message to Chip Marshall."

He already suspected the answer to the question he was about to ask. "Do you have the message prepared? Where would you like me to deliver it?"

In his gut he knew the communication wouldn't be words. More likely, the planned message would be disposing of the oil tycoon's family in some seedy neighborhood in Moscow where a vagrant would stumble upon them and maybe call the police.

Viktor took a puff of his cigar, luxuriating in his power, ignoring the question still hanging in the air. Only when the photographer pulled a vinyl tarp from a duffle bag near the door and spread it across the priceless antique carpet did Ryder have confirmation for his suspicions.

Artel puffed on his tobacco, on his feet, pacing like a dangerous animal about to pounce on his prey as his henchmen prepared the scene. Despite her fear, Mrs. Marshall had noticed the tarp, too. Like a protective mama bear, she'd moved her young daughters behind her, shielding them as best as she could. One by one, she frantically scanned the dangerous men in the room, desperate to find someone who would help her. Ryder held his steely gaze as their eyes met, giving her no reason to hope for his help.

When Artel pulled a heavy Glock from his shoulder holster, Ryder made his move. Pushing to his feet slowly, he deliberately kept his hands in the open, setting his half-smoked cigar into the heavy hand-blown glass ashtray before approaching Viktor Volkov.

Father and son tore their attention away from the doomed family to look at Ryder.

He spoke with confidence. "I would be honored if you'd allow me to prepare the message for the American."

He saw the surprise in Viktor's old, jaded eyes, quickly replaced with pleasure.

Artel was less pleased, eying Ryder with suspicion. Still, when his father gave his oldest son directions, Artel listened.

"Loan your weapon to Nicolai, *syn*. He offers a great service to the family."

It took almost a minute of silent standoff before the tallest Volkov in the room extended his hand, providing the only weapon in the room to a man he knew as Nicolai Romanovski. With a forced calmness, Ryder carefully closed the gap between them, grateful the bastard had been too arrogant to walk towards him. By making Nicolai come to him, he'd played perfectly into Ryder's plan.

The weapon was comfortingly heavy... sturdy. Out of habit, Ryder hit the magazine release, pulling the ammunition out to ensure all was as expected before slamming the magazine home and taking the weapon off safety.

His trained movements were so smooth, the Volkovs' sluggish reactions were no match for the seasoned operative.

Ryder closed the few feet remaining between him and Viktor Volkov. He grabbed the older man by the lapel of his suit, yanking him to his feet and pressing the nozzle of the weapon to his temple. His rush of adrenaline helped swing the now joined men around, putting the patriarch of the family directly in front of him, the perfect shield.

He'd half expected the other Volkovs to whip out hidden guns, but none did. Instead, they cursed loudly. The surprise on Vlad's face was almost comical, proving to Ryder he'd just blown a very successful cover.

"I'm sorry, but I can't let you kill innocent children. That's an unacceptable line to cross."

He'd spoken the words in Russian, but Artel answered him in English. "I fucking knew you weren't to be trusted. You have no idea how big of a mistake you made threatening my father."

Ryder smiled a menacing smile, switching to English as well. "Oh, I have a pretty good idea. But this is how this is going to go." The elder Volkov struggled half-heartedly to break free, but he was too old. Too frail.

He didn't dare take his eyes off Artel who was both the closest and deadliest man in the room, yet he spoke to the woman huddled on the floor crying. "Mrs. Marshall, stand up and gather your girls. Then walk to the man sitting directly in front of you in the black jacket. He's going to give you a set of car keys."

Alexi's eyes widened before turning dark with rage. Ryder knew that Alexi would pay a high price for not detecting the truth earlier, and for that he was sorry, yet the man was no innocent. When you play with fire, you need to be prepared to get singed.

Only when Mrs. Marshall had the keys in her hand did Ryder bark the next order. "Everyone except the Marshalls stand and go to the other end of the room." When no one moved into action, he pulled the muzzle of the gun away from Viktor's temple, only to bring it back with force. His pained cry filled the otherwise quiet room, jarring his sons into action, first rushing towards Ryder until he shouted, "STOP! NOW!" When the men did as they were told, he added, "To the other end, now."

Mrs. Marshall was stumbling towards the exit, pulling her girls with her, but Ryder needed to warn her of the dangers on the other side of the door.

"Don't leave yet."

Her eyes widened, desperation glaring at him. She swayed on her feet, still unsure why one of the Russians was helping her.

Ryder pulled the dead weight of Viktor Volkov along with him as he made his way to the door himself, keeping his back to the wall and the elder mafia king safely in front of him as leverage.

When he reached the door, he instructed her, "When we get outside this room, there will be many armed guards. We need to keep the old man between us and them. Grab a pool stick and put it into the door handles to this room to slow them down. We'll stay together."

"But who are you?" she asked with doubt.

"He's a dead man, that's who he is," Artel snarled from the far end of the room, too far away to help his father. Ryder made the mistake of making eye contact and knew if he didn't open fire and kill the men in the room before he left, he would forever be looking over his shoulder for the rest of his life. He'd never start his car again without wondering if that was the day it would explode, the Volkovs having found him.

He pushed down the thought of offing the entire family before leaving. As tempting as it was, he knew it would only destabilize things further in Russia. More importantly, it would alert the guards on the other side of the door.

Instead, he had the woman he was rescuing open the door slightly so he could glance out the crack. All of the guards were still playing cards, oblivious to the drama going on inside the private dining room. It gave Ryder the edge.

Going from slow motion to top speed, Ryder pushed through the door, swinging the old man in front of him as the henchman nearest the pool table recognized the threat. Ryder took aim and squeezed off a shot straight to his chest, quickly returning the muzzle to Viktor's temple.

"Hands where I can see them," he shouted to the remaining Bratva. At first, no one moved, but he quickly raised the gun and shot into the ceiling before returning the threat to the old man's temple. "Hands!"

It was then Viktor finally spoke. "I'm disappointed, Nicolai. Artel warned me about you, but I did not listen."

Nothing Ryder could say would change a thing so he kept silent, pushing their little party towards the exit while scanning the room for new threats. They had arrived at the door to the grand staircase when all hell broke loose. He reacted on instinct, lifting the gun and shooting at the armed guards in the room who dared to shoot in his direction, despite the patriarch of the family being at risk in the middle of the action.

They were almost out the door when he felt the impact of the bullets hitting Viktor. The old man grunted in pain, slumping in Ryder's arms making it harder to continue using him as a shield. By the time they got to the stairs, Ryder knew he'd have to make it the rest of the way without the shield. He let the old man slump against the bottom steps. Standing above him, Ryder could see the pained disbelief etched across his face.

"Why, Nicolai? I treated you as a son," the old man croaked.

"No, Viktor. You treated me like a henchman. Nothing more. Nothing less."

The old man coughed and a small line of blood dripped from his mouth. Not a good sign. An odd sadness invaded Ryder, recognizing he probably wouldn't make it. He may not have pulled the trigger that killed the *Pakhan* but he would be held responsible by the remaining family as if he had.

He didn't have time to mourn the years of work he'd thrown away in the space of a few reckless minutes. Knowing every second that ticked by made their escape harder, Ryder reached to grab up the smallest girl and barked his order.

"We need to run. Stay behind me. We're heading to the midnight blue Ferrari to the left as we leave the front door. Pile the kids in and have the keys ready for me when I get behind the wheel."

The frightened mother had morphed into a warrior, prepared to do all she could to assist in her family's rescue. They had made it almost all the way to the front door before he heard the dangerous cock of a weapon in the grand foyer. Spinning around, he got his shot off in time to neutralize the guard who'd come to investigate the shots fired.

Ryder cracked the front door, relieved to find the guards from the front gate had not already descended on mansion. He'd been counting on the communication blackout in the private meeting space paired with the confusion over Viktor being shot to give them the few minutes they needed to have a prayer of a chance.

He could see the bumping headlight of a souped up golf cart heading down the driveway in their direction. Their time was almost up. When he opened the driver's door to Alexi's beloved car, he practically threw the crying girl from his arms into the almost non-existent back seat. He had to hand it to Mrs. Marshall. She had kept up with him every step of the way, helping her older daughter into the car and handing the waiting keys to Ryder the second his ass hit the leather seat.

The engine roared to life as the first bullet punctured the back window, thankfully missing all occupants. He threw the car into reverse, spinning out as he screamed orders. "Everyone get down low and stay there." He maneuvered the sports car while adding, "There's another Glock on the floor under your seat along with my cell phone. Grab them and send a text that says 911 to my contact labeled 'Pizza'."

He'd pointed the car straight at the golf cart full of armed guards barreling down on them. Crouching low, he pressed the automatic window button to make the glass go down. The second there was room, he stuck his left hand out the window, peppering several shots into the crowded vehicle in their path. The cart swerved, but continued, now less than one-hundred feet away as Mrs. Marshall screamed, "It's locked!"

*Fucking of course it is, you idiot. It's also in Russian.*

"Hold on!" He had to focus on getting off Bratva property first and foremost, firing two more bullets at the guards, this time hitting the driver in time for the cart to jerk to the side, allowing Ryder to gun the Ferrari past it.

He pressed his foot to the floor, knowing he'd need all the speed he could get to break through the front gate with the sports car. He barked his next order, "Brace yourself. It's gonna get rough for a minute." The terrorized sobs of children in the backseat reminded him of what was at risk.

They hit sixty-five kilometers per hour just before they connected with the twelve-foot steel front gate. He was counting on the intel being correct and that they weren't about to hit an impenetrable wall. Certainly, the impact jarred the occupants of the luxury vehicle, but he shot out onto the snowy street so fast, he almost lost control on the slippery pavement. As the ass-end of the car fishtailed, more bullets shot through the back window, this time one grazed Mrs. Marshall's left arm. Only a small yelp told him she'd been hit, but he didn't have time to focus on that. They still had a lot of ground to cover to get to safety.

"Hand me my phone," he asked as he focused on exiting the winding streets of the upscale suburb, going as fast as he safely could to prevent spinning out or being pulled over by the local police who were on the Volkov payroll.

He used his thumbprint to unlock the smartphone, searching through his contacts to find the number he'd been looking for and pressing a simple '9-1-1-SEND' before handing the phone back to the rescued mother.

They drove in silence for a few minutes with only the sound of the young girls whimpering in fear in the backseat as their sound-track, and their mother whispering soothing reassurances to them that everything would be okay now. His first instinct was to tell her not to lie to her children, but with each mile they progressed, his stress level decreased marginally as chances for a successful extract from Russia went up exponentially for each minute his rearview mirror stayed clear. Still on high alert he finally asked, "You were hit. How bad is it?"

"It's a graze. I'm applying pressure."

He was impressed with the kidnapped woman's composure under the circumstances. Things could have turned out very differently had she fallen apart like he'd feared.

"Who the hell are you and why did you help us?" she asked for the second time.

His answer was gruff, even for him. "Who I am isn't important."

"I thought for sure we were dead. That Chip would be getting pictures of us murdered."

"That would have been the best outcome. More likely you would have been murdered and your daughters would have ended up being sold into slavery to some unknown pedophile whacko half way around the world, never to be seen again."

"Oh my God, that's even worse than I had imagined," the mother cried out in disbelieving anguish. "Is that why you helped us?"

He didn't owe her an answer. He'd already forfeited years of cover work in the space of a minute for her and her daughters, so no, he didn't owe her another fucking thing. He answered anyway. "I helped you because what they did crossed a line I won't cross. It was dishonorable bringing innocent women and children into the war."

"What war?"

Ryder's chuckle sounded out of place in the heaviness of the car. He forgot that most people around the globe were ignorant to the real depravity of the world. He didn't bother answering.

Normally he would zigzag his way to his destination to make sure he wasn't being followed, but not tonight. No one following them would be hanging back to observe, they'd be trying to run him off the road. He took the fastest route to the preplanned destination he and his local handler had agreed to meet if his cover was blown, knowing the only real obstacle between him and there were the hundreds of Moscow police cars now on the road looking for the 2015 Ferrari he was driving. With the chief of police in the Volkovs' back pocket, Artel would have the police working to find them. Not only would the Volkovs then get their revenge, but the police would try to pin the kidnapping on Nicolai Romanovski.

He needed to get the fuck out of town.

They were only a few miles from the tiny airstrip on the outskirts of the city, in the heart of the manufacturing district. Flights in and out served industrial fat-cats with private jets who liked to fly between factories. Most Americans would be surprised to know that an unmarked, nondescript Cessina was fueled and ready to take off within thirty minutes of an agent's call for help, no questions asked. He'd already been down this path after being shot on the job and was counting on tonight's flight being his last out of Russia.

He wasn't sure of the time, but suspected it was around four in the morning, so any lights would have alarmed him. As expected, the tiny tower used at the strip was dark. He turned off the headlights before driving the already crunched front end of poor Alexi's pride-and-joy through its second locked gate of the night, zigzagging through the warehouses turned hangars until he got to the appointed building.

The roar of the sports car was his only arrival announcement, yet the two-story metal door to the hangar slid open wide enough for him to drive in. He relaxed slightly the second the door slid closed behind them, making the distinctive car that much harder for the Volkovs to find in the game of hide and seek they were playing.

Emergency lighting was his only guide as he wove through the half-dozen small aircraft to park out of the way. After they were in the air, the car would be stripped and disposed of.

Mrs. Marshall had gripped the handle to the door, but he

stopped her, talking softly as he took his Glock from her, putting it back into his shoulder holster where it belonged and handing her the half empty weapon he'd taken from Artel Volkov.

"Take this. The safety isn't on so it's dangerous." When she looked confused he added. "We should be safe here, but let me check it out first. Don't exit the car until I come for you. Got it?"

Only now as he finally looked at her did he realize she was visibly shaking. Her bravery from before was beginning to desert her.

Ryder reassured her. "It's just a precaution. We'll be safely out of Russian airspace in less than two hours. Now, stay here and protect your family while I make the final arrangements. Can you do that?"

She nodded, tears in her eyes.

As he exited the car, he removed his Glock again, unwilling to approach the company jet without his weapon drawn until he confirmed all was as he expected. As he neared the only airplane with interior lights on in the cabin, Ryder's sixth sense alerted him. He didn't know what was wrong, but he trusted his gut explicitly and was suddenly glad he'd left the Marshalls in the car.

He was almost to the aircraft when someone finally stepped out of the shadows, blocking his way to the portable stairs leading to the luxury cabin.

"We've been waiting for you."

"Who the fuck are you? Where's Hansen?"

"He's on another assignment. I'm Burke. What's the nature of your emergency?"

He was deep undercover. He didn't talk to his handler daily. Hell, even weekly. It was possible that Hansen had been reassigned, but unlikely. He'd worked with Joe Hansen for three years and he'd never once sent anyone else to a meet in his place. When you're undercover, you learn to treat changes to the plan as a threat.

He trod lightly. "I burned my cover tonight. I need an extract.

The Volkovs won't stop looking for me this time. There is no going back in."

Burke drew a drag from his lit cigarette, acting too cool for his own good. "Why the hell would you burn yourself?"

He lied. "I fucked up. Made a mistake. They made me."

There was no way Burke was an agent. He let his emotions project on his face like a movie. Ryder saw disappointment in the man's eyes. His gut told him he'd been hoping for the arrival of the Marshall women.

Movement in the shadows caught Ryder's eye before he swung his Glock up, ready to down any threat. Just in the nick of time, he stopped from shooting the man stumbling forward, his weapon drawn. Joe Hansen emptied his magazine clip into the chest of Burke before the trusted agent fell to his knees.

Ryder checked the pulse of the traitor first, making sure he was dead before running to Hansen. The older man had fallen forward. When Ryder rolled him gently to his back, a pool of blood was left where his bullet-riddled shoulder had laid. His handler grimaced in pain.

"Sorry about that. The asshole ambushed me like I was a rookie."

Ryder quickly shucked his leather coat before taking off his shirt and pressing it hard against the fallen man's wound in an attempt to stem the bleeding. "It's okay. I made him."

"I don't know what's going on, but the police scanners are going crazy looking for you. We need to get you off the ground fast."

"I figured the Volkovs would call in all of their favors on this one."

"What'd you do? Did Vlad catch you fucking around with Irena?"

Despite the weight of the night's events, Ryder chuckled. "Naw. It was a bit more complicated than that. Let's get you onboard and I'll fill you in once we're in the air."

"But... I need to..."

"You need a doctor, and if they sent someone to take you out, you're burned too. We're both leaving Moscow tonight."

Ryder helped his friend get to the top of the stairs before adding, "I'll be back. I need to get something from the car. Tell the pilot we'll be ready in two minutes."

Ryder doubled back to the Ferrari and had a heart attack when he found an empty car. He had redrawn his pistol when Mrs. Marshall and her girls stepped out from behind the huge tires of a nearby plane. She approached warily.

"We heard gunshots so we hid."

"Smart. The good guys won. Time to go."

They took off running and when the youngest little girl had trouble keeping up, Ryder picked her up again, rushing to the stairs first. He settled the whimpering girl in a seat as far away from the bleeding Hansen as he could, shouting orders as he went.

"Everyone get buckled in. I'll go open the door to the warehouse and be back to take off." He stopped to shout into the cockpit where the pilot and co-pilot were completing pre-check. "I'll be back in one minute to close the hatch. Be ready."

Making another trip down the portable steps, Ryder now rushed to the heavy sliding door. He knew they didn't have much time. If Burke had known where to ambush Hansen, chances are others would be following him in. His suspicion was confirmed when the door slid open and a half dozen fast-moving vehicles could be seen weaving through the industrial park, several with police lights flashing.

Once the door was open wide enough for their departure, Ryder dashed back to the plane, hustling up the stairs two at a time and throwing the stairs back away from the door as soon as he was onboard. "We're about to have company! Let's get out of here!" he yelled to the pilots as he pulled the cabin door closed, latching it tight before leaning down to look out the small window.

*It's gonna be fucking close.*

The aircraft was mid-sized which meant it was slow to build speed. He rushed to the cockpit to strongly encourage the pilot to step on it when the first bullets hit the hull of the aircraft. They were taking fire.

"Step on it boys, or we're done for."

"Yeah, I'm sensing you really pissed someone off tonight, Helms."

Despite the danger, Ryder chuckled. "Yeah, you might say that. I have a feeling there's gonna be hell to pay when the dust settles."

It was a race to see if the advancing cars could arrive in time to block the runway. When one car went across a grassy berm in an attempt to block their departure, the pilot pushed the plane faster, pulling back the stick and lifting the wheels off the ground just in time to sail over the vehicle below. Several more bullets ricocheted off the fuselage, but luckily didn't do enough damage to down the plane.

"Nice work, gentlemen," Ryder added, patting each of the nervous pilots on the back. "Stay on your toes. I'm not sure if the Volkovs have the connections to scramble a military intervention, but I wouldn't relax until we're out of Russian airspace."

"Roger that. I saw you board. Please tell me that's the missing Marshall family back there."

"Yep."

"Holy shit, Helms. You have some balls."

"Yeah, well let's try to keep my balls intact long enough to get back to Langley where I'll be sure to get my ass chewed for burning years of work."

By the time Ryder returned to the main cabin, Mrs. Marshall was leaning over Hansen, applying pressure to his wound to help stop the bleeding. He went to her to take over.

"You should go be with your girls. I'll handle this."

She straightened, reaching to hand him the bloodied shirt.

Their eyes met and he saw such relief and gratitude pouring from her expression, it almost made the burn worth it.

"I think it's time you tell me your real name, don't you?" she asked.

"Does it matter?"

"It does to me. You saved my family. I'd like to know who I'm giving thanks for when I pray."

Ryder snorted. "No one's ever prayed for me before."

"Well then, there's a first time for everything."

"Ryder." He reached out to offer his hand, but she instead rushed into his arms to give him a big hug, finally letting her emotions go, dissolving into a sobbing mess. He finally had to help her take a seat between her frightened children so he could get back to caring for his handler bleeding out on the floor.

"It's all going to be okay now."

He sure as hell hoped he wasn't lying.

# CHAPTER 4

"K hloe!" Finally. The voice she'd been waiting for cut through the chaos swarming around her.

Guards at the door prevented Trevor from coming in. He stood a few inches above most men in the room. His buzzcut hair, broad shoulders, and visible tattoos gave him an air of danger, and the police were not inclined to allow entry. She was forced to push to her bare feet and head for the door.

"Please, Miss Monroe." The rookie who had been assigned to protect her in the lobby requested. "You're supposed to stay seated here until the captain gives us new instructions." She heard the pleading in his voice as he reached for her arm to stop her.

His touch was soft, but unexpected. She flinched away.

"I'm sorry. I didn't mean to frighten you."

She was barely holding it together. "Please. Let my guard... my friend... I need him."

"Okay, but please go sit back down. We wouldn't want you to faint again. I'll go get him."

She let herself be led back to the couch, but didn't sit. She fumbled with the belt of her robe nervously instead.

By the time Trevor was finally headed in her direction, she was ready to crawl out of her skin. She saw the fear in his own eyes as he scanned her, trying to assess the damage to his client and friend. But he wouldn't be able to see the damage done to her. It was internal... hitting her at her core.

Her guard and friend didn't stop as he approached. Trevor scooped her up into his arms and hugged her to him so hard it hurt. Any scrap of bravery she still clung to fled as soon as she was cocooned in his arms. She was safe again.

Trevor took a seat on the same couch she'd vacated, pulling her down into his lap. Muscled arms enveloped her while she cried on his shoulder.

"What the hell happened? I got a call from your doorman while I was at the hotel that there was a problem and to get over here fast." He paused, clearing his throat. "I'm afraid to ask why you're in the lobby in your bathrobe hanging out with a whole squad of police officers. And why is there an ambulance out front?"

When she couldn't stop the tears to answer, he added, "Shhh. Everything's going to be okay." She wanted to scream at him that he couldn't possibly make that promise to her, but the growing lump in her throat choked down the words. "Why not start at the beginning. What happened after I left?"

When she could speak, she took a deep breath and relayed the events he'd missed since leaving only an hour before. She was finishing describing the hundreds of photos in her bathroom when the captain rejoined them after exiting the elevator.

"How are you feeling, Miss Monroe?" he inquired.

"As well as could be expected, I guess," she answered truthfully.

"Good. Is this your boyfriend?"

"Oh, no," she quickly asserted. "This is my personal bodyguard, Trevor."

The older cop's eyes flashed. "I have a lot of questions for you, young man."

"Excuse me?" Trevor threw back defensively.

She felt Trevor begin to vibrate beneath her.

"What was Miss Monroe doing alone and unprotected?"

Trevor shot to his feet, cradling her in his arms while he handed it right back. "What the hell? She was in her own damn condo. I escorted her in. Made sure she locked the door behind me when I left."

"And exactly when was that?" The captain's questions continued, unfazed.

"About an hour ago, I guess." Trevor didn't wait to be asked the question Khloe knew would be coming next. "I dropped her at home and then went back to The Plaza. There was an after party in Khloe's suite."

This time, the captain directed his question at her. "So you're hosting a party you didn't even attend?"

She didn't appreciate his aggressive tone. He made her feel like she was the 'perp' instead of the 'victim'. It was awkward being interrogated while being cradled in Trevor's arms. She wiggled away from him enough that he lowered her legs to the floor, yet she was relieved he kept his arm around her as she answered the captain's question impatiently. "I wasn't hosting anything, clearly. I was tired and wanted to come home."

"Where were you before returning home an hour ago?"

Trevor answered the latest question. "Tonight was the red-carpet pre-opening party for Ms. Monroe's newest movie release. We were at The Plaza doing interviews and prepping for the release all day today. We were at The Lincoln Theater from about six to eleven tonight. The people who wanted to keep partying went back to The Plaza and I brought Khloe home."

A fresh commotion near the revolving door to the building drew their attention. Just in time, Trevor pushed Khloe behind him as he jumped in front her, standing between his client and the flashing cameras on the sidewalk outside the building.

How the hell had the media found out about this so quickly? It didn't make sense. Hell, nothing was making sense.

She'd never felt as trapped as she did in that moment. The

thought of having her photo splashed across the front of the gossip rags or trending on Twitter made her empty tummy churn. Disheveled, barefoot in a bathrobe. It would be a disaster.

The exit from the building was blocked.

She couldn't stay in the lobby.

Yet returning to her condo terrified her.

She was trapped.

It was Trevor who made the decision on their next move.

"We need to get out of this lobby. Let's go back upstairs," he insisted.

Another cop answered, "The forensic team is still up there working. We can't contaminate the scene."

"Bullshit. We can't stay here. We're sitting ducks for the media." While the police hem-hawed, Trevor turned his back to the front door and started shuffling Khloe towards the elevator. Her mind revolted at the thought of returning to her now soiled apartment, but shouts of her name from bystanders outside urged her into the elevator when the doors opened. Uniformed officers piled in around her and Trevor until she was pressed into the corner. Only Trevor's wall of muscles helped her fend off the claustrophobic panic attack threatening.

She put one foot in front of the other, in a trance, until she got to the threshold of her open door. The yellow and black 'Crime Scene' tape prevented her entry. A half dozen officers were mingling in her kitchen and living room, looking like they'd moved in. The flash of a police camera made her flinch.

Trevor seemed to understand, leaning in to talk softly against her ear. "It'll be okay, Khloe. I won't leave your side."

Her fear was obviously transparent to everyone around her as many pairs of eyes turned towards the celebrity in the room, pity shining bright and she hated it.

Ignoring the warning, Trevor reached to pull the tape away from the doorjamb to allow their entry before leading her to the leather couch near the sliding glass door to the balcony. Before she sat down, a cop warned them, "Don't touch anything if you can help it. We're sweeping your home for fingerprints."

Her guard left her long enough to retrieve a bottle of cold water from her refrigerator, returning and asking her to drink. She'd put the bottle down on the glass-topped coffee table in front of her when a police officer wearing a full-body white protection suit over his street clothes and blue latex gloves stepped into the living room. In his protective clothing, he looked like he'd come straight from the set of a sci-fi movie about a contagious epidemic. The seasoned-looking cop glanced around the crowded space until his eyes met with Khloe. Her pulse increased when he started walking towards her, but her heart lurched when she saw what he held in his hand.

She recognized the purple panties through the plastic baggie with the huge EVIDENCE splashed across the label. The forensic officer stopped to chat with the captain before approaching Trevor and Khloe where they sat.

"Good evening, Ms. Monroe. I'm Officer Effingham. I'd like to ask you a few questions if I may."

He may have asked politely, but the stern look in his eye told her he wasn't really asking for permission to interrogate her further. She managed to nod her reluctant approval.

Khloe used her acting skills to avoid reacting when he held out the plastic bag that held her soiled panties.

"We found these mixed in with your bed sheets. Do these panties belong to you?"

"Yes."

"We're going to send them to the lab for processing with the rest of the evidence, but would you mind sharing with us whose semen is present?"

Her heart lurched and she felt Trevor stiffen beside her. "Actually, I would mind."

"I'm sure you understand we're trying to help you, Ms.

Monroe. Avoiding simple questions isn't going to help us solve who broke into your home."

There was nothing simple about his question. An irrational anger took hold of her at Ryder that he wasn't there to help defend why the fuck his cum was in her bed months after he'd deserted her.

The cops near enough to have heard the question stopped to stare, waiting on her answer like they had a right to know jack shit about her sex life.

The cop pressed. "Was your boyfriend here earlier?"

Why the hell does he think she has a boyfriend? Ah yes, the lovely media.

Realizing the cop would out-wait her, she finally folded to answer with a simple, "No."

"Then..."

She cut him off. "It was from earlier, okay?" she replied defensively.

"Tonight?"

"This isn't important."

The captain pressed, "Let us decide what is important."

Anger helped her be brave. "No. I'm telling you he didn't do this."

"How do you know that? We need his name."

"I just know. No names." She held her ground while she felt Trevor's hand subconsciously squeezing her leg through the terrycloth robe.

The cop in charge took over the questioning. "Fine for now, but you'll answer my other questions. Do you have any known enemies you can think of who would have done this?"

"No," she replied.

Trevor jumped in to embellish her answer. "She has received several threatening messages over the last few weeks. They were either sent to her public email address, as a direct message to her twitter account. One was even delivered via U.S. Postal service to her agent's office."

Khloe startled, spinning to look Trevor in the eyes. She hated the guilt she saw there.

"Wait. You didn't tell me about the letter," she complained.

He hesitated before admitting, "Bernie and Natalie said you didn't need to know. That it would scare you."

Her voice screeched, "Are you fucking kidding me?"

"Khloe..."

She jerked away from him.

"Don't *Khloe* me. You work for me, Trevor. Don't you ever forget that, because if you do, you'll be gone." He sat stunned at her uncharacteristic anger until she added, "Got it?"

"I'm sorry." His apology was soft, but audible to everyone in the room that had silenced to witness the altercation.

The captain's next question broke the silence. "Were the messages threatening in nature?"

"Not really. They all have professed their love of Khloe and expressed a desire to spend time with her. Each message included a promise of being together in the future."

The cop wrote a note in his small notepad before asking, "Did you report these messages to the police?"

Trevor answered, "No."

She swung to glare at him again. "Let me guess. Bernie and Natalie didn't think it was a good idea to turn them over to the police?"

Trevor wisely kept his mouth shut.

The captain didn't allow him to dodge the question. "Why would you keep something this critical hidden?"

Trevor went on defense. "We protect more than her person. Things like this have a way of going public fast. We sent the messages off to an independent investigator to track down who is behind them."

"And?" The officer raised his brow like an impatient parent.

"The investigation hasn't nailed down any leads yet."

"Do you have anyone you've noticed hanging around Ms. Monroe or acting aggressive around her?"

Trevor's agitation at being interrogated was showing. "You have no clue how hard it is to keep a celebrity like Khloe safe. Every time she goes anywhere in public she is swamped by fans wanting photos of her. Autographs. To touch her." He turned towards her to accuse, "And then you do shit like tonight when you let those teenagers jump the stanchions and crowd you. I've told you over and over to stop letting fans get that close. They were waiting for you in the lobby when I got back there."

"Explain to me again why you didn't go back to the hotel?" the cop pressed her again.

"I told you. I was tired, and I wanted to sleep in my own bed."

"If you two aren't an item, are you seeing someone else?"

She hesitated. She hated the idea of lying to the police, but she equally hated the idea of pissing off the producers of *Dirty Business* who had insisted she and Dean hide their defunct relationship status until after the movie had been out for a few weeks.

"Yes."

When she didn't expound, he pressed her. "I'll need his name, Ms. Monroe."

"Dean Reynolds. My co-star on the soon to be released movie." She used her actress skills to her advantage to hide her disdain for her ex.

"And where is Mr. Reynolds?"

"He wanted to party with friends, and like I said, I was tired."

"I'm wondering why he isn't here to comfort you instead of your bodyguard?" That was a great question.

"Why does this matter? Dean didn't do this."

"We'll need to interview him and everyone else close to you."

"That's crazy. You need to focus on finding who broke into my house. My *home*."

"Oh, rest assured. We'll do that too, but we need to be thorough. This is a high profile case."

"No shit. I live a high profile life."

"I'm going to need a list of everyone who has a key to your condo along with the timing of when you were here last and can confirm the photos and threats were not in your bathroom. That will help us narrow our timeline down. The building has tight security, with surveillance cameras, so with any luck we should be able to get a photo of the perpetrator's entrance into your home."

She was close to losing her shit. Thankfully, Trevor sensed it and stood. "Are we about done here? I'd like to get Khloe out of here. She can't stay here tonight, obviously."

She bit her tongue. She didn't want to go back to the hotel, but only then did she realize she would never feel comfortable in her own home again. Some asshole had broken in and violated her private space, ruining what was supposed to be one of the best days of her life.

Surprisingly, the captain didn't try to stop them from leaving. "That's fine, but I need you to share your contact information and don't either of you leave town. We'll want to talk with you again tomorrow after we have a chance to evaluate the evidence. Are you going back to The Plaza?"

Trevor had pulled out a business card with his contact info on it, handing it over while answering, "We won't be going back there. The paparazzi will be expecting her there. I called her assistant, Ricky. He's securing alternate accommodations. I'll let you know where we end up."

Khloe was fading fast. All remnants of the adrenaline spike from earlier had worn off. All she wanted was to closet herself somewhere safe. A place where she could cry in private. She allowed Trevor to leave her parked on her couch while he went back to her bedroom and grabbed up a duffle bag with a change of clothes. She could hear him arguing with another police officer who didn't want him to disturb anything, but Trevor insisted that

Khloe Monroe would not be gallivanting around Manhattan without taking the most basic belongings.

The next thirty minutes were a blur for her as she let Trevor help her put on a pair of flip-flops before escorting her down to the lobby. She was relieved when they turned away from the front doors, heading down the hallway to the back door. Her personal assistant, Ricky, was waiting at the exit, looking worried.

They didn't speak as Trevor opened the door to the back alley of the building. Khloe wasn't surprised to find a Town Car waiting for them. Trevor opened the back door for her and then urged her, "Hurry up. There are photographers hanging around."

He didn't have to tell her twice. She dove into the car with Trevor and Ricky following, slamming the door as they saw two men running towards the car.

"Get us out of here!" Trevor shouted to Johnson who slammed on the gas, almost running over the photographers before they dove out of the way.

Ricky looked as shaken as she felt. To his credit, he didn't ask her stupid questions.

"I booked us a suite at the Marriott under my name. I alerted their security and they are waiting for us to arrive at the loading dock and will escort us up through the back of house to avoid any unwanted attention. We can regroup there."

Since she was still in her bathrobe, she was grateful for the VIP arrangements.

Khloe let herself be hustled through the bowels of the huge hotel, led by a pack of men who she had to trust to keep her safe. By the time they were unlocking the door to the suite, she felt ready to collapse. She hadn't had enough to eat that day and the trauma of her last few hours had drained the last ounce of her energy. When she stumbled against the loveseat inside the expansive living space, Trevor was there, scooping her up and carrying her towards the bedroom.

They didn't speak as he pulled back the covers to lay her down. Their eyes met as he stood over her.

"I'm so sorry, Khloe. I feel like this was my fault."

Her brain knew she shouldn't blame her bodyguard, but she didn't have the energy for any more talk. She wanted to be alone. When she didn't answer him, Trevor pulled the covers up and turned to leave her.

Only when he was at the door did the panic hit her. "Trevor!"

He turned back towards her, expectantly before she added. "You'll sleep on the couch out there, won't you? I mean... I... I don't want to be alone."

"I'm not gonna leave your side again until we catch the bastard."

After he'd left, she let the tears she'd been holding back fall. Khloe rolled to bury her face into the pillow, hoping to muffle the sound of her sobs.

Even knowing her guard was outside the bedroom door, she'd never felt as lonely as she did as she cried herself into an exhausted sleep.

# CHAPTER 5

"You look like shit."

He hadn't even sat down yet and his boss was starting in on him.

"Thanks. That's what happens when you have to beat it back to Langley at the butt-crack of dawn." Ryder gladly took the tall cup of coffee offered by Brandon Webster's personal assistant before she quietly left, closing the door on the top-secret meeting about to begin.

They'd landed at the U.S. Military base in Germany just after the sun came up last Friday. He'd spent less than twenty-four hours on the ground being debriefed before being summoned back to Langley for this early Sunday morning emergency meeting.

He'd been in this office dozens of times over the years, but this was the first time every chair around the long conference table was full. The fact that this many bigwigs had come in on the weekend gave him a hint of what to expect. There wasn't enough coffee in the world to fortify him for the shit-storm coming.

*Fuck me. This is gonna be a long ass day.*

He didn't recognize most people in the room, but it was his

boss's boss, George Fortin, who asked the first question before Ryder had even taken his first sip of caffeine.

"I don't need to remind everyone that this meeting is classified. Nothing said here leaves without my authorization." All heads nodded before he added, "Who the hell authorized you to terminate Viktor Volkov, Helms? Do you realize the trouble you've brought down on the agency with this stunt, not to mention the years of deep cover you've burned in the space of one night?"

He'd expected the question, but he hadn't planned on having an audience for his debrief. The sound of the agency stenographer typing away in the corner of the room reminded him he was on record, but he wasn't really worried. He'd had enough time to evaluate his actions on his last night in Russia, and he'd decided he wouldn't change anything that had happened other than possibly wishing he'd taken a shot at Artel Volkov before leaving. The world would be a much better place with that asshole six-feet under.

"As you know, sir, I'm authorized to use all tools at my disposal when faced with life and death situations. I made the best decision I could in the moment and I stand behind every action I took."

"That's easy for you to say, Helms. You don't have to deal with the fallout. Do you know I got a call from Director Ryan last night wanting to know what the fuck happened with the Volkovs?"

"Did you give him my regards?" Ryder deadpanned, taking his first sip of coffee, unwilling to let these assholes who pushed paper for a living second guess his decision from the safety of their cushy D.C. offices.

"Do you think this is funny, Agent Helms?"

"No, sir. I was there, and I can safely tell you there is nothing funny about this situation."

"So why don't you start by telling me how Viktor Volkov got dead?"

"Well it starts with pointing out that Maggie Marshall and her two young *children* are alive."

"Surely there was some way to accomplish their rescue without burning years of work and starting World War three by offing one of the most powerful men in a country that is not exactly on friendly terms with us right now."

Ryder fought to keep his voice steady through his growing anger. "First, it insults me to insinuate I wouldn't have thought of the consequences, particularly since I've had a front row seat to the power of the Volkov Bratva. More importantly, I've more than proven I'm able to evaluate risks and balance them with the desired outcome of my mission. If I hadn't taken action when I did, an innocent American woman and her two young daughters would be dead. Call me old-fashioned, but I thought we were going to the trouble of infiltrating one of the most powerful crime families on the globe to protect American lives."

The only man in a three-piece suit who'd sat silently at the other end of the table broke in, saying, "No one is denying you did a brave thing saving the Marshall family. We need to understand why you killed Viktor Volkov in the process."

Ryder chuckled. "I think you have been out of the field a little too long, sir." He was giving the men around the table the benefit of the doubt. He didn't have a clue if any of them other than Webster had served a day undercover or not. "We aren't factory workers. We have to make things up as we go. Gauge risks and weigh potential outcomes; making snap decisions with the information we have in the moment. I've reviewed the mission from every angle and I stand behind my actions."

Brandon Webster, the lowest ranking man in the room other than Ryder jumped into the interrogation with the first sensible question. "Helms, why don't you lay it out for us. We read the report you filed in Germany, but I'd like to hear you walk us through what happened once you entered the Volkov compound."

Ryder nodded a thanks to his boss for helping reset the room and then launched into a detailed verbal report of everything that happened last Thursday night, beginning with getting into the car with Alexi. He left no details out, talking through his actions as well as his decision making process along the way. It took him two hours of non-stop talking. He was grateful the men around the table didn't interrupt him with stupid questions, only asking for clarification a time or two. By the time he was done, he felt drained and wished he could go home and sleep for a week.

The men in the room had other ideas.

"Thank you for your detailed report, Agent Helms." It was George Fortin speaking. "While it's unfortunate to lose your connection with the Bratva, you won't be held personally responsible for Viktor Volkov's death."

He chuckled before he could stop himself. When every face was like stone, no one understanding why he was laughing, Ryder added. "Maybe the company isn't holding me responsible, but you can bet your ass that Artel Volkov and his brothers disagree." He sobered before adding, "I'll never be able to turn my car on again without wondering if today is the day I go boom. I'll be watching over my shoulder waiting for them to show up to collect their revenge. They aren't the kind of men to let a betrayal like this go unchecked. Worse, I know I put every agent on the ground in Russia in danger as the family turns over every rock looking for me."

Ryder could see agreement in the eyes of every man around the table. It was the man in the suit at the far end of the table who stood first, bringing the meeting to a close. "Gentlemen, let's let Webster finish debriefing Agent Helms so he can get some rest." He had walked towards Ryder, stopping short of where he sat before he finished, "Well done, young man. I realize that not everyone around this table would have made the same choices you did in the same situation, but I'm on record that it was a solid operation." He reached into his vest pocket and came out with a business card, placing it in front of Ryder. "I'll be debriefing Director Ryan personally. I want you to call me if anyone gives you shit, Agent Helms."

He barely got out his, "Thank you, sir," before the man was at the door. Only then did he glance down to find out he was Deputy Director, the man second in command of the Central Intelligence Agency.

*Fuck. I'm glad I didn't have a clue who he was before this meeting started.*

Understanding that the highest ranking man in the room had just dismissed them, the rest of the office's occupants stood, most quietly shuffling out without another word. Several stopped to pat him on the back or shake his hand.

Only when Ryder and his boss were alone did Brandon Webster whistle. "Holy shit, that was intense."

Ryder finished the last swig of his now cold coffee before answering. "After last Thursday, that was a walk in the park," he countered. He then asked the question he needed an answer to. "How is Hansen doing? Did he make it?"

"He came through surgery and is still hanging on. The last report I got listed him in critical, but stable, condition."

It was a good sign he'd made it this long. "He's tough. He'll make it." Changing the subject, he asked his next question. "So now what the fuck happens? I get put out to pasture?"

Webster took a pack of cigarettes out and lit up. It always cracked Ryder up that the federal ban on smoking inside government buildings was broken often inside the walls of CIA headquarters. Puffing out a line of smoke, he finally answered.

"You have some choices. At thirty-eight, you're young enough to start over. With your language skills, we could place you in almost any eastern European country tomorrow. We still need eyes and ears on the ground across the globe, whether you're in deep cover or not."

Ryder'd suspected that would be the first option offered. Starting over didn't sound like much fun at the moment.

"Next..." he prompted.

"You could retire. You have thirteen active years in. That's more than most."

"Retire and do what? I don't golf and don't feel like taking up knitting."

His boss gave him a dirty look as he puffed on his cancer stick. "Smart-ass. There's a lot of work for retired agents in the private sector."

"Are you trying to get rid of me?"

"Fuck no."

Ryder was getting impatient. "Then what else is there?"

"There are plenty of options. Stay in D.C. Become a handler. Work in mission control. Put your language skills to work in interpretation and logistics. Become a trainer. There are dozens of jobs you're overqualified for."

None of those sounded very exciting, but they did sound a bit safer. Still, he'd be bored in a week with a desk job. He knew it in his heart.

Finally, Webster mentioned something that sounded slightly better. "Hell, we could put you in interrogations with your success rate at breaking people. Don't worry about it for a while. You've earned some time off. Keep your phone on in case I need to get ahold of you, but take a vacation." When Ryder made to argue, he held up his hand. "This is not a request, it's an order. I don't want to see you back here for a few weeks. Get some rest. Eat some food, and for God's sake, take a shower."

Ryder was suddenly very tired. He couldn't wait to follow his boss's directions to the letter. Eat, shower, and sleep–in that order. Pushing to his feet, he reached out to shake Webster's offered hand. "Thanks for having my back with that crowd. I didn't know what to expect."

Webster chuckled. "Hell, I don't know half the time either. I'll try to keep them off you for a week, but I'd expect a call from Chip Marshall, unless you'd rather I not pass him through to you. He called yesterday looking to thank you personally for rescuing his family. The man actually started crying while talking to me."

Ryder had had time on the plane to research the Marshall family. He hadn't known anything about them during the mission and was glad. He wouldn't have wanted to figure in the fact that they were part of one of the countries ten richest families, making their billions in oil. Marshall had taken his family to Russia on oil business that apparently had been cutting into the Volkov's livelihood.

"Naw, that's fine. If he wants to talk, I'll listen."

He was at the door, about to leave when his boss shouted, "I mean it. Get some downtime, Helms."

Ryder didn't answer.

⁓

FORTY-EIGHT HOURS LATER, Ryder finally felt rested, having slept at least half the time he'd been holed up in his apartment. He'd been living off bad Chinese and pizza, relying on delivery, since he didn't have even the basic staples in his kitchen. He wasn't usually home long enough to cook.

He should feel relaxed, but instead, he was on edge. He'd spent the last hour pacing his small apartment located only a few miles south of CIA Headquarters. This was exactly how he'd spent the weeks of his recovery the last time he was back in the States, feeling a bit like a trapped animal. He needed purpose. A goal. Without it, his mind wandered to things he shouldn't think about that only put him more on edge.

He was resisting turning on the TV or getting on the Internet. Not because he wanted entertainment, but because he knew it would be hard to resist searching for information on *her*. He prided himself on his self-control, yet memories of a beautiful woman he'd had the pleasure of dominating for three short hours months before refused to be quieted. While he'd been working, he'd forced himself to focus only on his mission, but short of worrying if the Volkovs had uncovered his real identity yet, he didn't have any company business to distract him from his favorite pastime–thinking of Khloe Monroe. Remembering the feel of her thick hair in his grasp as he'd fucked her–the sexy sounds she'd made as she'd allowed herself to come apart in his arms–the tears in her eyes as he'd crushed her during their brief good-bye–it all made his chest compress with an odd, empty feeling that he loathed.

Even after he took a five-mile run and a long, hot shower, he couldn't shake visions of his temporary submissive from his mind. Finally giving in to temptation, he took a seat in the plush leather lounge chair, the only furniture in his living room, and turned on the television. He spent a few minutes flipping through global news channels looking for updates on events happening halfway around the globe. But as he knew he would, he eventually found himself stopping on the entertainment channels, looking for news out of Hollywood. It was a waste of time. What were the chances of them doing a story on Khloe?

When a small rectangle appeared over the anchor's shoulder with a smiling Khloe in it, his heart lurched. He scrambled to turn up the volume, not wanting to miss any part of the story.

"Inside sources on the set of Khloe Monroe's newest movie report the actress has received several threats. *Inside Edition* has confirmed that security in and around the Burbank studio where she is currently filming *Smuggled Dreams* is at its highest level. This coming on the heels of the police activity at her New York City apartment building last week have insiders concerned for Ms. Monroe's safety."

Ryder sat up in the chair, leaning forward with his elbows on his knees, getting closer to the TV as he watched footage of a burly guy with tattoos, his arm around her waist, pushing a frightened looking Khloe through a throng of fans gathered for her autograph. He gritted his teeth watching her bodyguard shielding her with his own body.

*Jealousy doesn't look good on you, Helms.*

The story continued. "Sources close to the studio are concerned that the Hollywood opening of Khloe's critically acclaimed movie, *Dirty Business,* might be in jeopardy. It's reported that Khloe Monroe is having second thoughts about taking to the red carpet this Thursday evening with her stalker still at large. Co-star and boyfriend, Dean Reynolds, is said to be very concerned for the love of his life."

The story cut to the close-up of some pretentious asshole who appeared to be enjoying his time in the spotlight. The words 'Exclusive Interview' crawled along the bottom of the screen as the *Inside Edition* reporter spoke with Khloe's boyfriend. "I'm not allowed to talk about the investigation. Just know that Khloe has been in danger and those of us who love her the most are working to protect her as best we can until the culprit behind the threats against her person is in custody."

*Of course she has a boyfriend now, asshole. Why would she be waiting for you? You threw her away at the end of Valentine's Day.*

It didn't matter that it had been for her own good. He'd still hurt her. What she didn't know was it had hurt him to leave her there, too.

When the story ended, he flipped off the TV, pushing to his feet to pace his apartment again until he found himself in front of his laptop. He spent the next hour Googling all the information he could find on the recent threats against Khloe. He found photos from her on the red carpet in NYC the week before, looking exactly like the princess that he had nicknamed her. It only angered him more to find the asshole Dean Reynolds had been at her side and the bodyguard followed a few feet behind her. Two men who had a place in her life, unlike him.

But it was the final photo he found, posted by some asshat paparazzo, of a terrified and barefoot Khloe being hustled to a limo in a dark alley wearing only a bathrobe. She was being carried by her bodyguard. Ryder stared at the photo for several long minutes, memorizing the tired lines of her face, a sick lump of pizza settling in his gut.

*Ah, Princess, what has you so spooked?*

# CHAPTER 6

$\mathcal{T}$he barricade gate at the security hut slid up, allowing the driver of the luxury SUV to proceed into the restricted area of the movie studio in Burbank, California. Khloe was comforted by the extreme vetting of all visitors to the historic studio. It gave her hope that the crazy stalker who'd been scaring the shit out of her wouldn't be able to get close enough to put her in danger.

Her driver today was Michael, an old friend of Trevor's. Together, the two men, who were each armed with pistols, bolstered her confidence. It allowed her to turn her focus back on the manuscript in front of her. She'd tried to study her lines for the last few days, but it had been hard to concentrate. Memories of the pictures plastered across all of the surfaces of her bathroom back in Manhattan continuously intruded into Khloe's thoughts at the most inopportune times. Worse, in the days following the break-in, new details had surfaced letting her know she'd been receiving escalating messages for months.

To say her confidence with the team of people who surrounded her had been shaken would be an understatement. She couldn't banish the feeling that it was time to make some major changes in her inner circle, but it would have to wait. Already juggling a busy filming scheduled for *Smuggled Dreams*, her current film, and public relations appearances for *Dirty Business*, adding on major personnel changes just wasn't a possibility. Layer on the threats and maintaining her pretend relationship with Dean, and her plate was overflowing.

Her stress levels were off the charts which meant she was only sleeping a little and eating even less.

They'd entered through the back entrance to the studio and it took them almost five minutes to wind their way through the narrow streets between the mammoth sound studios where hundreds of popular, and not so popular, movies and TV shows had been filmed over the years. Michael didn't bring the SUV to a stop until he'd pulled into the parking lot where a line of a half dozen luxury motor coaches were lined up in an impressive row.

Trevor got out first, opening Khloe's backseat door and holding his hand out to assist her from the vehicle. He may have been helping her exit the car, but his eyes were scanning across the entire area, assessing the space for danger.

She'd been locked down at the NYC Marriott for three full days with her bodyguard, refusing to leave her suite and making the police come to her when they'd insisted on another round of interviews. Flying back to California had helped her relax marginally. She may be naive, but since the break-in had occurred on the other side of the country, it was easier to pretend she was safe again in California.

The morning sun was already hot for late April. It was a good thing she didn't need to spend much time outside or she'd need another shower before she went in for hair and makeup. The gust of air-conditioning welcomed her as Trevor held the door for her as she scaled the few steps up to her personal trailer.

Being the lead female character did have its perks.

The brightness of the sun had temporarily blinded her, so she didn't see the Kaplans sitting in the middle of the living space of the luxury motorhome until it was too late to retreat. She shouldn't have been surprised to see them, but she was. Before a word was uttered, she glanced around the room to see her personal assistant, Ricky, already there, avoiding making eye contact with her. Her costume, hair and makeup crew was there, waiting to get started on her transformation. They were smart enough to stay seated at the other end of the space in front of the large mirror that doubled as Khloe's dressing room.

"I can't believe you cut off all contact with us, Khloe," Natalie attacked.

Khloe sighed, throwing her leather bag on the marble kitchen counter before crossing to the refrigerator to grab an ice cold sparkling water she'd asked always be stocked and waiting. Only after she took a swig did she answer her publicist.

"I was on lockdown."

"Not from us."

"From everyone," she answered flatly, refusing to let them intimidate her.

Natalie was so agitated she shot to her feet as Khloe took a seat in the comfortable lounge chair she liked to take a nap in if her schedule allowed for it.

"We've phoned and texted. You ignored us."

"Yes," she leveled, taking another sip of water, trying not to be drawn into the argument she should be having.

"How dare you! We need to strategize for your interviews!"

"We have all week for that. Opening night isn't until Thursday."

"I'm not talking about opening night." The tone of voice the elder woman chose to use assured Khloe she didn't want to ask the next question.

"What interviews?" Khloe pressed, glancing sideways at Ricky, her personal assistant. If she had appointments set up, it was his job to prep her. The guilt on his face wasn't a good sign.

Bernie finally injected, "Don't think we're going to let you lose this opportunity."

"Opportunity?" Khloe was genuinely confused until Bernie set her straight.

"Your stalker, of course. You can't pay for this kind of exposure. It gets you visibility and sympathy from the fans. So far your disappearance has enhanced the story, but we're at the end of the window now. We have an exclusive set up with ABC at one this afternoon. They need time for production to prep the segment for the evening and late night news. This is excellent free publicity."

"Free publicity?" Khloe asked incredulously. "Are you fucking kidding me?" Her shout made Ricky jump. "This is my real life we're talking about, not my movie."

Bernie lectured her as if she were a naive child. "You're an actress, Kalina. You have no real life. The day you hired us and asked us to get you Oscar winning roles, you took the stage. We turned you into Khloe Monroe, and you have a responsibility to your fans... to share what's happening in your life."

Like always, his use of her birth name was meant to remind her how far she'd come since she started modeling as Kalina Monawski the summer after she'd graduated from high school. They conveniently always forgot that she'd only hired them two years ago. The first six years of her career she'd launched Khloe Monroe on her own.

That's when it hit her. "It was you. You called the media and leaked the story of the break-in in Manhattan." She hoped she was wrong.

Natalie's haughty "Of course we did," was the final straw for Khloe.

She pushed to her feet and shouted, "Everyone out! Now!" The crew at the other end of the trailer bolted to the door as if they'd been shot out of a cannon. When Ricky looked lost, she added, "You too, Ricky. Out."

His relief was palpable. He followed the hair stylist out and closed the door behind him.

Khloe took a deep breath before turning back to face the Kaplans.

Bernie didn't wait for her to speak, jumping on the attack first. "We only did what you pay us to do. It's that simple."

Khloe's body vibrated with energy she was so angry. "There is nothing simple about this! I have a lunatic stalking me. The messages are coming faster and getting more aggressive." A new thought came to her in her rant at them. "In the three days since the break-in, you've left me voicemails and text messages. Dozens of them between the two of you."

"Yes, and you were rude enough to ignore them all," Natalie countered.

"Funny, out of all of those messages, not a single damn one asked how I was doing. Not once did you say you were sorry for all I was going through or offer to help me get to safety. No offers to send over new clothes or personal items since everything I owned was now part of a criminal investigation. No flowers, card or hell, not even an email to let me know you were worried about me and hoped I was feeling better after my ordeal." Khloe was on a roll. Her uncharacteristic rant had effectively stunned the Kaplans into silence, allowing her to continue. "I'm just a Goddamn paycheck to you. You'd run me over with your car and then back up and run over me again if you thought it would get more publicity and a bigger pay day."

Her words had hit home, yet the crusty old couple was too jaded to take her concerns seriously. "You're being melodramatic and emotional. Are you PMSing?"

"Are you fucking kidding me? Did you just ask me if I had my period?"

Bernie visibly blanched, "Okay, I might have taken that a little too far. All I meant was you are being overly emotional."

For the first time in her life, Khloe wanted to reach out and slap someone. Not someone. Bernie Kaplan. Her ears were ringing from the effort it took for her to keep from losing her shit.

"Get out. I don't want you here."

Natalie tried to smooth things over for her husband. "Let's not overreact. Bernie didn't mean anything by his insensitive comment. We really do need to prep you for this afternoon's interview."

"There is no interview this afternoon. I'm not going to use the illegal stalking by some crazed lunatic as a publicity stunt." An inkling of doubt made her add, "And if I find out either of you have had anything to do with these threats, not only will I fire you, but you can bet your ass I'll be giving interviews then to every news outlet that will listen to make sure they know what kind of bullshit you would go to for your clients."

"Why... I never..." Natalie was speechless.

Trevor's voice cut through the space. She'd missed him coming into the trailer. "You heard Khloe. She needs some privacy now."

Her eyes met his and she saw his approval for how she'd handled her agent and his wife.

The older couple headed to the exit, addressing Trevor as they left. "The ABC crew will be setting up in the front office of the studio at noon. You need to have Khloe prepped and ready for filming at one. They're sending Robin Roberts. This is a big deal, Trevor."

He didn't answer Natalie at first, but finally let her know, "Khloe and I will discuss it. We'll do whatever *she* decides."

The couple huffed out, slamming the door behind them and leaving Khloe and Trevor alone.

"Are you okay?" he asked.

She tried to lighten things up, not wanting to worry him. "Oh sure. Never been better." She took a long swig of her bottled water, trying to calm her rattled nerves.

"Apollo and Paul are asking for you. They want to get started." He hesitated, before adding, "I can tell them you aren't feeling well and that you need to leave."

The idea was so tempting, yet she had spent three days holed up in a hotel room, and it hadn't really helped her feel any safer so she knew spending the day barricaded in her LA rental wouldn't help. No. The only thing that would really help was the police catching the asshole responsible for terrorizing her.

"Thanks. It's tempting, but I'll pull it together. Thanks for backing me up with them this time."

The shadow of guilt crossed his face before he replied, "They conned me into hiding the fact that Dean was going to be in New York last week and I regret it. They also conned me into keeping some of the threats from you, but that was a mistake, too." He took another few steps closer to her before stopping so close she could reach out and touch him. "I am so sorry, Khloe. I don't ever want you to doubt where my loyalties lay. I'd do anything for you."

For a minute, Trevor's monologue was heartwarming, but as he took another step closer into her personal space, she saw a look in his eyes that shouldn't be there.

Sexual attraction.

She was in his arms the next second as he pulled her into a tight hug. When she tilted her head to ask him what he was doing, he leaned in and planted his lips on hers in a kind of kiss they'd never shared before. Before she could jerk away, she felt him tightening his embrace until their bodies were flush against each other, making it impossible for her to miss his erection.

She yanked away from him, twisting out of his arms until she was able to take a step back, putting distance between them again.

"What the hell was that?" His kiss had been passionate enough that her lips felt swollen. She lifted her fingers up to touch them, subconsciously trying to wipe away his touch.

"Khloe... Surely you have to know I care for you. Very much."

Her ears were ringing.

"Trevor... "

He stuttered his way through his declaration, "These last few weeks, when you've been in danger, I've had to face my feelings. The thought of something happening to you on my watch. Well, I couldn't deal with that. These last few days, being with you 24/7, well... it's shown me what I want."

"What you want?"

"You, Khloe. Well, *us* really."

"Trevor..."

"I know I'm surprising you, and maybe my timing sucks, but..."

"Stop. Please." She turned away from him, pacing to the other side of the room to put distance between them so she could think.

She didn't need this. Trevor was one of the only steady people in her life and now he was ruining it. Unwanted tears sprung to her eyes. She fought to hide them, but by the time he stepped up behind her, she felt drops overflowing, spilling down her cheeks.

"Talk to me. Please. Tell me I didn't just make the biggest mistake of my life," he pleaded.

Only she couldn't say that to him, because he had.

Khloe took a deep breath and turned to face him. She flinched away from him when he reached out to swoosh her tears away. Surprise was replaced with sadness in his brown eyes. She hadn't even said a word, but he knew her answer. He could read her like a book.

Would dating Trevor be that bad? He'd be the first man she'd go out with since Chase whom she felt actually cared about the real her. Not her public persona. Yet as she thought about the kiss they'd shared, she knew there was no way it would work. She cared about Trevor, but he was like a brother to her. A substitute for her own brother, Milek, whom she missed like crazy.

"I'm sorry," she whispered.

"So am I. I don't suppose we could pretend the last ten minutes didn't happen. Maybe just go back to the way things were?"

Damn it was tempting. "I'm not sure..."

"I insist. At least until we catch this asshole who is after you. I won't trust your safety to anyone else." He paused before adding. "You need me right now. No one else can protect you like I can."

Her pulse spiked. The only way she'd gotten through the last few days since the break-in was because she knew Trevor would give his life for her. He did make her feel safe. He was right. The thought of him not protecting her right now scared the shit out of her.

"Are you sure you can handle it?"

His smile was wan as he answered, "Not being able to protect you right now is the only thing I couldn't handle. I promise. I can keep it professional if that's the way you want it."

She didn't miss his hopeful inflection. "It's the way it needs to be."

They stood silently until it turned awkward.

"I'll go out and tell the crew to come in and get started."

She nodded. "Thanks, but I'd like a few minutes alone first. Ask them to give me five."

"You got it." He paused, like he wanted to say something more, but then decided against it, turning and heading out into the sun, closing the door softly behind him.

The silence of the trailer was a welcome change. She'd had almost no time alone since the break-in to think, and God did she need to think. Everything was closing in on her and she felt like she might suffocate if she didn't relieve some of the stress weighing on her.

As if fate wanted to say 'fuck you' to her need for silence, she heard her cell phone ringing in her leather bag on the counter. She let it go to voicemail as she paced the small space, trying to think through all she had on her plate. A ding alerted her to a voicemail message. Within seconds, the alert for an incoming text rang next.

"Jesus, it better not be the Kaplans." She wrestled her phone from her purse and her heart lurched when she found it was Chase Cartwright trying to reach her. There'd been a time when hearing from her ex, Chase, would have brightened her day, but since Valentine's Day, she couldn't think of Chase without remembering the dangerous game of Valentine Roulette he'd conned her into playing. How disastrous it had been.

Okay, the event itself hadn't been disastrous, but the aftermath of having to walk away from the man who'd turned out to be her sexual soul mate was draining her. She should have moved on by now, yet she felt stuck, unable to forget how Ryder Helms had mastered her perfectly for exactly three hours and then walked out of her life without a backward glance, leaving her to wonder if it had all been some figment of her imagination.

MESSAGE FROM CHASE:
*I heard about your stalker. Am worried about you. Check in when you can and let us know if there is anything Jaxson, Emma and I can do to help.*
*XOCC*

AS TEMPTING AS IT WAS, she didn't think it was a good idea to ask them to get in touch with Ryder for her and tell him... what? What the fuck would she say to him right now even if he were here? He'd made it clear he had no room in his life for a silly actress. Ryder Helms was a dead end for her.

MESSAGE TO CHASE:
*Thanks, but I'll be okay. Police investigating and have beefed up security. My love to you, Jaxson and Emma.*
*XOKM*

HER FIVE MINUTES had flown by. The knock at the door followed by six hustling people invading her trailer assured her that her meditation time was over, and it was time to get down to work.

Sandra, the costume designer, worked to get Khloe poured into the full leathers she'd be wearing for that day's filming schedule. She'd been having fun playing the daughter of the leader of a motorcycle gang.

Hair was next. Randy, her stylist, worked his magic to create the messy up-do for today's scene with her long locks.

"Working with you is like a dream, Ms. Monroe," he flattered her. "Your hair is the perfect base for all of my special creations. I'll stick around the set in case you need a touchup later."

"Thanks, Randy."

It was Cathy's turn next to start on her makeup. The award-winning makeup artist stepped in front of Khloe, blocking her view of the hairstylist in the mirror. "I need to get started because we're running out of time. Mr. Lancer wants you on the set in five minutes, and we're never going to make that."

For several minutes, both professionals prepped Khloe until Randy was finished. "All done! I can't wait to show you the back." He stepped around her to the long counter that held all of the supplies. Randy spent several minutes rummaging through the drawers and cabinets. Finally, Cathy prodded him.

"What are you looking for?"

"The big hand-held mirror so I can show her what the back looks like."

Cathy helped with a suggestion. "I think I saw it in the bottom drawer."

Randy leaned down, opening the drawer and reaching out for the long-handled mirror and then handing it to Khloe while swiveling the chair sideways so she could angle it to see her hair.

Only when Khloe's eyes focused on the reflection in front of her, it was the message scribbled on the glass with what she hoped was red lipstick and not blood that she saw.

Her reflexes were sluggish, not immediately recognizing it for the threat that it was. But when she did, her blood-curdling scream coincided with her releasing her grip on the offending accessory. The handle had become like a proverbial hot-potato. She flung the threat away from her, crashing it into the huge mirror, shattering it into a web of cracks.

*Run. I need to get the fuck out of here.*

Khloe shot out of the plush chair, pushing her way through the crowd of studio employees standing in a dazed confusion, unsure why she was screaming.

Even in her panicked state, Khloe suspected she was overreacting. She was surrounded by people she knew. People she trusted. Yet she felt so violated. Like in her NYC apartment, this bastard was slowly ruining the places she'd previously felt safe by proving he had access.

She met Trevor at the door. Having heard her screaming, he was rushing in as she was rushing out. She flung herself into his arms, hanging on for dear life while crying out, "He was here! Get me out of here!"

To his credit, Trevor didn't stop to try to rationalize with her. Instead, he turned and jumped from the steps to the pavement below before taking off running as if the boogieman were chasing them.

Khloe clung to him like a monkey to her mother, letting him weave through the trailers, trucks and cars in the lot towards her waiting SUV.

Michael must have seen them coming because he pulled out and met them in the middle of the driveway.

Only when both she and Trevor were in the backseat did he take off again, slamming his foot on the gas to rush towards the exit of the studio grounds.

"You're safe now, Khloe," her bodyguard reassured her.

She wanted to believe him, but knowing that her stalker was close enough to her to gain entry to both her home in NYC and her private trailer in California rocked her to her core. She was grateful she hadn't been hurt... *yet.* But it was clear anyone could get to her at anytime if they were determined enough.

# CHAPTER 7

"*P*lease take a seat, Ms. Monroe. We'd like to start."

They'd saved her a seat at the head of the mammoth table situated in the boardroom of the producer's upscale offices in the heart of Burbank. The problem was there was only one and she needed two.

"We need a chair for Trevor."

Bernie who had saved her the lone seat spoke up, "There are seats around the wall for support personnel," waving his hand in the general direction where a line of skimpily-dressed personal assistants sat waiting to jump to their male-executive's beck and call.

"Trevor isn't support personnel. He'll need a seat at the table." When not one of the dozen men around the table moved to assist her, she turned to the row of assistants to add, "Can one of you bring in another chair?"

The woman closest to her looked at her boss sitting at the long table before she'd help. It made Khloe want to laugh wondering if she could take a piss without permission.

Once they were all seated, Edward Rivera, the executive

producer for both *Dirty Business* and *Smuggled Dreams* opened the meeting. Khloe took a minute to glance around the table of over a dozen people. The only women who got to sit at the 'big boy' table were Natalie and herself. She didn't recognize most of the people present and that made her nervous.

"Thanks for coming in, Khloe. I know it was difficult for you to leave your apartment."

She caught the exasperation in his tone. After all, he had two major box-office projects in motion with Khloe as the female lead. Considering one of those films was set for its grand opening the following night and the second was in the middle of production, he had a lot riding on Khloe's ability to pull it together.

She was grateful that he'd been a big supporter of hers. Rivera had taken a chance when he'd chosen her over more seasoned talent with *Dirty Business*. She'd been awarded the even juicier role in *Smuggled Dreams* because she'd exceeded his expectations in the first film.

Well that, and the fact that she was 'low drama' as he liked to call her. She could sense his impatience with her now that she was squarely sitting in the 'high drama' category.

"I've asked everyone to come to this joint planning session so we can nail down plans for tomorrow's opening of *Dirty Business* as well as the shoot schedule for Khloe's scenes for *Smuggled*."

She was furious when he launched into a review of an already printed schedule straight away without any discussion of the main topic she'd come for. Glancing around the table, she noticed everyone was focused at the paper in front of them, refusing to make eye contact with her.

Fuckers. Not one of them would stick their neck out with the powerful producer.

"Excuse me, Edward," she interrupted, waiting for him to stop talking before continuing. "But I think we've skipped a major topic that has to come first." She was proud of how steady she kept her voice. Their eyes met despite the distance between them.

"I came today for an update on the police investigation into my stalker case and how it will impact the projects. They go hand in hand."

All eyes in the room looked at the financier. She got the impression they all knew something she didn't know and he'd been elected their spokesperson.

"I'm afraid the investigation hasn't concluded yet. The stalker is still at large."

"I'm aware of that. Or at least I would hope the police, or someone, would advise me otherwise had he been captured. Did they get any fingerprints from my trailer? Or how about the security footage. People can't waltz on the lot without credentials."

"Precisely, so it does narrow the suspects, but..." He paused before adding, "Our investigators haven't drawn any conclusions yet."

Trevor picked up on it too. "What do you mean, your investigators?" When no one answered, he asked the general room, "Who in here is from the police department?"

When no one identified themselves, he cursed under his breath, but loud enough for those seated close to them to hear.

An eerie calmness came over Khloe, not unlike the one that had come to her rescue when she'd walked in on Dean and Gloria fucking in her bedroom. Remembering that moment had her seeking out Dean who was seated about halfway down the table. He was one of the few people brave enough to look her in the eye.

Edward had picked up where he left off, ignoring Khloe's previous concerns. Her mind raced, thinking through her options instead of paying attention. The thought of going on with her life as if nothing had happened felt impossible. Both invasions into her private space had to have been accomplished by someone with close access to her. She didn't have some random stalker sitting far away in his mother's basement stroking off to her magazine covers. Someone who knew where she lived in NYC and had access to her apartment had also gained access to her locked trailer on the secure studio lot. Based on the photos he'd left in her apartment, she suspected she knew the person. Hell, for all she knew, he could be in the room at that very moment.

Khloe shot to her feet, bringing Edward's speech to a halt while all eyes in the room turned to her. She was grateful when Trevor stood next to her. Even if he couldn't help her with what she had to do next, he could at least catch her if she toppled over from the crushing stress she was under.

"With all due respect, Edward, I'll be making changes to the proposed schedule." She took a deep breath before dropping her bomb. "When any of you become the victim of a stalker who is resourceful and bold enough to break into not one, but two private and locked personal spaces of yours, then you can make the decisions. But since it was my home... my personal trailer... my vote is the only one that counts."

She let that sink in before continuing. "So here is what I am willing to do. I will attend the opening tomorrow night, but I expect at least two more personal bodyguards assigned to me to assist Trevor starting this afternoon and until the perpetrator is caught. I also want to limit the amount of interviews on the red carpet so let's set up press interviews earlier in the day at a hotel suite so I can limit my time in public."

She paused, before dropping her next bomb. "I will be hiring my own private investigators who will be taking over the investigation–at the studio's expense, of course. I understand your reluctance to call the police in. After all, then you'd have to admit that the studio's security had failed to keep me safe, which could turn into a liability problem for all of you. But let me be clear. When my investigators find the culprit, we will be calling the police, and I will be pressing charges. Get any thoughts of trying to sweep this under the rug out of your heads, gentlemen." She then turned to address a smiling Natalie, "And no, we're not turning this into a publicity stunt, either. The interviews tomorrow will be focused on the movie and nothing else. Prep the press accordingly, Natalie."

Turning back to the rest of the room she concluded. "This is *my* life. Some lunatic broke into *my* home. He left *me* a note yesterday describing how he couldn't wait to get me to the secret hideaway he'd created where he could fuck me all day and night for the rest of my life. If that had happened to any of your wives, sisters or God forbid, daughters, you all would be losing your shit. Maybe you should keep that in mind the next time you decide to sweep bodily threats to a woman under the rug. Email me the final press schedule."

She'd used up every ounce of her bravery. Had anyone in the room chosen to rebut her speech, she'd have burst into tears. Thankfully, the room sat in stunned silence as she leaned down to grab her big purse and then loop her arm through Trevor's, allowing him to lead her out of the room. The glass door to the boardroom was at the other end of the room, and she felt all eyes following her until they had left the room.

Her blood was pounding in her ears by the time they exited into the mid-day sunshine. Trevor had texted Michael from the elevator, and he arrived with the SUV as they emerged. She felt eyes on her as she leaned heavily on her guard, finally letting him lift her into the backseat, sliding in behind her and quickly closing the door.

Khloe's mind raced as they sped away from the office building. How she wished she could drive to the airport and get on a plane going somewhere, anywhere. But then what? She'd worked too hard to get where she was. She wasn't going to give some asshole the power to take it all away.

It was time to go on the offense.

Swishing the tears away impatiently, she dug her phone out of her purse. She didn't have many people in her life she trusted explicitly, but she did have a few, and it was time to ask for their help.

Flipping through her contacts, she found who she was looking for and pressed *SEND*. When she heard the concerned voice at the other end of the phone say her name, she choked up with emotion and could only gush out "Chase" in reply.

She felt safer already.

# CHAPTER 8

"Good evening, Mr. Helms. Welcome back to Black Light."

Ryder was surprised the employee standing behind the counter in the middle of the locker room at the entry recognized him on sight, particularly since he hadn't been back for a visit since Valentine's Day.

"Good memory. I'm sorry, I don't remember your name."

"It's Danny, sir."

"Danny, I meant to give Spencer a call to let him know I was coming. I'm not sure if you have..."

The young man cut him off. "You're on our pre-approved entry list, sir. I'm afraid I do need to see your identification as a formality. If you'd please put all electronics into the open locker to your left, I can then let you proceed into the club. I'll warn you. It's pretty quiet tonight, even for a Wednesday night. There aren't many single subs here to play with, yet."

Ryder crossed to take his watch off and deposit it along with his cell phone and concealed Glock in the small locker while he answered. "That's okay. I needed to get out of the house and thought I'd check in with your boss."

That much was the truth, although if he was honest with himself, he was here to pump Spencer for information on Khloe. He hadn't been able to bring himself to call in favors over at the FBI to try to track down a private phone number for her. As a celebrity, it wasn't like her contact info was readily available to the public, but he was sure his buddies in the intel community could track her down.

Even if he got her number, he probably wouldn't call.

But he would be more subtle. She was friends with the owners. If Davidson had heard from her, Ryder wouldn't mind listening to an update on how she was doing.

The music was more subdued on this visit than in the past. As Danny had warned him, only a smattering of couples were already there playing throughout the expansive club. The lights seemed brighter too, allowing him a good view of the submissive currently getting her body lit up by her Dom and his flogger on one of the raised platforms. He couldn't see where it was coming from, but the distinctive sounds of bodies slapping together in heated sex added to the ambiance of the club as he wove his way through the sex equipment and nearly empty seating areas towards the bar.

He recognized the bartender on duty. She'd been one of the fifteen submissives to play roulette back in February, and if he wasn't mistaken, she was the one Spencer had lost his shit over. He took a seat at one of the open stools as she came to take his order.

"Mr. Helms, it's good to see you back at Black Light."

*Why the hell does everyone remember me? I have no clue what the fuck her name is.*

Apparently, his face registered his thoughts because she introduced herself. "I'm Klara, the bar manager. What can I get you tonight?"

"Bourbon on the rocks. Make it a double and I want top shelf shit."

The beauty grinned, "Is there any other kind?" Her bright red lipstick made her pale skin almost translucent in the club's neon lighting, and as she turned to grab the bottle of booze, he admired her lean legs peeking out from her short skirt.

His friend was a lucky guy.

Only after she'd served his drink did he finally ask, "Spencer around tonight?" He hoped he sounded more nonchalant than he felt. He wasn't sure why, but he felt embarrassed to come scrounging for gossip on a woman. It all felt so... high schoolish.

"Yeah, he's back in his office. He tells everyone he's busy, but I know he's really playing Candy Crush. He's addicted." She smiled mischievously.

Ryder chuckled. "I haven't fallen prey to that trap yet. Go tell the old man it's time to put away his toys. He has company."

"I'd love to."

Ryder sipped the liquor, welcoming the burn as he swallowed. She was gone long enough for him to empty the rock glass and get a nice buzz on.

When the bartender reappeared behind the bar with Spencer following, Ryder knew immediately they'd made him wait while they got it on in the back office. Klara's red lipstick was smudged and she was walking a bit bow-legged as if she either had a plug up her ass or cum dripping down her thighs. Her inability to look Ryder in the eye combined with the shit-eating grin on his old friend's face sealed his conclusion.

"Nice of you to join me," he quipped. "You have lipstick on your collar."

Spencer slapped Klara's ass, and she squealed before giving him a deadly look and moving to the other end of the bar to check on her other customers. The Master Dom stopped in front of Ryder, leaning over and placing his forearms on the wide bar before stating, "My collar's not the only place I have her lipstick."

"Get a room," Ryder deadpanned.

"This is my room."

Ryder couldn't really argue with that.

"So to what do I owe this honor? I thought you were overseas. I didn't expect you back for a while."

His friend had served with Ryder at one point so Spencer had a pretty good idea how things worked when on a deep undercover assignment. Ryder made eye contact with his friend before answering with a simple, "I got burned."

The Dom's eyes widened. "Fuck, that sucks. At least you lived to talk about it. Who the hell burned you?"

Ryder made a motion to Klara to bring him a refill before answering honestly. "I burned myself."

Spencer held out his own empty rock glass for his girl to fill when she returned with the bottle of bourbon. Once she left, he held up his glass as a salute. "To living to talk about it."

The men clinked glasses, both downing more of the amber liquid before the next question arrived from his friend. "So now what?"

"Who the fuck knows. I'm on leave for a while, trying to figure it out. At least I have options."

"Does this mean you'll be coming around more often?"

Ryder doubted it. Being at the club reminded him of his time here with Khloe. He already thought about her more than he wanted to. The last thing he needed to do was have memories of her thrown in his face.

"Naw, probably not. I'm here for the booze and privacy more than anything."

His friend eyed him up suspiciously. The men knew each other well and were both trained in interrogation methods. Keeping subtle secrets was hard.

Spencer's focus shifted to someone coming up behind Ryder just before he felt the slap on his back between his shoulder blades. Ryder turned in time to see Jaxson Davidson sliding into the stool next to him.

He'd come here hoping to talk to the owner of the club, only now seeing him here Ryder suddenly regretted drinking so much. He could see the intensity in Jaxson's eyes he'd forgotten about. This was the kind of man he needed to keep his wits about himself when interacting with, not get sloppy drunk.

"Helms. Your timing is impeccable."

He didn't know what the newcomer meant by that cryptic message.

"Davidson." Ryder raised his glass as if to salute him.

"How much have you had to drink?"

"Don't worry. I'm not playing tonight."

Jaxson reached out and pulled the glass out of Ryder's hand as it was almost touching his lips. "I don't give a shit about that. We need to talk. I was happy when Danny let me know you'd checked in." The owner looked at Spencer and added, "Give us a minute, will you, Spencer?"

"Sure thing. I'll go back and finish up the payroll."

Only after Spencer had disappeared did Jaxson grab the departed man's deserted glass and down the last swig of bourbon before turning on the stool to talk with Ryder. "He's so full of shit. I know he's going back there to play fucking Candy Crush." Jaxson's friendly grin disarmed him.

Only after the men shared a chuckle at their mutual buddy's expense did Jaxson get serious again. "I'm pretty good at reading people, Helms. I hope I haven't read you wrong."

Ryder jabbed the taller man. "Do you use tarot cards or crystals for your readings?"

"I'd love to spar, but I don't have time to dick around. We're leaving for the airport in less than an hour and I have other calls to make before we go."

"Heading out on vacation?" He heard the slight slur in his speech.

"No." He waited to answer more until Ryder looked up into his eyes. "I'm flying to California to try to help protect Khloe."

Fuck. That got his attention. He'd come hoping for news of

her. Now he wasn't so sure he wanted to hear more. What the fuck was he going to do with information anyway?

Jaxson pressed him. "Did you hear me? Have you been watching the news? Some asshole is terrorizing her."

Hearing that she really was in trouble got his adrenaline flowing. His brain was clearing. He needed to think clearly. "Terrorizing her how?"

"Stalking her. It started a few weeks ago with threatening letters and emails. Now it's escalated to him gaining access to both her New York apartment and on-set private trailer. He left candid photos he'd taken as he stalked her with messages saying she was only his. His last note talked about how he had a secret hideaway ready to take her to and how he planned to fuck her every day for the rest of her life once he got her there."

An angry growl escaped as Jaxson finished filling him in.

*I need to find this asshole and make him wish he'd never been born.*

He forced himself to approach the problem like the professional he was. "Do the police have any leads?"

"No, and her production company and publicist are giving her the run around about working with the police."

"What the fuck? So who's protecting her now?"

"Her normal detail. They added another personal bodyguard, but she's freaking out. She called Chase this afternoon because the studio is making her go through with the scheduled red-carpet opening of her newest movie release tomorrow night. She begged Chase to come be with her for the event. All three of us are going instead."

Ryder remembered bits and pieces from the report on TV the day before and replied bitterly, "Why isn't her precious boyfriend, that Reynolds asshat, taking care of her?"

Jaxson grinned, clearly hearing the unguarded jealousy in Ryder's voice. "That's a sham. They broke up before Valentine's Day. He's the reason she'd come to visit Chase in the first place that weekend. She'd come home early and caught Dean with his dick stuck in one of their mutual friends."

Ryder hated himself a little for feeling relieved. "So why keep up the charade?"

"They're starring together in the movie that's opening. The studio demanded they keep up public pretenses that they're still together until after the movie is out for a few weeks."

The men sat in silence until Jaxson finally stood, looking at his watch before adding. "She called. She needs help. She asked for Chase and me, but it's you who she needs."

"Bullshit. She doesn't want to ever see me again."

"Don't bullshit me. I was there. I saw the chemistry between you two."

"It died when I walked out of the club."

Davidson changed tactics. "So why are you even here? And why aren't you playing with someone else?"

"I'm not in the mood for one thing, but more importantly, you don't have any available singles here to play tonight."

"Sure we do." Davidson waved over a scantily clad server girl who'd been flirting with other patrons. "This is Ling. She's available."

Jaxson was calling his bluff and he knew it. "Fuck off. Stop trying to stick your nose in where it doesn't belong."

Jaxson waved off Ling before answering. "Fine, Chase and I will take care of her while you stay here and get shitfaced like a loser." Before the taller man left, he pulled a business card from his wallet and threw it down on the bar in front of Ryder. "If you get your head out of your ass, give me a call. You're trained in what needs to be done to keep her safe. You can deny it all you want, but I know you have feelings for her. I just hope you call before it's too late."

Ryder didn't answer him. He didn't have anything to say. Instead, his mind raced with the possibilities of her being in danger. Jaxson left him to wallow in his self-doubt on if Khloe'd even want his help or not and then getting angry with himself for even considering what she wanted. He was the fucking Dominant. She was the sub.

Only he knew it wasn't that simple. Not with Khloe Monroe.

He waited long enough to make sure he wouldn't run into Davidson on his way out before pushing to his feet, not bothering to say goodbye to Spencer.

He made it back to his depressing apartment despite having a blood alcohol level that could have thrown him in jail if he'd been pulled over on the drive. Weary, he plopped in front of the TV again, flipping through news programs looking for new reports on Khloe. Instead, he found an update on the miraculous return of the Marshall family to the United States. Chip Marshall's grateful speech about the unnamed agent who'd gone undercover to extract his family filled him with pride.

He was about to nod off when one of the leadoff stories on *E!* was about the growing rumors of Khloe Monroe's problems. They reported they had no confirmation, but inside sources had disclosed she had a stalker. Ryder watched footage from earlier that day of Khloe leaving a downtown high-rise, the same body-guard from earlier reports snuggled close to her as he hustled her to a waiting SUV.

Ryder grabbed the remote control, stopping the screen on a close-up of Khloe. He hated the worry lines on her brow and the sad terror in her eyes. Those eyes were too beautiful to be clouded with panic. When he resumed the feed, he watched the guard scoop her up and place her into the back seat of the waiting SUV before sliding in next to her. A pang of something impossible to ignore constricted his heart, finally forcing him face it head-on.

*Fuck me. Some asshole wants to hurt her, but I'm the only one who gets to hurt Khloe Monroe.*

# CHAPTER 9

*K*hloe watched as tourists walked along looking down at the sidewalk, reading the names of the A-list celebrities who were forever memorialized with stars on the famous Walk of Fame. One day, those pedestrians would be taking their photo next to *her* star, but tonight, the smoky glass of the slow moving limo protected her from their prying eyes.

They weren't far from the Chinese Theater, the destination of her dreams. She'd been in the historical movie house many times, dreaming of the day she'd get to watch her own film on the mammoth screen.

Tonight would be that night.

She tried not to feel bitter that her stalker had put a damper on what should be one of the best days of her life.

Khloe jumped when a hand caressed her arm gently. She'd been lost in thought and almost forgotten she wasn't alone.

Dean moved to weave their fingers together intimately, but she snapped her hand away from his defensively. She may not have the option of pulling away when they were in public, but in the privacy of her own limo, he could keep his fucking hands to himself.

"Sorry. I didn't mean to startle you," he said.

He was conceited enough to attribute her reclusiveness as fear, when disgust was a closer description.

He babbled on, unaware of her feelings. "I've wanted to tell you how impressed I was with how you handled yourself in the boardroom with Richard yesterday."

Okay, so maybe he was sincerely trying to get back in her good graces.

Dean added, "It gave me a boner."

Or, maybe not.

Khloe glanced at her assistant, Ricky, and found a scowl on his face she wished she could clone.

Within minutes the driver was pulling up in front of the red carpet lining the sidewalk in front of the historic building where their grand opening of *Dirty Business* would be playing in a few hours.

It was still early by Hollywood standards. The sun pounded down on Hollywood Boulevard making her wish she'd held her ground and insisted that they cancel all red-carpet interviews. By the time she got to the air-conditioned theater, she'd be sweating like a bitch.

"Ricky, make sure there's someone to touch-up my makeup in private after we get inside."

"You got it," he replied, updating the tablet he never went anywhere without.

Trevor stood waiting near the curb, so tall he was a head above the pressing crowd. He'd gone ahead to do a security sweep before her arrival. Her newest and temporary security guard, Darius, had been provided by the studio. He exited the limo first to confer with Trevor. As the door opened, the shouts of fans screaming for Khloe and Dean grew louder, suspecting the stars of the night's premier were behind the thick windows of the luxury vehicle.

Once the door slammed closed behind Darius, Khloe's stomach gurgled in the quiet car, complaining at her constant neglect. At least her elegant floor-length champagne-colored satin gown wasn't as tight as the dress she'd worn at the pre-screening party in NYC. Her days of starving herself combined with the lack of sleep due to worry about her stalker had at least helped her lose a few pounds.

She jumped when fans got close enough to the car to start pounding on the windows, screaming her name. Her heart swelled with gratification. They loved her. They wanted to touch her–talk to her.

*And one of them could be the one who wants to hurt me.*

The thought turned her empty stomach. She tried to focus on the fact that, unlike in New York, tonight she'd have more people on the red carpet with her whom she trusted. People who would watch her back, refusing to let her psycho fan close enough to hurt her. She relaxed slightly.

When Dean tried to open the door, she stopped him. "Not yet. Not until Trevor opens it."

Dean looked annoyed at not being in charge.

The door finally opened, allowing the rowdy shouts for the stars to surround them.

Trevor leaned into the back of the car, looking serious. "It's showtime." He stared into her eyes. She could see his worry, and something else they hadn't talked about since he'd kissed her. When he glanced at Dean she suspected it was jealousy as he finished, "I'll be right behind you, Khloe."

Dean got out first and turned to help her out of the limo, already playing the role of the doting boyfriend he no longer was.

As they pressed through the throng of fans, she heard Trevor cursing behind her. Anger bubbled inside her. The studio's security should be keeping everyone held back. She felt hands touching her and she fought to stay calm, her public smile plastered on her face as she leaned heavily on Dean to press them through until they finally got far enough up the long sidewalk entrance to get to the secured area. She recognized several of her fans, including the trio of pimple-faced teenagers who'd made the trek across country to see her again in Hollywood. They screamed out to her, but she kept going, only throwing them a small wave.

A long line of media interviews awaited them. In typical fashion, Natalie hadn't done what she'd asked. Bright lights, photographers, microphones and pushy interviewers intent on talking only about her stalker instead of the movie she'd worked so hard on, stood between her and the cool lobby of the building. To his credit, and Trevor's displeasure, Dean didn't leave her side. He supported her when she became unsteady on her feet. They kissed and snuggled like the lovers they no longer were and the cameras loved it. It pissed her off, knowing that the sensationalized photos of her and her cheating ex would be plastered across the Internet and magazine covers, forever memorializing them together.

It was how the game was played in Hollywood.

What felt like an eternity later, she detected the first gust of air-conditioned coolness as they entered the opulent foyer of the theater. Goosebumps sprung up on her damp skin at the sudden change of temperatures, and for once, she was grateful for Dean's arm pulling her closer against him.

A waiter greeted them with tall flutes of expensive champagne. She lived dangerously, drinking one down, filling her empty stomach. The slight buzz it brought was welcome and helped fortify her for the additional interviews and photo ops that waited inside. It also dulled her constant fear that one of the hundreds of people pressing into the foyer was her stalker, intent on getting her alone to do the despicable things he'd described in his notes.

It took them another thirty minutes to finally reach the end of the gauntlet where the director, producers, support personnel and supporting actors from the movie who'd gone ahead of them already mingled, waiting for the two main stars of the film to catch up to them.

She was headed towards the Kaplans to give them a piece of her mind when the studio's coffee runner, Peter, stepped in front of her, this time with a tray full of her favorite treat–chocolate fudge. As if it sensed the nearby temptation, her stomach grumbled.

The young man with the unfortunate acne was near breathless as she approached. "I've been waiting for you, Khloe. I brought your favorite food in the whole wide world. You told me and I remembered!"

The producer's nephew had a way of turning up at the most inopportune times, but considering who his uncle was, Khloe always tried to take a moment to say hello to the young man who wasn't quite dealing with a full deck in life.

"Peter, you shouldn't have. If I eat that much fudge, all of my dresses would stop fitting," she teased as Dean reached out to take one of the biggest pieces from the tray. He must not worry about fitting into his tuxedo.

The look of hatred on Peter's face was alarming. "I made this for Khloe, not for you!" Peter actually reached out to try to snatch the sweet snack away from her ex, but Dean was too fast.

"Chill out there, coffee boy. There's plenty, and anyone who knows her knows she isn't going to eat more than one bite anyway."

Khloe placed a hand on Peter's arm, trying to stop him from making a scene. He calmed immediately, forgetting about the stolen treat to turn a smile towards her instead. "I appreciate you bringing me one of my favorites. You're so thoughtful, but I'm too nervous to eat anything right now. Please save me a piece, and I'll be sure to eat it after the screening, okay?" She gave him a celebrity smile that had him bumbling like the inexperienced novice he was.

"I'll save them all for you, Miss Monroe. I promise."

He leaned closer, invading her personal space until she snatched her hand away from his arm, stepping back to put more distance between them and then chastising herself for acting like everyone she meets was her stalker. She was seriously getting paranoid.

She didn't have time to obsess like normal, though, because she heard a voice she recognized calling out her name from behind her.

"Khloe! Wait up. We want to sit near you in the screening."

She turned, her heart expanding with palpable relief at seeing Chase, Emma and Jaxson approaching. They looked breathtakingly perfect on the red carpet in their tuxedos and flowing gown. Breaking away from Peter and Dean, she rushed towards her friends.

It wasn't until Chase had wrapped her tightly in a bear hug that she realized her error. Tears pricked at her eyes as she allowed the first real feeling of safety she'd felt in weeks wash over her. It was stupid really, but it was as if her body recognized that nothing could hurt her. Not with Chase Cartwright and Jaxson Davidson next to her.

*I can't start crying. I'll cause a scene and ruin my makeup.*

Chase pulled out of their hug enough to look down into her eyes. She saw his concern as he examined her. Before he could even speak, Jaxson stepped closer on her left and Emma on her right. Seconds later she was wrapped into the six arms of the infamous trio. What they had together was extraordinary and tonight, they were sharing their love with her, their friend. It almost felt like they were wrapping her in an invisible force field that would protect her from any bullshit. Emotional tears streaked down her cheeks.

Dean stumbled forward against her back, unwittingly testing the strength of the protection by trying to pull Khloe out the trio's clutches. "Hey, sweetheart. Maybe you'd better introduce me to your friends. I'd like to know who it is who's trying to move in on my girl."

It was Jaxson who left their embrace, turning to lean closer to

Dean, speaking softly so only their small group and Peter could hear his warning.

"She's not your girl any more than she's mine. You gave up the right to call her that the day you fucked Gloria Mining." Jaxson paused to let his words sink in with Dean. "That's right. I know all about it. I also know she's being forced to play out this sick game of star-crossed-lovers for the press. We'll keep your little secret for Khloe's sake, but don't for one minute think you're gonna get back in her good graces. She has enough shit on her plate with the fucking stalker."

Dean moved forward, bumping his chest with Jaxson aggressively until Khloe moved away from Chase to try to break it up. "Guys, not here. Jax, I really do appreciate you protecting me. I'm so glad you guys could come, but please don't make a scene. The press knows who you are. That would only make things worse." She tried to brush away her tears without the press noticing.

She was relieved when Jaxson smiled outwardly while passing along his next threat under this breath. "If I find out you've had anything to do with this stalking business, Reynolds, you're gonna wish you'd never been born. Got it?" He grinned a fake smile while Dean's smile grew comical as he leaned even closer.

"Fuck you, Davidson. Yeah, I know who you are. I don't need to stalk anybody. I can have a dozen women in my bed by midnight if I want it."

It was Chase who stepped up to the other side of Dean to counter, "You have a pretty high opinion of yourself, but until the charade of your romance with Khloe is over, you won't take anyone to your bed, got it? You know damn well your groupies will talk and I won't let you drag Khloe's name through the mud with rumors of cheating, got it?"

Dean growled lowly. "What the hell is it with you guys? Your girl not keeping you happy enough? You got to move in on mine instead."

It was Emma to the rescue when Jaxson and Chase looked like

they might deck Dean where he stood. "I think we've had enough chit-chat. Let's all go in and find our seats. I can't wait for the movie to start."

Emma linked her arm with Khloe's and headed towards the theater, pulling her friend along.

"Do you think we should leave them together like that?" Khloe questioned.

The beautiful brunette giggled. "Jax and Chase will come along. They hate it when I get out of their sight, particularly since I'm with you." When Khloe looked at her inquisitively at that remark she added. "They almost left me in D.C. They know you're in danger and don't want me exposed to anything dangerous with your stalker. I had to promise them I wouldn't leave their side."

The women had already passed through the huge entrance to the main theater and were headed down the long, angled aisle towards the VIP section. She tried to pull her new friend to a stop. "Then shouldn't we hold up and wait for them? I mean, I don't want to get you in trouble."

Emma smiled mischievously, continuing to walk. "It's okay. Don't tell the guys, but I kinda like getting into trouble every once in a while, if you know what I mean."

The twinkle in her eye made Khloe's insides do a somersault, realizing her friend was talking about enjoying the kind of punishment scenes she herself had savored playing out with Ryder Helms. No matter how much time she spent obsessing about her few short hours with the sex-god who'd mastered her at a game of roulette, she still couldn't fathom why she'd loved that night so much. The incredible sex she could understand, but the pain... humiliation... debauched kinkiness... submission... those darker emotions she just couldn't reconcile.

The men eventually caught up to them. True to their word, her celebrity friends had the seating arrangement changed around so that Chase sat on her left while Dean took the seat to her right. Only after she was seated did she see Trevor staring at her from the shadows of the theater, watching over her, yes, but she suspected from the scowl on his face that he was about as happy to see Chase and Jaxson as Dean had been.

Edward Rivera stepped to the podium on the stage, spending several minutes thanking those who had helped make the creation of *Dirty Business* possible, saving his thanks for Dean and Khloe for last. Her heart swelled with pride as they rose to a standing ovation, fans and co-stars pressing in to congratulate them again. From the corner of her eye, she saw Trevor still watching over her, a stony face hiding any emotion.

The crowd settled down, returning to their seats when the lights dimmed and the two-story red-velvet curtains parted to reveal the screen. Khloe held her breath as the opening credits began, the pounding beat of the title song, *Dirty Business*, filling the theater. Her heart expanded when Chase reached for her hand in the dark theater, linking their fingers in his show of support.

He had really come through for her tonight. She was under no illusion that he had any lingering romantic feelings for her, and honestly was grateful for that. Anyone looking at the threesome next to her knew they were crazy in love with each other and Khloe couldn't be happier for him and Emma. But she trusted Chase and Jaxson and, right now, that was a rare thing in her life. Having them there to support her meant the world.

As the movie started, she let herself get lost in the story. The week before in NYC, she'd spent the pre-release showing picking apart her performance, examining it from every angle to understand how she might have improved each scene. Tonight, she let herself forget it was her on the screen, trying to enjoy the picture as a fan might instead. By the time the lights came up and the credits were rolling, she was trembling with emotion. As the entire theater pushed to their feet, clapping their approval for the film, Khloe sat frozen in her seat.

It had finally happened. For the first time in her career she felt like she deserved the praise directed her way. Fame could be a poisonous thing. So many people sold their soul to chase it, yet it was slippery, often shining down on those undeserving while eluding those who worked the hardest. She'd been enjoying her own growing fame for the last few years, but until tonight, she'd felt a bit like a fraud. Like she'd achieved the successes she had only because of how she looked or who she knew. She'd never felt quite worthy of the VIP treatment, as if she were simply the actress she was, playing the role of a celebrity.

But tonight she basked in the accolades, feeling vindicated against all of the talking heads who had written Khloe Monroe off as just another pretty face in Hollywood. Relief coursed through her as she allowed herself to acknowledge she had real talent.

Edward Rivera approached her, holding out his hand to pull her to her feet and hug her to him. He spoke quietly against her ear as the applause continued around them. "Thank you, Khloe, for being here tonight. I know it's been hard on you, and I'm sorry for not being more understanding. I'm very pleased with how *Dirty Business* turned out and thrilled I was able to snag you for *Smuggled Dreams* before the rest of Hollywood starts knocking on your door offering parts. Don't forget I was the one who gave you your first big shot when you're accepting your Academy Award for best actress." He pulled away, grinning as he winked at her.

His encouraging words bolstered her, giving her the courage to look around at the mammoth room. Those involved with the film's creation congratulated each other on a job well done. Fans in the balcony shouted out to her and Dean. The couple turned and waved to the throngs who would be leaving the theater and spreading the word on how good the film was. Nearby, industry bigwigs and movie critics mingled with dozens of media outlets, giving snippets of quotes for the next day's news programs.

It all felt surreal. She'd looked so forward to this night that now she didn't know what came next. In the commotion of the celebration, she was jostled from person to person, getting moved farther away from Chase, Jaxson, Emma and even Dean. An uneasy feeling settled in her tummy when she didn't recognize anyone surrounding her. She frantically searched the room for Trevor or Darius. Hell she'd be happy to have Ricky or the Kaplans near her. She spotted them all, too far away to comfort her.

"I have your fudge for you now, Miss Monroe." A friendly face, she reached out to link her hand through Peter's bent arm, feeling better to be with someone she knew. She even reached out to pick up the smallest bite-sized piece of the luscious dessert and popped it into her mouth, letting the sweet chocolate melt in her mouth slowly. It was heavenly. Her low groan of delight lit the coffee-boy's face up in a lopsided grin.

"That was without a doubt the best fudge I've ever had. Thank you, Peter."

He had picked up another piece and was holding it out for her to take another bite when Jaxson wrapped his arm around and pulled her away from Peter.

"I let it go before the movie because I knew you were nervous enough, but you've lost too much weight. We're gonna take you out for a big, healthy dinner and try to put get some good food in you. Let's head out."

Peter looked crestfallen as Jaxson pulled her away. She barely had time to call out to him, "Thanks again," before trying to pull away from Jaxson and his heavy-handed crap.

"I'm not a child, Davidson. I think I can decide what I'll eat and when," she complained.

He stopped them long enough to lecture her quietly. "You called us for our help. Sorry, kiddo, but this is how I help. If you can't take better care of yourself, I'll be happy to help."

"But--"

He cut her off, leaning in to talk against her ear. "Chase told me about your past eating disorder. I understand how being stressed can trigger old habits."

"Chase has a big mouth," she muttered.

Jaxson's naughty grin disarmed her anger. "Yes, he does, but it feels oh so good." It took her a second to realize his meaning, but when she did, she could feel the heat rising in her cheeks as she broke out into a full-body blush. He teased her. "You're almost as adorable as Emma when you blush. Now come on. Let's find you some food."

Trevor met them in the lobby of the theater. The party was in full swing with drinks flowing freely as fans, studio personnel and the media mingled. The scowl on her bodyguard's face as he caught up with her told her he wasn't happy.

"I thought I told you to stay put in the theater until I could escort you out. I lost sight of you for almost five minutes. You gave me a fucking heart attack."

"I'm sorry. The crowd was too heavy. I kinda got swept away there for a few minutes, but Jaxson was with me."

For the first time Trevor had to acknowledge the only man as tall as he was in the room. "I was with her when she phoned you and Chase for help." He stopped talking, but she knew the words he'd left unspoken; 'I tried to talk her out of it because I don't need your damn help to protect her'.

Jaxson was unfazed by Trevor's grousing attitude. "Being old friends with Khloe, it was great that we could be here on her big night. We're on the same team, after all."

Trevor took the bait. "What team is that?"

Jaxson took a step closer, leaning in to answer. "The 'keep Khloe safe from assholes' team."

The tall men stood chest to chest, sizing each other up for a few long seconds before Trevor sighed, stepping back and replying, "Yeah, I guess I'm good with getting help from people we can trust for that team." He finally looked back at Khloe before adding an emotional, "I'll do anything to make sure she stays safe."

Memories of his kiss... his declaration of love... they flooded back, making her feel uncomfortable. She loved Trevor like a brother, but the look he was presently devouring her with was anything but brotherly. Of course, Jaxson noticed.

"Is there something going on here I should know about?" her friend asked.

To his credit, Trevor answered in unison with her in their joint, "No."

The emotional ups and downs of the night were taking their toll on her. She'd had exactly one glass of champagne and a bite of chocolate fudge in the last twelve hours. The thought of eating the heavy food of the party terrified her because she knew it would be followed by a nearly uncontrollable urge to purge. She fought to remain calm as a waiter stopped with a tray of appetizers, waving him off before Jaxson could lecture her more.

The press of the crowd grew worse, but she was grateful for Jaxson and Trevor working together to help her weave through the throng of guests, stopping for photos and quick hellos as they slowly made their way towards the exit. They eventually met up with Chase and Emma near the door to the outdoor red carpet. Remembering she was supposed to be in love, she looked around the crowded lobby, but Dean was nowhere to be seen.

*He's probably off banging some groupie. That'll be a great headline in the tabloids. Good thing I'm not counting on him to protect me.*

Trevor peeled off to meet Darius who had called to bring her limo around, leaving her in Jaxson and Chase's care. She kept her celebrity smile plastered on her sweaty face as they finally made it out into the now cooler evening breeze. Her three famous escorts were garnering as much attention as she was, making forward progress slow.

She was shocked that the studio hadn't made the public crowds disperse. If anything, there were more people crowding the sidewalk and entry plaza as they tried to make their way to the curb. The stanchions that had held fans back on the way in were now pressed aside, allowing shouting admirers to surround her– touch her– as she made her way through the throng.

Within minutes, things went from packed to mild chaos. Trevor shouted to her from the curb, but she lost sight of him as people pressed in. Remembering that any one of these people could be her stalker filled her with renewed terror. She took comfort that Jaxson, Chase and Emma were pressing through the crush alongside her. A stalker would have to go through them before they could whisk her away.

When the paparazzi pressed through the mob to start taking photos, Trevor shoved the aggressive photographer aside sending his expensive camera to the concrete. The cameraperson lashed out, trying to tackle her bodyguard. Darius jumped into the fray as all hell broke loose. Women screamed, not knowing what was happening. Men either moved out of the way, or a few aggressors joined in the fisticuffs, happy for a little excitement.

Jaxson yelled to Chase, "Stick with Emma! Don't let anyone touch her." He then stooped to pick up Khloe in his arms before pressing through the crowd assertively, making a path for them and his lovers who followed close behind. She could feel her flowing satin gown hanging down, trying to trip up Jaxson as he made slow progress through the pushing and shoving. All she could do to help was grab up her dress, trying not to flash the swarm in the process.

As they got to the curb, they discovered her limo had not arrived yet. Jaxson raised his hand, ready to flag a passing cab in the crawling traffic. Before a taxi could weave to the curb, a rumbling Harley Davidson motorcycle came barreling through the street, weaving between the gridlocked cars, limos, and SUVs. It was the only vehicle making any progress at all. As it neared the theater, the roar of the engine temporarily doused the chaos as everyone stopped to watch the lone rider drive the heavy bike up onto the sidewalk. The crazy driver barged through the throng, prepared to mow over anyone who got in his way until he ground to a fast halt directly in front of Khloe and Jaxson.

Her heart almost stopped with fear. This was it. This had to be her stalker making his move–riding in to whisk her away on his two-wheeled, powerful chopper. She suspected if he got her on that bike, there would be no saving her as only another motor-cycle could cut through the traffic on Hollywood Boulevard to pursue them.

She held her breath, shrinking away from the motorcyclist to burrow into Jaxson's embrace as the driver stood, holding his ride upright between his leather-covered legs. Fight or flight instincts had Khloe wiggling in Jaxson's arms, willing him to move his feet in the opposite direction–away from the danger. But instead, he moved forward, almost as if he was ready to hand her over without a care. Regret mingled with her fear. Regret at trusting the wrong men.

They were only a few feet away from the motorcycle when the cyclist removed his helmet. Time ceased, paralyzing her with shock. Khloe was figuratively knocked silly as the driver's identity became clear.

"Hi, Princess."

It was Ryder. The man she'd dreamt of almost every night since they'd parted. The man who had mastered her–body and soul.

The man who had left her, telling her they would never see each other again.

She was speechless, but Jaxson didn't suffer from the same affliction. "I was beginning to think you'd changed your mind, Helms, and had decided that taking care of Khloe wasn't your job."

"Fuck you, Davidson. It's no one else's job but mine." He turned his piercing blue eyes on her again, this time demanding, "Hop on, Princess."

She somehow found her voice. "Are you nuts?"

A loud bang cut through the air. It was probably a car backfir-ing, but to an inexperienced ear, it could easily have been a gunshot. She frantically searched the crowd, relieved to see Trevor still on his feet, detaining several photographers. He glanced her way, worry on his brow, but too far away to be of any help to her.

Her heart had restarted and now banged hard in her chest, a combination of adrenaline and the appearance of Ryder Helms its fuel. When Trevor realized the motorcycle was next to her, he started pressing through the crowd, desperate to get to her. Another loud clap and she flinched.

Jaxson set her feet on the ground, but thankfully kept his arm wrapped protectively around her. She realized too late he was moving them forward, closing the last few feet until she was only inches away from Ryder.

He was more handsome than she remembered, dripping dominance as he dared to look her up and down, examining her as if to evaluate her for injuries. She didn't like his assessment.

"Jesus Christ, you're fucking starving yourself."

His words woke her from her trance. "What's it to you?"

His hands clamped onto her bare upper arms, yanking her so close she could feel his breath on her cheek. "I don't take kindly to anyone harming what's mine, and that includes self-harm."

"Yours?" she scoffed. "You're delusional. You left, making it abundantly clear you couldn't wait to slink away after you'd had your fun debasing a celebrity." She was practically shouting to be heard over the motor.

He flinched, but didn't apologize. "I came back as soon as I could. We don't have time for a chitchat. Let's get the hell out of here. Now."

He really was crazy. Even if she wanted to go with him... as if every fiber of her being wasn't already drawn to him like a powerful magnet... how was she supposed to ride on a motorcycle in her ten-thousand-dollar satin, beaded gown? Unaware she thought he was crazy, Ryder pulled a second helmet from the back of the bike, reaching out to jam it over her coifed hair that Randy had spent an hour on, effectively smashing it to her head.

If she thought Jaxson would help her, she was wrong. On the

contrary, he was helping Ryder fasten her helmet and then scooped her up to place her on the back of the bike, leaning down to bunch up her flowing skirts and lifting them to her waist, exposing her long, thin legs to the screaming crowd. He pressed the wad of fabric between their bodies, using his left hand to press her forward, closer to the man she'd never thought she'd see again.

Jaxson yelled against her ear to be heard, "It's getting out of control. I'll tell your bodyguard who you're with and let him know you're safe with Helms."

Their eyes met as she questioned him. "Am I?" She couldn't stop the words from spilling from her mouth. "Am I safe?" she pressed her friend, truly not knowing who to trust anymore.

Jaxson looked her in the eyes and answered with what she recognized as confidence. "I never would have told him where to find you if I didn't trust him. He has the right skills. He's the best man to protect you right now."

He didn't give her a chance to argue, lowering the smoky visor on her helmet before taking a step back towards the curb. Behind Jax she saw the flash of cameras taking her photo as fans pushed and shoved against the line of security, trying to get to her like a rabid mob.

She forced herself to look away from the chaos as it made her want to puke. Ryder had put his own helmet back on. Just before he put the motorcycle in motion again, he leaned back, shouting to her over the roar of the engine. "Hang on tight, Princess."

As the bike jutted forward, ready to weave through the cars moving at a snail's pace, she did as she was told, clutching at him to avoid falling off and finally hugging him so tight she heard him chuckle.

"I missed you too, baby"

## CHAPTER 10

*R*yder was grateful that it was impossible to have a conversation over the roar of the powerful motorcycle beneath them. He'd need every minute of their trip to get his head on straight. Driving up to find Khloe surrounded by the out-of-control crowd, cradled in Davidson's arms, had affected him in ways he was afraid to examine too closely.

He'd come prepared to be her protector, telling himself he would resist the temptation to be more. What he hadn't been prepared for was the vulnerability he saw in her expressive eyes as she'd recognized him. On the one hand, he should be happy she hadn't been afraid of him. Considering how far he'd pushed her out of her comfort zone the last time they'd seen each other, he wouldn't have blamed her if she'd run screaming from him.

The engine roared louder as he picked up speed. Traffic thinned once they were outside of the congested tourist area. As he banked around a corner at the entrance to the expressway, he reveled in the way his beautiful passenger hugged him tighter. The press of her breasts against his back revved up his libido.

Before he merged with the northbound traffic, Ryder brought the bike to a stop along the edge of the highway. He shook out of his leather jacket, turning his body to wrap it around Khloe's shoulders.

When she didn't move to put her arms through the sleeves, he prodded her. "Put it on." There was no arguing.

She eyed him suspiciously, but followed his directions. He should tell her to zip it up, but he was a dickhead, preferring to feel the chilled nipples he could see straining against her evening gown pressing against his black T-shirt instead.

Their eyes met. He saw so many questions there. Questions he wasn't sure he had answers to. He couldn't resist the urge raise her visor, cupping her rosy cheek through the opening as he gave her the only information she needed at the moment.

"We're heading north about twenty miles. Hang on tight, Princess."

"Ryder..." He saw her confusion at his sudden appearance.

"I know. We have a lot to talk about. For now, just try to enjoy the ride."

He lowered her visor and waited until she'd wrapped her arms around his waist again to pull the powerful machine out into fast moving traffic.

It had been a while since he'd ridden. He'd forgotten how much he loved it. Like it or not, motorcycles were an important part of his life. Having Khloe riding with him made it close to perfect, yet as much as he enjoyed the warmth of her body pressed against his back, he couldn't entirely ignore the nervousness growing in his gut with every mile he put behind them. Figuring out how to protect the celebrity on the back of the bike without getting dead first was just one thing weighing on him.

Three years. That's how long it had been since he'd been home for a visit, if he could call it that. He'd been home less than twenty-four hours last time before he'd packed his bag and left. As he passed an exit with several low-end motels, he contemplated changing his plan. No one was expecting him. They could check-in to a seedy hotel and none would be the wiser.

But Khloe Monroe deserved better than that, and like it or not, he needed to try to clear the air with his father before it was too late. He'd pretended his aunt's emails hadn't impacted him, but the truth was that facing death so many times in the last year on the job had forced him to face his own mortality, something deep cover agents normally avoided at all costs.

By the time they reached their exit, he had his emotions in check. He observed the town he'd grown up in with reserved interest. Southern California expansion had reached Santa Clarita, making it a medium sized city now. New mixed with old, bringing back memories, both good and bad. There was no avoiding The Office as it was on the main highway that ran through the heart of the town. He slowed, but didn't stop, observing the dozens of motorcycles parked in the oversized parking lot of the building he'd spent most of his formative years in.

Except he was no longer welcome there and that was fine with him.

He turned onto Canyon Ridge Trail. The road in front of them inclined sharply as he began the last leg of their trip for the night. The path was dark, street lamps few and far between on the edge of the protected federal parkland where hiking trails were more common than paved streets. Up ahead he saw the bright lights of the last all-night gas station they'd pass. He pulled in, parking at the door to the small but well-lit convenience store attached to the station.

They were plunged into silence as he turned off the engine. Despite stopping, Khloe still clung to him and he almost hated to break their connection. His hands found hers at his waist, twining their fingers together for a few seconds before gently pulling her arms apart, He took off his helmet, but as she moved to do the same, he stopped her.

"Leave it on. I don't want anyone to recognize you." Even

through the visor, he saw understanding in her brown eyes. "Stay here. I'll only be inside a few minutes."

She argued, "I don't want to be alone out here. Can't I come in?"

"In your elegant gown? I don't think so." He reassured her. "It'll be okay. I promise."

She didn't look convinced.

He unbuckled his duffle bag from the back of the bike and headed inside. They'd need supplies for at least a few days. True to his word, it only took him a few minutes to pick up what they'd need and pay. He could see the relief in his passenger's eyes when he returned, enjoying the extra tight hug she gave him once he was seated again. After months spent apart, he couldn't shake the feeling that he was finally home, but he suspected the feeling had nothing to do with their physical location.

*She feels perfect against me.*

The final few miles to their destination were so different from the first few miles of their trip. Thick forest and ground brush surrounded them where concrete and buildings had been in the city. Even in the dark he could tell that the recent rain had greened the area nicely; the smell of spring flowers was evident as winding turns replaced flat streets. Here, the near-full moon was the only light besides the single headlight of his bike. They didn't pass another vehicle the final two miles of their trip, reminding him of how remote the family homestead was.

Family. The word could be misleading. In this place, family was linked by loyalty, not blood. He may have the right blood flowing in his veins, but he wasn't stupid. Many here would not be happy for his return, which was why he'd like to keep his presence under wraps for as long as he could and that meant going to see the one person he was pretty sure would be happy he was here.

He pulled into the dark parking lot of The Canyon Ridge Resort, the last public establishment before hitting the private family compound. A few older model cars were parked at the far edge of the lot, looking abandoned.

In the distance he could see the campfires of the residents of the neighboring RV park that sat along the smaller of the two lakes on the property. Once he cut the engine, he could make out the laughter of people having fun.

Ryder turned his attention to the mammoth A-frame lodge in front of them. It hadn't changed at all. The log frame, gigantic windows and wraparound porch called to him. He was home.

Or close enough.

Like at the gas station, he got off and told Khloe to stay put, but she was ready for him this time.

Ready to argue.

"Where the hell are we and who do you think you are, stealing me away like you did?" she growled, anger brewing in her beautiful eyes as she lifted her visor.

He'd missed her fire. The spark he'd masterfully tamed for three short hours months before. Only tonight, he didn't have a roulette wheel and consent form giving him the right to master her. Here... tonight... they were in uncharted territory, playing with no carefully crafted rules to their game and they both knew it.

He spoke softly, recognizing the growing fear on her face in the dim lighting. "I haven't stolen you. At least not in the way you're worried about."

"So why?" Despite his leather jacket, she shivered visibly. From fear or the chill of the night, he wasn't sure.

Ryder stepped closer, pulling her torso flush against his chest as he enveloped her in his arms, sharing his own body heat with her until she stilled. Her eyes sought answers he didn't have. He replied with the only truth he could come up with in the heated moment.

"I need to protect you, Khloe. The thought of someone out there wanting to hurt you... fuck..." He was unprepared for his own emotions bubbling up as he squeezed her tighter as if to prevent her from disappearing like a mirage. She really was in his arms again, and it felt damn perfect.

The shouts of the nearby campers reminded him they had a potential audience. This was neither the time nor the place for their little reunion discussion.

He released her, stepping back to give her directions before he got further swept up in the growing tension. "Leave your helmet on again. We don't need anyone recognizing you and posting something on social media sites. It's gonna be hard enough protecting you in public. We don't need to be looking over our shoulder out here."

"Where is here, anyway? Why not take me back to my place in Malibu, or even a hotel closer to town?"

He held his fingers up to her lips to stem the spew of questions. "Shhh. I'll try to answer all of your questions when we get settled. For now, stay put, got it?"

He enlisted his best Dom voice, hoping to channel the power he'd held over her the last time they'd been together. From the widening of her eyes and slight 'o' of her mouth, he'd say it worked.

He didn't stay and gloat. Instead, he lowered her visor again before securing his helmet to the seat and headed down the long brick sidewalk to the entrance of the hotel. The rustic luxury of the expansive lobby welcomed him home. Despite the heat during the day, it got cool in the evenings so he wasn't surprised to see the roaring fire in the two-story high stone fireplace. A couple snuggled on the leather couch, looking like the newlyweds they probably were.

He hadn't even approached the front desk when he heard his name shouted from across the room. He turned in time to see an attractive woman in her fifties rushing towards him.

"Ryder! Is it really you?"

She pulled him into a hug as soon as she reached him. He chuckled. "Hello, Aunt Ginny."

"Would it kill you to drop a line every once in a while? You know, they make this thing called a telephone. Hell, even an email or text would do."

They pulled out of their embrace. His aunt was several inches shorter than he was. Small webs of wrinkles crinkled around her eyes as she smiled up at him reminding him they'd both aged since they'd seen each other last. He could see she was assessing him for changes as well.

"Yeah, well my job isn't exactly conducive to staying in touch."

His family didn't know exactly what he did for a living, but they knew enough to know he couldn't talk about it.

His aunt smiled good-naturedly. "A likely excuse. You probably work in an office in L.A. and don't want to bother with family." He knew she was teasing him. His father's sister was listed as his next of kin with the agency. She'd been the one who'd got the phone call each time he'd been injured in the line of duty.

"So don't get me wrong. I'm thrilled to see you, but to what do I owe this honor?"

"I was hoping you had an open cabin I could borrow for a few days, maybe weeks. I'm not really sure." He paused, "I know I should have probably called ahead but..."

His aunt cut him off. "You're welcome here any time. No need to call ahead. This is your home."

His heart constricted at her words. The emotions pressing in were unexpected. He finally choked out, "I hardly expect you to keep a cabin empty on the off-chance I'll come by."

A sad smile played at her lips. "Ah, honey, I don't keep a cabin empty. I keep *your* cabin empty."

"But..."

"Come. I'll get the key." Ginny smiled wryly.

He followed her to the small front desk where a teenager sat behind the counter looking bored out of his mind.

"Go ahead and take your break early, Mikey. I'll take care of this customer."

"Sure thing." The kid was more than happy to get lost. Ryder appreciated her discretion, helping to keep his identity under wraps, at least until he was ready to deal with the fallout of his appearance. Still, she didn't ignore the elephant in the room.

"You're welcome here any time, you know that, right?"

"I'm not sure everyone feels that way," he countered, slipping the set of keys she'd handed him in the pocket of his leather pants.

"He's changing. Mellowing. You need to at least stop in to say hi." His aunt's face look pained. "Even if you don't stop at your dad's, at least look in on Axel. We're all so worried about him."

Christ, he didn't need this guilt trip. The motel back on the highway was starting to look better, but he tried to appease his aunt.

"I'll think about it," he conceded, anxious to get back out to Khloe for more than one reason.

He could see she didn't believe him. "So stubborn. Just like him."

His aunt's eyes left his to focus on something behind him. The crinkles around her eyes returned as she smiled. "So who's the beautiful woman in the long gown headed this way?"

Of course she didn't listen to him. He didn't need to turn to know Khloe had followed him into the lodge.

"No one. Just a job." Ginny had the audacity to grin at him knowingly, so he tacked on. "She's in danger. I'm protecting her, that's all." He wasn't sure if he was trying to convince his aunt or himself.

"Uh-ha. If you say so." Her smile slipped. "Always looking for that adrenaline high?"

He agreed reluctantly. "Something like that."

He turned to see Khloe making her way across the lobby. Seeing her here, in this familiar place was surreal-unexpectedly calming. Still, he didn't want her to get close enough to be recognized.

He turned to say goodbye. "Listen, I gotta go now, but I'll stop by to catch up before I leave town. I promise."

"Go." She smiled mischievously before adding, "I'm sure you're anxious to get Khloe Monroe alone to yourself." She patted his arm to reassure her nephew. "Don't worry. Your secret is safe with me."

He took off, meeting Khloe before she got to the desk. She'd taken the helmet off and her thick mane of blonde hair was a hot mess, molded to her head at the top with the ends that had extended outside of the helmet a tangled mess from whipping in the wind on the drive there.

*She's still fucking perfect. Well, other than not following directions.*

"I thought I told you to wait for me outside," he admonished, grabbing her elbow, attempting to turn her in an abrupt about face.

She stood grounded, looking conflicted, but finally admitted. "It was really dark and spooky out there. I got kinda creeped out." Fear lingered in her voice. The night they'd met, he'd reveled in pushing her to her edge. Seeing her like this, vulnerable and afraid, by someone else's hand––that infuriated him.

For a city girl like Khloe, the remote resort probably was like visiting another country.

Aunt Ginny came up behind him, scolding him and reminding him why coming here had been one of his more boneheaded ideas. "He never should have left you out there in the first place. He was trying to avoid having to introduce us." Khloe's eyes widened before his aunt took the plunge and added, "I'm Ginny Helms, Ryder's aunt. It's a pleasure meeting you, Ms. Monroe."

His hand had found its way to the small of Khloe's back, snaking under the bottom of his leather jacket she was still swimming in. That hand ended up helping stabilize Khloe when his aunt rushed forward, pulling his protectee into a tight hug.

"Jesus, Ginny, what the hell?" His hands found Khloe's too-thin waist, trying to pull her back towards him, suddenly feeling like he and his aunt were playing a game of tug-of-war.

Ginny won when Khloe unexpectedly returned the older woman's hug.

"What the fuck?" he blurted in frustration.

Khloe didn't seem fazed as the women parted. "Nice to meet you."

His aunt grinned before adding, "Don't let his bark scare you."

"It's not his bark I'm worried about. It's his bite."

He'd never seen his aunt blush before, but he enjoyed watching her fumble to answer, "Well... I've heard rumors about his... but... oh, never mind."

He couldn't stop his chuckle. "Alright, that's about enough from you two. I can see coming here was a mistake."

"Oh I wouldn't say that. You actually just jumped up in standing with me," Khloe teased, adding, "Your aunt is lovely."

"Figures," he groused, unable to be angry.

He tried to pull Khloe back towards the door, but Ginny kept pressing for details. "So, how long have you two been seeing each other?"

"Oh it's not like that, is it, Ryder?" The beauty in his arms turned to deliver her under-cut. "We went out once, months ago, and then he ditched me, not even bothering to get my number."

"Woman, you don't have a clue what the hell you're talking about," he defended.

He couldn't believe she was picking a personal fight with him in the middle of the thankfully quiet lobby. Could they possibly be more conspicuous?

He moved his grip to her bicep and had started dragging her back towards the door when his aunt unexpectedly tried to defend him, calling after them as he tried to get to the exit.

"You can't hold leaving against him."

Khloe pulled free of him to turn back towards Ginny, her

hands on her hips. "Oh, and why not?" He heard the vulnerability in her voice. It was then that it hit him that Khloe probably didn't have many men walk out on her.

Ginny leaned close to speak softly. "Trust me, sometimes he has to leave, even when he may not want to." His aunt's gaze found his and he saw her understanding of his secretive job that had torn him away from his family most of his life. The corner of her lips curved up as she added, "You're welcome here any time. Any friend of Ryder's is a friend of the family."

*Christ, not that.*

"Khloe, we really need to go. We have a lot to talk about." He finally got her feet moving, but the women still both shouted out their 'good-byes' to each other across the lobby.

Only when they were out next to the bike did he complain. "I told you to stay out here."

"And I told you it's spooky out here."

"Nice try, Princess. Aren't you a little too old to be afraid of the dark?"

He had reached to put her helmet back on her, but she yanked out of his arms, her eyes sparking with anger. "I'm not afraid of the dark, jackass. I'm afraid of the lunatic who is after me, promising to take me away and fuck me every day for the rest of my life. Call me crazy, but yeah, that has me a bit spooked."

Raw anxiety mingled with exhaustion, clouding her beautiful face. He'd seen that expression on her briefly on the TV, but tonight she reeked of fear, and it gutted him.

When he'd made the decision to protect her, he'd also pledged he would keep her at arms length. In his line of work, no good could come from him getting involved with a woman, let alone a celebrity. Yet, they had a combustive history, and in that moment his normally unfailing self-control fled.

The urge to hold her was undeniable. He didn't fight it, pulling her into his arms. For a brief moment, she let her guard down, relaxing into his body, molding them together so tightly he was unprepared for her to shove him away, losing his balance and almost knocking over the bike at his back.

"How do I know you aren't the stalker? This is a pretty remote location. How do I know this isn't where you'd planned to take me?" Her voice quavered with emotion.

He didn't know if he should laugh or yell. "You must think I'm the stupidest criminal alive. Driving up to take you with thousands of witnesses, most with cameras snapping. Then stopping for supplies at a well-lit stop with security cameras everywhere. And then dropping in to say hi to the family on the way to my hideout." He took a step closer and her eyes widened as he added, "You think I need to kidnap you to take you to my own cabin to do things to your body I've already done and could have again at the snap of my fingers?"

At least fear had vanished from her expression, leaving misplaced anger. Khloe scoffed. "You have a pretty high opinion of yourself if you think you'll snap your fingers and I'll fall to my knees, under your spell again. Look around. There is no roulette wheel here tonight, and we sure as hell aren't at Black Light."

His patience was at an end. Ryder yanked her against his body, twining his fingers through her long, messy mane and snapping her head back. He towered above her, so close he could feel her gasping for breath against his cheek.

"This is not the time for this. Or the place. Like it or not, you're stuck with me, Princess."

"And why is that?" she asked breathlessly.

"Because I'm the best person to protect you right now. Trust me when I say that as long as you listen to me, I'm not gonna let anyone hurt you. Period."

"Why the sudden interest in my welfare? You walked out, making it clear you didn't give a shit. You said it had all been a game." Her vulnerability was back.

"Well, game time is over."

Her breaths were sporadic. She had the exact same hurt look

on her face that haunted him when he closed his eyes at night. The one she'd had just before she'd left Black Light. She wiggled, trying to free herself from his grasp while shouting, "Why now, Ryder?"

Crushing her to him was easy. She was tiny, but he admired her spunk as she struggled against him. Like the bastard he was, the harder she fought, the harder his cock grew in his leathers, until lust demanded he subdue her like the dominant he was.

His lips crashed down on her, taking what he needed. His tongue conquered her mouth as his free hand cupped her perfect ass, yanking her against his body, ensuring she felt the erection straining for release.

Once she melted like a candle in his arms, it took every ounce of his will power to pull out of that kiss. There would be plenty of time for that after he got her to real safety. His body screamed with need, recognizing the proximity to his kryptonite. They spent several seconds looking into each other's eyes by the bright moonlight before she pressed him again, this time with a whisper. "Why now, Ryder?"

The urge to tell her the truth couldn't be denied. "You really want to know?"

"I *need* to know."

"Because. No one gets to hurt you but me."

# CHAPTER 11

*K*hloe let Ryder lift her onto the back of his motorcycle, stunned into compliance by his shocking words. She welcomed the loud roar of the engine as he put them into motion, hoping it would drown out her pounding heart.

She'd been living on the edge for weeks. The events of the last few hours threatened to drown her. Her mind raced to make sense of the barrage of details she'd learned about her mystery man, Ryder Helms. In many ways, he was a complete stranger. Other than his use of his pet name for her, nothing about the last hour resembled the three hours they'd spent together at Black Light. Still, she couldn't deny feeling safer with him than she had in weeks.

It made no sense.

She was forced to hug him tighter as he banked around a sharp corner, taking another stone path through the thick woods, yet she barely paid attention, too busy remembering his kiss and the crush of his erection throbbing between their pressed bodies.

Ryder's left hand left the handle bar of the Harley to link with her grasp at his waist. It was so innocent, the twining of fingers, yet the intimacy of it warmed her from the inside out. Memories of the kinky things they'd done together closed in. He'd debased her, yet she'd loved it. She'd never felt more alive—or devastated—than she had when he'd entered and then fled her life in a matter of hours. He'd mastered her, then deserted her so fast she'd had whiplash, yet the uncontrollable urge to beg him for a round two had her rocking uncomfortably against the vibrating seat.

Her brain wrestled for control, determined to disappoint her tempted body. She wasn't going to give in so easily this time. Not when she begrudgingly admitted how much power he wielded over her happiness.

They rode less than five minutes before entering a clearing in the trees. A large cabin with a wrap around porch came into view courtesy of the moon, landscape lighting and a bright overhead lamp.

They were plunged into silence when he released her hand to cut the engine. They sat in the quiet stillness looking at the house so long, she wondered if something was wrong. Ryder eventually got off the bike, helping her to climb down without ripping her designer gown.

She couldn't resist asking, "Whose place is this anyway?"

He threw the strap of the duffle over his shoulder before grabbing her hand while guiding their walk up the dark path to the house with his light from his smartphone. They were half way to the porch when he answered her.

"Mine."

His answer shocked her. She'd always assumed Ryder lived in D.C. She didn't know what he did for a living, but she'd always pictured him doing something larger than life. Maybe that was because he'd become the center of her universe in the matter of minutes. Not once since they'd said good-bye had she pictured him as a southern California cabin kinda guy.

He wrestled with the lock and key until the front door finally opened. She followed him into the dark cabin, grateful when he flipped the switch, blanketing the large open interior in warm lighting.

White sheets were dropped over every piece of furniture in the space, their brightness in direct conflict with the rich browns of the wood paneling and floor. From the dust that stirred on the uncovered front table where he threw the keys, she guessed it had been a long time since he'd been there.

"I love what you've done with the place," she deadpanned.

He released her hand, barking orders, sounding more like the Ryder she remembered. "Take off the sheets. Pile them in the corner there," he said, pointing. "Ginny will send someone to collect and wash them tomorrow."

The silence was awkward and she was grateful for something to do. Feeling vulnerable in his presence, she purposefully moved to the far side of the open space to give herself a chance to regain her composure.

The first set of sheets she removed uncovered a plush brown leather sofa and loveseat. Near exhaustion made it look like the perfect place to collapse to take a twelve-hour nap, but she pressed on, removing smaller drop cloths from end tables full of books, some even open as if the home's occupant had gotten up one day and simply walked out of their life.

The next treasure she uncovered was two tall built-in bookshelves. As the sheets fell away, hundreds of books came into view filling every shelf, some stacked two deep.

*I never would have pegged Ryder as a bookworm.*

Khloe started reading the spines of books, trying to make sense of what made Ryder Helms tick, but the more titles she read, the less she understood him. Classic stories like George Orwell's *1984* and *The Count of Monte Cristo* by Dumas were piled with Woodward and Bernstein's *All the President's Men*, a biography of Nelson Mandela, and titles like *Good Hunting*, *The Polish Officer* and *The Circle of Treason*. Stephen King and James Clancy shared a shelf with Hemingway and Truman Capote.

When she got to the next bookshelf, the selection got even more interesting. Titles in multiple languages mingled together. She recognized Polish and Spanish, but there were others she couldn't make out.

*Who the hell is this guy?*

Finally moving on, she felt like she hit the jackpot uncovering a credenza full of picture frames filled with dozens of photos, giving her a glimpse into the man across the room unpacking supplies in the kitchen. She fought down the urge to pick up each frame, wanting to examine each closely in hopes of unearthing clues of what made Ryder Helms tick. Khloe settled with quickly perusing them. Most had motorcycles in them with groups of men looking like they had come from the set of *Sons of Anarchy*. There were fewer shots of Ryder in a military uniform surrounded by equally fierce looking men.

One particular photo caught her eye of a twenty-something Ryder, shirtless with his tanned six-pack on display, his dog-tags shining in the desert sun. There was no grey yet in the short, cropped hair. Even through the photo his ice-blue eyes pierced her, as if he'd been looking at her as the photo had been shot many years before.

It unnerved her.

She almost missed the one picture of a teenaged Ryder. She picked up the smallest frame, pushed to the edge of the display. Its size wasn't the only remarkable attribute of this treasure. It was also the only candid shot that contained a woman. A beautiful woman... with piercing blue eyes exactly like the teenager she hugged as she smiled for the photographer. They both looked so happy that a feeling of regret came over her that she hadn't been there to share that moment with him.

"That's my mom." His quiet voice behind her made her jump. She'd been so enthralled with unwrapping the hints of his past that she'd forgotten to keep tabs on his presence. He stepped close enough to brush against her. She glanced sideways to see a sadness in his eyes.

Khloe had to ask, even though it wasn't really any of her business. "What happened to her?" she whispered.

He stood frozen, and she was sure he wouldn't answer, but she was wrong.

"She died just over a year after that photo was taken." He sighed before adding, "Fucking cancer."

"I'm sorry." And she meant it.

"Yeah, well it was a long time ago."

That may be true, but she felt a chink in her protective armor melt away as she watched a man she'd have sworn yesterday had a heart of nails grieve for a woman he clearly had loved. A drop of jealousy fell into her empty stomach, realizing he shared something with the dead woman in the photograph she'd longed to have with her own distant parent who still lived, but couldn't care less about her actress daughter's life.

"I'm gonna make us a late dinner. We need to get some calories into you while you fill me in on the investigation."

Bossy Ryder was back. She didn't know what bothered her more; that he was gonna try to make her eat or that, short of the kiss they'd shared in the parking lot, the man in front of her was acting like they barely knew each other.

*We do barely know each other.*

The thought of eating nauseated her. "I'm exhausted and not hungry. All I want is to take a hot shower and sleep for a day or two. I don't suppose you picked up a change of clothes back when we stopped."

The bastard had the nerve to grin. "Sorry, they were fresh out of designer casuals at Mac's. You'll have to settle for the robe on the back of the bathroom door. Go in, take a shower and change. I'll have food ready when you get out."

"I told you..."

His hand squeezed her bare bicep, cutting her off. "You're

gonna eat tonight. And again in the morning, and every chance I get until you've put on ten pounds." The asshole dared bark at her as if he had the right.

"Fuck you," she said yanking away from his grasp. "You can't tell me what or when to eat. Ten pounds would be a death sentence to my career."

This time he latched onto both her arms and yanked her against his chest to lecture her. "Bullshit. You're too thin. Any director who can't see that is a moron."

Before she could find a proper retort, he was pulling her behind him in the direction of a hallway that shot off from the main living space. More pictures lined the walls, distracting her until they arrived in what had to be his master suite. More sheets were draped over most furniture, but the king-sized four-poster bed was the focal point of the masculine room. He didn't release her until they got into the connected master bath. With the flip of a switch, warm lighting illuminated the surprisingly modern bathroom.

She eyed the whirlpool tub, longingly.

He'd loosened his grip, caressing where he'd gripped moments before leaning closer, talking softer in her ear. "That's fine. Take a long soak."

She caught a whiff of his cologne, the same scent on the handkerchief that she'd been masturbating to since Valentine's Day. It acted as a sexual trigger, and the temptation to kiss him was strong. She closed her eyes, trying to hide her conflicted attraction to him and getting angry at her disappointment when he released her and started rummaging through drawers and cabinets, coming out with the supplies she'd need for a bath.

He was all the way to the door when she called out to him, "Ryder!" When he turned, he'd masked all emotion, leaving her more confused than ever. "Can you..." She hated to ask. "I need your help unzipping my dress."

A wolfish glee she hadn't seen since Black Light adorned his handsome face as her stomach flip-flopped with sexual tension. His long, slow strides back to her reminded her of a predator stalking his prey. The final gap was closed as he lunged at her, pouncing, roughly twirling her in a one-eighty to face the huge mirror that had been at her back.

Gone was the stranger. The blue-eyes that devoured her in the mirror as he yanked her back to his chest and held her immobile were as familiar to her as they were frightening. Her breath hitched as Ryder's right hand found her zipper, slowly opening the back of her gown as if he were opening a present. Their eyes never broke their connection as she felt hands on her shoulders, pulling the slinky fabric outward until the weight of the flowing gown and gravity pooled the bodice at her waist. Only then did Ryder's gaze drop lower, taking in the sexy strapless bra perfectly showcasing her breasts.

Khloe trembled when Ryder's lips latched onto the crook of her neck–where her nape met her shoulder. What started as a soft kiss escalated to a nibble and finally she cried out in pain as the bastard dared bite her.

"Ouch," she complained.

Her complaint only made him wrap his left arm around her waist, squeezing her harder as he sucked his way up and down her shoulder until she was a jumbled ball of confusion. Her brain might be screaming for him to stop, but every other body part felt like it was just waking up from a long winter's rest.

His body tensed before yanking his lips from her skin. In the reflection, she could see him internally struggling for control just as she was.

Trying to push him away emotionally, she blurted a question her gut already knew the truth of. "Tell me again, how do I know you aren't my stalker?"

"Baby, I take what I want. If I'd wanted you, I'd already have you."

His words hurt. He'd left which meant he hadn't wanted her. She lashed back, "You mean like tonight."

He didn't like her analogy, but barked back. "Exactly like tonight."

"So I have two stalkers," she reasoned, trying to stay calm.

The grasp on her hair tightened, hurting her so good. "Princess, I'm not a stalker. I'm the Big Bad Wolf who's gonna keep you safe."

At her core, she recognized his words as the truth, but had to press. "And who will protect me from you?" When he didn't answer, she asked the question she wanted the answer to more than anything. "Why now? Where the hell have you been?"

Her vulnerable question of, '*Why did you leave me?*' hung silently in the air between them. His face softened slightly.

"It's not important where I've been. I'm here because I was at Black Light. Davidson told me you were in trouble. That someone was trying to hurt you." He paused before adding vehemently, "I'm not going to let that happen."

Her body almost collapsed with relief, recognizing the truth in his words. As fucked up as things were, she knew deep down he spoke the truth.

Awareness of her near nakedness made her blush as the room filled with a sexual electricity she only felt in his presence. From the expression in his eyes, he felt it too. She tried not to be disappointed when he stepped away from her, moving to the tub to start the water, liberally pouring in bath oils as she forced herself to brush her teeth one-handed, pulling the bodice of her gown higher to hide as much of her torso as possible with her other hand.

He was at the door when she finished brushing her teeth.

"Have a nice soak. When you're done, throw on the robe on the back of the door and come back out to the kitchen." Their eyes met in the mirror before he finished. "We have a lot to talk about."

He was gone then, leaving her truly alone for the first time she could remember. It might be for the first time since she'd been alone at her apartment back in NYC the week before. She welcomed the unexpected solitude, desperate to have time to mull over all of the events of the last few weeks.

Khloe stripped naked, flipping the switch to turn on the many jets in the now full tub before stepping in. She let the water run until it grew almost too hot, refusing to douse the fire that had started burning between her legs at the sudden appearance of her long-lost lover.

*Lover.* That felt like the wrong word. They'd been intimate to be sure, but she reminded herself it had only been a twisted game to him. The debauched medical examination–the time in the medieval torture chamber, the intimate blowjob on her knees in the shower. He'd probably played the same game with a dozen women in the months they'd been apart. The thought that she was jealous of even that possibility was sobering.

It was hard to stay focused on anything for long, though. Weeks of sleep depravation closed in fast as her body relaxed in the knowledge that she was safe, at least for now. She fought to keep her eyes open, eventually giving in to the temptation to close them. She'd take a short nap to help fortify her for the certain argument ahead with the bossy man she could hear rummaging around out in the cabin's kitchen.

CHAPTER 12

The feel of fingers massaging her calf felt heavenly, easing her slowly from the haze of sleep. She'd been having a wonderful dream, but her mind was clouded, unable to recall the details. Snippets of a sexy Ryder dressed in leather refused to be pushed down by her exhaustion, and intensified when the fingers moved higher to her thigh, massaging what felt like slippery soap across her skin. She heard the distant sigh, not immediately recognizing she'd made the soft sound.

It wasn't until the mystery fingers of her dream moved higher still, grazing against her pussy before applying swirling pressure to her hooded gem that slumber was pushed out by sexual hunger. The reality of the last few hours poured in until she shot upright, moving the now cool water so hard a wave sloshed over the edge of the tub, splashing the grinning man still touching her intimately.

Unperturbed by the water, Ryder released her long enough to pull his now drenched T-shirt over his head, flashing her with a muscular chest covered with a smattering of chest hair. Like the salt and pepper hair on his head, shades of silver woven with dark hair, reminding her he was all man. Her mouth felt dry and

146

her heart hammered in her chest as she gawked at his perfection.

For the first time, she wondered how old he was, begrudgingly acknowledging she was secretively happy he was older than her. She was sick and tired of being pursued by boys like Dean who were too self-absorbed to know the first thing about how to treat a woman.

"You should take a picture. It'll last longer." The sexy grin on his face made him look younger.

Despite the cool water, Khloe felt her body heat from embarrassment, caught red-handed gawking at Ryder's body. She grabbed for the bath sponge in his hand, needing to get busy doing something that would distract her from his proximity.

"Hand me that. I can wash myself," she quipped.

Releasing the sponge, he threw his wet hands up as if to surrender. "Little Miss Independent," he teased her.

"Yes, you can get lost now."

Reaching for something on the floor, he came up with a paddle hairbrush. For a split second, she saw a feral desire in his eyes before the icy blue cooled. "You'll have your hands full getting the tangles out of your hair. Let me help."

Her protest died on her lips as the brush made contact with her scalp, finding a growing nest of knots as he raked through her long locks. As gentle as he was, her hair pulled at her scalp, wrestling a moan of pain and pleasure from her lips.

"We'll put your hair up in the helmet next time we ride to avoid this."

She wanted to argue that she wouldn't be riding with him again. Didn't he know? She rode in limos... chauffeured luxury SUVs... not on the back of motorcycles.

Her retort died before she spoke, recognizing the truth was she'd loved riding on the back of the powerful machine. It had made her feel alive. Less like a celebrity and more like plain Khloe, something that didn't happen often enough these days.

He worked silently on her hair as she closed her eyes, focused on keeping her breathing steady to hide the impact his touch was having on her body. Only when the cup-full of cool water fell over her head did her eyes pop open in surprise.

"Hey, that's cold," she complained.

"Maybe if you hadn't fallen asleep in here for over half an hour, it would still be hot," he retorted.

"So shoot me. I'm tired."

Their eyes met long enough to remind her of how much danger she was in. It dawned on her that she'd just traded in the danger of her stalker for the danger of falling deeper for a guy who had the power to destroy her emotionally when he left again.

And he would leave again. Of that she was certain.

He didn't help when he added, "I have a lot of things I want to do to this body, but shooting you is not one of them."

The words came out playful, but the heated gaze that devoured her naked body was dead serious. A full-body shiver shook her, and she was grateful he blamed it on the water temperature.

"Let's finish washing your hair before you catch a chill."

His hands were as gentle tonight as they'd been demanding and harsh in February. This new version of Ryder Helms confused her, contrasting with her memories of his stern dominance over her body... over her soul.

Only when he turned off the jets and pulled the stopper to the water did it really dawn on her that she'd been naked and on display. How long had he gawked at her while she slept before waking her? When he turned his back to put away the bath supplies, Khloe shot to her feet and lunged for the pile of towels on a stool next to the tub, anxious to wrap herself up as quickly as she could.

When he turned back to her, laughter danced in his eyes as he taunted her, of course knowing what she'd been doing.

"It's a bit late for that, baby. I've seen it all already," he teased.

Too late did she realize her sudden push to her feet left her lightheaded. Too much stress, not enough food and a healthy dose of sexual tension sent her toppling sideways, thankfully into the open arms of the man directly responsible for at least some of her distress.

Ryder scooped her up into his arms, half wrapped in the towel that dragged behind them as he hurried back into the bedroom. He'd put bedding on while she'd been in the bath. His efforts had the room looking like a five-star hotel. The sheets had been turned down, inviting her to sink into their comfort. The only thing missing was a mint on the pillow.

He sat her on the edge of the bed before pulling the towel she clung to away from her body. She wrestled for the cloth briefly, but gave in quickly, realizing she didn't have the energy to fight him. Instead, she let her body be dried like a child before he moved the towel to her dripping hair, squeezing out the excess water as he leaned closer.

She had people wait on her all day, every day. They drove her places, brought her food and drink, applied makeup and even did her hair. So why did what Ryder was doing feel completely different? Randy touched her hair every day on the set, but not once had his fingers left a trail of fire against her scalp.

They were so close, his legs leaning in, pinning her against the bed where she sat. Unexpected tears pricked at her eyes. She slammed them closed in an attempt to hide her weakness, not wanting to let him know how affected she was by his proximity. Her plan was ruined when she let herself fall forward, her fore-head touching the heart of his six-pack abs as she embarrassed herself further by wrapping her arms around his waist, not stopping until she hugged him.

"Khloe..." Her name came out as if she were torturing him, guttural... raw.

It was a warning... one she ignored as she let the tears fall, dripping onto his skin.

His desperate, "Christ," was synchronized with the hard yank of her wet hair, snapping her head back so they were face to face, inches apart as he towered over her. A storm brewed in his eyes as if the dominant normally in control of everything was lost. His confusion made her feel powerful, knowing she had some level of power over him as well. She suspected he didn't let that happen often in his life.

Time stood still long enough that she had to gasp for a breath she hadn't known she'd been holding. His pull at her scalp increased until she cried out, in pain.

He released her as fast as he'd grabbed her, shoving her shoulders so hard her body flung back to the soft bed, bouncing slightly from the sudden impact. Ryder pounced on her like a predator, trapping her beneath him like a prized animal he'd wrestled under his control. His hands were near each of her ears, holding his body above her to stare into her eyes. Her legs had fallen open, allowing his crotch to grind against her sex, only his leather pants protecting her from penetration. A dangerous glare had turned his eyes almost black in the dim lighting.

She was helpless to stop herself. She'd spent too much of their time apart missing him. Her body remembered how he'd played her like a maestro played a violin. In that moment of weakness, she needed to hear their music again.

"You're playing with fire, little girl."

She finally found the courage to whisper, "So burn me."

THEY HADN'T EVEN MADE it a few hours. The entire cross-country flight, he'd lectured himself on how he would need to keep his emotional distance from the A-list actress. He'd come to protect her. No good would come from confusing his mission to keep Khloe safe with anything personal. He was a Goddamned machine at controlling his responses while on the job. It was why he was alive today and exactly why he needed to keep whatever was happening between them as strictly business.

Yet, looking into her water-filled eyes, filled with desire and a vulnerability that he might reject her... he acknowledged he'd been a fool to think he could possibly ignore the pull of their powerful attraction. He was in uncharted territory and it terrified him more than having to face down the Volkovs.

He was a dominant to his core. Control over his environment and even his own self-control was what kept him grounded in life, confident in achieving any goal he set out to grab.

But the woman staring up from the bed held a power over him he had naively thought was just an exaggerated memory of one spectacular night spent together in February. He didn't like it. He didn't even understand it. But he couldn't deny it.

*I fucking need her.*

His lips crashed down to her mouth a second later. Her arms and legs reaching up to pull his body down on top of her, crushing her to the bed. He tasted the minty toothpaste he'd left out for her as his tongue explored, boldly taking what he needed from her. When she ran her fingers through his hair, he wrenched their bodies apart to lean up, grabbing each hand in his own and pinning them above her head. Their fingers intertwined as she was splayed out beneath him like the sexual offering he so desperately needed.

His mouth found the sensitive skin at the nape of her neck, sucking hard enough to leave a mark in a childish show of possession. She tried to thrust her hips off the bed in hopes of taking his erection inside her. Her guttural groan only made his already hard cock ache for release.

He tried to reach the pebbled tip of her breast with his mouth, but couldn't. He knew how to fix that.

"Do not move your arms," he ordered as he released her hands before sliding lower and latching onto her tit with his mouth. He sucked her hard, as if he would magically pull a mouthful of warm

LIVIA GRANT

milk from her full breast. Allowing their passion free rein, he let his teeth graze the sensitive tip, pulling a cry from his gorgeous captive as she wiggled beneath him.

Ryder's hands kneaded her breasts, crushing them together roughly, creating a valley he looked forward to thrusting his hard-on into. The image of hot cum spurting from the tip of his cock onto her fresh face, branding her as his, consumed him. He knew he wouldn't be able to resist playing that vision out later.

But not tonight. Raw instincts took over, demanding that he sheath his sword deep in her sex, taking from her what he needed. Base human hunger drove them both until he was forced to push off her long enough to stand between her legs at the edge of the bed.

God, even without a stitch of makeup on, she was the most beautiful woman he'd ever seen. She looked younger... more vulnerable than he remembered. It only made him want to protect her that much more.

His hands moved to the buttons on his leather pants, anxious to be naked, moving inside her. Her gaze fell lower as he pushed his pants down. A surge of dominance reared as her eyes widened, a touch of fear there as she remembered how thick he was.

A glob of pre-cum wet his tip. He suspected if he were to fuck her right away, he wouldn't last more than a minute. Knowing he needed to slow things down, once naked he fell to his knees, hugging each of her bent legs and pulling her pussy to the edge of the bed. Like a starving man, he lunged forward, sucking her clit as she cried out his name.

She was so wet and her cream tasted fucking fantastic. He had to tighten his grip around her bent legs, holding on tight as she bucked her hips with her passion. Memories of how beautiful she looked as she orgasmed tempted him to drive her over the edge, but he released his suction on her gem before she came, drawing a frustrated growl from her instead.

Slowing things further, he brought the tip of his tongue lower, pressing it inside her wet slit and slowly moving it upward, scooping her juices onto his tongue as he went. When he brushed against her swollen nub, he drank her as if he'd been dying of thirst and then started all over again.

He had no clue how long he lapped at her. He only knew the more he drank, the deeper his hunger for her became. He drove her to the edge again and again until she was crazed with the need to come, writhing beneath him, and mumbling sexy, nonsensical groans.

When he finally stood, he didn't resist grasping his erection, stroking it slowly as he watched Khloe gasp for breath on the bed. The whole room smelled like her.

It smelled like sex.

Need drove him. His hands found her ankles, yanking her legs up, out wide and finally, back over her head, folding her lithe body in half and opening her bare pussy perfectly to receive him.

Their eyes met briefly before they both shifted their gaze to where he was about to claim her. She whimpered as he squeezed her ankles tighter, trying to hold off plunging inside her like a Goddamn rookie. He rocked his hips as his heavy shaft hung between them, the crown rubbing up and down through the slick path his tongue had tasted.

He waited until she tore her gaze away from the spectacle of their sex, linking them together visually instead. He changed angles, pressing the tip of his dick into her as he stood on his toes, a powerful animal, ready to pounce.

He wasn't sure if it was her tight pussy or her scream as he bottomed out in one hard thrust that affected him more. Ryder stilled, buried balls deep as he watched the woman beneath him struggle to take his girth.

He held perfectly still. He'd like to think he did it because he was a gentleman, but he knew the truth. The only reason he wasn't pounding her hard and fast was because he refused to shoot his wad in less than a minute. Her vaginal walls squeezed him, as if anxious to milk him of his white gift.

Sexual anticipation hung heavy in the air as they each breathed heavily. Lust filled her gaze, making her even more fucking gorgeous than she'd been only a minute before.

Unable to wait longer, he pulled his shaft free of her body slowly, only to plunge deep. Again. And again. He lost himself in her reactions, knowing he could become addicted to watching the unique cocktail of pleasure and pain on Khloe Monroe's face as he staked his claim on her body in the most traditional of ways.

He fucked her like she was his, because... well... she was. He drilled her hard and deep, reclaiming the intimacy they'd shared months before until it felt as if no time had passed.

An ugly thought took hold, threatening to dampen the magic. He felt like an idiot, but he had to know.

Not missing a beat, he grunted out his serious question. "How many cocks have been in this pussy since me?" He thrust so strong on the word, 'me' she cried out, pain mixing with pleasure in her eyes.

She didn't answer. Pictures of her holding hands with that fucker Dean Reynolds flashed red before him. His rhythm grew erratic as he became distracted by flashes of her bodyguard lifting her in his arms to put her in the back of the SUV.

"Answer me, Princess. How many men have you slept with since Valentine's Day?"

The corner of her mouth turned up in the smallest of smiles. He saw the spark of humor in her eyes as she pieced together the truth. He was jealous at the thought of her being with anyone else.

His angry growl finally convinced her to give him the answer he had wanted to hear.

"Zero." She hesitated, looking vulnerable again before adding, "No one was you."

Their bodies slapped together until the woman beneath him shocked him, begging permission to come. It was a rule he'd enforced months before in their three-hour tryst. It humbled him that she remembered and deferred to his authority over her body, even without Black Light and the roulette wheel there to direct their game.

"Come with me, baby. Let me see you lose control."

Her pussy clamped his cock tighter, coaxing him to deliver his load deep inside her womb. When he could catch his breath, he couldn't help but praise her.

"Such a good girl. I've been saving it all for you, too."

He'd made them food. She needed to eat, but all of his energy left him with his ejaculation. Suddenly feeling as tired as she looked, he collapsed, his weight crushing her to the bed in her uncomfortable position until she protested, breathless.

"You're squishing me."

Ryder reluctantly lifted himself, letting his softening erection slide out of her swollen flesh. It was gratifying to see remnants of his pearly seed slipping out of her gash, sliding onto the clean sheets. If he were a gentleman, he'd get her a warm, wet cloth, but he settled for reaching for the bath towel he'd thrown aside earlier, using it to dab at her leaking sex.

Pushing to his feet, he reached out to scoop her relaxed body up into his arms, depositing her head and still damp hair on one of the pillows at the head of the bed, pulling the covers over her naked body and then sliding in beside her to pull her into his arms.

Having a sex life that usually consisted of pole dancers and sex workers, Ryder rarely snuggled, yet that was exactly what they were doing as they each came down from their sexual high. He tried not to think about how pleased he was that she'd not slept with other men while they'd been apart. They'd had no commitment to each other. No understanding of monogamy to consider. Not even a pinky swear of fidelity.

Khloe's voice broke the silence. "Wow..."

He chuckled at her embarrassment at her exclamation.

She giggled, poking his chest playfully. "Some gentleman you are, laughing at me."

He hugged her tighter, pulling her until she lay almost on top of his body before answering. "Hey, at least I'm not making you sleep in the wet spot."

# CHAPTER 13

*K*hloe woke to the sun shining in her eyes and the smell of bacon cooking. The aroma drew a grumble from her empty stomach. She felt like she'd been asleep for days. Her brain rebooted slowly, enjoying the rare feeling of calmness that had eluded her for weeks. For the first time in a long time, she enjoyed waking slowly, not being jarred awake by nightmares of a faceless man stealing her away to torture her.

She stretched, reaching her arms up with a yawn and that's when her body screamed at her. Every part of her ached in the best possible way and she had the sex-god, Ryder Helms, to blame for it.

Not that she was complaining.

She forced her eyes open, squinting until she grew accustomed to the bright California sunshine streaming in. She knew before looking that she was alone in the bed. She knew that because if Ryder had been there, he'd have been touching her. Squeezing her. Pinching her. Caressing her. Fucking her.

Like he'd done all night long.

After getting a few hours of rest after their passionate reunion, he'd woken her by roughly rolling her onto her tummy, lifting her hips and thrusting his engorged cock deep before she was even fully awake. As if it had been waiting for it, her body let him slide home, already slick for an encore performance of their first rendezvous of the night. Unlike their initial coupling, he'd had the staying power of a racehorse, riding her hard through not one or two, but three orgasms before finally emptying himself inside her again.

When they'd caught their breath, he'd pulled her up to spoon, her back to his front, using his right arm as her pillow. They each fell back into a satiated sleep, his softening appendage still buried inside her.

There was no clock in the room, so she had no clue what time it was. Based on the sun alone, it had to be after eight. She'd been out of communication, without her cell phone, for over ten hours now. A part of her didn't feel whole without her twenty-first century technology, but a bigger part felt relaxed for the first time in a long time, knowing no one could find her... get to her... mess with her. Not her stalker and not even the Kaplans.

It was liberating.

Just knowing Ryder was so near calmed her in a way that didn't make sense to her. She knew Trevor cared for her. That he'd give his life for her if it came down to it. He was solid. Dependable.

Ryder had shown himself to be the opposite of those qualities. He'd pushed her hard, in unpredictable ways. He'd deserted her, without explanation or apology, before showing up again from out of the blue, acting possessive one minute and aloof the next.

He was an enigma. Unknown.

Her brain told her to run the other way, yet deep down, that inner voice she'd learned to listen to told her to trust him. It confused her greatly.

A full bladder and empty stomach eventually coaxed her from the warm bed. The towel she'd used the night before was gone so she padded her way to the bathroom naked.

The full-length mirror next to the sink welcomed her, the reflection reminding her of the aggressive nature of the other occupant of the cabin. Shadows of forming bruises were visible on her boobs and upper arms where he'd been particularly passionate with her. She should be furious considering she was in the middle of filming. Instead, she was confusingly pleased to have his marks on her body, proving last night hadn't been a figment of her imagination.

She eyed up the shower, tempted to steam away some of her aches, but decided to go in search of coffee first. The robe on the back of the door turned out to be at least three sizes too large, almost dragging on the ground. She could have wrapped the faded terrycloth fabric around her three times. Only the matching belt held it together as she walked down the hallway, into the open great room of the cabin.

Being barefoot made her trek silent, allowing her a few minutes of undetected reconnaissance on the handsome man moving effortlessly through the upscale kitchen. In all of the daydreams she'd lost herself in thinking of Ryder, not once had she pictured him frying bacon and eggs. He was shirtless, wearing only a pair of comfortable lounge pants. She'd done her share of modeling before getting into acting. The scene looked like a photo shoot for an Eddie Bauer catalog. Ryder could play the hunky model teaching men how to relax in the woods.

Yet the closer she looked, she knew he wasn't relaxed. Muscles rippled and tensed as he looked out the window over the kitchen sink often as if satisfying himself they were still alone. She'd seen that look of concentration on his handsome face before. He had a lot on his mind.

The promise of coffee eventually got her moving again. When he saw her approaching, the scowl on his brow deepened, hurting her ego. She'd hoped he'd be as happy to see her this morning as she'd been admiring him. Instead, he looked angry.

"Good morning," she offered quietly.

Only when she got to the kitchen island that also served as an eat-in dining table did he acknowledge her verbally with a simple, "Morning."

She didn't have to ask for coffee. He placed a large mug in front of her, pouring the hot liquid to the top, barely leaving enough room for a splash of creamer and a packet of zero calorie sugar substitute. She didn't want to evaluate how he'd known how she took her coffee. Not that it was a matter of national security, but they'd never shared a meal together. Not even a beverage, other than bottled water during the Valentine Roulette event. Was it a lucky guess on his part?

She doubted it.

Khloe took a seat on the high stool and had only downed one sip when the second half of his breakfast delivery arrived. Ryder slid a platter in front of her. The sheer volume of eggs, bacon, and a stack of pancakes, topped with melted butter and syrup nauseated her. It was more calories on one plate than she normally ate in two or three days combined.

Pushing the plate away, she complained. "I'm not really hungry."

"Too fucking bad. I got sidetracked last night. It won't happen again." There wasn't a trace of negotiation in his voice.

Since the first words out of his mouth when he'd seen her were that she was starving herself, Khloe suspected he would be digging in on this subject. She contemplated her options, deciding between telling him to fuck off because what she ate was none of his business or placating him by taking a few bites. Her stomach growling helped her decide.

Ryder had stopped his cleanup activities to lean his ass back against the kitchen counter directly in front of her, crossing his arms, watching her intently, making his expectations clear. There was nothing sexual about the scene, yet her heart raced, recognizing he was determined to take his proven natural dominance of their sex lives into other aspects of their relationship.

*What relationship, Khloe? He hasn't said shit about a relationship.*

The thought annoyed her. Part of her wanted to press him on what kind of game he was up to coming back into her life like a tornado. Would he be blowing back out as quickly? If so, she owed him nothing, including modifying her eating habits, even if deep down she'd known for a while she was skating dangerously close to the edge of her previously diagnosed disorder.

She felt his stare as she looked down at the plate of food, suddenly fighting the urge to cry. Damn him to hell. She'd been relaxed for the first time in ages and he was ruining it, acting like he couldn't care less about her now that he'd gotten what he wanted from her the night before. At least last time, he'd made a clean break after the life-altering sex.

Picking up her fork, she decided to eat the whites of the over-easy eggs. She'd learned to take small bites, psychologically trying to fake her body out that it had received a full meal. She knew it was stupid, but it didn't stop her. She could feel his glare as he focused on her slow progress.

If she were alone, her breakfast would be over once the whites were gone, yet a quick glance in his direction told her he wasn't satisfied yet. Looking at the remnants of her options, she picked up the glass of orange juice next, slowly sipping down a quarter of the cool beverage.

This time when she glanced his way, she detected a small lift at the corner of his mouth. It was the first sign of levity from him since they'd woke. She wasn't sure she wanted to know why it was there.

"I know what you're doing. It isn't going to work."

"I don't know what you mean. You said eat, so I ate," she said as she pushed the plate away from her toward the edge of the counter.

"From now on you'll eat like a woman, not a bird. Today, you'll eat at least half of what's left."

Her temper flared. "What the hell? I'm not some toddler being told to clean their plate."

"No, you're not. You're a grown woman who knows better which means you should also know what the consequences are for disobeying."

"Excuse me? What the fuck are you talking about... consequences?"

"Don't play coy with me, Khloe. We may not be at Black Light, but you know damn well what I'm talking about."

She argued back, despite her heart rate spiking at his mention of their only other night spent together–him, her master–her, his sex slave. "Look around you, Ryder." She waved her hands widely to make her point before continuing. "Like you said, we aren't at Black Light. That means you can't make me do shit. Hell, you couldn't even then. It's all just a big game, remember?"

It felt good to throw his hurtful words from their goodbye up in his face. She jumped down from the stool, grabbing her coffee mug and heading back in the direction of the bathroom. That shower was sounding better.

She barely made it to the couch when he pounced on her from behind. Hot coffee sloshed out onto her hand, burning its way down to the area rug beneath them as Ryder wrestled the mug from her before placing it on the coffee table.

The sudden escalation of their disagreement unnerved her. Khloe used the distraction to take off running towards the bathroom, hoping to get behind the locked door before the angry man chasing her caught her. But she didn't have a chance in hell. Ryder's arms squeezed around her from behind, dragging her to a halt before she even got across the room. If the strength of his hold meant anything, he was pretty pissed.

*That's fine by me. I'm not too happy myself, asshole.*

She put up a nominal struggle to be free, giving up quickly. Beating almost anyone in a physical altercation was a long shot for the slip of a woman. Besting a man like Ryder Helms physically was impossible. A thread of danger sparked as she realized she was at his mercy, alone in a remote cabin, her closest possible help might be his own aunt, miles away.

Memories of the real danger she was in returned with a rush. The constant panic she'd pushed down returned, making her gasp for breath, coming close to hyperventilating within a minute. She was alone with an aggressive near stranger. The recklessness of it closed in.

"Goddammit, breathe for me, baby." Recognizing her distress, he'd loosened his grip on her in an attempt to help her take deeper breaths. When it was clear it wasn't working, she felt his lips on the shell of her ear, talking softly, but demanding. "You're safe. No one's gonna hurt you." He paused and then demanded, "Breathe! Now!"

Her body obeyed, sucking in precious air, even as her brain resisted. They stood in the middle of the cabin for several minutes, Ryder whispering calming assurances into her ear until her panic receded and her breathing returned to normal.

By the time he released her to scoop her up into his arms, she was exhausted. The fatigue of constant stress blanketed her again, like an old friend. She didn't put up a fight when he walked them back to the kitchen, this time sitting in the stool she'd vacated, holding her in his lap with his left arm while pulling the platter of food she'd shoved away back towards them.

His tone of voice was eerily calm when he spoke next. "I'm sorry I scared you. It wasn't my intention."

Had Ryder Helms just apologized to her? The absurdity of it cut through the fog of her stress, forcing her to look into his eyes to see if he was serious. Real regret shown in his eyes.

"I know you're afraid. It's why I'm here. I meant it when I said no one would hurt you."

His words from the night before came back to her. "Except you. You said you were the only one who got to hurt me."

Frustration was evident on his handsome face. His day-old

growth of facial hair only made him look more sexy... and danger-ous. "I shouldn't have said that. It was..."

"Barbaric? Presumptuous?" she filled in the blank.

He finished for her in an unexpected way, "It was wishful thinking."

Those were some of the few words he could utter to make her feel even a bit better. They worked.

"Wishful in what way?" she questioned quietly.

His free hand that wasn't holding her on his lap moved to cup her cheek, unusually gentle considering their physical history.

This time he used words instead of strength to hurt her. "It was a mistake sleeping together last night."

Instant tears made him swim before her. Her fluctuating emotions felt like she was on a rollercoaster ride. Up... down... She hated that they were so close. There would be no hiding them from him. She felt so foolish. He was already ready to ditch her all over again.

Khloe slapped his hand away from her face, doing her best to swish the tears from her eyes before they hit her cheeks. She wouldn't give him the satisfaction of knowing how much he could still hurt her. She wiggled to escape his clutches, but he only hugged her tighter.

"Fuck, woman. Will you sit still and let me finish?"

"Oh, I think I've heard enough. I want to go home. Now."

"You aren't going anywhere. Not until you listen to me." He paused and then added, "And not until you've eaten at least half this food."

The man was seriously brain damaged. "Screw you."

"We've already tried screwing. It only complicated things."

That was an understatement. "Well, welcome to my world. It's complicated."

The asshole had the nerve to smile. "Yeah, I've noticed. I can't say my world has been a cakewalk lately, either."

She didn't know what he meant by that, but she saw the truth in his eyes. "So why are you here? Really. Or is it like you said, all a big mistake?"

The normally controlled dominant in front of her was left speechless for a long minute. He swished his free hand through his hair, fidgeting in his seat as if he were uncomfortable. Several arguments were on the tip of her tongue, but she held them back, more anxious to hear what he had to say.

When he finally spoke, his words gutted her. "I never wanted to leave you. Not then. And not now."

"Then why?"

"I had to, for my job."

"Even if that's true, why are you here then? Did you quit?"

"Not exactly. Let's say I took a leave of absence."

"Why would you do that?"

"Because I know I'm supposed to be protecting you now, instead of..." His voice trailed off as if he were afraid he'd said too much.

He may be telling her the truth, but there was a lot he wasn't saying too. She was still hurt. "Except now you regret it. You said it yourself."

He held her chin still, forcing her to look at him again. "I meant what I said. It would be easier to protect you if things weren't so... *personal*... between us." When she didn't reply, he continued. "I'm distracted around you. I'm worried that I'm going to spend too much time thinking about all of the delicious things I want to do to your body instead of focusing on any danger in your environment." His voice cracked as he added, "I'll never forgive myself if anything happens to you on my watch."

She was stunned into silence. He sounded sincere. God, she wanted him to be telling the truth.

Their visual standoff was interrupted by the ringing of a nearby phone. Ryder released her chin to dig a phone out of the pocket of his pants. He didn't even look at it before answering it with a simple, "Helms."

He listened intently to whoever was on the other end of the phone as he stared at her with that unreadable glare he had perfected. Several minutes ticked by while he listened before finally answering with two simple words. "Hold on."

He looked down long enough to mute the call before looking back at her. "It's Davidson. Seems your asshat of a bodyguard is threatening to call the police if he doesn't get to speak to you within the hour."

Guilt closed in. She hadn't even thought about calling Trevor to check in. He must be frantic, not having a clue who Ryder was.

"Is that him?" she asked.

"He's there, yes."

She reached for his phone, taking it off mute. "Trevor?"

"No, Jax. But he's here. I tried to tell him you were safe, but it seems he'll only listen to you."

"He's only doing his job."

Jaxson hesitated, "Are you sure about that? It seems to be more than that." It took her a second to understood what he was hinting at. She blushed, remembering Trevor's declaration of love less than a week earlier.

"I'm sure. Put him on, please." She felt heat rising under Ryder's glare.

"Khloe? Where the hell are you?" Trevor was seriously pissed.

"I'm safe. You don't need to worry."

"The hell I don't. I don't know what's going on around here, but since when do you take off with some stranger without even a word of who he is or where he's taking you. Fuck, you didn't even take your phone with you."

"I'm sorry. I really am." Her gaze locked with the man who's lap she was wiggling in. "Ryder is an old friend. I didn't know he was in town or that he'd be coming to see me."

"That's bullshit. I know all of your friends. Your enemies. Your business partners. This guy is a complete unknown. Now of all times, I can't believe you'd be stupid enough to take off without my protection."

He was right, of course. It had been foolish of her. "I said I'm sorry."

Trevor sighed. "We'll talk about this when you get home. Apollo called. He needs you on set in two hours. They're doing the retakes on the courtroom scenes today before he releases the extras."

"Dammit, we're supposed to be off until next week."

"That's not how this works, and you know it." She detected the simmering anger he was barely containing. Even if he was right, he'd never talked to her like this before.

"I'm not sure if..."

"Listen, I'm trying to be a sport here, but don't you dare stick me with having to tell the director you can't come in today because you're off gallivanting with some old boyfriend."

She was pretty sure he was fishing for information, but she didn't like it. "I'm not gallivanting," she defended lamely. She stopped short of explaining Ryder's relationship to her, in part because it wasn't any of Trevor's business, but more importantly, because she didn't have a clue what he was to her either. "Hold on."

It was her turn to put the call on mute. "The director needs to do some retakes on some scenes we did last week. We're about to lose the extras from the scene and that would force an entire re-shoot and cost a lot of money. Can you have me at the studio in two hours?"

Instead of answering her question, he asked his own. "What's going on with you and your bodyguard?"

"For crying out loud. There's nothing going on with Trevor. He's my personal guard. That's all."

"Personal, eh?"

There was a sliver of her that was thrilled at the idea of Ryder Helms being even a tiny bit jealous of another man. The dominant was so confident. So self-assured. Jealousy didn't fit his profile. Still, she wasn't crazy about being the prize in the two men's present tug-of-war match.

"Knock it off. Can you have me there or not?"

He hesitated, but finally agreed. "Yeah, I can have you there." She was reaching to unmute the phone when he added, "But before we leave, I'm gonna lay down the ground rules, and you're gonna agree to them."

She held off returning to her call with Trevor. "Excuse me? What rules?"

"Just one rule, really." His eyes had frosted over with that icy-blue that made her quiver with a cocktail of emotions. She held her breath waiting for him to finish.

"I'm in charge. Period."

"In charge of what? My protection detail?"

"Yes. And where you go, who you see, what you do..." His eyes shaded darker, as he added, "How and when we fuck." Her core clinched with sexual excitement, just before he added, "And yes, even what you eat and drink."

Not that again. Who did he think he was, anyway?

The phone shook in her hands, almost toppling to the floor as she internalized his words. Sensing she was on overload, Ryder grabbed his phone back and took it off mute.

"Helms here. I got the message. I'll have her there in two hours. Not a minute before."

She could hear Trevor shouting as Ryder pulled the phone away from his ear and ended the call, hanging up on a still yelling Trevor.

"You didn't have to be so rude to him," she complained.

"He's a big boy. If he's just your employee, he'll get over it."

"What do you mean, if he's just my employee?" she countered, already knowing exactly what he meant. She was relieved when he let the argument die, unwilling to dig too deeply into Trevor's motives herself.

Not wanting to continue with the current line of questioning, Khloe tried to squirm out of his clutches in hopes of heading to the shower. He only hugged her tighter, reaching out for her fork and using it to cut off a big bite of pancakes.

She clamped her mouth shut as he rubbed the food against her lips. "Open up."

Even as she shook her head no, she felt childish. But whether she liked it or not, they'd entered into a battle of wills. Holding her ground was now a matter of pride, or at least principle. Letting Ryder control their time between the sheets was one thing. Controlling her everyday life was something completely different.

"I know you think you're gonna win in our little war, but you're a rookie, baby. You will eat half this food." He paused, before making it clear he knew at least some of her tricks. "And you'll keep it down, too. The only question left to answer is how sore your ass is going to be by the time you're chewing the last bite."

Her mouth popped open from the sheer shock of his words. Ryder was ready, shoveling the forkful of food inside, depositing the sweet syrupy goodness on her tastebuds. She froze, tempted to spit it back out at him, but unwilling to see what that stunt might earn her.

"Chew," he demanded, their eyes locked in a battle of wills.

It galled her that it tasted fantastic. Pancakes and syrup was one of her favorite breakfast foods.

*Don't panic. One bite won't kill you.*

Slowly, her mouth moved. She expected him to gloat, but instead, the icy blue of his eyes melted a bit. He looked pleased.

"Swallow."

Testing a theory, she did as she was told and this time was rewarded with an actual smile.

Interesting.

Still, she wasn't going to let him treat her like a child. She

LIVIA GRANT

opened her mouth to tell him so, but the bastard scooped another big bite in instead. She finished that bite without prodding, but then clamped her hand over her mouth to protect it from incoming projectiles while she tried to set him straight.

"You don't understand. This is how it is in Hollywood," she mumbled.

He wrestled her hand away from her mouth, shoving a slice of bacon in as he answered her. "I understand perfectly. I just don't give a shit about Hollywood." He chucked her chin as she tried to spit out the greasy caloric nightmare, preventing her from spitting it out as he added, "I only care about you."

His simple words worked like magic. He only cared about her.

Instead of looking embarrassed by his admission, the blue in his eyes melted into an inviting pool she wanted to lose herself in. She had no idea what it was called or how it happened, but there was no denying the almost magical attraction they had for each other. It had been there the minute they'd met and he'd chased her down at Black Light. It had nearly destroyed her when he'd turned his back on it, walking out on her and making her think she'd imagined the whole thing.

As if he could read her mind, he answered her unspoken question. "I don't really understand it either. But I know this is where I'm supposed to be." He hesitated before adding, "Please, Khloe. Let me take care of you. At least until we find the bastard behind the threats and get them neutralized."

He was asking her. She should be happy, but it felt like they were treading in new waters. Renegotiating their scene. Only this time, there would be no roulette wheel calling the shots and there was more at stake than pushing each other's sexual buttons.

She needed more information.

"What do you mean by take care of me? What exactly are we talking about here?"

His eyes hardened again. "Effective immediately, I take over your personal security. Twenty-four, seven. I put together my

170

own independent team of investigators to dig into the threats against you and ferret out who's behind them. I won't stop until they're behind bars." He paused and she was about to tell him that sounded perfect when he held his finger up to shush her.

He continued. "I also call the shots on who has access to you. You'll go where I tell you, when I tell you. I approve your schedule, publicly and privately, with your safety my number one concern." He squeezed her chin, ensuring she wouldn't look away as he added with the yummy authoritative tone that melted her core, "And... when we're alone, I'm your Master. Like we were back at Black Light, only I call the shots instead of the roulette wheel."

Khloe's heart lurched at his unexpected proposal, her brain and body at war. She'd half expected him to drop her off at the studio and then ride off into the sunset, never to be seen again. Relief that he obviously planned to stick around for a while warred with terror at the thought of turning herself over to him as he wanted. She was a successful, independent twenty-first century woman, and he was asking for unprecedented control over every aspect of her life.

This was not normal. But then again, nothing had been normal for them since the minute they'd met. But what if she couldn't do it? He was asking too much.

"Just like that? You waltz back in and demand complete control?"

"I rarely waltz, but yeah... pretty much."

The bastard had the audacity to grin the sexiest smile in his arsenal. It almost made her waver, but she stuck to her guns, grateful for the clarity of what she needed to do. She pushed away from him until she was standing on her own two feet, her hands on her hips.

"Here's my counteroffer, Mr. Helms. I agree to turn the investigation over to you, including control over my personal safety and schedule, but Trevor stays on. Until the culprit is found and behind bars, I will defer to you for all things regarding my protection." She paused, reaching out to hold his chin as he had hers, sending a loud and clear message. "As for being my Master behind closed doors... that one you're gonna have to earn back." His eyes widened at her demand. "You walked out. It hurt me, more than I'd like to admit." His eyes softened. "So, you have a bit of work to do before you earn that kind of unwavering trust from me again. Got it?"

Several long seconds went by as she held her breath, worried she'd overplayed her hand in the complex game they seemed to be playing.

He moved so fast, she had no warning. One minute she was standing in the kitchen with her hands on her hips in complete control, the next she was spun around, her torso bent over and pressed into the hard kitchen counter. Ryder opened her robe and ripped it away from her body, leaving her naked before him. He yanked her arms behind her back and used the belt from her robe to effortlessly wrap her arms together from her wrists to her elbows, subduing her completely under his control in less than a minute.

Electricity sparked where he touched her body, his hands roaming... exploring. She gasped for air, feeling lightheaded as he slapped her ass hard before using the same hand to slide through her shamefully wet pussy.

She didn't understand it. She didn't even know if she liked it, but there was no denying her body loved everything he did to it. The problem was, her brain couldn't quite get wrapped around it.

He pinched. He squeezed. He slapped. He caressed. He played her body, driving out all cognitive thought until she was nothing but a sexual blob, desperate for release. He edged her until it hurt.

"Ryder! Please!" She couldn't stand it any more. She needed to come more than she needed air. She trembled at his victorious growl of satisfaction as he finally buried his cock inside her, lifting her at the hips, her feet now dangling as he plowed her from behind like a man possessed.

She screamed as her first orgasm consumed her. Still in the throes of ecstasy, she was like putty in his hands as he lifted her off the counter by placing his hands on the back of her thighs, holding her still linked body in front of him as he effortlessly lifted her off his rod before letting gravity impale her again. He was like a machine–a piston at work–lifting and dropping her to a fast rhythm until he grunted his own release, hugging her to him as she felt the heat of his wetness filling her.

As she came down from her sexually-induced high, she felt Ryder trying to catch his own breath as he hugged her folded body against his chest.

Her arms were starting to hurt having been sandwiched uncomfortably between their grinding bodies, but he distracted her from the pain by sucking her earlobe into his mouth, nipping it intimately until he released her to speak softly against her ear.

"Challenge accepted, Princess."

CHAPTER 14

*H*e zoomed in on the grainy photo on his tablet, his blood pressure rising. Ryder had spent the last thirty minutes reviewing the evidence collected so far in Khloe's stalker case. He owed Davidson one. The model turned club owner had used his celebrity connections to pressure the studio's investigators to forward over everything they'd collected to date on the case to Ryder's secure email account.

He didn't know what infuriated him more. That there was so little evidence other than that provided by the crime photos themselves, or that the people surrounding the actress presently drying her hair in his bathroom didn't seem to be taking the threats against her seriously.

He'd have to read everything more thoroughly later, but his early analysis of the evidence was that he didn't trust anyone in her inner circle. He'd started a list of possible suspects based on the photos, emails and threatening messages along with who had access to her private locations that had been breached.

The list was unfortunately long and growing. And her bodyguard, Trevor McLean, was at the top of his list. Something didn't add up with the guy. His first instinct was to fire his ass and keep him as far away from Khloe as he could, but he knew Khloe herself would dig in to try to protect him, which only made Ryder hate the guy that much more.

No, better to keep him close–watch him carefully.

He jumped when Khloe stepped close. He'd been so focused, he'd not heard her approaching.

"Where did you get that picture?"

Something about the tone of her voice made him turn to watch her. "Why?"

"Tell me! Where did you get that?" Her voice cracked with anxiety.

"Davidson sent it over. It's part of the evidence the studio investigators collected. Why does it upset you?"

Of all of the photos he'd reviewed, this one of Khloe talking to Trevor seemed pretty benign. She was facing away from the camera and the shot was taken too close for him to sort out where they were located. Taking a closer look, he didn't care for the look on McLean's face as he spoke with his boss, Khloe.

"Where was this taken?" he asked again. When she didn't answer, he added, "And when?"

She'd turned pale. The photo clearly unnerved her. "It was taken in the lobby of my New York apartment building the night of the first break-in. I was scared shitless. The police held back all photographers though. We didn't want any photos like this floating around and making it into the tabloids."

Ryder made a mental note to find out exactly who had authorized the secret photos.

He knew she wouldn't like it, but he had to speak up. "Tell me more about Trevor McLean."

She glanced up at him, curious, but answered. "What do you want to know? He's been with me almost two years now." She must have sensed where this was going because she added on, "I trust Trevor completely."

"That may be, but you have to admit, he has more access to you than anyone else. I've only seen photos and news feeds, but even I can tell he has the hots for you. How do you know he isn't behind the threats, trying to drive you to depend on him more?"

"Oh come on. That's ridiculous," she protested verbally, but even her Oscar-worthy acting skills couldn't hide the worry line on her brow. She wouldn't admit it out loud, but he knew Khloe had already given that possibility some thought.

"I have a lot more questions, but we need to head out if we want to get you there by eleven."

"I can't believe you're gonna make me wear this ridiculous outfit," she complained.

He'd called Aunt Ginny for help with a woman's wardrobe change, not wanting to put his passenger back into her elegant gown for the ride back to the city. It hadn't been as conspicuous in the dark of the night, but in midday Friday traffic on an L.A. freeway, her gown would draw unwanted attention. The sizes-too-big jeans held up with a belt and the black T-shirt would have to do.

"Aw come on. You look great," he teased.

He grabbed his already packed duffle before taking her hand and heading out to the Harley. It made him smile to see how excited she was to be riding the bike again. He'd half expected her to be afraid of the powerful machine. He punched the address of the studio into his smartphone before taking off for the drive back to civilization. He looked forward to the trip, especially when his passenger hugged him tighter as he gunned it.

Fifty minutes later, they pulled up to the guard shack of the Burbank studio where Khloe's next movie was being filmed. He'd asked Davidson to have his name added to the approved visitor's list, but was anxious to see exactly how much security vetting took place at the studio gates. Unfortunately, he wasn't surprised when all he had to do to gain entrance was give his name to the guard who checked his computer, and finding Ryder Helms on some list, granted him access to the grounds without even asking to see any identification.

He'd definitely be discussing the breach with the head of security right before he chewed him a new asshole for putting Khloe at risk with their amateur crap.

He hadn't even cut the engine to the bike when Trevor McLean rushed out of the luxury trailer. The asshole had the nerve to pull Khloe from the back of the bike before he'd even taken his helmet off.

"I can't believe you took off like that. You gave me a Goddamn heart attack." The asshole was turning her around, inspecting her as if she'd been injured.

As soon as he had their helmets secured, Ryder stepped next to Khloe, wrapping his left arm around her waist possessively as he reached his right hand out for a handshake. "Ryder Helms."

He wasn't surprised when the greeting wasn't returned. He watched Trevor's reaction carefully, catching the flash of jealousy just before he schooled his expression to mere anger.

"I don't know who the fuck you are, but you have some nerve pulling a stunt like that last night."

"What stunt was that? Pulling Khloe out of a chaotic mob and taking her to a safe house where she could be properly protected?"

The taller man's face turned bright red with anger. "I had things under control."

"Yeah, right. That's why Jaxson had to scoop her up and carry her to me at the curb."

Khloe wiggled from his embrace, stepping between the men. "All right, you two. I think we've made a big enough scene for the day."

Ryder glanced around. Small groups of people, many in period costumes, had exited nearby trailers, interested in watching the altercation.

"You're right. Let's go inside," Ryder agreed.

Trevor did not. "You're not going anywhere. I'll take it from here."

It galled him when Khloe placed her hand on his chest, trying to keep her guard calm. "Come on, Trevor. Let's go in and talk."

McLean wasn't listening. "Jesus Christ, you're actually gonna put up with this? What's going on? Are you firing me?"

"Of course not. Ryder is gonna be joining my security detail, that's all."

They were setting the tone for all things to come. He couldn't let her explanation stand. "Correction, Princess. I'm going to be *leading* your security detail." His eyes locked with McLean's before adding. "You're welcome to stay on, or resign. Up to you."

Trevor looked like he wanted to deck him, and despite his cool facade, Ryder felt exactly the same way in return.

The crowd around them was growing. He ended the standoff by grabbing Khloe's hand and pulling her into motion towards the steps to her trailer. The rush of cold air greeted them as he swung open the door, catching the group of people red-handed who'd been hovering near the entrance to eavesdrop on the altercation in the parking lot. Most dispersed quickly, looking embarrassed.

The only two who stayed near the door were the older couple he assumed were Khloe's agent and publicist. He'd been looking forward to asking them some questions. He didn't like the tone of several emails they'd exchanged with the police, almost as if they'd hoped to sweep the criminal investigation under the rug while still ensuring leaks of the details made it to the press.

He had expected them to react to his presence as McLean had, but he'd been wrong. Before he could even acknowledge them, Natalie Kaplan was hugging him, a broad grin on her face.

"I need to congratulate you, young man. Riding in and stealing Khloe on that motorcycle of yours was a brilliant idea! I don't know why I didn't think of it myself." She released him, but proceeded to pat herself on the back. "Of course, it would have been nice to have a heads up in advance so I could have prepped a few photographers. As it was, there were only a few freelancers in range to get the best shots of the stunt."

She leaned over to the counter and grabbed a tablet, pulling up a photo taken the night before out front of the theater. He'd been so happy to see Khloe, he hadn't noticed how scared shitless she'd looked as he drove up to the curb, prior to taking his helmet off.

Ryder prided himself for living life on his terms, rarely letting guilt factor into his choices, but in that moment, guilt was what he felt staring down at the photo of a terrified Khloe in Jaxson's arms.

She'd stepped close to see as well, giving him the chance to hug her and whisper softly against her ear. "I'm sorry I scared you like that."

She looked up, surprise registering before she smiled. "That's twice." He didn't have a clue what she meant so she added, "You've apologized to me twice in one morning. I'm not sure, but I'm guessing that's a record for you."

*Damn.*

"Smartass," he retorted, hating that she had his number and wasn't afraid to call him on it.

Natalie was rambling on, unaware of their intimate sidebar. "You can't buy this kind of publicity. Such a good buzz going today. You're trending on Twitter, of course, but the real coup is Harley Davidson just announced a surge in business. Their stock is up four percent!"

Ryder interjected, "I got news for you, but last night wasn't some stunt. My only goal was to protect Khloe, not draw more negative publicity."

Natalie babbled on, totally missing his growing anger. "Young man, there is no such thing as negative publicity."

Her husband, Bernie, was equally animated. "This will get you an added three million easy on your next contract. Moving a national brand's stock like that proves you have real star power with advertisers."

Ryder's blood pressure was going through the roof listening to them babble on as if the nightmare Khloe was living through was the best thing since sliced bread. For once, it looked like he had something in common with McLean because the bodyguard looked like he wanted to dispose of the Kaplans almost as much as Ryder did.

He gave Khloe a reassuring hug before stepping away and towards the older couple in the room. He didn't stop his forward movement until he had invaded their personal space, getting up in their faces, his most menacing expression on his mug, the one that he usually reserved for criminals and low-lifes he was about to interrogate. The gasp of shock from Natalie as she stumbled backwards into her husband was gratifying.

"Now listen up, because I'm only gonna say this once. You're done turning the illegal threats against your client into a publicity stunt. I'm taking over the investigation, and I'm gonna be digging deep, leaving no question unasked." He looked around the room, making sure he had everyone's attention before adding. "And if I find out anyone in her inner circle has anything to do with the threats against her, I'm gonna make it my life's mission to make sure the offender doesn't see anything but the inside of a jail cell for the next twenty years."

"Why I never! How dare you speak to me like that? Mystery man or not, you're out of line." Natalie turned to Khloe, looking for support. "Are you really going to let him speak to me like this?"

Before Khloe could answer, McLean decided to take sides–a major mistake.

"I'm with Natalie on this. I don't know who the hell this guy is or why he's here, but he clearly is a hothead prone to violence. You need to fire him."

Ryder barked a bitter laugh. "That would be a little hard for her to do since I'm protecting her for free."

Trevor's eyes widened, "Why the hell would you do that?"

Ryder stepped into *his* personal space, inches away before adding, "For the same reason you would if Khloe asked you to." The taller man's eyes widened with understanding.

"All right, everyone... stop arguing. We don't have time for this. Randy and Cathy, I'll be over in a minute. We need to get started on hair and makeup." Khloe turned to the Kaplans next to add, "Ryder is right. I'm done letting you turn the threats against me into an advertising opportunity. Cooperate with him, or go home."

He didn't think it was possible for her to be more beautiful, but watching her take charge and stand up for herself gave him an instant boner. She was so strong and yet so fragile. A dichotomy of nature wrapped up in a too-small package that all he wanted to do was steal away to keep all for himself.

*Fuck. Not unlike her stalker.*

The irony of his realization was unsettling, although it gave him a lead on a possible motive.

Khloe'd turned her attention back to the tall men in the room. "And you two... grow up. The pissing contest is already getting old. I trust you both, so you'll have to figure out how to work together."

*She isn't nearly as cute when she's mouthing off to me, though.*

Even as he thought it, he knew it was a lie. Her strength was refreshing.

She didn't wait for an acknowledgment, stomping away from the drama to sit in the makeup chair at the other end of the trailer.

The remaining occupants of the room dispersed to all corners of the trailer. It felt a bit like prize fighters going to their corner between rounds, resting up for the next bout of punches. He couldn't stop a small smile from forming, acknowledging that, so far, he was having a surprising amount of fun with his unexpected side-job.

He filled the time organizing a few items from his duffle bag. It only took her crew twenty minutes to transform Khloe from the girl-next-door to gorgeous actress. As she stood before him, he could tell she was looking at him nervously, her previous confidence hidden.

Aware every set of eyes were on them trying to figure out who the new guy was to their boss, Ryder pulled her into his arms for a tame hug, leaning low to whisper in her ear. "You're stunning... but, not quite as beautiful as you were around three this morning."

Her sharp intake of breath at his mention of their encounter was followed by a full-body tremble that had her falling against him in a way that told everyone in the room the real nature of their relationship. When they separated, she had an adorable blush shining through her layer of makeup.

Ryder pulled a small gold bracelet from the pocket of his slacks. A rather lame decorative four-leaf clover charm hung from the chain.

"Hold out your arm. I want you to wear this."

He wasn't surprised at her reaction. It hadn't been his first choice either, but he had to take what he could get on his hasty supply run on the way to the airport.

"Um... thanks, but it's not really my style," she said diplomatically.

"Yeah, well, it's not meant to be a fashion statement. Just wear it. I'll explain later." He didn't have time to explain that there was a tracking chip in the charm that would allow him to track her with his cell phone anywhere in the world. For now, he didn't need to worry her further with such details.

They were five minutes late leaving the trailer. Someone had sent a souped-up golf cart to pick up Khloe. With the driver and one other passenger already in the back seat, there were only two seats left. The asshole McLean rushed to take the front seat, assuming he was leaving Ryder without a seat in the impromptu game of musical chairs.

Unfazed, Ryder held Khloe back while he took a seat in the only empty slot and then reached back to lift her into his lap. He knew he was being a jackass, but he couldn't stop flashing a grin at the disgruntled McLean.

"Problem solved," he gloated.

"I'd have thought you were too old for childish games like this," she chastised him quietly.

His palm squeezed her ass through the thin pencil skirt she was wearing for the courtroom scene she was about to film.

"Are you kidding me? I love this game." He was happy to see his hands were having the desired effect. She shifted in his lap, her eyes widening as she encountered his thick erection under her bottom. He added suggestively, "In fact, I could play all day."

They'd arrived at the entrance to the lot they were filming in. Ryder gave her ass a pinch as he lifted her up and out onto her own feet. He took her hand as they left the heat behind them for the darkened hallway.

A few minutes walk took them to an opening where a replica of a traditional courtroom appeared. She adorably smiled up at him before taking off to talk with a group of men about a dozen feet away. Ryder's trained eye started evaluating the environment for threats... clues to who might be behind the threats to his princess.

He stayed on the sidelines on purpose, out of the way, but where he had the best vantage point to watch the cast and crew interacting with Khloe. Makeup was touched up, costumes were checked, refreshments delivered, dialogue reviewed. He made mental notes of people and actions so he could ask her questions about them later. It wasn't ideal that he hadn't had more time to debrief with her and the evidence prior to being thrown into her detail.

It also wasn't lost on him that Trevor had purposefully taken a protective stance exactly opposite Ryder on the far side of the set. He begrudgingly admitted the guy looked to be taking his job seriously.

They were about to begin filming when his cell phone started ringing in his pocket. He pulled it out in time to see his boss's name on his caller ID. Flashbacks of the diplomatic disaster he'd thrown the country into the week before invaded his thoughts, distracting him from his current mission. He hit the *IGNORE* button on the call.

*If he really needs to talk to me, he can leave a message.*

He flipped the phone to silent and threw it back in his pocket. When he looked up, several crew members in the area where giving him dirty looks for making noise. They distracted him momentarily and when he glanced back to where he'd last seen Khloe, she was gone. A quick scan of the area proved she was no longer on the set.

And neither was McLean.

His heart lurched. He'd only looked away for a few seconds. He'd never forgive himself if anything happened to her. There were faux walls, doors to nowhere, and large recording equipment making the area a mini-labyrinth. He took off to the last location she'd been standing in hopes of seeing where she might have gone.

He was standing in the middle of the now empty courtroom when he spotted her waiting off-stage with the guy he suspected was the director.

A grizzly looking guy with a beard like Santa Clause shouted at him. "Hey, who the hell are you? We're about to start shooting! Clear the set!"

The hardened undercover operative forced on his best placid facade as he stalked toward Khloe. Their eyes met as he approached, and he could tell she was already in character, preparing for the upcoming scene. That was too damn bad. He'd forgotten to lay down some important rules.

"I need to talk with you."

The director answered before she could. "You haven't delayed us enough? Don't know who you are, but there's no time for chitchat. We have hours of work ahead of us."

He towered over the shorter, portly man with an out-of-place fishing cap on. "I need one minute with Khloe." When the man started to object, Ryder raised his hand like a stop sign. "I insist."

He squeezed her elbow, pulling her into motion beside him until they had a modicum of privacy amongst what looked like some old props and new cleaning supplies.

"I can't believe you embarrassed me like that. I'm working here," she hissed.

"Yeah, well so am I, and I don't appreciate you getting out of my line of sight."

"You're kidding, right?"

He hesitated, not wanting to scare her, but knowing she needed to take the threats more seriously if she was going to stay safe.

"Where did the first break-in take place?" Her caramel-brown eyes widened in alarm. When she didn't answer, he added. "In your locked, private home. And where was the second threat left?" He again answered for her. "In your locked, private trailer."

He had her full attention. Drudging up the scariest moments in a person's life will do that.

"If he can get to those places, he can get to you anywhere." Tears welled in her eyes. It struck him that in his past, seeing a woman crying usually meant he was having fun at one of the BDSM clubs he frequented. Things had changed the night he met the remarkable woman standing in front of him. These tears weren't fun.

"I swear to you, I won't let that happen, but you need to be smart. Don't go anywhere alone. Don't leave the area without me or McLean with you."

She protested, "Don't you think you're being a bit melodramatic? I mean what if I need to pee and you aren't around to escort me?"

He reached on the shelf behind her to pull out an empty five-gallon bucket. He grinned. "Then, like you did at Black Light, you can pop a squat over the bucket here in the corner." He was rewarded with a mortified groan from Khloe before he got more serious. "I mean it. Do not leave the area without me, understand?

I think you can guess how I would likely deal with your defiance on this."

Her eyes widened with understanding before she teased him with her best imitation of an Army salute. "Yes, sir."

Little did she know, she'd be saying 'yes, sir' often to him in the future if he had anything to say about it.

"Can I get back to work now?" He heard the snark in her tone, but nodded yes. Only when she turned to retrace her steps back to the director did he pop her on the ass with a swat. She swung around, surprise on her face. "Hey, what was that for?"

He leaned in, loving the scent of his own soap on her. "Just a preview of what to expect if you get too sassy, young lady."

Raw desire mingled with apprehension in her beautiful eyes at the thought of being spanked. Little did she know, he'd be lighting up her ass just for fun, regardless of whether she earned it or not. The only thing she could control was whether it would be a good girl spanking or a naughty girl spanking. For her sake, he hoped it was the former.

The next thirty minutes flew by. Ryder found another out-of-the-way place to observe, thoroughly enjoying watching her working her magic with her co-stars. Before he'd met her, he'd assumed, probably like the rest of the world, that Khloe Monroe was another pretty face in Hollywood, working her way to the top on her knees. Not that he was an expert in these matters, but she was the utmost professional. He watched the rest of the cast and crew defer to her, showing her respect he guessed was hard-earned in an industry like show business.

The vibration of his phone distracted him again. This time he wasn't surprised when it was Webster calling. If he was calling twice in less than an hour, something was up. He looked around, spotting McLean nearby. He was tempted to take the call, to see what they had to say to him, but he couldn't do that unless he trusted McLean to handle solo protection duty.

Ryder approached him, finally leaning in close to speak softly. "I need to take an important call. You think you can..."

The bastard cut him off. "I've been protecting her for almost two years on my own. I think I can handle it."

Ryder raised his hands in the universal surrender motion, before weaving away from the set, down the hall they'd entered through and back out into the mid-day heat. A feeling of dread settled in his gut as he found the number to Langley and hit *SEND*.

Brandon answered on the first ring. "Glad you called."

"Yeah, well you're not an alarmist so two calls in less than an hour while I'm supposed to be on vacation got my attention. What's up?"

"We got confirmation. Viktor Volkov is dead."

Ryder didn't need this call to confirm that. He'd seen many men die over the years. The old man may not have breathed his last breath when Ryder left, but he'd known Viktor wasn't long for this world when he'd left him bleeding out on the floor of the Bratva mansion.

"Not surprised. What's the fallout been like?" That was less predicable.

"That's why I'm calling. Artel is calling in favors from everyone he knows. He's not even trying to hide that he's looking for you." His boss paused before adding, "There's a hit out on you. A big one."

"I'd be disappointed if there wasn't," he quipped. "Who'd he farm it out to?"

"Everyone. He's made it an open field on your head."

Okay, that was a surprise.

"Do I want to know how much?"

"Probably not. You should be honored though. I think it breaks the agency record." The seasoned agent on the other end chuckled as if they were talking about winning a bowling trophy.

"Great. Not exactly the kind of award I was going for."

"So far there's no indication he's uncovered your real identity, but if he's willing to pay enough, it's only a matter of time before he gets it. I don't need to tell you to stay lost until we work this out."

"I should have fucking offed him when I had the chance," Ryder groused.

"I'll deny I ever said it, but I wish you had, too. He had a hard-on for you even before you burned yourself. Artel has serious money and absolutely no conscience. I'd sure as hell hate to have him out for me."

Ryder's feeling of dread was growing. He'd never even considered it before, but his presence could actually be putting Khloe into more danger than she'd been in before he'd arrived. A vision of Artel Volkov hurting Khloe the way he'd seen the monster hurt dozens of other women had Ryder's breakfast ready to make an appearance on the pavement.

"Did you hear what I said?" His boss regained his attention.

"Sorry. Can you repeat that?"

"Chip Marshall wants to meet you. Something about thanking you in person for saving his family."

"That'll have to wait. I've got too much shit going on to deal with that right now. Anyway, I was just doing my job."

"Maybe, but not many agents would have gotten them all out alive. Listen, I gotta run to a damn budget meeting. Watch your six, will ya? And check in in a few days so I know you aren't road kill."

"Nice. Thanks for the heads up."

He stayed outside long enough to regain his cool composure despite the growing heat. It would do no good to panic. He needed some time alone to think through his options and make some decisions on next steps, but that would have to wait until they got back to the cabin.

Anxious to get back to the set to catch Khloe in action, Ryder opened the door, noting that it wasn't secured in any way. The head of security was not going to like the shit about to fly his direction when Ryder finished his analysis of the studio's security, or lack thereof.

It didn't take long to retrace his steps to the courtroom set, but instead of filming in progress, he found a bunch of extras milling about in the jury box. A quick glance around found the director and Khloe gone along with several other men who'd been loitering in suits. His blood pressure was rising with each second that ticked by without Khloe in sight.

It wasn't lost on him that he'd be happy to see McLean in that moment, but even that asshole was missing.

*Stay calm. McLean is probably with her, as he should be.*

He asked one of the remaining crew, "Hey, did you see where Khloe went?"

The guy didn't look up from the piece of furniture he was staining. "That's above my pay grade. They don't tell me where they're going. They don't tell me when they'll be back." Nice. A disgruntled employee.

Ryder went back to the secluded area where he'd talked with her less than an hour before, pretty sure he wouldn't find her squatting over the bucket, but he had to check just the same. He searched for five minutes before he remembered the tracker.

*What a dumbass.*

It only took a minute to pull up the tracking app on his phone. He'd tested the accuracy before giving the bracelet to her. The homing device would track within six feet. When the pinpoint marker showed she was still in the building, he sighed with relief. Using the app's map, he wound through the maze of darkened sets until he arrived at a huge door labeled *Costume Department*.

The world's largest and most eclectic closet greeted him when he went through the door. The room had to be almost one-hundred feet long and fifty feet wide with triple layered rods hung in row after row–thousands of costumes and accessories from every genre... every time period...

"Can I help you?"

A portly woman with thick glasses looked up from the sewing machine she was working on behind the entry's counter.

"Yeah... I'm looking for Khloe Monroe."

The costume designer smiled indulgently. "Honey, she doesn't come to me. I go to her."

"But... I..." He didn't want to disclose he'd put a tracking device on her. "I gave her a gold bracelet, and I was told it was in here. Did someone bring in..."

While he was talking, she'd stood and walked to a pile of suits and dresses waiting to be rehung. When she turned, she held up the bracelet.

"This what you're looking for? I wondered where it had come from."

For the first time in a long time, Ryder panicked. Truly started to lose his shit. Snatching the tracker from her without another word, he took off running in the direction of the courtroom set while he switched over to his phone and called McLean.

"Hello." At least the asshole answered.

"Where the hell are you guys?" he shouted.

"Who is this?"

"Don't be stupid. This is Helms. Put Khloe on."

He waited for Trevor to dish shit back. It didn't come.

"She's not with me."

"What? I told you not to let her out of your sight."

The jerk tried to defend his stupidity. "I had to take a piss. These sessions can last hours. I'm sure she's still filming."

"Do you really think I'd be calling you if she were on the set, asshole? You had one job. One fucking job!" Ryder ended the call before he lost his shit.

*Think. Where the hell would she go?*

He retraced his steps, heading back to check the courtroom one last time before he would head out to her dressing trailer to see if she'd gone there for a break.

Trevor met up with him in the hall just before the set. If he wasn't so frantic to find Khloe, he'd take the time to beat the jerk to a pulp. As it was, the taller man's ashen face filled with concern was punishment enough for the moment.

In a moment of silence, only his exceptional hearing picked up the faint sound of Khloe's laughter in the distance. It has been so brief, it was hard to triangulate her location, but the sound calmed him enough to allow him to think again. To focus. He closed his eyes, listening intently. There were men's voices, muffled in the distance. His gut told him to follow the sound. Finally, another short laugh confirmed he was on the right track.

Suddenly the voices boomed louder as the door labeled Production Office swung open and a line of bigwigs in suits filed out with tiny Khloe Monroe sandwiched in the middle of the group.

The broad smile on her gorgeous face slipped the second she saw him. No doubt, her woman's intuition had picked up on the fact that she wouldn't need to worry about her stalker anymore.

He was going to kill her before anyone else could get to her.

# CHAPTER 15

"Where the hell did you go?"

Ryder's grip on her arm above her elbow was so strong, she suspected he was bruising her. Khloe tried to yank away, but he only clamped down harder, pulling her to a stop and roughly swinging her to face his anger straight on. As his icy blue eyes bore into her, she could swear she saw sparks flying from his glare.

"Is there a problem, Khloe?" Edward Rivera asked her, concern in his voice as he stepped up behind her.

An involuntary tremor raced through her body, making her shaky in her high heels. She struggled to keep her voice steady as she tried to reassure the half-dozen men surrounding her. "No problem."

The heat of Ryder's eyes taunted her. Calling her a liar.

*There is definitely a problem. I pushed him too far.*

The director, Apollo, announced, "Good. Let's get back to work. I want to finish this scene before we take a break."

"Khloe will be there in fifteen minutes." Ryder contradicted, never taking his eyes off hers. She wanted to look away, but his gaze held her hostage, commanding her full attention.

"No, Khloe will be on set in three minutes. We left the crew waiting and have wasted enough time."

"Ryder..." Her plea was cut off.

"Fifteen minutes. Not one minute before."

The relief of his breaking eye contact was short-lived when he turned and started stalking towards the door at the end of the hallway. With his grip only tightening on her arm, she had no choice but to run in her high-heels to keep up with his long, angry strides. She heard the men behind her asking who the hell that guy was while one of the crew started yelling "Security!" as loudly as possible. The last thing she heard before they shot out into the mid-day California sun was Trevor trying to reassure them all that Ryder wasn't her stalker.

Khloe's heart was in her throat. As angry as she was at Ryder for embarrassing her, she knew she'd made a huge mistake by underestimating his resolve to keep her safe at all costs. Flashes of the scary man who'd chased her down at Black Light months before swarmed her, reminding her how dangerous he could be.

When she almost fell trying to keep pace with him, Ryder stopped long enough to stop, turn and crouch down. Without warning, his left shoulder jammed into her tummy. As he stood, her feet left the ground and her torso and head flopped over, slamming her face into his lower back. In her surprise, she thrashed, afraid she was falling. Only the three fast swats of Ryder's open right palm across her now upturned ass stopped her from flailing like a fish on the hook at the end of a line.

From her upside-down vantage point, she knew he was headed towards her trailer. While she was grateful he was moving their upcoming knockdown, drag-out argument to a private location, she was equally petrified of being alone with this angry version of her newest bodyguard.

As her panic grew, she started pounding her fists ineffectually against his ass. Within seconds, his palm was back on her butt with much greater effect.

193

"Keep it up, baby. I'm sure we're putting on a great show for anyone who's watching."

She stopped immediately. She felt her face turning red, unsure how much of it was from the blood rushing to her upside-down head versus the heated embarrassment of being spanked like an errant child in the open parking lot, surrounded by trailers busy with entertainment professionals who would be more than happy to stop what they were doing to watch an A-List actress getting her ass blistered by her bodyguard.

The only way she knew they'd arrived at her trailer was Ryder's strides up the steps to the door. The gust of air-conditioned coolness confirmed their arrival as Ryder shouted at Randy and Cathy, her hair and makeup artists waiting to touch her up.

"Everyone out." They must not have started moving fast enough to suit Ryder because he added a stern, "Now!"

Khloe was relieved she was upside down so her employees couldn't see how mortified she was. Relief was short lived when Ryder followed them to the door. Khloe caught a glimpse of the murderous look on a running Trevor's face as he rushed towards the trailer just as the door crashed closed behind them. She heard the lock being engaged and then the deadbolt being slammed into place.

Trevor's "Open up, Helms!" was muffled. The pounding of his fists against the door as he tried to get in went unnoticed by her present captor as he turned and stomped into the dressing room of the opulent trailer.

He dumped her back on her feet as unexpectedly as he'd snatched her up only moments before. Things were moving so fast, she had no time to react. No time to fight back. No time to try to wiggle free and get to the door to let Trevor in.

Even as she thought of her original bodyguard, in her heart she knew there was nothing he could do to help her right now. The only consequence of Trevor getting inside the trailer would be him being beaten to a pulp by the furious man standing behind her. He'd swung her to face the huge makeup mirror, each of his hands now digging into both her arms above her elbows, holding her stationary as he slammed his rock-hard chest against her back, locking them like two puzzle pieces glued together.

Their eyes met in the mirror and all breath left her. As frightened as she was, Ryder was magnificent in his dominance. Unbelievably, in her breathless moment, Khloe realized she could read the emotions in his glare as easily as she could a book she'd read a thousand times before. The anger she'd expected, but there was so much more there. Concern. Worry. *Panic.*

She'd scared him with her childish disappearing act.

The realization helped her begin breathing again. She gasped for sips of air as she realized he was doing the same. They stood frozen, each taking calming breaths until Khloe could muster her voice to call out to the panicked man still pounding on the door.

"Trevor, it's okay. I'll be back inside soon. I'm fine."

The pounding stopped immediately, but she doubted he'd be stepping away from the door until his client emerged safe and sound.

Ryder's voice was oddly distant when he finally spoke. "That was optimistic of you." Her confused look urged him to expound. "I'm not so sure you're going to be fine after I get done with you."

"Ryder, I just..."

"Stop. There is no excuse you can give me that is going to get you out of the hot water you're in with me."

"Listen, I'm working. This is my job. You can't wrap me in bubble wrap until you find my stalker."

"The hell I can't. I agreed to keep you safe and you agreed to follow my every direction without hesitation. If I want to wrap you in bubble wrap and lock you in a padded room for safe keeping, then that's exactly what the fuck I'll do." He paused as if he was contemplating his words. "The threats are real, Khloe. I'm not an alarmist, and I'm telling you the threats are real."

She saw the truth in his eyes. It helped douse the last righteous anger she was clinging to at being treated like a piece of property. He was genuinely concerned about her welfare.

It's strange how reality can slap you in the face at the most inopportune times. That was the moment she realized that as fucked up as his methods were, and as furious as she was at him for deserting her in February and then showing up again to consume her life as if he had every right to, Ryder Helms cared about her. The *real* her. Not the A-List actress. Not the fashion model. Not the person who signed the paychecks for everyone else who professed to care about her.

He wasn't here to get famous or make a buck. Hell, he almost seemed to hate that she was rich and famous. As the possible reasons for his being so angry narrowed, the truth became so obvious to her.

Ryder Helms genuinely cared about her.

The realization didn't calm her completely, but it did allow a slight smile to play at the corner of her lipsticked lips.

"You find this funny?" he growled.

"No. Nothing about this is funny."

"On that we can agree."

"If you'll just let me, I can explain."

He ignored her comment. "What were my instructions before I left the set?" His voice reminded her of the calm before a brewing storm.

"I wasn't to leave the set until you got back, but--"

"If you needed to pee?" he prodded.

Embarrassment flooded her neck, rising up to her cheeks before she whispered, "I could piss in the empty bucket in the corner."

She saw the flash of satisfaction with her answer in his eyes. "Where the hell is the bracelet I gave you?"

That question was unexpected. "What?"

"The bracelet. Why isn't it on?" He demanded, lifting her arm and pointing at her empty wrist.

"The continuity director made me take it off. I wasn't wearing it in earlier takes and we can't change anything about my appearance until after this scene wraps."

He looked frustrated with her answer, adding a cryptic. "I'll have to get something different that they can't take off... or out... of you."

Before she could ask him to clarify what the hell he was talking about, his questions continued. "So what do you think is going to happen next?"

Her heart rate spiked. The implication in his voice was obvious. He'd told her what he'd do if she didn't follow directions. At the time, it had sounded like a good idea to attend the production meeting without telling him where she'd gone, but now that his stony glare was devouring her in the mirror, she realized she'd made a tactical error.

"Khloe?" he growled.

"I'm sorry. It won't happen again," she promised.

"Oh, I'm quite certain it won't. Not after I get through with you."

She wasn't sure what he meant, but the skin on her ass physically prickled as if it knew it would be paying the price for her foolishness.

Ryder released her abruptly, shoving her upper body forward, pressing his hand against her back until she was bent over the back of the makeup chair in front of her. She thrust her hands out in time to catch herself on the armrests of the stationary chair. While she struggled to stop her forward trajectory, she felt his knee inserted between her legs as he then used his shoe to kick her high-heeled feet wider and wider until she felt obscenely open. Instead of stabilizing her, the awkward position forced her body weight to rest against the padded back of the chair she'd spent hours in having her makeup and hair attended to in the recent weeks.

Once he had her positioned the way he wanted her, he gave his next order. "Don't move a fucking inch."

Too afraid to disobey, she stood frozen as she felt him lift the hem of her dress up and across her back, exposing her thong panties and milky white ass cheeks to his hungry gaze. Not that they gave her even an ounce of protection for what she suspected was coming, it still shocked her when he hooked his fingers in the waistband of her underwear and yanked them down to her knees. With her legs splayed open, the fabric stretched, digging into the flesh of her legs.

She waited anxiously for his palm to connect with her now-bare ass. As much as she dreaded the pain that was certain to come, she couldn't deny the equal measure of excitement coursing through her, injected into her veins by his raw dominance.

When he reached around her to pick up the wooden paddle brush Randy had left on the counter, she tried to stand, but he anticipated her move. His palm laid on her lower back, holding her in place easily.

"Khloe..." Her name was a warning to obey.

"Please..." It was a futile attempt at changing his mind. Manipulating men had become rather easy for the talented actress. She could usually get her way one way or another with most men, but in Ryder Helms, she knew she'd met her match. She'd witnessed him in his dominant glory at Black Light on Valentine's Day and she knew he wouldn't be swayed by begging or tears. In a sick way, she respected him because of it. He didn't let anyone manipulate him or his decisions, once made. And right now that meant she was about to have her ass lit up.

He didn't pull any punches. There was no warm up. The first crash of the flat wooden paddle-brush on her right butt cheek made an alarmingly loud splat that filled the trailer. The pain of the swat caught up to her brain just as the next strike connected with her left ass cheek. It had only been two smacks, yet already her bottom felt like she'd sat on a nest of wasps. The skin of her butt prickled and stung from the heavy thud of continuing lashes against her behind. While Ryder kept his attention on her bottom, Khloe watched his profile in the mirror, trying to focus on the masculine scruff on his chin or the salt-and-pepper grey streaks through his dark hair, both reminding her he was all man. Dominant. Aggressive. Sexy, man.

Tears pricked at her eyes as she struggled not to call out, not wanting Trevor to be alarmed that she was being hurt, yet her paddling continued on with pounding regularity until she couldn't hold still any longer. The burn was too intense. She tried to stand, but he easily subdued her in her prone position. She wriggled her ass wildly, trying to move away from her punishment, but he only used his left arm to hug her around her waist, pulling her flush against his body as his right hand rained down even harder and faster. Back and forth until she started begging him to stop.

"Please, stop! It's enough! I've learned my lesson." When her begging failed, she changed tactics. "I can't cry like this. It's ruining my makeup and we don't have time to redo hair and makeup! Apollo is gonna kill me if I fuck up the shoot!"

It was the truth.

He finished her off with a half-dozen wallops a bit lower that hurt so bad she lost the battle and cried out, "Please, stop!"

Her cries triggered Trevor's pounding on the door again. "Goddammit, Helms, open the fucking door."

Through her tears she watched him in the mirror as he inspected his handy work as if he were admiring artwork on a canvas. Satisfied he'd properly roasted her bottom, he looked up and caught her glare. She could see his panic had receded, but that was the only emotion that had diminished. His eyes shone with raw authority that had an odd way of making her feel safe. He rested his right hand on her bottom as if he enjoyed feeling the heat of her skin, but she didn't complain. His light caresses helped take away a bit of the sting.

"What do you have to say, Khloe?"

His question confused her. She stumbled on her words a bit until she forced out, "I already apologized."

"I'm glad you're sorry, but that's not what I'm waiting for."

Genuinely at a loss, she waited until he instructed her. "You'll thank me after a punishment."

The man was a lunatic. The look on her face must have portrayed her sentiment because his hand lifted and swats started raining down again.

"Stop! Enough!" Those words had no impact on her situation until she added, "Thank you!"

The thrashing stopped as soon as she said the two small words, and she finally let go of the tension of her body when he stepped away from her, letting her collapse with relief, dropping herself across the back of the padded chair where she struggled to catch her breath.

She was too lost in her own thoughts to wonder where Ryder had gone until he returned, resuming his position on her left. The light stroking of his left hand on her hair and back calmed her farther so when she felt the cold, wet finger pressing against her exposed pucker Khloe tried to shoot out of the chair like a cannon. He was ready for her reaction, pressing her body back into her prone position as she felt one of his fingers slip inside her anus.

Damned if what he was doing to her most private body part didn't feel confusingly glorious. The insertion and removal of what felt like his middle finger gained speed until he was slowly finger fucking her ass. As nice as it felt, it was her pussy that was desperate for his touch. Instead, he removed his finger altogether, much to her regret.

Only seconds later, the press of something much larger than Ryder's finger was pressing for entry in her backdoor. As the first inch of the toy disappeared inside her, the stretch began to hurt. The sharp pang of pain as he forced the hard object deeper had her tensing and renewing her struggle to wiggle away, but he was having none of it.

"You had problems remembering the rules and consequences. This is my reminder to keep you on track. If it bothers you, then I suggest you follow instructions in the future to avoid being plugged."

His words marked his sincerity because he gave the thick dildo a hard push and it shoved home, the widest part right before the end flange stretched her puckered hole obscenely wide until it slipped inside her lubed opening. Once the flange was the only part sticking out of her body, the pain stopped, leaving her feeling uncomfortably full.

Khloe collapsed over the chair again, suddenly feeling completely drained of energy. When she felt his continued touching in the area, she looked into the mirror in time to see him take the cheesy bracelet he'd asked her to wear out of his pocket. She couldn't see what he was up to, but he was focused on the hitchhiker protruding from her ass and realized too late that he was oddly wrapping the bracelet around the flange.

Unable at first to understand his motive, she allowed Ryder to lift her feet one at a time to move them to a more comfortable position before pulling her tiny panties back up her legs, settling the thin strip of fabric of her thong against the portion of the plug sticking out of her body.

"I'm glad to see you like thong panties. They will serve you well to help keep the plug nestled in your ass. I'm guessing it would be a bit embarrassing for you if you lost your hold on your little hitchhiker and it fell to the floor in the middle of a scene."

"Oh, God..." She was too overwhelmed with physical and emotional feelings to fend off the confusing intimacy she felt towards the man who was helping her stand upright as he gently smoothed down the skirt of her dress before pulling her into his arms for a bear hug. In addition to the obscene fullness, she also felt the naughty jewelry dangling down, rubbing against her inner thighs.

It was suddenly harder to hold back her tears as he cradled her close, stroking her hair softly while he whispered, "Shhh... it's over now."

This man confused her like none other. So stern. Strict. Dominant. Yet now gentle and even comforting.

Trevor's pounding had stopped at some point. When her tears waned, Ryder pulled a hankie from his pocket and spent a minute dabbing at the wetness. The smoke rising from his eyes told her he was as turned on as she was, but they didn't have time to do anything about it at the present moment.

"Ready to go back?"

She nodded, looking down, too shy to hold his eye contact. She took a few tentative steps away from him towards the door to the trailer. He was beside her when he opened the door, letting the bright sunlight flood the space, temporarily blinding her. Ryder grabbed her above her elbow again to help her navigate the steep steps.

Only when her heels hit the parking lot pavement did she glance around to see a small crowd had gathered near her trailer. If looks could kill, Trevor's glare directed at Ryder would have dropped him dead.

Khloe kept her eyes down, trying to avoid looking anyone in the eye for fear they would know what had happened. It was humiliating enough to be spanked as a grown woman, but she prayed no one else knew what had happened behind the closed door.

Her hopes were dashed when Ryder pulled them to a stop next to Randy. Only then did Khloe see he'd picked up the heavy wooden paddle brush before they'd left the trailer. His hand held the implement out, but Randy was almost afraid to touch it.

"Thanks for the use of your hairbrush. It came in handy."

The jerk had the audacity to crack into a wide grin, enjoying the uncomfortable awkwardness that had fallen on the small crowd as they put the clues together to know that the actress they all knew had just had her butt roasted by the man who'd now placed his arm around her waist, pulling her closer as they resumed their walk towards the studio.

Before they got too far away, he shouted back to her hairdresser. "I'll try to pick up one for my duffle so I won't have to borrow yours next time."

Khloe groaned, wishing the pavement would open up and swallow her whole. She was so embarrassed. Having Ryder there to protect her was proving to come with an unexpected price tag.

Her dignity.

# CHAPTER 16

*H*e was about ten minutes away from pulling the plug, literally. Khloe looked exhausted. They'd been at filming for almost five hours straight with the asshole of a director who was clearly on a power trip, demanding take after take from the cast and crew. He knew she'd be furious with him for interfering, particularly after it had taken more than a few minutes for the whispers and pointing to die down after he'd returned her after her butt blistering. News traveled fast in the petrie dish of a closed set and while he was perfectly comfortable with every single person knowing the kind of relationship he and Khloe had, he was conscious of the fact that he was in her world right now.

Her world or not, he wasn't going to stand by and watch her dehydrate or work to exhaustion. And he sure as hell wasn't going to let her starve herself to death either. She needed a break.

For the twentieth time, Ryder let his vision scan the crowded area of onlookers watching the courtroom battle in progress. They'd gotten to the crux of the story and he wasn't too crazy about watching Khloe breaking down into tears over and over with each take.

*Yet her tears while I lit up her ass were beautiful.*

He didn't bother to examine how fucked up that was.

When Apollo yelled out, "again," Ryder moved into motion, pushing his way through the small circle of crewmembers and stalking out into the middle of the regal courtroom set.

He beelined it straight to Khloe sitting in the witness chair where her makeup artist was touching up her red and swollen eyes. "I think Khloe's had enough for now," he demanded, stepping into the box and taking her by the arm.

The fact that she didn't object told him he'd made the right call. She moved slowly, walking a bit stilted. He was an asshole to smile, knowing the secret no one else did, which was that she'd been filming for hours with her cute back passage stretched with his butt plug. Their eyes met briefly as she looked up at him, silently pleading with him to remove the uncomfortable accessory.

Ryder had a better idea.

He escorted her backstage, away from the cursing director who didn't care for his star performer being taken away from him. He didn't stop until they arrived at a food and drink cart setup in an out-of-the-way corner where a grinning young man with a lopsided smile looked like he might pee his pants as they approached.

"Khloe! I brought you an éclair. Mary wanted to eat it, but I wouldn't let her. I told her it was yours."

The young man's speech was slurred, his movements jerky. Ryder was a bit surprised the studio would hire disabled staff, but then again he was serving coffee and donuts so how hard could it be.

"Hi, Peter. You know I don't normally eat..."

Ryder cut her off, taking charge. "We need a sparkling water for Miss Monroe and then I'd like you to warm up that ham and cheese sandwich. Do you have any carrots or maybe an apple instead of all of these sweets?"

An out-of-place anger filled the kid named Peter's face at Ryder's curt demand. His sixth sense kicked into gear telling him he needed to do a bit of research on this one.

"I'm not hungry, Ryder. I only want to drink and... I need to go to the..." She was adorable when she blushed. "You need to take the damn thing out..."

Instead of answering, he reached to take the small bag of baby carrots and the apple from the out-of-place worker, examining them before opening the bag and taking one carrot out.

"Open up, baby."

Anger flashed in her eyes. "You're nuts. I'm too tired to eat."

He leaned closer, talking softly into her ear. "I'm not big on excuses. It's late. You've barely eaten and you're clearly exhausted." He pressed the carrot to her lips as they stood in a silent standoff. When she delayed, he added a stern, "Open."

He watched her pupils register surprise just before her lips parted, allowing him to slide the healthy snack into her mouth, adding a "Chew" for good measure. Only after she'd swallowed did he add a pleased, "Good girl."

Pleasure replaced defiance in her eyes, as he repeated the routine with a half dozen more carrots before reaching for the now ready sandwich. He led her to an empty chair lined up along an out-of-the-way wall, taking a seat and pulling her into his lap.

Her *humph* as she sat coincided with the end of the plug jamming into his thigh, shoving deeper into her stretched channel.

Her protests were back, "I don't want..."

He shoved a bite into her mouth as she spoke, telling her with actions that he didn't care what she wanted. He knew what she *needed*.

It was a testament to how tired she was that she didn't fight him harder as he fed her half the sandwich, a bottle of water and the rest of the carrots. The fact that he suspected it was the biggest meal she'd had in days pissed him off.

Her eyes were drooping by the time he set aside the rest of the food. He pulled her into an intimate embrace, rocking slightly in a calming way as she snuggled her head on his shoulder and closed her eyes with a sigh.

"You're safe. I've got you," he whispered.

His next scan of the room found a pensive Trevor stationed about a dozen feet away, arms crossed and a glare on his face. The men's gazes connected and for the first time since they'd met, Ryder saw approval staring back. With a small nod, Khloe's guard retraced his steps, giving them some privacy.

He held her like that for fifteen minutes while the rest of the cast and crew enjoyed the impromptu break. Only when the director's patience was at an end did Ryder reluctantly wake the beauty in his arms.

"Princess, time to wake up."

She startled awake. "I can't believe I fell asleep. What time is it?"

"Time to get back to work."

"Can I..." she paused and finished quietly, "go to the bathroom?"

"Of course. I'll take you."

"That won't be necessary..."

"Yes, baby, it is. I'll need to get you put back together again."

"But..."

He put his finger to her lips, shushing her. Once on her feet, he led her to the ladies' room, not bothering to knock. Two older women who were extras in the film quickly rushed out, leaving them with a bit of privacy. He threw the deadbolt on the door to ensure it stayed that way.

Khloe's eyes were wide when he turned back towards her. He suspected she had planned on some privacy.

"Turn around, baby. Hands on the counter."

"You aren't gonna spank me again, are you? I mean I didn't do anything wrong this time."

"As much as I'd love to, naw. I'll help you with your hitchhiker."

Their eyes were locked in the full mirror in front of them as he lifted her skirt and pushed aside her panties to grab onto the end of the plug. "Exhale for me and push it out."

The plug was larger than he'd have liked, but she'd taken it like a champ. It took a sharp pull to get the widest flare past her stretched pucker. He looked down, loving how she gaped open for several long seconds once she was free of the hard intruder.

With a smack to her ass, Ryder let her up. "Go take care of business. I'll get it ready to go back in."

"Please, not again. I've learned my lesson. I promise." Her submissive pleas did nasty things to his rod tucked into his slacks. He pushed down the temptation to shove the growing hardness where the toy had just been, knowing they didn't have time.

Instead, he pulled the small bracelet from the end, and reached out to attach it to the tiny waistband of her panties. He liked the way it dangled down at crotch level.

He saw the question in her eyes and answered. "It's got a tracker in the charm. Until we get the asshole behind bars, I don't want you going anywhere without it on. I'll conceal it in something better when we get home. Now, hurry up. I'll wash this bad boy and then wait for you outside."

True to his word, he finished cleaning up and took off for the exit. When he pushed the door open, it slammed into the back of Trevor who had taken up a protective stance in front of the portal. It pissed him off that the asshole was probably there thinking he had to protect Khloe from Ryder.

The men stood chest to chest in a standoff of sorts. Ryder wished he were taller, hating that the jerk had a few inches on him. As the guard eyed him up and down, his gaze stopped on the wide plug still in Ryder's right hand. He suspected Khloe would be pissed at him for holding it out so McLean could get a better look at it, but he did it anyway.

Several emotions passed over the guard's expression starting with anger and ending with what looked like acceptance.

"I get it. I don't like it, but I get it."

Ryder slipped the sex toy in the pocket of his sports coat before answering. "I'm glad. I'd hate to have to paint you a picture."

"You don't have to be such an asshole, you know. I really do care about her," McLean protested.

"That's exactly why I'm being an asshole." He moved closer until their chests bumped aggressively. "Keep your fucking hands off her and do your job."

"That's all I've ever done." He looked sad for a moment before adding, "Now I see she needed more." Ryder was about to deck the jerk until he added, "You worked a miracle getting her to eat that much. I've been worried."

After an awkward pause, Ryder stepped aside, putting some distance between them to de-escalate that discussion. "Yeah."

Just as the words left his mouth, he heard it. The unmistakable sound of someone puking. Not someone. Khloe.

Trevor must have heard it too because the men met at the door, each fighting to get through first. Ryder had the edge from his angle and pushed in ahead of the taller man, beelining it to the only closed door, pounding so hard the entire three-stall structure wobbled.

"Goddamn you, Khloe, I'm gonna blister your ass so hard it makes our earlier *discussion* look like love taps. Get your fucking finger out of your throat and open this door right now."

The sound of her depositing the contents of the food she'd eaten into the toilet stopped, but when he leaned down to look under the door, he could see her still huddled over the porcelain. He detected her body shaking, fighting the urge to purge. When she leaned forward ready to resume against his orders, Ryder kneeled, reaching under the door and grabbing both of her ankles.

He yanked her hard, furious that she couldn't see the damage she was doing to her own body. She struggled and kicked, barely missing slamming her face against the toilet by pushing back in time for her torso to fall to the ground before being dragged under the bottom opening of the still closed stall door.

Her dress rode up as he pulled, exposing the still-red patches on her butt cheeks where the hairbrush had done a number on her. He'd be adding belt marks in a few minutes.

He'd expected her to fight him, but instead she'd started crying, laying limp in a heap on the cold tile floor, curled up into a ball on her side. Her sobs cut through his anger, temporarily stunning him into non-action.

McLean had surprisingly stayed on the sidelines, standing a few feet away looking as lost as Ryder felt. As angry as he was at her, a little voice was shouting at him that this wasn't a submissive's defiance. The woman at his feet was falling apart before his eyes, trembling from fear or cold, he wasn't sure. He ran his hand through his cropped hair with uncertainty until he knew what to do.

Ryder took his coat off and slid to the ground, placing his back against the closed stall door. He reached out and scooped the broken woman in front of him into his lap, wrapping her in his coat and hugging her to him.

"Grab me some wet paper towels," he yelled to a still frozen McLean before talking softer to Khloe. "It's gonna be okay, baby."

He rocked her as she cried into his chest. He suspected she was too ashamed to look at him, which was fine by him. He needed the time to get his anger under control.

Trevor handed him a handful of wet towels, standing close by as if waiting for orders. Ryder held her chin, forcing her to look up at him. Her eyes were bloodshot from crying and the exertion of purging. Her makeup was a running mess and her coifed hair was jumbled.

"Go tell the director Khloe isn't feeling well. She needs to call it a day." She opened her mouth to protest, but he lifted her chin to stop her. "Trust me. You're done, baby."

Trevor stood grounded until Ryder looked up to see why he

was still there. Anger emanated from her guard. "You better not lay a hand on her for this."

He wasn't sure what pissed him off more. That the jerk actually thought he would spank her for hurting herself, or that he had actually contemplated it himself first.

"Relax. She's sick, not in trouble."

Only when they were alone did he use the towels to start patting at her splotchy face, wiping away drops of spittle and tears along with snot running from her nose. He wiggled until he could retrieve his hankie from his pocket, holding it up to her Rudolf-red nose and asking her to, "blow for me."

The loud honk of her nose made them both smile, breaking the heavy blanket that had been thrown over them. Fresh tears welled in her eyes as she tried to explain.

"I panicked. I felt so full. It scared me."

He didn't know what to say, so he said nothing.

"You don't know what it's like, being a woman in Hollywood. Always having someone slightly younger, or thinner, or more talented nipping at your heels, trying to take away every part. Every appearance. Every opportunity."

He took his time, formulating his response. When he was ready, he drove his hand through her ruined hair, grasping close to her scalp and yanking her head until he was certain she couldn't look away.

"I want you to listen to me well, little girl. You have one body. One life. What you're doing to it may help you today, but what about tomorrow? And the next day? Trust me when I say, you're on a fucking slippery slope. One day, you'll get so tired from holding on, you'll let go and fall so hard and fast, there won't be any recovery. I see it in your eyes. You're exhausted, pushing yourself so hard, but by refusing to refuel your body, you'll be burned out before you're thirty.

"You're a beautiful, talented woman, Khloe Monroe. I've watched you all day, and you have serious talent. *Dirty Business* is a box-office smash hit. You're being offered dream roles. You're so close. Don't fuck it up by judging yourself by some antiquated vision of what asshat producers want. You're the real deal. Make them take you on your own terms."

"Why are you being so nice to me?"

She really didn't know?

"Because I think you are amazing. Because as much fun as I have hurting your body, the thought of you hurting yourself infuriates me. I'm not a doctor, but I know enough about this to understand you need help, so I guess I'd like to apply for the job."

"Since when do you ask? You barged in and made yourself the head of my security without asking." She must be feeling better; she was teasing him.

"Guilty. I guess I know I can't just spank you into submission on this one. Not without getting this straightened out first." He tapped her temple with his index finger.

She melted into his arms, trembling as he rocked her. He wasn't sure how much time passed until McLean returned. "Apollo is pissed as hell. I think we should get out of here."

Khloe wiggled in his arms. He knew she was going to try to pull it together, but he knew it would be sheer hell for her trying to walk out there and pretend nothing had happened. She was an amazing actress, but he didn't think she could pull it off.

Instead, he would play the role of overprotective guard. "I think that's a good idea. As much as I love seeing her on the back of the bike, she's too tired for that right now. I'll leave the bike here. Bring the SUV around. Do you have a key to her Malibu house?"

"Yeah. I have a key to everything."

The men's eyes locked, recognizing Trevor had just admitted he was one of the few people on the planet who had access to all of the locations where the actress they protected had been threatened. It was also in that moment that Ryder knew in his gut that the guard was innocent. He'd trusted that inner voice dozens of times in more dangerous situations than this.

"That's good. We'll stop and pick up clothes and supplies and then head back out to the safe house." Trevor had turned and was at the door when Ryder added, "Pack yourself a bag too. I'll need your help watching our six and I want to run through all of the evidence with you and get your input."

The tall man nodded slightly, his only acknowledgment of Ryder's official offer of a truce.

"Let's go home, baby."

~

THE NEWS VANS lined the street in front of Khloe's beachfront home, making the few photographers who had been outside the studio gate look insignificant. Their driver, Michael, slowed to avoid hitting people brave enough to approach the moving SUV. Ryder was grateful for the tinted windows, hiding the three occupants in the back seat as shouts of Khloe's name could easily be heard.

There was no way he was going to subject her to this throng, but that wasn't the only reason he wouldn't be getting out of the luxury car.

*The last thing we need is for me to have my face plastered all over the media.*

Artel Volvo's hired guns would find him in a hot minute. Uncharacteristic guilt gnawed at him as he remembered he could be doing more harm than good with his presence. He felt trapped. An almost desperation to keep the slip of a woman next to him safe warred with knowing that despite his unique skill set, he probably should stay as far away from her as possible.

Her stalker was a boy scout compared to the likes of the Russian Bratva.

"Let's get inside the gate and then, McLean, I'd like you to go in and grab what she needs. I'll wait in the car with Khloe."

She protested. "I don't understand why we can't just stay here? They aren't stupid enough to go past the locked gate."

"You mean like they wouldn't go into your locked New York apartment or VIP trailer?"

Her eyes widened before agreeing. "Fine, but why can't I at least go in and pack my own bag?"

Against his better judgment, he compromised. "Fine, have the driver pull into the garage. We can close the door and never be seen by the photographers."

McLean answered, "The garage is detached. We'd have to make a run for it. It's no big deal."

Fuck, he felt trapped. "Fine, you two run in and grab what she needs, but don't be in there too long. I need to go see someone who's gonna help us with the investigation."

Khloe grabbed his hand, ready to pull him along. "You can come in."

Uncharacteristic anxiety helped him yank his hand back. "No, I can't."

Confusion clouded her gaze. "But..."

He tried to reassure her by cupping her face as he replied. "I can't explain now, Princess. Just know that I can't have my picture splashed around on social media or TV."

If anything, she looked more confused, but McLean seemed to accept his explanation. "You stay here. We'll be back in ten minutes."

Ryder bit his tongue as Trevor stepped out and then reached back to take Khloe's hand to escort her inside. Only once they had disappeared did it dawn on him that they could be walking into a trap. The stalker had entered two private locations of hers already. What if he was waiting inside for them now and she was in danger?

With each minute that ticked by, he got more anxious. He felt neutered and he hated it. He was the one who was always in control, yet he sat trapped in a car in Malibu, California, unable to get out without putting his picture into circulation.

He had just sent a text to Trevor's phone when he saw them exiting the front door. Nothing looked amiss. He exhaled the breath he hadn't realized he was holding.

Trevor was schlepping a huge roller suitcase behind him and went to the back hatch door to secure the load before hopping back in the vehicle. Khloe was sandwiched between the men again.

"Everything okay in there?" he asked when they'd gotten in, forcing his usual calm into his voice.

"Yeah, fine, but Khloe packed heavy for the trip to D.C. tomorrow. If you're sticking around, we should contact Ricky to have him get you on the same flight as us tomorrow. He flew out a day in advance to make sure everything is ready at that end."

Ryder's anxiety intensified. "Who the hell is Ricky and why are you going to D.C.?"

The Volkovs may not know who he was or exactly which organization he worked for, but it didn't take a rocket scientist for them to figure out he'd been working for an American agency. Washington would be brimming with eyes, looking for him in hopes of receiving a sliver of the big bounty on Ryder's head.

Things were going from bad to worse.

Unaware of his internal struggle, Khloe rattled on, excited she was to take her turn on the red carpet again—yet another place an active duty undercover agent could never go.

"...since *Dirty Business* was set in D.C." She turned to him then, a shy, almost wary expression in her eyes. "I thought maybe we could go visit Jaxson, Chase and Emma."

She'd left any reference to Black Light out, of course, but he knew exactly what she meant. An idea took hold. He'd have to give Davidson a call.

Ryder looked over Khloe's head to the taller guard on her

other side. The men exchanged a knowing look as Ryder explained. "Don't worry about my flight. I'll probably fly separate and meet you there."

She was a smart cookie. "But we haven't even told you when the flight was yet. How could you know you couldn't take it?"

In that moment, he almost came clean. He hadn't thought this through. A deep sadness formed in the pit of his stomach as he faced reality head on.

There was no way he could form any sort of relationship with Khloe Monroe. Not with the enemies he'd made in his lifetime. If it wasn't the Volkovs, it would be any number of other equally horrific criminals, more than happy to fuck with someone he cared about. It was why most agents stayed single. Why they didn't form attachments.

Ryder Helms was a time bomb. The only question was when, not if, his dangerous career would blow up, potentially taking out the woman looking at him expectantly. The woman he finally admitted to himself he cared deeply for. She'd wormed her way past his defenses somehow.

His instincts had been right. He should have turned Davidson down when he'd asked him to help with Khloe's security. If the petite woman had been hurt by his disappearance in February after only three hours together, how would she take his ultimate desertion once they caught her stalker?

He needed her to stop looking at him with those puppy-dog eyes of hers.

He needed to hold her.

Ryder scooped her tiny body into his arms, pulling her to sit in his lap as the driver picked up speed as they merged on the highway headed north. He hugged her so tight she mewed, safe for the moment in the cocoon of his arms.

McLean hadn't taken his eyes off the couple, watching like a trained observer. Ryder knew he was putting things together on his own, and while it galled him to acknowledge it, he was grateful Khloe had the guard in her life. She'd need Trevor more than ever after Ryder left.

Only after he'd swallowed sufficiently to get rid of the lump that had formed in his throat did he speak.

"When we get to the cabin, let's go through the evidence first, McLean. Then I'm going to see an old friend who can help us dig in and find who's behind this shit."

Khloe hugged him tighter. "Can I go with you?"

"No, baby. You need to take a shower and then rest. Before I leave, I want you to make a list of all of your favorite foods. The ones you've been avoiding. And then a list of foods you allow yourself to eat. We're gonna tackle this eating thing together."

She tried to push away, but he was too strong. "You can't tell me..."

"The hell I can't. I'm in charge, remember?"

It dawned on him that any progress he made with getting her to embrace eating again would fly out the window the day he left her again. He pushed the guilt aside, refusing to think long-term.

He'd been shot, beaten, and pushed out of moving vehicles in his illustrious career, but he'd never regretted his choice in professions until that moment. His heart hurt with a foreign pain as Khloe hugged him tighter just before falling asleep in his arms.

*So this is what love feels like.*

$\mathcal{R}$ yder parallel parked the SUV between two pieces of shit cars that lined the run-down street in the seediest part of town. He'd known his best friend from ages ten to twenty-two had fallen on hard times in the last few years, but seeing how far he'd fallen was yet another harsh blow to Ryder's normally aloof conscience.

He sat in the car, analyzing his options. Walking up the uneven sidewalk and into the tiny, rundown house turned business would be opening a can of worms he wasn't sure he was ready for—emotionally or physically. It had been almost four years since the old friends had seen each other. It felt like a lifetime ago, and yet he suspected their reunion would be worse for Axel. Seeing Ryder would remind him of better times. Times he could never regain.

"Don't be such a pussy, Helms," he spoke out loud to the empty vehicle.

He grabbed his duffle and got out into the waning sun, starting up the path before he could change his mind.

A cheap metal sign labeled *iSpy Investigations* hung in the front door window, confirming he was at the right address. They'd come up with the stupid name as kids, planning even then to go undercover for hidden answers as their life's work. The two friends had taken very different paths to that end; Ryder traveling the globe mixing with the world's most dangerous crime families–Axel stuck in their old hometown, taking grainy pictures of husbands cheating on their wives.

He shoved down his sadness at the thought, knowing a deteriorating career wasn't the worst thing that had happened to his friend. He pushed the button for the doorbell, hearing a distant buzz, ensuring the bell was working. Several minutes passed with no answer, so he pressed again, holding the buzzer longer.

It was Friday night. Axel could be in the bag by now down at The Office. There was no fucking way he'd step foot in the watering hole turned clubhouse. Before he gave up, Ryder walked through the mostly dead yard to stand at a dirty window, cupping his hands over his eyes to look inside. The flickering light of a playing TV bounced off the dark walls, demanding further investigation.

He was about to turn to retrace his steps to the door when the click of a weapon cocking behind him made him freeze. Instinctively, he threw his hands up in the universal show of submission.

"Who the fuck are you, and what the hell are you doing snooping around here?" A hint of Axel's Mexican heritage mingled with the slur of a man who'd been drinking.

"Some kinda welcome, Square." Ryder purposefully chose his childhood nickname for Axel Alvarez–A squared–not only because he knew it bugged the shit out of the man who had groaned, but because it reminded them both of their unbreakable childhood bond.

To the rest of the world, he was just plain Axe.

Ryder turned slowly, unsure what he'd find behind him. It was worse than he'd feared. The men were only one year apart, yet Axe looked like an old man. His once jet-black hair was now a long mass of silver and grey, matted together with his out-of control grey beard. Deep crevices left behind by years of worry and anguish were now a permanent fixture on the brown-skinned man's face. Despite the smile that crept to Axe's mouth, a profound sadness permeated the air surrounding them, blanketing Ryder in anger.

"Ryder? Is that really you?"

"I was gonna ask you the same damn thing." He stopped short of criticizing his friend's appearance. If anyone in the world deserved to fall apart, it was Axe. Still, Ryder had held out hope his strong friend would have recovered by now.

*Does anyone ever recover from the hell he's been through?*

His friend lunged forward, pulling Ryder into a man-hug while asking, "What the hell are you doing here? I pictured you in some far off shit-hole of a country stirring up trouble."

Axe's assessment wasn't far from the truth.

"That was last week. Now I'm here trying to stir up trouble instead."

Axel'd uncocked his revolver, shoving it into the waistband of his too-big shorts. The men were the same height at just under six-foot, but a very fit Ryder had forty pounds on the guy. Not unlike Khloe, the dude was wasting away, although he knew the underlying reasons for not eating were as different from the actress's as they could be.

"Well, you gonna invite me in or am I gonna have to stand out here with your dead bushes?"

Axe hesitated, no doubt not wanting to invite his old friend in to see how far he'd fallen in life. Well fuck that shit. It was time Axe Alvarez joined the living again.

The men walked back to the front door. For a second, Ryder worried he'd be turned away, but Axe reluctantly pushed through the screen door, holding it open for his old friend.

A stale odor saturated the air. It was the perfect scent to accompany the deteriorated-looking occupant and possessions that lived there. Stopping shy of being declared a hovel, the space was appalling. Old wrappers from past carryouts mingled with dirty clothes, heaped wherever the wearer had shed them. A thin sheen of dust covered anything that wasn't used regularly, telling a tale of long-term neglect.

His friend cleared a place to sit in one of the few comfortable looking chairs in the living room. Ryder sat first, with Axe taking a seat in the worn recliner that looked like it doubled as his bed, based on the pillow and blanket in a basket next to the seat.

He scanned the space before locking eyes with his friend and hitting the elephant in the room head on. "I love what you've done with the place."

"Fuck you." Ryder was satisfied with the spark of anger that leapt into Axe's eyes. It meant there was still something there. A piece of his old friend that he might try to ignite like kindling at a bonfire.

Anger was better than apathy.

"I'd ask how you've been, but I know."

"You don't know shit."

Ryder took a deep breath, exhaling before admitting, "You're right. I couldn't possibly understand what you went through."

As the words left his mouth, the nightmare of Artel Volkov victoriously standing over a naked Khloe flashed before his eyes. It was the closest analogy he could come up with to fathom the pain Axe had lived through in the last three years. Still, he knew the torture wasn't even close.

"You mean what I'm *going* through," Axe corrected him.

His Aunt Ginny had warned him in an email that Axe still clung to hope like a life-raft adrift in the ocean. He suspected it was none of his fucking business how Axe chose to handle his grief. Who the hell was he to barge in after all these years and judge his friend?

But then he remembered Axe was the closest thing Ryder had had, and would ever have, to a brother. Both had been only children, growing up in the shadows of their powerful fathers. When Axe's father had been killed in an MC deal gone bad, Ryder's own father had taken him in as if he were his own son. The inseparable teenage boys had shared a bedroom like brothers for the two years leading up to Ryder's father's arrest on his seventeenth birthday.

The teenagers had been placed at a crossroads in their lives at a young age–to follow in their fathers' footsteps at the helm of the powerful motorcycle crime family they'd grown up in, winding up dead or in jail... or enlist in the Marines and use their pent-up anger as fuel to fight evil in the world. They'd enlisted together, fighting the good fight for four years in Afghanistan and Iraq before Ryder had been recruited by the Central Intelligence Agency and Axe had come home to be a husband and father.

Now, fourteen years later, Ryder had burned himself and would forever have to look over his shoulder for a boogieman named Volkov, and still, he knew he'd gotten the better end of the deal.

"Have you gotten any new leads?" he asked, hopeful Axe wasn't just in denial.

His friend polished off the last swig of the warm beer next to him, before pushing to his feet and heading towards the galley kitchen. "I'll get you a beer."

"No thanks. This isn't a social call."

Axe stopped, turning to stare back at Ryder. "I should have known. You only stop in when you need something."

"That may be true, but it's still good to see you."

"Don't try to blow sunshine up my ass. Why the fuck are you here?"

Ryder was actually nervous. He was in serious need of someone with Axe's technology skills, but having seen his friend, he wasn't entirely sure that part of Axe was still alive and well.

"I need your help tracking down a stalker. It's a high profile case, and I don't know anyone I can trust here in the states."

"Bullshit. Call your boss or your handler. They'll fire up the shiny computers in D.C."

"I'm trying to keep this on the down-low, for many reasons."

"Sucks to be you."

"Just like that. You aren't even gonna hear the facts. Not gonna open a file or look at a picture?"

"You said it's high profile. I don't do high profile."

"Yeah, well neither do I, normally. This is a special occasion."

"Special in what way? Big bucks?" For the first time, Axe's eyes sparked with interest.

"Why, you interested if so?"

"Maybe. I'm always looking to pick up cash that I can use to keep my other investigations afloat."

Ryder knew by other investigations, he meant he'd refused to accept that his now fifteen-year-old daughter, Mia, who'd been kidnapped at the age of twelve, was dead. It had to be a father's worst nightmare, knowing or at least hoping, his daughter was out there somewhere, waiting for her daddy to come in and rescue her, and not knowing where to find her.

He couldn't even imagine the nightmares Axe saw when he closed his eyes at night. He'd spent the first year of her disappearance focused solely on finding her. Calling in every favor. Spending every dollar he and Marielle had.

As his wife's hope died, he'd had to carry the faith for both of them until she'd been killed just over a year ago in a single car accident. Ryder'd read the news story online. 'A tragic accident' the reporter had said. 'Another sad blow for a family already under siege.'

But Ryder suspected the truth was Marielle couldn't live with the nightmare of not knowing where her only child was any longer. Not knowing if some pervert was hurting her. Helpless to protect her baby.

He remembered his Aunt Ginny's words as he'd called home from Moscow, looking for an update on the case. *"Losing a child to death is the second worst thing a parent can live through. Having your child snatched, stolen away from you and never knowing where they are or what's happening to them... that is the worst pain a human can suffer."*

Looking at the shell of his friend Axe, he knew those words to be true.

"Listen, I have some time off. In a few weeks, after I wrap up the job I'm on now, why don't I come back. We can go through the evidence again with a fresh eye. I can..."

"Why now?" Anger bubbled up in his friend's accusation.

"What do you mean, why now?"

"I mean, where the hell were you three years ago–when the trail was hot and I needed you the most?"

"You know damn well where I was. I was in deep cover, in no position to tell the Bratva I needed a few weeks off to fly back to California to help my old friend."

"Fuck vacation. Fuck the Bratva." Axe threw the empty beer bottle against the wall in his anger, punching a hole through the drywall.

The men had never spoken about the nightmare Axe and his family lived through. On one level, Axe's anger was understandable, yet it still caught Ryder off guard.

He got defensive. "What did you want me to do? Throw away my career? Burn myself and years of Russian language studies. Throw away the dozens of unspeakable tests I had to pass to get into their inner circle?"

"Yes! That's exactly what I expected from my *brother*." He spat the final word as if it were a curse.

Ryder was floored. Truly taken aback. Had it really been so selfish of him to stay in Russia? He'd sent over ten grand to the online fund setup to collect donations to help fund bringing Mia home safely. Sitting in that dingy living room, facing the shell of Axel Alvarez, he realized the gravity of his mistake.

That he'd come here to ask for Axe's help with Khloe's case as if nothing had happened since the last time they'd seen each other was unforgivable. He sat stunned, unsure what to say–how to recover from his error.

For a moment, he allowed himself to feel sorry for himself. What a fucking emotional rollercoaster week he'd had. First burning years of work, yet miraculously rescuing the Marshall women and saving Chip Marshall from the nightmare Axel was going through times three.

Second, reconnecting with a woman he had no right to, realizing too late that he'd only hurt her worse than he already had when it was time to leave. The irony was, he knew it was going to devastate him, too.

Now, walking in on a time bomb he'd been too selfish to detect.

Ryder leaned forward, his elbows on his knees as he hung his head in his hands, trying to think his way out of the shitshow he'd backed himself into. He forced deep breaths until he could think clearly again, a technique that had served him well undercover.

He sensed Axe moving around the room and finally looked up when a cold bottle of beer was shoved in his line of sight. He reached to take it, thankful for anything that might help numb the emotions.

Axe had taken a seat again, looking pensive as he swigged his own beer.

Their joint "I'm sorry," was simultaneous.

His friend smiled. "Holy shit. Who are you and what did you do with Ryder?"

"Fuck you," he quipped, still off base.

"Touché." Another swig, before he added. "Seriously, man. You've never been one to apologize."

Their eyes met as Ryder contemplated his words. "Yeah, well I've never fucked up before."

Axe smiled a sad smile. "Oh you fucked up plenty. You just never would admit it, you hard-headed bastard."

Yep, that sounded about right. "I can't help it I'm never wrong." Ryder chuckled.

They sat in an awkward silence, drinking beer and remembering the past. Ryder was about to stand to leave, when Axe pressed him for details.

"So why don't you tell me why you're here."

"It's not important. Forget..."

"Hey, a job's a job. As you can see, I need to bump up my income if I hope to maintain this lavish lifestyle." His friend was making fun, but neither man laughed.

"Like you said, you don't do high profile."

"Listen, asshole. Do you want my help or not?"

The spark was back in Axe's eyes. That's when Ryder realized he might be doing his friend as much of a favor by possibly getting him excited about an investigation again as Axe would be doing helping him nail Khloe's stalker. It was clear the man was going through the motions of life, no longer having purpose. Maybe working a case together would jumpstart his rejoining society.

"Promise you won't laugh."

"I promise no such thing, although, to be fair, I don't do a lot of laughing these days, so you're probably safe."

Ryder's pulse went up, about to say words he never thought he'd say out loud. "I think I'm falling in love."

The bark of Axe's laughter was like music to his ears, despite the fact it came at his own expense.

"Only you could make it sound like it was a death sentence."

Ryder didn't laugh. "Yeah, well, considering what I do for a living, it might be one for her."

That brought the humor out of his friend's face. "So what's really going on? This doesn't seem like the kind of case most men would hire a PI for. She cheating on your ass or something?"

Oh how he wished life with Khloe Monroe could be that simple. "We met in D.C. in February. Had one spectacular night at a club together before I shipped out, back to Moscow. I should have fucking left it alone, but when I got burned, I got sucked back in. Now I find out I have a hit on my head, and I'm putting her in danger by being in her life."

"No offense, brother, but Russian hitmen are a bit out of my league these days. I think I'd better walk before I run again."

"I don't need help with the Volkovs. I'll have to handle that on my own."

"Volkov... Why does that name sound familiar?"

There was no way he was disclosing top-secret details. He'd already said too much. "Focus. I don't need help with them. She's a public figure, and she's been harassed by a stalker for a few months. It started with some relatively harmless emails, but has escalated to mailed threats and now two break-ins into her personal space. I've promised her no one will get to her, but now I'm not so sure I'm not making things worse by being on her detail."

"Detail? You make it sound like she's a government bigwig."

"Try Hollywood bigwig."

Axe's eyes widened as he whistled a surprise whistle. "Landed yourself a starlet, eh? You always did go for the elegant ones. Don't think I don't know your secret."

"What secret is that?" Ryder was genuinely surprised at his friend's assertion, although not denying it.

"You love turning women from elegant to needy slut. It's all part of the power games you like to play."

"You can stop psychoanalyzing me now."

"Hit a bit close to home?"

More like a bullseye. "Like I said, fuck off."

"Does your mystery woman have a name?"

Ryder hesitated. Saying her name out loud would make it all seem more real. Finally, he surrendered, softly answering "Khloe Monroe."

Axe's whistle was louder this time. "Holy shit, you go big when you decide to jump in."

"It was supposed to be one fun night. No strings. No future."

"I've heard that before. Then I got the call in Afghanistan that Marielle was pregnant. Things got serious pretty quick."

Ryder had been with him the night he'd gotten that call. He'd seen the sheer terror on Axe's face at the thought of being responsible for a wife and child. Now, all these years later, look how fucked up that had turned out. He had no interest in following in Axe's footsteps. It was too hard, caring so much for someone that it hurt. It distracted him when he needed to focus. It fucking hurt just thinking of being without her again.

*I'm so fucked.*

"Talk to me about the threats."

He was almost relieved to have something to take his mind off hurting Khloe. Instead of talking, Ryder reached down for the duffel he'd thrown down next to his chair and pulled out his encrypted laptop. "You still have the same email?"

"Yeah."

"Okay, I'm sending all of the info I have to your account."

The men spent the next half-hour looking through the evidence, talking through the motives and suspects on Ryder's short-list of suspects. With each minute, Ryder grew more tense, the threats becoming more real. Ironically, Axe seemed to almost relax, relieved to have something to focus on other than his family's misfortune.

"Okay, let me do my thing on the computer forensics. I have a new hacker program that's great at sniffing out electronic footprints. Make sure I have your number. I'll give you a call when I've got something."

"Thanks, man. I owe you one. We're leaving for D.C. tomorrow sometime for some big red carpet event on Sunday afternoon. Obviously, I won't be attending, at least not on the carpet. I'll probably stay concealed, watching the crowd. The sooner we track down the asshole responsible, the sooner..."

He let the sentence die, unwilling to say it. He was already on the train. Like it or not, he was barreling down the track towards his exit. He couldn't stop it. All he could do was make sure he'd leave her safe and sound for when he was gone.

# CHAPTER 18

The hot shower felt spectacular. She'd been under the water so long, her fingers were starting to prune. Khloe tilted her head back, letting the spray wash out the deep conditioner. Once she'd rinsed thoroughly, she reluctantly turned off the water and grabbed the bath towel.

She avoided her reflection in the mirror as she reached for her satin loungewear and robe, afraid to glimpse her own body. She burned with shame remembering being caught purging earlier that afternoon. She'd brushed her teeth three times since then, but she still felt dirty.

Khloe knew the cycle well. She was in her *'I'll never do that again'* phase, swearing to herself after the shameful expel that she would control it the next time. By tomorrow, that promise will have faded as panic over her weight returned, overshadowing guilt with fear. She'd become so good at starving herself that she rarely had to push into where she'd gone today–euphoria while eating followed by uncontrollable regret.

Rinse and repeat.

She took a seat on the stool near the counter, picking up one beauty cream after another until she'd lathered herself with the full array of expensive products she used to fend off wrinkles and age spots. Tempted to brush her teeth one more time, she realized she was stalling, hiding in the bathroom to avoid eating. To avoid Trevor's knowing glares as he made it very clear how he felt about Ryder calling all the shots.

But mostly to avoid Ryder himself.

They'd only been together again for such a short time, yet in some ways, she couldn't remember what life was like without him there. That was how larger than life he was, sweeping her off her feet, not unlike back in February. She closed her eyes, remembering snippets of their time together, trying to understand the complexity that was Ryder Helms.

The strict structure of the Valentine Roulette game had kept their BDSM activities at Black Light focused only on sex. It had given her a false sense of understanding of what made the sexy dominant tick.

But outside of Black Light, Ryder was much less predicable. Surprisingly warm and loving one minute, dominant predator the next. But it was the Ryder in between those extremes that confused her the most. His need to protect her, yet refusal to be seen with her. His early jealousy and suspicion of Trevor quickly turning into a blanket trust, almost as if he were forging a partnership with her long-time guard.

Something fishy was going on, and Khloe was determined to figure out what it was.

The smell of pasta greeted her as she arrived in the open great room of the cabin. Ryder was back from his errand, moving effortlessly through the kitchen as if he'd studied in culinary school. Trevor sat on a stool opposite the stovetop. The men were deep in conversation, talking too softly for her to hear what was said.

It was the ring of her cell phone in the pocket of her robe that drew the men's attention to her arrival. Two pairs of eyes glanced up, as she pulled her phone from her pocket, sending the call to voicemail.

She didn't need to look at caller ID to know who was calling. She'd given her parents their own distinctive ring tone, *Such a Disappointment*, her theme song with them. She put the phone back into her pocket as she walked slowly to the kitchen.

Her eyes fell on the crusty Italian bread, butter and olive oil. The appearance of her favorite foods had her moving back into her temptation phase a bit early. By the smell of things, an array of her favorite pasta dishes awaited her, too. She could feel the men's stare as they waited for her reaction.

Ryder spoke first. "Dinner is almost ready, baby. I hope you're hungry."

She scoffed as she took the seat next to where Ryder was standing. "Being hungry is never my problem." She paused, before adding, "It's the choking it down and keeping it there I struggle with."

"Well then, we'll have to take it one bite at a time, won't we."

Her phone rang again. She pulled it out, this time turning it off completely.

"Who was that? Is someone harassing you?" Ryder's concern was touching.

"Harassing, no. In fact, quite the opposite."

He didn't like her cryptic answer. When she didn't expound, the traitor, Trevor, answered for her. "That's her parents' ring tone."

She gave him the evil eye for mentioning them.

Ryder's eyes widened. "Why is that a bad thing? I bet they're worried about you."

"I wouldn't know. We barely speak. I was supposed to have dinner with them in New York last week. It was the only good thing that came out of the break-in. I had a legitimate reason to cancel on them."

Ryder looked distressed at the news, which struck her as funny considering how he'd been avoiding seeing his own father who, as best as she could tell, was only a few miles away from him at the moment.

"Far be it from me to give advice on parent-child relationships, but since they rarely call, don't you think they might have something important to say if they phone again?"

"Oh I know what they'll have to say. I have it memorized. I'm immoral, chasing fame instead of religion. Then they'd remind me that my brother Milak would be a priest by now. He was the perfect child in their eyes. They never forget to remind me how much they wish he were alive. Oh, they leave off the part about wishing it had been me instead of Milak in the car that night, but I know. I can hear it loud and clear."

She heard the bitterness in her voice, recognizing her normal shrew-like tone she always got when she spoke of her parents. In many ways, she wished they would just cut her out of their life completely. That would be easier to take than this hot and cold savior routine they insisted on putting her through randomly, fucking with her mojo.

An awkward silence fell while she watched Ryder strain the cooked pasta and bring the hot dish to the island counter table where small salads and the bread already waited. She was glad to be seated as her heart rate raced watching Ryder putting a portion of each type of food on the plate in front of her. She felt lightheaded, almost faint in her panic. Her brain knew he'd given her small portions, yet for a woman who normally ate less than half that amount of calories in an entire day, the serving looked enormous.

*Maybe I'll go for a couple miles run later to work this all off.*

That was her other trick. Exercising until exhaustion.

"Give me your phone." His request surprised her. She'd expected him to lay down the law about how much she'd have to eat. She handed over the smartphone and watched him turn it on before setting it aside.

His next order came seconds later. "Pick up your fork. Stab the lettuce and take a bite of salad."

They may be seated at the dinner table, but Ryder was using the same stern tone of voice as he had barked his orders to her on the first night they met. That deep, yummy tone that went straight to her girlie parts. It surprised her that it didn't seem to matter what words he uttered, only that he used that melting hot dominance.

The first bite of salad tasted good. Almost as if he'd known, he hadn't drowned the veggies in heavy dressings, making it easier for her to justify. The men tore into their much bigger portions as she slowly chewed and swallowed, determined to eat slow enough to time the end of her salad with the end of their meal.

As if he knew her trick, Ryder slowed his bites, finally putting down his own fork to watch her intently. When her salad was gone, she wanted to stop. Had Ryder Helms not been there, she would have.

"Now take a bite of pasta and sauce."

This would be harder. The food was heavier, full of unwanted calories. The carbs would make her feel bloated. She resisted pushing away from the table, instead filling her fork with the tiniest bit of food she could and still call it a bite. Her hand trembled as she raised the pasta to her lips, finally opening and savoring the heavenly taste on her tongue.

She closed her eyes, determined to enjoy the flavor as much as she could before panic prevented the next bite.

The renewed sound of her phone ringing broke the silence.

"Answer it and see what they have to say," Ryder asserted, back to giving orders.

Funny how it's all about choices. Minutes before she couldn't be bothered to talk with her parents, but now, faced with talking to them or eating a heavy dinner, they suddenly looked better.

"*Cześć, Papa. Do czego mam ten zaszczyt?*" She almost laughed out loud at the surprised look on Ryder's face as she carried on the conversation with her father in Polish. It distracted her enough that she almost missed the animated shouting at the other end of the phone.

"Wait. Slow down. What did you say?" Only after she'd spoken did she catch that she'd flipped back to English.

Her father answered her in the same. "A package came for you this evening at the house. Your mother and I thought it strange since you have not called this your address for over seven years."

She had to agree, but that hardly warranted his panicked call. "I'll have my assistant contact you and arrange for you to forward it." Feeling snarky, she added, "I'm sorry it inconvenienced you."

"Stop, Kalina. Listen to me. There was something odd about this package. It smelled funny and the address was filled out with words cut from magazines and newspapers. It was, oh how you say in English... *tykanie.*"

Her brain translated the word, taking a few seconds to understand its true meaning. "Ticking? The package is ticking?" Awareness of the danger must have shown on her face because Ryder grabbed the phone from her hand and then blew her away.

"*Nie otwieraj opakowania. Natychmiast wezwij policję.*"

Had Ryder Helms just spoken in fluent Polish? She translated in her head. Yes. He'd said, "Don't open the package. Call the police immediately."

The conversation went on, her gleaning what was happening by Ryder's side of the exchange. She sighed with relief when she heard they had opened the box already and the ticking had been an old-fashioned wind-up alarm clock. An odd thing to mail a celebrity, until you factored in the threatening letter that accompanied it, warning that the next one would be a real bomb if Khloe didn't get rid of her newest bodyguard, effective immediately.

Ryder and her father's dialogue continued as she tried to make sense of the threat. Feeling left out, Trevor was standing, pressing her for details of what was being said in Polish. She couldn't talk, listen, and translate at the same time so she shushed him, listening to Ryder directing her father to call 911 immediately and report the delivery. He explained that Khloe had a stalker and that they needed to record the threat so when Ryder caught the culprit—and he would catch them—they had the evidence they'd need to put them away for a long time.

It was only when Ryder started lecturing her father that she wondered if her Polish was getting rusty from lack of use. Was he really telling her father to "get his head out of his ass and support his wonderful and talented daughter?" She had to have the translation wrong for his, "Khloe is so special. She deserves your love. She deserves the world."

Ryder's gaze was so intense. So protective. So *possessive*. It scared her. It wasn't what he was saying that frightened her. It was that despite his passionate defense of her, she could feel him pulling away. She felt it in her bones. He was constructing a wall around himself, treading careful not to let her get too close. Little did he know, he was already too late. She'd known in February that what they had was extraordinary. She'd let him walk out once.

She wouldn't make that mistake again.

Trevor finally insisted on an update so she filled him in while Ryder got additional details about the package. When had it been sent? What did the return address look like? Had it been delivered by ground or air? By an express shipper or the USPS? The interrogation went on in Polish, telling her Ryder did not just speak some of the language. He was completely fluent, his accent perfect.

The call lasted until the police arrived at her parents' small bungalow in the Bronx. Ryder switched to English, barking orders to the responding officers as if he were the Chief of Police. Despite being thousands of miles away, chilling pictures arrived on her phone, making the threat more real.

By the time they hung up, the delicious food Ryder had

prepared sat stone cold on their plates. The trio sat silently, each taking in all that had happened in the bizarre turn of events.

Trevor spoke first. "I'm trying to interpret this clue. On the one hand, everyone in Khloe's inner circle knows she is estranged from her parents. At first I thought the stalker had tipped his hand that he didn't know her as well as we'd thought he did. But I'm not so sure. My gut tells me it's the opposite."

Ryder pressed him. "Why's that?"

"They mention you for one thing. That means it's someone who has been close enough to her physically in the last few days to know you're not only here, but they're afraid of you. They want you to back off. For Khloe to fire you. With that in mind, I think whoever it is was afraid to send the package to anywhere you might intercept it and have a higher probability of tracking them down. I think they purposefully sent this message to her parents knowing we wouldn't be monitoring their house."

She hated that Trevor's explanation made sense to her because that meant that it really was someone in her inner circle responsible for terrorizing her.

Ryder didn't comment, instead pulling apart the crusty bread and dipping a bite in the olive oil before holding it to her lips. "Open up, baby."

"I'm not..."

Like at breakfast, he shoved the food in when she opened her mouth to protest. And so the game went on, this time lasting longer than the standoff that morning. When she zipped her lips closed and pushed to her feet about halfway through the entree, Ryder was ready for her. He hugged her to him, pulling her to sit in his lap as she wiggled to be free. She didn't fight hard. She was a realist. If he wanted to subdue her, he would.

"There's no use in fighting me on this. You're gonna eat the whole portion. Period."

She choked down a few more bites, but by the time she got to the last quarter of the pasta, the food threatened to come back up even without her finger's help. She tried to tell him, but every time she opened her mouth to speak, he'd shovel another bite onto her tongue.

Her panic spiked until she was cursing him and fighting like a madwoman to be free from him. His hand cracked her ass through the thin robe, surprising her more than anything.

Trevor intervened, coming around to their side of the island. Tears of gratitude for his help, turned to sobs of frustration when her long time guard and friend picked up her fork and held the food against her lips, helping Ryder.

She was furious. How dare they gang up on her? How dare they force her to do something she clearly did not want to do? How dare they...

Gone was his dominant demand. Ryder's soothing voice cut through the loud hum of dread in her head, calming her. "Shhh, it's gonna be okay. Every bite you take, tell yourself it's going to keep you healthy. Every bite you eat makes you stronger. To hell with Hollywood rules. You're Khloe Fucking Monroe. It's time you make your own rules."

And so it went, for what seemed like forever. Ryder holding her, rocking her, soothing her with his smooth words while Trevor fed her, slowly... with small bites... like he knew she needed, until the miraculous happened.

Her plate was clean.

She felt over-full... fat even. She'd be lying if she said she didn't want to run to the bathroom that very minute.

But overshadowing her need to purge was a sense of accomplishment.

"How are you feeling?"

"I can't believe you guys did that," she pouted.

Ryder smiled, unfazed. "Would you have finished on your own?"

She didn't answer. There was no use incriminating herself. He knew the truth anyway.

"Listen, I need to go call Axel and fill him in on the newest threat. If there are any clues with the delivery, he'll figure it out. Can I trust you to stay out of the bathroom, or do I need to tie you down?"

The sexy smoldering in his eyes challenged her to defy him. They also broadcast how much he'd love to tie her down.

Trevor stood, clearing his throat as if he were an uncomfortable third wheel. He started clearing the dishes as he offered, "I'll keep an eye on her to make sure she doesn't head in that direction."

"Traitor," she whispered under her breath.

"Nope. Friend." A sad smile on his face.

"Same thing."

~

RYDER'D BEEN GONE for almost two hours, and while Khloe was grateful to have Trevor there with her, she longed to be alone so she could cry.

It didn't make any sense, really. She had every right to be upset about some asshole stalking her—scaring the shit out of her and disrupting her life. She had more than earned the right to be angry at the Kaplans and even the producers for being more interested in capitalizing off the danger than stopping it. And sure as hell, the feminist in her was furious at the way not only Ryder, but now Trevor too, had manhandled her, particularly when it came to her eating disorder.

But in her heart, those were not the reasons she fought back tears, or at least not the only motivations.

No. At the heart of her pending meltdown was a need so deep, she had no label for it. She'd been sitting curled up on Ryder's comfortable couch, a bestseller novel open in her lap, but her eyes didn't see the words on the page. Instead, her mind raced to retrace every moment of their time together, trying to understand how she could possibly feel so connected to someone she barely knew. Sexual chemistry aside, it didn't make sense.

Still, there was no denying that uneasy ball in the pit of her stomach that had nothing to do with the food lodged there and everything to do with the man who'd put it there.

Where had he gone? Why wasn't he back yet?

*Why do I care so much?*

A litany of questions was on auto-loop in her brain. The most frequent being... when would he leave again?

He was as much of a mystery to her tonight as he had been the night they'd met. All she knew with any certainty was that he had changed her. He had drawn out desires inside her hidden so deep, she hadn't even known they were there, and it was throwing every part of her life into a spin.

"It's getting late. Why don't you go to bed?" Trevor was only trying to be helpful, but she resented his interference, especially because she suspected he only suggested it because her staying up to worry about Ryder annoyed him.

"I'm not tired," she lied. She was exhausted. "But you can head to bed if you want. I'll be fine out here reading my book."

The corner of her friend's mouth curled up in an attempt at a smile. "You actually have to turn the pages to read a book, you know."

*Busted.*

She slammed the hardback closed in an exaggerated huff, leaning forward to throw the book onto the coffee table.

"I know it's none of my business, but it's driving me nuts. I'm with you almost non-stop. Where the hell did you two meet? He's clearly not part of the Hollywood scene."

Trevor was sitting in the chair across from her, his feet propped up on the ottoman. Despite having changed into jeans and a T-shirt, he didn't look relaxed. She'd been so wrapped up in her own worries, she'd missed that he looked to be wound tight enough to explode.

She didn't owe her security guard answers to his personal question, but Trevor was so much more than an employee.

She sighed, deciding that maybe talking to her friend might help her make sense of her jumbled feelings. "We met on Valentine's Day." When he didn't acknowledge, she added, "Chase, Jaxson and Emma set us up."

Technically, that was true, in the strictest of definitions. She wouldn't explain that, in reality, it had been the turn of a roulette wheel that had sealed their fate.

She watched him internalize her answer before he dug deeper. "I've never asked you, but how did you end up in D.C. that weekend? I know you flew to New York, not Washington. You came back acting so different. Upset even. I thought it was because you and Dean had broken up."

Funny how it was easier for her to talk about being humiliated by Dean than it was to explain her and Ryder's confusing connection.

"I went back early to surprise Dean, only I was the one who was shocked. I walked into my bedroom just in time to watch him fucking Gloria Mining as she hung from a hook he had the balls to install into the ceiling of *my* bedroom."

"Ouch."

"Can you believe Daniel Mining invited me to a foursome with him, Gloria and Dean in New York? That was why I didn't want to stay at The Plaza. They were pressuring me to join them."

He looked furious. "I wish I'd known."

"Why? What could you have done about it?"

"Well for one, I would have told Natalie to fuck off when she told me she'd arranged for Dean to be on the red carpet waiting for you at the theater."

They'd never discussed it, but now was the perfect time. "You should have told her to fuck off anyway," she protested. "I expect that kind of shit from her, but I need you to protect me, not just from the public, but even from her bullshit."

"I told you I'm sorry for that, and I am. But..." he stopped abruptly, looking tempted to say more.

"What?" she coaxed.

"You like to pick and choose what you want me to protect you from." She heard the anger in his tone as he continued. "I mean, seriously. Who the hell is Helms to swoop in on a motorcycle and steal you from right in front of me? No warning. It gave me a fucking heart attack, Khloe. Then when I have the audacity to try to protect you from him today at the studio, you side with him even though he beat you!"

Embarrassment warred with surprise, yet she couldn't let his statement stand without correction. "He didn't beat me."

"I don't know what else to call it. Don't you dare lie to me. I saw the marks on your ass as we pulled you under the door in the bathroom this afternoon."

She felt the heat rushing to her cheeks. "He didn't beat me." Their eyes locked, he waited expectantly. "He spanked me. There's a difference."

"Why the hell would he do that? You're a grown woman, for Christ's sake."

"I don't expect you to understand. Hell, I don't even understand. It's just the kind of relationship we have."

"Some kind of relationship. Where has he been since Valentine's Day?"

She was about to lose her cool. He was digging into the very heart of what she didn't know herself.

"I have no idea. We haven't even spoken. And before you ask, he knew where to find me from Jaxson."

"So it was his semen in your apartment."

She was confused. "What?"

"On the underwear. The forensics guy found semen on your underwear. I assumed it was Dean's."

"It's none of your..."

"Bullshit. You don't get to pick and choose when you want me to be more than your bodyguard, remember?"

Okay, he was right. "Yes, it was Ryder's."

She felt like she was under a microscope. Trevor glared at her silently before asking the million-dollar question.

"Do you love him?"

She tried to laugh it off. "I barely know him."

"Yet you let him completely control you. Today on set, pulling you out of an active scene. Hell, even your eating."

"It's just how he is..."

"I see that. What bothers me is how you've reacted to it, not just letting him do it, but... you like it."

"I'm tired, Trevor. I don't have the energy to fight him."

"It's more than that. You seem less tired, not more, since he got here. You seem..." He hesitated, unsure if he should continue, but he did. "Calmer."

She certainly didn't feel calmer. But then she realized the only thing she wasn't calm thinking about was wondering when Ryder would leave her again. How she could be so upset over someone she barely knew, outside of his sexual prowess, didn't make sense to her.

"Don't ask me to explain it. I don't understand myself. All I know is..." She paused, trying to decide if she could say the words she could barely comprehend internally. "He makes me feel different. Like... not Khloe Monroe, the actress. Just Khloe."

He whistled. "You have it bad."

"I do not," she protested. "I'm just off-base is all."

"Uh-ha."

"Stop it."

"What?"

"Analyzing me. I don't like it."

"I'm not analyzing, although I am curious about who Ryder Helms really is. I haven't been able to dig up anything helpful at all."

"That's because I do my best to stay under the radar." Ryder's voice boomed from the doorway where he'd arrived undetected. She blushed, wondering how long he'd been listening.

Trevor seemed embarrassed, as well, at being caught doing a background check. "Hey, you're back." He reluctantly added, "Sorry for invading your privacy."

Ryder was moving closer, slowly, finally admitting, "I'd be disappointed if you hadn't. What kind of a personal bodyguard would you be, especially under the circumstances, if you didn't check out the new guy." He turned his attention to Khloe. "You look tired. Time for bed, baby."

"Excuse me? First eating and now you get to tell me when to go to bed?" Her pulse raced, in part because he was so near, but more because she remembered the things he'd done to her the night before in that waiting bed.

He was next to her when he answered, holding his hand out for her to latch onto for help standing. Only once she was on her feet, pulled into his open arms did he add, "If memory serves, I offered to control all things in your life."

She countered, flirting. "And I distinctly remember telling you you'd have to earn it."

"Ah yes, I do remember something like that. I guess you'll have to decide for yourself if you want to share my bed again tonight." The invitation was anything but innocent. Ryder held her against his chest, humping his body into hers in an age-old dance.

She was acutely aware that Trevor was a few feet away, watching their dynamic carefully. She bit back her reply, unwilling to egg him on with his overt advances even as his hands reached lower to cup her ass, feeling her up.

Self-conscious, she tried to make light of the sexual overtones. "I guess I am tired, and we'll have a long day tomorrow, so we should get some sleep."

Ryder may be talking against the shell of her ear, but she knew damn well he spoke loud enough for Trevor to hear his naughty challenge. "You can try to get some sleep, I guess, but I'm planning on being up most of the night." He lifted her feet off the ground, hugging her to him until she instinctively wrapped her legs around his torso as he started walking them towards the master bedroom. "I'll sleep on the plane."

# CHAPTER 19

"*I*'m sorry, sir, but we'll need to wake up Ms. Monroe. The captain has put on the fasten seatbelt sign for our descent into Reagan National. You'll need to get her buckled in."

Ryder'd been dozing off himself. While he didn't look forward to the trip from the airport, it would be good to get settled for the night behind locked doors again. Being in public with the threats against Khloe made him jumpy enough, but knowing the Volkov's hitmen were out there combing the world for him and that Washington D.C. would be one of the first cities they looked, he was on edge more than normal.

He had planned to fly separate until that ticking package had been sent to her parents' house. After that, there was no way in hell he'd allow her to travel without him.

He looked down at the sleeping woman who was stretched across the plush first-class seating, using his lap as her pillow as he stroked her silky hair. The poor baby had been exhausted this morning when they left for the airport. He should feel guilty for keeping her up half the night, but he didn't. Not in the slightest. With hyperawareness, he knew their time together was short. He was determined to make every moment count.

Despite the flight attendant's evil eye from the galley, he leaned to his right to nudge Trevor across the aisle. "Hey." He waited for the bodyguard to take his earbud out before continuing. "I'm not going to be able to travel through the airport with you guys. I'll follow behind about twenty-five feet, watching your six. You take her straight to the limo. I'll wait inside and pick up the checked bags and then meet you at the curb."

Trevor nodded at the plan, but then added, "When are you gonna level with me about who you really are?"

"You know what you need to know."

"Bullshit. I get the impression nothing scares you, yet being seen in public with Khloe clearly terrifies you."

The guard wasn't wrong. "The less you know the better. Just make Khloe's safety your top priority."

"It always has been, which is more than I can say for you."

"What's that supposed to mean?"

"You talk a big game, but I think you're just here for the booty call. Don't think I don't know why she's slept the whole way here. The walls at your house aren't that thick."

"Jealous much?"

"Will you two stop it? I'm not sure the people back in coach can hear you." Khloe's sleepy admonishment coincided with her pushing to a sitting position, stretching her aching muscles. He suspected she was pretty sore considering the workout he'd put her through.

Ryder leaned back into his own seat, enjoying watching Khloe's ritual as she prepared herself to walk out onto the public stage after they landed. Light makeup and lipstick was applied. Her long hair was brushed and pulled back in a high ponytail. The flight attendant delivered an unordered protein bar and energy drink on a tray, the anorexic's go-to meal.

Damned if she didn't even have the airlines trained to support her unhealthy habits.

She smiled victoriously as she took a small bite of the low-calorie bar. He'd let her win this round in public, looking forward to the rematch behind closed doors.

The landing was uneventful. Traveling with a celebrity did have its perks as they were escorted off the plane first. Khloe pulled a pair of sunglasses from her big bag as they walked the jet way, getting into the zone for her dash to the limo. Even though he couldn't see her eyes behind the glasses, he felt her tense as he pulled them to a stop long enough to release the waist he'd been holding and hand over her arm to Trevor before they exited the tunnel.

"Where are you going?" she questioned.

"I'll be right behind you. I want to watch the crowd. I promise, I'll be making sure nothing hurts you."

It was the truth. Not the whole truth, but the truth nonetheless.

She looked hurt at his rebuff, but let Trevor lead her out through the throng of passengers waiting to board the plane at the gate. He hung back far enough that he easily heard the voices whispering, "Hey, I think that's Khloe Monroe." And, "Wow, she's even more beautiful in person than in pictures."

He agreed.

The trip through the arrival hall was uneventful. He texted with Trevor and the limo service, observing until Trevor and Khloe were safely ensconced in the back of the car before going back to the luggage carousel.

Ryder kept his own dark glasses on, trying to throw off facial-recognition software that he knew was snapping photos of all travelers. Each waiting passenger was evaluated by his trained eye, looking for threats and relieved when he found none.

Once he had her bag, he stopped outside the exit long enough to pull his pistol from the checked luggage, securing it in his shoulder holster. He then zigzagged his way to their location, stopping several times to turn and check his six.

*You really are turning into one paranoid bastard, Helms.*

Finally, confident it was safe, Ryder hopped in the back of the limo.

"What took you so long? Did they lose my bag?"

"Nope. Just slow today." He made eye contact with Trevor who was sitting opposite them on the bench seat facing backwards. He wished he'd remembered to tell the guard that he wanted that seat.

"Don't worry. I'm watching," Trevor reassured him.

The bastard was on to him.

"Watching for what?" Khloe asked, oblivious that the men were worried about a tail.

Ryder answered with a hug, pulling her into his lap to distract her. "So I have a surprise."

He saw the worry line, the one she often applied creams to avoid, crinkle on her brow. "I hope it's a good surprise. I've had my fill of bad ones lately."

"Well, at least I think it is. I called Davidson and we're gonna stay at his secure apartment above Runway while we're in town."

Khloe's face lit up like sunshine, understanding the implications of the location. Trevor was less impressed.

"What the hell? We already have a suite reserved at the Marriott. We spent a small fortune on security sweeps."

"That's fine. You'll need a place to stay and it's a good thing that everyone thinks she'll be there. It could flush out the stalker."

"Thanks for turning me in to a decoy," Trevor grumbled.

"Don't mention it."

"Seriously, will you two grow up?"

Trevor wasn't going to let the subject drop. "That makes no sense. Why the hell would you want to take Khloe to a popular dance club full of people on a Saturday night? That's the last place we want to try to secure."

Khloe's eyes widened at Trevor's probing question.

"You don't need to worry about it. We won't be going to the dance club."

He snuggled Khloe closer, enjoying the feel of her in his arms as they watched the national monuments passing by outside the tinted windows. Only the vibration of his cell phone could distract him.

The text was from Axe. It was a simple *'call me when you land'*.

He put his phone away, not wanting to call his friend back until he was alone.

"Everything okay?" Trevor questioned.

"Yeah. Just great."

The men's eyes met over Khloe's head. He should be pissed that Trevor was so suspicious, but wasn't that exactly the kind of protection Khloe would need when he wasn't there? He pushed down his jealousy, determined to make an effort to cut the asshole some slack. After all, it wasn't that he was in a competition with the guy for Khloe, but he was still jealous of the taller man, knowing he was free to go anywhere, do anything with Khloe... something Ryder could not do without putting her in danger.

He'd been lost in thought, not paying attention where they were going until the limo driver pulled up in front of a psychic shop. Khloe's eyes looked up at him in surprise.

Trevor injected before Ryder could redirect the driver. "Why the hell did we stop here? This isn't the hotel or the club."

The driver called back over his shoulder through the open partition. "Mr. Helms, this is the address you sent me in a text, is it not?"

"Yeah, but you need to drop Mr. McLean off at the hotel first." Trevor eyed him suspiciously so he added, "They have a backdoor VIP entrance to the club through this shop. Just one of the reasons I told you not to worry about her being safe. This place is like a fortress."

Trevor leaned over and opened the door. "I'll help you get the bags inside and then I wouldn't mind throwing back a drink or two. I can grab a cab to the hotel later. I'm not in any rush to see the Kaplans since they are in the adjoining room to the suite."

Khloe looked like she was about to hyperventilate. He reassured her, "It's okay, baby. I'll take care of this."

The three of them piled out, grabbing their bags from the trunk before heading into the psychic shop. It was late afternoon on a Saturday in Georgetown and the shop was not nearly as empty as it had been the other nights Ryder had arrived. It made him nervous, pulling Khloe against his body, shielding her face as they meandered to the back of the store. He was actually glad he had Trevor to follow behind with their bags.

The Hispanic security guy, Luis, must never take a day off. He'd been there to greet Ryder on every visit to the club.

"Good evening, Mr. Helms. Ms. Monroe. We've been expecting you. Mr. Davidson asked that I give him a call to let him know you'd arrived. He said he'll meet you at the bar."

Ever nosy Trevor edged closer. "God dammit, I thought you said you wouldn't be taking Khloe out in public."

It was Luis who answered. "Are you a member, sir?"

"A member of what? Runway?"

Luis looked to Ryder for help.

"He's part of Ms. Monroe's security detail. We're gonna pass through to Runway. Can you have Jaxson meet us at the elevator to the private suite instead?"

"Of course. I'll call him now. Have a nice evening," Luis said, pulling the door open to reveal the well-lit stairs that would take them under the alley separating the building from Davidson's property.

Khloe's heels clicked on the cement flooring of the tunnel and stairs at the other end until they reached the carpeted landing. To the right was the unmarked door leading to the very exclusive and private Black Light, but Ryder headed up the neon-lit stairs straight ahead, knowing they led to the open-to-the-public Runway dance club instead.

Ryder had never taken this path on previous visits so he was surprised and confused when he opened the door at the top of the stairs and found himself inside a dark broom closet.

"Do you know where the hell you're going?" Trevor grumbled.

To be fair, he really didn't, but he sure as hell wasn't going to tell the guy that. Instead, he barged ahead, pulling the curtain at the entrance of the closet aside only to nearly run into the back of a burly security guard.

The guy had obviously not heard them coming over the music because he whipped around, looking ready for a fight, especially when he saw Trevor and Ryder. It was when his eyes landed on the petite Khloe he backed down.

"Ah, Ms. Monroe. You surprised me. Blake told us we were expecting you. He briefed us on your unique security concerns. I must have misunderstood. I thought you'd be secluded at Black Light tonight where we can keep you locked down easier."

Ryder wanted to deck the guy.

Security 101. Don't say more than you need to.

He tried to do some damage control before Trevor asked questions he didn't need answers to. "We're meeting Davidson at the elevator. He's loaning us the apartment upstairs."

"Sure thing. Let me escort you there."

Ryder could feel Trevor's distrustful glare on his back as they went down the long hallway, past the public restrooms where he had to shield Khloe again from being recognized by the long line of women waiting to pee. From the looks of things, they were backstage of Runway. Dance music pounded loud around them, gratefully making it hard to converse as they approached the elevator.

The guard used an electronic keycard to call the lift and a minute later, the doors opened and Jaxson, Chase and Emma appeared before them.

Leave it to Emma to welcome them first, bursting forward to give Khloe an excited hug. "I'm so glad you made it here safe and sound! That was so scary the other night at the theater." She turned towards Ryder, hugging him next. "You saved the day riding in on your motorcycle. It was so exciting and romantic!"

Jaxson stepped forward to peel his woman away. "I think that's enough hugging for one night, don't you?"

Emma grinned up at him, "Not quite yet." She shrugged out of her Dom's grasp to give Trevor a hug, too. "I'm so sorry we panicked you by arranging Ryder to pick up Khloe. I never dreamed you wouldn't know who he was."

It was Chase who pulled her away from McLean. "All right, now that everyone got their Emma hug, I think you and I should head on downstairs and let these guys get settled, don't you?"

Emma looked like she disagreed, but Chase pulled her along behind him, stopping long enough to place a platonic kiss on Khloe's forehead and say, "You look good, kiddo. I'll talk to you later. Come along, Emma."

Jaxson stepped aside, waving his arm as an invite for them to board the elevator. "I'll take it from here, John. Let's get your bags upstairs."

Once the lift was in motion, he pulled an envelope out of the inside pocket of his designer suit jacket and handed it to Ryder.

"These keys will allow you to get off the elevator on any floor as well as gain entry to the apartment. The master key to the suite is locked in the security office safe. Chase, Emma and I enter with a biometric retinal scan, so unless you give someone this key, you're one-hundred percent locked down. In addition, the entrance to the safe room is through the master closet. Once inside, if you engage the locks, it will call 911 and put you on generator backup so even if electricity is cut to the building, you're safe with supplies for up to one week."

"Jesus Christ, are you expecting Armageddon?" Trevor seemed impressed. In truth, Ryder was too.

"Naw, not really, but the world is getting scary. I need to know that I can protect the people I love." Jaxson's passion was admirable.

"Well, let's hope we don't need that extreme. Based on the threats so far, Khloe's stalker isn't nearly that sophisticated," Trevor observed.

Ryder didn't comment. The safe room may be overkill for her stalker, but it might be the only kind of fortress to keep them safe from the Volkovs if they were to catch up to them.

*I'm not going to let that happen.*

An opulent foyer greeted them as they exited the elevator. The security pad for the key and retina scan was mounted on the wall to the right of the thick double doors. Davidson leaned down to provide his scan, and the sound of the lock disengaging told them they could enter.

The suite was stylishly elegant, the modern decor in almost all white with colorful pillows providing occasional splashes of color. The walls were lined with shelves that housed a combo of what looked like expensive artwork, hardback books, and dozens of candid photos. Fresh cut flowers in crystal vases were interspersed throughout the space making it smell like a springtime garden, and despite the warming weather, a welcoming fire roared in the fireplace.

But it was the huge round bed that was the focal point of the room. It had to be custom made. Ryder had no trouble at all imagining the debauched activities that took place on that bed between the trio, particularly when he noticed the mirror on the ceiling above it and tucked-away rings every few feet around the base he assumed had been used to tie down Davidson's submissives.

"As you can see, I think you'll have more than enough space to spread out and relax." Jaxson wasn't very successful at hiding his sly grin, knowing damn well that Ryder and Khloe would be putting the custom bed to good use.

Trevor was less jovial at being relegated to bellhop. "Where do you want me to put this stuff?"

Ryder was getting anxious to call Axe to see if he'd turned up any leads yet now that he'd had some time with the evidence. "Just park them over next to the table. I'll help her with them in a bit. I need to make a call."

He leaned down to kiss Khloe lightly, aware that they had an audience. "Jaxson, I don't suppose we could order up a light dinner by chance? It's time to get some more food into this one."

"I ate on the plane!"

"Half a protein bar is not dinner. We slept late and you missed breakfast and we had a tiny lunch when we boarded. We're going to eat a good dinner."

She looked as if she wanted to yell obscenities until he graced her with his most dominate glare. The pout that replaced her anger was adorable, and her quiet "yes, sir" went straight to his cock. He may be the Dom, but little did his submissive know how much control she wielded over him. Her happiness and safety felt like his new air and blood.

"I'll order up a good selection." When Khloe appeared panicked, he added, "Don't worry. I was on the runway for years. I know what to order that will make you both happy. I'll give you a call when the food arrives so you know when to expect one of my staff with the delivery."

"Thanks, Davidson. For everything." The guy had turned out to be a great ally. Yet another man he would have to trust to keep Khloe safe when he couldn't.

Jax was headed to the door when he stopped and prodded Trevor. "Why don't you come down with me? I'll get you settled on our VIP floor where you can unwind with some drinks and entertainment."

Trevor looked back at the hugging couple and then nodded, understanding his work was done for the night. For a minute, Ryder felt sorry for him, but he pushed it aside. He didn't have time to think of anyone but Khloe.

When they were finally alone, he scooped her into his arms bride-style and stalked to the giant bed, plopping her down, loving her giggle as he watched her petite body bounce before he pounced on top of her, smothering her against the mattress.

"Finally. I didn't think those guys would ever leave," he complained.

A radiant smile lit up her face, making his heart physically ache. He'd been looking forward to spending time dominating his submissive on the unique BDSM equipment in the bowels of the building, but in that minute, he realized if they never left this room again, it would be too soon.

He crushed his mouth down on hers, grinding his body against her, all finesse went out the window. She had a way of making him feel more like a giddy teenager than the sexual dominant he was. Only the feel of his phone vibrating in his pocket reminded him that Axe was waiting on his call.

With regret, Ryder separated from her enough to peer down at her, loving the look of sexual carnality staring back at him.

"Hold that thought for a minute. I need to call Axe and check in. Why don't you check out the rest of the suite?"

"Really? Do you have to call him right now?" Her hands roamed his body, pulling his button-down shirt from the waistband of his pants to get to his back. She hugged him tighter, trying to stop him from pushing to his feet.

With a chuckle, he answered, "I'll only be a few minutes and then we can resume where we left off."

"Promises, promises," she teased.

Still, when he'd rolled off her, she stood and took off for the other side of the room where there was a dining table and an opening to what looked like a small kitchen. Her hips swayed beautifully in her skinny jeans. Only when she was out of sight did Ryder ring Axe.

His friend answered with a, "I was getting worried."

"I waited to get us settled before I called. What do you have for me?"

"Nothing conclusive yet, but plenty of interesting things to explore. I have a few questions."

"Shoot."

"You told me who McLean and the Kaplans were. I know from the media about Dean Reynolds. I'm seeing the name Ricky Covasse popping up pretty often with a lot of intimate details about her travels."

"I haven't met him yet, but he's her personal assistant so that would make sense, unless the messages are threatening."

"Not so far. How about Apollo Starling and Edward Rivera?" Axe asked.

"The director of her current film and according to McLean, Rivera has produced two movies for her."

"Interesting. He is having some pretty substantial cash flow problems right now."

Ryder had only met the guy for a few minutes, but he didn't seem the type to stalk anyone, unless he was looking at it as a publicity stunt.

"Okay, I'll see him tomorrow at this event. I'll be sure to dig in on him a bit. What about the douchebag, Reynolds? I'd sure love to throw him behind bars if for no other reason than being an asshole."

"The only thing I've turned up on him is closer to my normal kind of job. He's hitting a married woman on the side. Woman by the name of Gloria Mining."

Ryder had heard the story from Khloe, so he wasn't surprised.

"I think he's a dead end."

"Me too," his friend agreed.

"So who does that leave us with? The package to her parents proves to me that it's an insider. Who haven't we looked at?"

Axe agreed with him. "Technically, it could be a fan, but I think you're right. The evidence points more to someone she works with. Did you meet anyone on the set who concerned you?"

Ryder reran the prior day on a loop in his head. "I emailed over the crew names that I collected yesterday so you could run a check on them. There were about twenty names on the list. Now that I'm thinking about it, there was this one guy I didn't have on my original list. I had to ask around to get his name. It's Peter Hernandez. When I asked Khloe about him, she said he's the nephew of one of the producers or something. He's not playing with a full deck."

"I'll check him out. I'm expecting the security camera footage from the studio tomorrow. You did a good job scaring the shit out of the head of security. But the best gift we got was that package to her parents. I dug in and found the service the stalker had deliver it was a custom delivery service. At first, I almost eliminated everyone on the west coast due to the timing of the delivery. It came so soon on the heels of your arrival, that clearly scares them by the way, and just the logistics of physically getting a package to the doorstep of her parents in the Bronx after nine on a Friday night."

"Yeah, whoever is behind this is either stupid or has one big set of balls," Ryder reasoned.

"I'm going with stupid. It didn't jump out at me immediately, but up until now, all of the messages focused solely on Khloe. How they planned to be with her. Professing their love and devotion. This message barely mentions her. It's like all they care about is getting rid of you, someone they clearly see as a threat."

He should be flattered, but he was more relieved. He was used to playing with danger. If his presence drew the danger off Khloe and made the stalker make stupid mistakes, then he couldn't be happier.

"We need to find out where that package was sent from."

"I'm on it. It's getting late there. Keep your phone on."

"Yeah, I will, but we may go downstairs for a bit. I won't be able to take my phone in with me. You still have that number for Spencer, right?"

The men had served together in the marines what felt like a lifetime ago.

"Yeah, but I'd rather not call him," Axe groused.

"It was fourteen years ago. You need to let it go," Ryder urged, remembering how the slightly older Spencer and Axe had always argued like siblings, picking at each other incessantly, but always there to cover the other's back when needed.

"It's not that." Ryder could hear the frustration in his old friend's voice. "Every time I talk to someone from the old days, the first thing they do is tell me how sorry they are for me. I don't want anyone's fucking pity." Axel's voice quavered with pent up emotion.

"I get that. I do, but it's hard to know what to say, man. Cut us some slack if we botch it." Ryder spoke from his heart, his own guilt for not being there for his friend when he needed him crowding in again.

"You're right. Fuck it. I'll call him if I can't reach you."

Axe ended the call without a goodbye. Ryder threw his phone down on the coffee table a bit too hard and looked up to see Khloe watching him from across the room, her arms folded across her chest. When their eyes met, she began her trek across the spacious room towards him. She didn't stop until she'd mounted his lap facing him, her legs spread so that her knees touched the leather couch and her clothed pussy pressed against his flaccid shaft.

"So when are you going to tell me what's going on with Axe? You barely told me anything last night when you got back from visiting him." He didn't want to waste their precious time together talking about or even thinking about how fucked up Axel's life was, but one look at Khloe's determined face as she wiggled her ass, grinding against him like a cat in heat trying to scratch their itch, reminded him of her control over him.

"You don't want to know."

"Of course I do. You said he's one of your oldest friends. I know next to nothing about you, Ryder. The only reason I met Aunt Ginny is because I didn't listen to instructions."

He let his hand squeeze her tight ass through her jeans. "Thanks for the reminder. I never did punish you for that, did I?"

She wasn't deterred. "Please. You know almost everything about me. It isn't fair."

Ryder didn't want to be the one to tell her that life was rarely fair in his experience. Considering all of the scary truths he was keeping from her, he decided sharing some of his history with Axe was some of his safest secrets.

"We were childhood friends. Our fathers were in the same motorcycle club. We were in high school when his dad was killed and he came to live with my father and me for a couple of years until we both enlisted in the marines together. That's where we met Spencer."

"Where was his mom?"

"She took off when he was a kid. Couldn't handle the MC lifestyle."

"And she left him behind? That sucks."

Ryder didn't want to get into what it was really like to be part of an MC family. Axel's mother had understood well that she would never be allowed to take her son away from the family.

"That isn't the worst thing that happened to him." He paused, unsure if he wanted to say the horrific things his friend had survived. It somehow made it all more real. She waited expectantly until he continued. "He was married. They had a daughter. About three years ago when she was twelve, some asshole kidnapped Mia on her way home from school. There were witnesses. He's spent the last three years spending every waking hour and every dime he had looking for her."

"Oh my God, that's horrible! Why is he helping us then?"

Ryder sighed. "Because he needs to move on. As horrible as it is, he needs to find a way to live again."

"His poor wife. I can't even imagine the pain she is going through."

Ryder was uncomfortable talking about such depressing topics, but at the same time, knew it would help him to talk it out with Khloe.

"It killed her. Literally. Yeah, the coroner might have called it an accident, but she wrapped her car around a tree at sixty miles per hour."

Tears streamed down Khloe's cheeks. Genuine anguish filled her eyes thinking about the pain Axe must be going through. "How does he wake up each day and find the will to go on?"

It was a fantastic question. One he wasn't sure he knew the answer to. "Axe has always been the strongest bastard I ever knew. As long as there is a tiny chance of finding Mia alive, he'll keep fighting. I went to him for help because he has always been stronger at technology than I have been, but I also wanted to try to give him something to think about other than losing Mia. The investigation has been good for him."

The ding of a text on his phone gratefully ended the depressing conversation.

"That's probably Davidson with news about dinner."

"I'm not hungry," she complained.

"Liar. You said it yourself. You're always hungry. You just don't want to eat."

"Same thing."

He grinned as he hugged her closer, squeezing her ass through her clothes. "You need to get some calories in you so you'll have the stamina to keep up with me when we get downstairs."

The heat in her eyes melted, turning her glare into pure passionate longing. "Are you sure we should go down to Black Light?" He didn't miss the hopeful hint in her question.

Ryder pulled her closer, nibbling at her neck as he answered. "Hell yes. Your body has a date with your Dom. He can't wait to remind you who's in charge."

Her full-body tremble as she crumbled into his arms like a noodle humbled him. She'd already turned herself over to him. Body and soul. As he pulled back to look into her eyes, he witnessed her slipping deeper into her submissive role, shucking her Khloe Monroe larger than life persona and leaving only his princess in her place.

And just like that, they were in a scene. That suited him fine. His first act of dominance over her for the evening wouldn't be on the medical table or in the dungeon below. It wouldn't be sexual in nature at all. No, it would be her kneeling naked at his feet as he spoon-fed her every fucking bite of her dinner.

*Being a dominant over a woman you love sure is different than a sub in a Moscow dance club.*

# CHAPTER 20

*K*hloe couldn't remember feeling so alive. So expectant.

*On the edge.*

She knew that was exactly Ryder's plan as he took her hand and escorted her from the elevator on the ground floor of Runway, still relatively safe in the private backstage area. As they neared the hallway leading past the perpetual line of partying women waiting to pee, Ryder pulled her body close, wrapping his arm around her waist as she huddled against him to hide her face. It felt sinful to be naked under the oversized robe, the only clothing he'd allowed her to don for their trek downstairs.

He'd already primed and readied her body for the sexual adventure their visit to Black Light promised. Memories of his dominance from months before mingled with this more confusing current version of Ryder, making her uncertain as to what to expect. He was a pro at keeping her off base.

She felt the blush burn on her cheeks as she burrowed closer against him, remembering how it had felt to be stripped naked and made to kneel at his feet where he'd fed her bite after bite of the light dinner Jaxson had had delivered. He'd edged her between bites throughout dinner and she was already desperate to have him inside her.

She was hoping to relax when they got to Black Light, but being a Saturday night, the locker room where they checked membership IDs was already busy. A small line waited to check-in, giving her a chance to take a few calming breaths.

Danny greeted them by name when they were at the front of the line. "Mr. Helms. Ms. Monroe. We've been expecting you. Mr. Davidson said he'd buy you a drink when you got here."

"Thanks, Danny."

"Of course, sir. You know the drill. Please leave all electronics in your locker. Ms. Monroe will need to leave her cell phone as well."

Ryder flashed a devilish grin. "We left her phone upstairs, didn't we, Princess? In fact, I think you should demonstrate to security that you're not hiding anything. Let's leave the robe in the locker."

Khloe's heart pounded hard in her chest. She'd thought she was prepared for her return to Black Light, but the idea of stripping naked suddenly terrified her.

Ryder stepped closer, pulling her into his arms so he could talk softly against her ear.

"I've got you, baby. Trust me. Turn yourself over, like back in February."

That night had been magical––right up until he'd ditched her without explanation at the end. What if he tried the same again after tonight? She shook her head as if to chase the negative thoughts away, remembering that at least for tonight, they'd sleep together upstairs in the luxurious round bed.

Her body responded to his dominance. He knew the secret code to tap into her carnality. Her fingers moved to the opening of the robe and she pulled the sash loose, letting it fall open before she shrugged it off her shoulders to pool at her feet. She felt the eyes of the other couples in the small room on her, but she kept her focus on her Dom, swept away by the heat of authority in his icy blue eyes.

Ryder reached into the pocket of his slacks, coming out with a thin black choker that he attached around her neck. Khloe liked the surprisingly heavy weight of the jewelry, as if it was his calling card, marking her for all to see. From his other pocket, he pulled out a delicate chain with a jeweled clip on the end. The last of her reticence fell away with the snap of the clasp attaching to the ring of her collar.

Tonight she was not Khloe Monroe, the actress. She was simply Ryder Helm's submissive, Princess, being led naked by a leash onto the main floor of the BDSM club. To those watching, she suspected she'd appear to be playing her newest part as many who role-played in the D/s lifestyle did for fun. Yet the invisible connection she felt to the man proudly leading her had never felt so real. So unlike play.

Pounding music mingled with sounds of sexual adventures creating a captivating soundtrack. It was impossible for it to not intrude into her jumbled mind. Naughty snippets intersected with naughtier memories. Where would he lead her? What was his plan?

As hard as she tried to tune out everyone but her Dom, it was impossible when she'd catch fragments of conversations talking about her. She tried not to think about being naked and on display, yet if she were honest with herself, it felt a bit like coming home... being here in this place again and with the man who had rocked her world.

She followed a few steps behind, keeping her head bowed, watching her slippered feet pad along the carpeted floor. Stopping when he stopped to chat with other Doms. Following as he wound them through the maze of debauchery in motion, as if she were on parade. With each moment that passed, she relaxed more, becoming accustomed to the crack of paddles and screams of passion.

By the time Ryder sank into a plush leather chair not far from the long neon-accented bar, Khloe had quieted her inner angst, subconsciously slipping deeper into the submissive mindset she'd begun to think had been an exaggerated dream from Valentine's Day. Gone was her Type-A career woman disposition, seduced by the sex-God presently tugging gently on the chain linking them until she was kneeling between his open legs facing him, his right hand reaching to stroke her silky hair as if he might pet a long-haired feline.

His soft petting comforted her, allowing Khloe to slip deeper, blocking out the sounds around them even as Ryder chatted with this Dom or shook hands with that Master. Between visitors, he leaned forward, using his dress shoe to tap at her inner knees, wordlessly instructing her to spread her legs wider. Instinctively, she laid her hands on her spread thighs, palms up, chin to her chest.

That earned her a soft, "Good girl," which melted any final remnants of reticence she had. She tried not to think about why she felt proud, and not embarrassed, at Ryder's chauvinistic show of ownership over her body and soul. She watched the chain linking them sway, a symbol that she was his. But then it hit her. He was hers too, and that knowledge thrilled her.

Only the sound of Jaxson's voice was able to jar her back to the present, cutting through the din of commotion in the club around them.

"I tried to make it over to the bar, but the place is packed. I figured you'd find us here eventually." Ryder was talking to Jaxson who'd nabbed the matching leather chair next to Ryder's as the previous Dom got up to leave.

"I couldn't be happier with the turn out. We've only been open a few months, but already we're exceeding our membership goals," Jaxson answered, setting his rock glass filled with an amber liquid down on the small table between the men.

Only through her peripheral vision did Khloe sense someone kneeling next to her, inches away. A quick glance confirmed a nearly naked Emma was kneeling in front of her Dom, just as Khloe was, only she didn't have a leash attached to her collar. Of the many times she'd met Emma, this was the first time seeing her deep into her submissive role in the trio's complicated relationship. The fact that Jaxson had stretched his long leg out and was presently rubbing the tip of his leather shoe against Emma's pussy while he chatted with Ryder helped Khloe feel less on display when she could share the spotlight with Emma.

But where was Chase? She had to admit that, much like the rest of the world, she was more than a little curious about the sexual dynamics of the trio's relationship, particularly after seeing their unique bed and its accessories upstairs.

She didn't have to wait long. Within minutes, a shirtless Chase arrived carrying an armful of scary looking punishment devices.

"Princess, I didn't give you permission to look around. Eyes on the floor unless instructed otherwise." Ryder's voice rumbled low in the noisy room, his chastisement enhancing her need to surrender.

The "yes, sir," slipped from her lips as easily as her next breath, sinking her deeper still--calming the anxious noise that so often accompanied her every waking moment. Khloe stopped straining to hear what was happening around her, understanding her Dom would let her know what she needed to know.

Ryder may be talking as if he weren't paying attention, but she felt the steady pull on the leash, moving her torso slowly closer until her head was cradled in his lap. His muscular thigh formed her pillow as he stroked her long, flowing hair as he would a beloved pet. Nervous tension receded, helping her relax and fall into an almost trance-like state as she allowed her brain to slow down long enough to quiet her demons.

She wasn't sure how much time had passed when Ryder and Jaxson pushed to their feet, each reaching out to stroke the hair of the women at their feet. Only the tug of the leash against her collar told her it was time to move. She had started to push to her feet when a strong palm pressed the top of her head, silently instructing her to stay on her hands and knees. Khloe was relieved to be low to the floor as they wove between the growing crowd, grateful it made it harder for people to recognize her and her blushing face.

Having only been to Black Light once, she didn't have the layout of the club memorized by any means, but if memory served her, it felt like the dominants were heading them in the direction of the main stage where the roulette wheel had been set up in February. Her suspicion was confirmed when Ryder started climbing the carpeted steps, slowing down to make sure his submissive didn't injure herself as she crawled up the steps on all fours, aware she was moving into a central focal point of the room.

Khloe was relieved when Jaxson and Emma followed them to the center of the stage where Chase waited for them all. Only now could she see he was wearing tight-fitting black leather pants, identical to those Jaxson wore. The glint of the gold rings piercing his nipples caught in the spotlight illuminating the center stage. The rings were thick and sturdy and Khloe couldn't help but be curious about how it would feel to have her body marked so personally. As if he could read her mind, Ryder's fingers pinched her right nipple as he leaned down to talk against her ear.

"This is your second reminder to keep your eyes on the floor. If I wanted you to gawk at other men, I would have told you to kneel up."

Was that jealousy she detected in his voice? It couldn't be, yet the mere thought of influencing the emotions of an all-alpha man like Ryder Helms thrilled her. Their eyes met long enough for her to see a vulnerability shining back at her from his intense icy blue eyes. She had to force herself to tear her gaze away and return her attention to the stage floor.

Her ears perked at the sound of heavy furniture being dragged across the stage floor. Her pulse raced as she imagined the possibilities the men were preparing for their submissives. She had to force cleansing breaths, trying to remain calm by reminding herself that she could trust Ryder. The last time they'd been here, he had been completely unknown to her. He'd nearly scared the bejesus out of her at first, and yet they'd ended up connecting in a way that had held them together, even for the months they'd been apart.

The pull of her leash told her it was time to stand. Her knees were stiff after kneeling for so long, and Ryder was there, helping to pull her upright. Her line of sight fell on a now naked Emma being fastened into restraints. Jaxson pulled her arms high above her head, attaching her wrists into hanging fur-lined manacles while Chase spread her ankles wide, locking her into matching padded metal brackets about three feet apart in the floor.

Only when Ryder stopped them directly in front of Emma did Khloe notice identical restraints waiting for her. He worked silently and she offered no resistance as he started with her arms, securing her tightly before kneeling before her to bind her legs spread eagle. Only when he finished the final point and stepped away from her did she realize she couldn't keep her feet flat on the floor as she hung from the constricting device above her head.

Unable to look her submissive friend in the eye, Khloe focused her attention on Emma's own toes straining to hold her steady as she swayed from her high hook as well. They didn't have to wait long for relief as Ryder and Chase returned from a brief absence, pushing what looked like two pommel horses used in gymnastics, only the handles on top where a gymnast might hold on were missing.

The leather of the six-inch wide sex furniture was cool against her bare tummy as Ryder moved it against her abdomen, instantly bringing some relief to her arms already becoming fatigued from holding up her weight. Yet she quickly realized the farther he pressed the leather forward, the higher her feet left the ground. Worse, the horse was the perfect height to present her ass as a ready target for whatever devious plans Ryder might come up with.

Khloe dared a glance up to lock eyes with Emma, recognizing the same excited anticipation reflected back at her. The walls of Khloe's pussy contracted with expectation of the coming sexual exploration reminiscent of Valentine's Day. Familiar fear and excitement mingled into a heady cocktail as the women hung waiting for their men to return to the center stage. For now, the Doms had left their submissives displayed on the main stage acting as the delectable centerpiece of the smorgasbord of debauchery being enjoyed around the room.

She focused on the sound of a paddle rhythmically connecting with the tender skin of a nearby submissive. From the sounds of it, the recipient was enjoying the attention her dominant was paying her body because with each connection, her moans turned more feral until the unmistakable sound of her screaming through a powerful orgasm briefly silenced the din around the sex club.

It was impossible to gauge the passing of time as she hung there waiting, but with each minute that passed, her arms ached a bit more and the wetness between her legs produced a steady stream of cream she could feel dripping down her inner thighs. If he was gone much longer, she feared there would be a wet spot on the floor beneath her.

Only when Chase suddenly appeared from behind the nearby black curtain backdrop of the stage did she realize the men had probably been close all along, watching over their submissives. Her ex looked different than she'd ever seen him. Gone was his trademark jovial smile, replaced with a serious dominance that reminded her more of Ryder and Jax. The leather flogger he carried matched the tight leather pants that hugged him in a way that showcased his ample cock, already pressing for release.

Chase stepped close to Emma whispering something in her ear so softly Khloe couldn't hear. She pushed down the pang of jealousy as she witnessed their intimacy as he snuggled his submissive, clearly making sure she was okay before he proceeded with their scene.

The funny thing was, she wasn't jealous watching her ex-boyfriend. No. She was truly happy for him that he'd found love with Emma and Jaxson. What she wished more than anything was that she could have the kind of long-term commitment from Ryder that the trio clearly had made to each other. For all she knew, tonight could be their last night together. The fear of Ryder deserting her hung over her like a black rain cloud.

The first impact of the flogger against Emma's back was soft, drawing a purr from her friend. Chase moved from side to side, changing the angle of the strikes, peppering Emma with light kisses of leather until she closed her eyes, absorbing the increasing thwacks, and taking deep breaths.

Khloe had been so enthralled with the scene playing out in front of her she'd missed hearing her own Dom arriving until she felt his clothed body press against her ass, leaning in to talk softly against her ear.

"You're leaving a wet spot, Princess."

She could feel her face heating with embarrassment that only grew deeper when she felt his fingers sliding through the lake between her splayed legs. His sexy growl of desperation doused her humiliation, reminding her of the power she wielded in their complicated relationship.

As if he'd been thinking the same, he asked, "Again, what's your safeword tonight, baby?"

She had the power to make the scene stop at any time. In February, it had been the only reason she'd continued on with the game long after she'd left her comfort zone. How quickly things could change. She was no more experienced as a submissive, and while she and Ryder had only had a few short days together, something had shifted between them. He still intimidated her with his larger than life dominance, but underneath that was an inherent trust in Ryder Helms.

*He will never hurt me. Not really. Not physically anyway.*

She pushed down sadness of his coming desertion to answer. "I don't need a safeword. You won't hurt me."

The growl in her ear corresponded with his pressing harder against her. "Don't be so sure, Princess. You drive me crazy in a way that makes me want to lose control."

She heard the truth in the emotional rumble of his voice. She paused, watching Chase's continued thrashing of Emma's ass only feet away until she could formulate her response.

"I trust you, Ryder."

She felt his teeth biting into her shoulder proving just how on edge he was. He ground his hard cock into her hip, hugging her against him while squeezing her heavy breasts in his palms. Khloe recognized that he was making his mark on her, body and soul. He was claiming her body in every way except the way she wanted the most.

As suddenly as he'd pounced on her, he pulled away, leaving her chilled. "Red. That's the word that will stop everything. Got it?"

She nodded slightly, forcing him to command, "Say it. I need to hear it from you."

Khloe should be relieved at his gallant actions, but instead she was annoyed. "I told you..."

A line of fire ignited across her ass, the worst pain striking her right hip. The sudden sting took her breath away as Ryder jammed his hand into her long tresses and yanked her head back, exposing her long neck as he growled against her ear. "We play by my rules. You'll have a safeword when playing at the club. Say it. Now."

Memories of almost screaming the word in February flooded back, giving her the courage to whisper, "Red."

"Good girl. Don't be afraid to use it."

The next line of fire fell fast, as if he were testing her promise. The pain was all consuming, drowning out everything else but the need for relief. Khloe panicked. She'd forgotten how real the game was that they played in the secret dungeon. For the briefest of moments, the word red sat at the tip of her tongue, ready to fly, but she held it back, not wanting to fail Ryder so quickly.

"Take a deep breath, baby."

He was there, lightly tracing the welt that had to be adorning her ass like a badge of honor. Comforting where he'd hurt. It was an odd game they all played. A dance of pain and pleasure. If she wasn't experiencing it first hand, she'd say it was crazy, yet the wetness between her legs and the peaked nipples hanging heavily towards the floor proved she loved every minute of it.

The third line he painted on her body was lower, catching the underside of her ass and drawing her first wail as she jerked against the restraints, unsurprised when finding no give whatsoever.

Ryder's hands were on her, cupping her bottom, squeezing her tenderized skin until the pain fled, leaving pleasure in its wake.

Again. Fiery streak. Tender caresses.

High. Low.

Pain. Pleasure.

She closed her eyes, blocking out everything but her connection to the man mastering her body until she longed for the pain, knowing his loving caresses would soothe it away. A dichotomy of dark and light, culminating after a strong dozen strokes when

LIVIA GRANT

Ryder stepped close and cupped her sex in his large, calloused hand, squeezing her pussy so hard she cried out as he growled, "This is mine," against her ear.

Hell yes, it was his.

"Prove it!" Her own voice was hoarse, thick with emotion.

It was a dare. A sassy, bold temptation. She wanted him inside her and his low groan betrayed his mirrored desire, but the crack of his open hand slapping her punished ass proved how disciplined her Dom was.

"That will be enough topping from the bottom, Princess. Just for that, I think I need to give these beautiful breasts of yours a bit of my attention."

As he moved in front of her, she finally saw the implement he'd been using on her ass. That he was tapping the tender skin of her boobs with the end of a heavy riding crop alarmed her. Surely he wouldn't strike her...

"Ouch!" A small patch of pink stood out against her milky skin just above her tit. Instead of caressing the pain away as he had on her ass, Ryder leaned down to suck her pebbled nipple into his warm mouth, distracting her sufficiently as the sting dissipated, leaving sexual need in its wake.

As Ryder stepped away, she again felt a chill at the loss of his body heat. With nothing to block her view, she couldn't help but admire her friend Emma's protruding nipples and heavy breasts on display only a few feet away.

The grad student's curvy body was so very different from Khloe's thin frame. As Khloe watched Jaxson squeezing and caressing-- slapping and tickling--all of Emma's curves, Khloe understood why Jaxson and Chase adored their submissive so much. Emma was the antithesis of the stick-figure models they had been surrounded by since the beginning of their modeling career together. She was genuine... real. Anyone watching the trio's current display could see in ten seconds flat how much the three loved each other.

Jaxson stepped between the submissives, blocking Khloe's view of her friend just as Ryder renewed the cropping of her breasts and nipples. She was grateful he was only using the snappy end to flick the leather against her skin again and again, slowly stoking the fire between them instead of laying a line of heat with the length of the leather. She closed her eyes, focusing on the physical sensations Ryder was fueling.

The sound of a mechanical winch engaging pulled Khloe out of her sexual haze. She opened her eyes to find Jaxson using a remote control to lower Emma's arms, allowing her tummy to rest completely against the top of the horse. He didn't stop until her head was at his waist level. While she couldn't see Jax's insertion, there was no mistaking the gagging and gurgling as he grabbed Emma's long hair and started thrusting his length down her throat. For Khloe, it was like watching a live porn show, only she was frustrated that all the best parts of the scene were blocked by Jaxson's body.

"I thought I told you not to stare at other Doms, Princess." Ryder had caught her again red handed.

"I can't help it. They're right in front of me," she sassed, earning her another line of fire across the width of her bottom. Three more quick licks to her cheeks and Khloe was flying high on adrenaline and pain.

Just when the word red was on the tip of her tongue, her Dom stepped close and demanded, "Open your mouth. Wide."

Her lips snapped open in time for him to place the center of the warm leather crop into her mouth.

"Bite down. Don't let go until we're done or unless you decide you need to use your safeword, understand?"

She nodded, although her vision had blurred from the tears the pain had produced.

Khloe used her peripheral sight to watch her Dom unzip his slacks and pull out the hard-on she admired so much. Like always, her pulse increased as she thought about where that flesh would soon be buried.

Ryder moved behind her, rubbing his erection through her soaking folds. She was so turned on by the sights and sounds that she couldn't wait for him to claim her, yet it didn't happen. A long minute passed as disappointment at remaining empty warred with relief the pain was subsiding.

Unable to communicate with him or move, she felt helpless. She was held hostage, desperate for him to claim her and getting hornier by the minute watching and listening to the spectacle in front of her.

She was relieved when Jaxson removed his erection from Emma's throat and stepped away from her, allowing Khloe to admire the sexy picture of a messy Emma. There was no doubting her own submissive tendencies because the sight of her sub friend trussed up and having been face fucked almost made Khloe come without even being touched by Ryder.

Things heated up when Chase returned to the scene, pulling his own thick tool out and stepping up behind Emma's spread legs. She was relieved that her ex wasn't looking at her, but instead seemed to be distracted by something happening behind Khloe. She figured out what it was a few seconds later when Chase slammed into Emma balls deep at exactly the same moment Ryder penetrated her.

From the sounds of it, both women came undone immediately. Khloe saw stars, the pleasure was so intense. She'd been aching to be filled and the relief of Ryder claiming her made her almost drop the crop from her clenched teeth.

The Doms were on a mission, fucking their submissives hard and fast. Khloe's eyes met Emma's and the subs shared an intimate moment of understanding. She felt Ryder's fingers digging into her hips as he held her hard while fucking her impossibly deep. She was sure he was about to explode when he stilled, buried deep inside her while they watched Emma and Chase both cry out as they orgasmed together.

Khloe felt cheated that her own grand finale was cut short, but she was helpless to complain about it with the crop still wedged in between her teeth. Her jaw was starting to become fatigued.

Frustrated tears filled her eyes when Ryder removed his thickness from her pussy, leaving her bereft.

She was contemplating opening her mouth to complain when she felt the first drops of warm liquid on her ass, more specifically near her puckered hole. Her pulse raced as she felt Ryder's fingers prying her punished cheeks apart to uncover her most private body part. She felt more liquid just as something small penetrated her bottom. It wasn't his cock, of that she was sure. She remembered how full she'd felt Valentine's Day when he'd claimed her there. Her cheeks had to be bright red as she recognized both Chase and Emma were catching their breath and watching.

She was blind to what was happening behind her, but she had a front row seat to watch a fully erect Jaxson, cock protruding proudly from his groin, step behind Chase and begin dribbling lubricant in exactly the same hole Ryder was for Khloe. As best as she could tell, Chase's penis was still buried inside Emma's pussy, yet with each passing second of Jaxson's finger fucking, she could see Chase shedding his dominance and embracing submission.

As if it were choreographed, Jaxson and Ryder completed the preparations of their sub's bottoms and each stepped closer. Khloe felt Ryder testing her pucker with the tip of his erection, pushing in a bit before retreating. In. Out. Each attempt a bit deeper. Stretching her a bit wider until the tight ring of muscles at her entrance were trained and ready for what she knew was coming.

The Doms claimed their subs together. One minute she longed for Ryder. The next she was impossibly full, stretched so wide it burned. Relief was short as he withdrew, only to slam back into her ass. That was when she opened her mouth to cry out his name and the crop fell to the floor.

Ryder frozen, still buried inside her. She knew he was on the brink of coming by his pained question, "Are you safe wording?"

"God no! More!" Khloe should have been embarrassed at the grins all three of the trio's faces as they witnessed her desperate plea, but she was too excited to come to care. In fact, when Ryder seemed reluctant to claim her at the same pace as before, she added, "Harder!"

His open-handed smack to her bottom arrived with his warning, "You're topping from the bottom again, little girl. I decide how I fuck you, remember?"

Oh boy, did she ever and it turned her on.

His hands were back on her hips, fingers digging into her to once again, holding her still to act as the receptacle for his rod. She was distracted watching Jaxson servicing her ex with the same dirty rhythm. Each Dom's thrusts were getting harder... faster... as if they were racing to the end. Ryder's pounding became erratic when he leaned into her back, reaching his right hand lower until he could reach Khloe's pussy.

She waited for him to stroke her to climax or maybe pinch her clit, but instead he used his open hand to begin slapping her as if he were spanking her pussy. More pleasure. More pain. Sensory overload. It was oh so close, but not nearly enough. Khloe lost track of how long their sexy dance went on, turning herself over to the cocktail of sensations consuming her body and soul.

He drove her over the cliff into a mammoth, screaming orgasm that club members playing across the entire space had to hear. She was vaguely aware of Ryder shooting waves of his sticky cream into her bowels.

The climax zapped her of her strength, leaving her a limp noodle strung up from the restraints. She was grateful the leather horse propped her up or she would have been hanging completely from her wrists.

Khloe felt the warm washcloth and towel gently cleaning her inner thighs, pussy and bottom hole. She closed her eyes, enjoying the sensations buzzing through her body until she felt Ryder lowering her restraints. Then he was there, scooping her into his arms, and she felt like she was coming home.

Khloe loved the sound of his beating heart against her ear as she snuggled against him, feeling closer to him than she had anyone ever before. The pain of possibly having to say good-bye to him again was more than she could fathom, yet it was already too late. Khloe knew she'd already given him the power to break her heart.

# CHAPTER 21

The clock read four-thirty-three. What was the date again?

Ryder would be marking the occasion in the encrypted, online journal he kept. The log that held all of the important details of his life. Conversations or actions he might need to remember. Details for some future report he'd need to file for Langley.

Only he would know that tucked in between details of dangerous arms deals and a plethora of other illegal activities he'd witnessed as a deep cover agent, that he'd hidden the most important statement of fact he would ever record.

It was the first moment of his thirty-eight years that he knew with every fiber of his being that he was in love. Not sexually addicted or in lust, but head-over-heels, Romeo and Juliet, till-death-do-you-part kinda shit.

And there couldn't be a worse person in the world to have it happen with.

The irony was not lost on him. He never dreamed he could feel as he did for Khloe, but had she been a schoolteacher or a nurse, they might have had a small chance at happiness. It was rare, but a few of his peers had managed to make it work, taking their families with them across the globe. They'd stepped back from the most dangerous missions, but still managed to have it all. Others had retired. Walked away from their life's work for the one they loved--successfully changing their identity and staying under the radar to start over again.

But he knew the depth of the Volkovs' global reach paired with Khloe's extraordinary fame combined for an impossible combination. She didn't know it yet, but their budding relationship had been sentenced to the death penalty before it had started.

The beautiful woman inches away from him sighed softly in her sleep, subconsciously snuggling closer to him even in her slumber.

He'd left on the small lamp next to the mammoth round bed in Davidson's loft so he could watch her doze, knowing he wouldn't sleep that night, refusing to miss even a moment of their limited remaining time together. He'd lain awake memorizing every fine laugh-line around her eyes that she had frantically applied expensive creams to before she'd come to bed.

He loved that he knew that tiny secret about her. And that she took forever to eat a damn meal, or the best secret... how gorgeous and vulnerable she looked as she orgasmed. As a public figure, there was so much the world knew about Khloe Monroe, and that made him treasure his private memories of her that much more.

And that, right there, was exactly why they were doomed.

He'd already taken too many chances--put her in too much danger. Regret for not emptying his weapon into the head of every Volkov man before leaving the underground fortress outside of Moscow had never been so heavy. He'd acquired other enemies over the years, but those he could have dealt with. The Russian crime family was in a rare echelon of criminals with unprecedented global reach. He knew that as long as one of Viktor's sons were alive, he would be a hunted man and that made appearing in public with one of Hollywood's biggest starlets out of the question.

"What are you thinking about?"

Her voice startled him in the quiet of the dark loft. When he didn't answer, she added, "You look sad."

It was his turn to sigh. "I guess I am sad," he answered truthfully.

Several seconds passed before she quietly confronted the elephant presently jammed into the few inches between them. "You need to tell me."

"Tell you what?" He played dumb, pushing down the temptation to tell her the truth.

"I'm not stupid. I know you're keeping secrets from me."

He may not be able to tell her everything, but he sure as hell wouldn't let her think what he had to do was her fault. He reached out to push a messy lock of hair away from her face as he replied. "I know you aren't stupid, Princess, but it's for your own good."

He was unprepared for her burst of anger as she slapped his hand away to retort. "Bullshit. You think you're protecting me, but you're wrong. We can deal with whatever it is, but we need to do it together."

If only that were true.

"It doesn't work like that for me."

"Maybe it never has before, but that's how it's going to work this time. You know why?"

Her eyes flashed with determination in the dim lighting, stunning him into silence until she finished her thought. "It's going to work because I refuse to let you walk out on me––on *us*–– again. It nearly killed me last time, and we'd only been together three hours."

Her bravery was wavering, leaving vulnerability in its wake. Before his eyes, the angry actress was reduced to his fragile lover, her heart figuratively bared before him.

The old Ryder might have been able to pull it together and

gloss over the moment, but in light of his own personal revelations, he could no more do anything that would injure her emotionally than he could have stabbed that bared heart with his hunting knife.

That left him in uncharted territory.

She waited, watching him intently as he weighed his words.

"It's difficult," he said softly, clearing his throat of emotion before adding, "I've never talked with a civilian about it before."

Her perceptive gaze sparked with recognition of new information. "You're still in the military?"

He danced around her question. "Not exactly."

"Well, what then--exactly?"

Her impatience brought a sharpness to her tone. His inner-Dom raised an eyebrow, bringing an adorable blush to the bridge of her nose, spreading across her pale cheeks. The simple exchange only served to solidify their tenuous connection, reminding him that for the first, and only, time in his life, he understood what it meant to share his life with someone.

And not just anyone. With the remarkable, strong woman he was lucky enough to be sharing his pillow with. He hadn't known he'd been carrying around an empty lockbox in his heart all of these years, but now that she'd somehow unlocked the small compartment, it was as if he had lost the key.

He couldn't imagine going back to life with it closed again.

Yet, he'd have to try. It was the only way to keep her safe.

"I'm not allowed to share the details. Just know that my only motivation is, and has only ever been, to keep you safe." He paused, hating to add the words he knew would hurt her. "It's why we can't ever be together. At least not in the way most couples can be."

His words were a direct hit. Instant tears flooded her expressive eyes, but she angrily swished them away, refusing to accept his answer.

"That's such crap. I can't think of a single thing you could tell me that would convince me we aren't supposed to be together." A tear escaped, sliding down her left cheek, across her nose and towards the pillow below. "I know you feel the connection like I do."

It was supposed to be a statement, but he heard the reflection in her voice, turning it more into a hope.

His acting skills had kept him alive through the most dangerous scenarios, so he knew if he wanted to, he could summon the skill to lie––to look into her eyes and tell her it had all just been fun and games for him, bagging a famous actress.

*If I really did love her, that would be the best thing I could do for her.*

This time he cried bullshit on himself. Before factoring in love, keeping her physically safe had been all he'd thought about. It was still his primary objective.

But being in love changed everything. Her emotional well-being was equally important. He thought of the precarious nature of her eating disorder, certain she would revert into full blown anorexia if he handled this wrong and wasn't there to care for her.

Deep anger took hold. He'd never been one to lament about the fairness of life, in part because he'd always felt like one of the lucky ones. He'd seen a lot of fucked up shit in his travels. Yet in the middle of the night, looking into the watery eyes of the woman who had changed him forever, anger at how unfair it was that they couldn't get their shot at happiness like all the other sets of lovers galled him.

The scent of their quickie after returning from Black Light still permeated the room. It calmed him, reminding him that what they had was real––tangible.

She waited for her answer, looking more distressed with each second that passed until he blew out his breath and said words he'd never said before. "I do feel the connection, baby. In fact, I'm going to tell you two things I've never said to another woman in my entire life. Things I never dreamed I'd need to confess."

The excitement on her face waned as he added, "But there's a hitch." He waited until he knew she was listening. "You can't tell anyone. Ever."

"I would never..." she quickly objected.

He cut her off. "Your life depends on it, Khloe."

"I think you're being a bit melodramatic, don't you?" She tried to play it off nonchalantly, but he could see the worry that he was telling the truth in her gaze.

Ryder took a deep breath and broke the vow he'd taken the day he'd been sworn in as a CIA operative. "I'm not military, but I do work for the government. My job is dangerous. I've made many enemies."

"I hate the idea of you being in danger."

"I can take care of myself. It's you I'm worried about."

"Me? Why would I be in danger?" She didn't understand. She hadn't put the dots together yet.

"Baby, my enemies have deep pockets and long memories. It isn't a problem retiring can solve."

She was quiet as she internalized his words, coming to the conclusion he knew would dawn on her eventually. "And my fame has the potential to put you on the front page of magazines and lead off stories on the nightly news."

He didn't affirm her statement. There was no need.

"So I'm the one putting you in danger and not the other way around?"

Whoa. What the hell?

"Are you fucking kidding me? Don't you dare put an iota of blame on yourself. You've worked so hard. You deserve every award coming your way. It's your dream, Khloe, and I couldn't be happier for your success."

"But being seen in public with me puts you in danger of being recognized, right?"

"Yes, but..."

"So I'll retire."

"Over my dead body. And anyway, fame doesn't work like that

and you know it. You could retire tomorrow and for the rest of your life, people will recognize you. And you deserve that. You worked hard for it."

"Fine, then you'll retire."

"Honey, I'd do it in a heartbeat if I thought it would help, but like I said, the damage has been done. The men who hate me will stop at nothing. If it were just me, I'd say bring it on. But being seen with you scares the shit out of me because before you, the worst they could do to me was end my life. You would be a gift to them they couldn't pass up. I've seen firsthand what they do to women. The thought of them discovering how important you are to me terrifies me."

His voice quavered with the emotion he was struggling to hold back. He had to make sure she understood how grave the situation was. Make sure she understood how critical it was to keep their brief affair hidden from the world.

Her tears were coming harder as his truth seeped in. "So that's it? Just like that? We give up?"

He reached for her, pulling her into his arms and rolling to his back until his chest was her pillow as she let loose, sobbing hard enough for both of them. He had to swallow often to choke back his own anguish, thinking about the corner they'd been backed into. The only thing that helped him was being able to stroke her long, velvety hair and whispering a lie, "It's going to be okay," over and over, wishing it were true.

After ten minutes, her sobs had turned to sniffles. He felt the pool of wetness on his chest, hating that he couldn't magically fix her sadness.

Her quiet question felt loud in the silence. "Why did you finally tell me the truth?"

He'd hoped that telling the truth would get easier, but it wasn't working. "Because you deserve to understand. I left you last time because I had to return to my mission but..." He paused, hating the next words more than any he had ever uttered in his life. "But the next time I leave, it'll be because it's the only way to keep you safe."

She hugged him harder, clinging to him as if she could physically force him to stay. "What is the other thing?"

"Sorry?"

"Before. You said you were going to tell me two things you've never confessed before. What is the second thing?"

His heart lurched with a cocktail of emotion he'd never felt before. Desire to tell her the truth warred with his normal practical intellect telling him to say whatever would help her forget about him the fastest. He'd listened to that voice the last time they'd parted ways on Valentine's night, forcing him to say the hurtful words that their time together had just been a game to him. In that moment, he remembered the pain in her eyes as his words had struck her.

God help him, but he would never do that to her again.

In one swift motion, Ryder rolled them closer to the center of the mammoth bed. Khloe's back was pressed into the mattress as he let his weight blanket her, grinding his semi-hard cock into her as he grabbed her hands, intimately linking their fingers as he forced her arms up and out, spreading her before him like an offering.

Their faces were inches apart. Red blotches surrounded her wet, swollen eyes. Snot dripped from her nose. And yet to him, she'd never been more beautiful. This was the Khloe Monroe the rest of the world would never get to see. The one meant for him alone in their intimate moments where she let her public facade fade and bared herself to him, allowing him to glimpse the woman at the core of the celebrity.

The woman he'd fallen in love with.

"I... well..." The confident Dom who kicked ass and took names most days had fled, leaving him to chart the new emotional waters alone. He took a deep breath and plunged forward. "I decided you deserved to know the whole truth about why I to have to leave again." Her tears were back, rolling down the outside corners of her eyes, down to soak her hair. Khloe started to struggle to free herself, unwilling to lay there as he talked of deserting her again.

"I love you, Khloe Monroe." It was a declaration. Loud and clear.

She froze beneath him, surprise and relief warring on her face. "Oh, thank God. I've wanted to tell you I loved you too, but I was so afraid I'd scare you off. Everything's going to be okay. It has to be."

He couldn't take the sound of her crying again. He crashed his mouth against hers in an attempt to end the painful confession hour.

He'd said his piece, not that it changed what had to happen. He'd find her stalker and make sure they regretted ever threatening the woman he loved. He'd see them sent to jail and then make sure Trevor had all he needed to form an impenetrable security blanket around Khloe in case the Volkovs ever found out his deepest secret.

*And then I'll disappear again. It's the only way to keep her safe.*

The deep sadness of not waking up beside her every day in his future tampered the passion of his kiss, slowing it to the tender exploration of lovers. He released her hands, letting her hug him tightly around his neck as he cupped her damp face in his own palms. She clung to him holding him close, while opening her legs wider, thrusting her ass off the bed as if desperate to take him inside her.

He was happy to oblige, letting his now hard cock slide through her wet folds, piercing her core slowly... reverently... lovingly. He yanked his lips from hers, needing to look into her eyes as he consciously made love for the first time ever.

Ryder Helms had fucked many women in his life, performing any number of extremely intimate actions between the sheets, but nothing in his life had prepared him for the intensity of his connection to the woman moving beneath him. She'd ruined him.

These few days together would never be enough, yet they would be all that they had. As he stroked his shaft deeper with each thrust, he again started memorizing everything about this moment. He knew he'd recall it many times over in the coming years, his only tenuous connection to what he was losing. In that moment, he knew it was so much more than Khloe herself. He was losing his shot at a family. Children. The house with the white picket fence, or in the case of his love, the beach house in Malibu.

He felt his own tears streaking down his face, refusing to hide them from her, hoping they would bring her comfort later, helping her understand he'd told her the truth.

Khloe turned their D/s dynamic topsy-turvy by pressing against his chest, rolling their still linked bodies until it was Ryder's back flat against the mattress. She straddled him, pressing her slight weight down and holding his phallus as deep inside her womb as it could touch. His little minx rocked against him, treating him to a sexy ride like none other, lifting and falling erratically as they each enjoyed the sound of their bodies slapping together.

She toyed with him, proving how much power he'd ceded to her, bringing him close to his peak again and again, and then backing off, leaning down to suck on one of his nipples. He watched her confidence growing as she pushed his buttons in a way he'd never experienced before.

He was supposed to be letting her say goodbye in her own way, but too late he realized the error in his strategy. She had pulled him in closer. Giving him a glimpse of the *more* he'd be walking away from.

The emotions were too much. He wanted... no *needed*... control again.

He had her on her back in a flash, driving so deep she cried out. He let his desperation flare, yanking her knees up and out, pinning them down next to her ears and folding her in half.

Her only warning was his anguished cry of her name into the dark. His "Khloe!" marked the tip of his hardness bumping against her cervix, pulling a cry of physical pain from her to mingle with their emotional ache. He turned his body over to the sentiment, possessing her pussy with long, demanding strokes.

"Come with me, baby," he invited as hot spunk threatened to spurt from his cock.

He was hanging on by a thread. Precarious. Her request caught him off guard. "Promise me, Ryder."

She paused and he had to slow down his thrusts to keep from orgasming. "I'm not sure I can promise anything, baby."

Their bodies stilled in unison, recognizing they needed to sort things out before finishing.

She was panting as she continued. "Promise me... you won't leave without saying goodbye. At least give me that much."

He shouldn't make that promise. Any number of things could happen that would call for his sudden disappearance. He made the only promise he could in that moment.

"I promise I won't leave without at least getting a message to you through Davidson. I don't trust many people with your safety, but I do trust him."

"But..."

"Princess, I'll do my best to not disappear on you, but don't make me make a promise I may not be able to keep." He paused, their bodies still primed and ready to explode.

Her simple, "Okay," sealed their dealings. They loved each other. He'd promised to do his best not to leave her without saying goodbye. As sad as that was, that was the best they could muster at the moment.

He moved his hips again, slowly pumping into her, building their joint pleasure until they exploded together in one shattering completion. As his spurts of cum emptied into her body, he felt the last shred of control desert him, leaving him completely bare before her.

He pulled her to him as he rolled their linked bodies until he had her cradled on top of him again. The room was beginning to lighten with the coming dawn. Too soon it would be daylight and they would have to move forward, no matter how much each of them dreaded it.

They were both exhausted, but he was sure neither would sleep again that night, each refusing to waste one minute of their limited time together. He wasn't sure how much time had passed before he heard her quietly say, "I love you, Ryder."

If only love was enough.

CHAPTER 22

"Whoa. What the hell happened to you?" Trevor greeted them at the elevator on the main floor of Runway the next morning.

"Shut up," Khloe quipped, unable to handle the pity she saw in her friend's eyes as he looked her up and down. Even though they weren't outside yet, she pulled the large sunglasses out of her purse, anxious to hide her bloodshot eyes. With any luck, Trevor would think they were hungover.

Her security guard turned his attention to Ryder next to her, reaching to pull her suitcase away as he added, "You don't look much better."

Ryder dished it back. "You heard the lady. Shut the fuck up."

Trevor grumbled, "Good morning to you, too," as he turned to lead the way towards the two-story glass entrance.

Khloe leaned heavily on Ryder as he stepped closer, wrapping his arm around her waist as they crossed the expansive dance floor. The only sign of life in the closed club was the distant sound of a vacuum cleaner and the burly security guard standing at the entrance, ready to unlock the door to let the VIP guests depart.

She was relieved they wouldn't see their trio of hosts in the light of day. Not only because she was unsure if she could look them in the face after watching them fucking each other like rabbits on the floor of Black Light the night before, but more importantly because she knew they would pick up on her utter despair.

The night before had been one of the best... and worst... of her life. She tried not to feel bitter that some of the highest highs of her personal life and career were colliding spectacularly with equally low lows, leaving her confused and shell shocked. She was still trying to internalize all that she'd learned from Ryder the night before, unable to accept with the same certainty as him that they had no future.

The simple touch of his hand as they dashed from the building into the waiting limo made her heart constrict with a desire so deep she thought she might die if he let go. She'd never felt this way about anything or anyone, and it terrified her.

Ryder pulled her into his lap as soon as he was seated in the luxury car. Her panic receded as his arms enveloped her. She snuggled against his shoulder, inhaling his unique scent to help calm her.

She hated how clingy she felt, but it couldn't be helped. She'd begged him to tell her the truth and like it or not, he had. Now she had to deal with the knowledge that he could, and probably would, leave her again as soon as her stalker was caught.

How ironic that twenty-four hours ago the worst scenario she could have thought of was never finding who had been terrorizing her, leaving her feeling forever insecure. Now, a few hours later, she'd give anything to never get to the bottom of the case if it would mean Ryder would stay with her.

She had tuned out the men, lost in thought. Ryder's words jarred her back to the present.

"I'll be in the theater office, watching the security monitors." To his credit, Trevor listened as Ryder took charge, laying out the plan to keep her safe at that day's event. "I emailed my office.

They're sending over a package of top-end security equipment by courier. I'll need a few minutes alone with you to go through everything before we leave for the theater."

"Got it." Trevor hesitated before adding, "The office, eh? Which office would that be?"

"The 'none-of-your-damn-business' office," Ryder groused.

"Bullshit. You're nervous, and I get the impression nothing makes you nervous. So understandably, now I'm nervous. All I'm asking is for you to level with me on what has you watching out the back window, afraid we're being tailed by the boogieman. And don't tell me Khloe's stalker has you rattled like this."

Khloe hugged Ryder closer, understanding for the first time the agony he must have been going through since returning to her life. Wanting desperately to protect her... yet knowing his presence put her in a different kind of danger.

"You should tell him," she whispered against his neck where she'd snuggled in.

"Khloe." It was a warning.

She didn't listen. "I trust him. You should too."

Ryder growled, running his fingers through his cropped salt and pepper hair with frustration. "I trust him too. That's not the problem. The more you both know, the more danger you're in."

"So you're active duty then?" Trevor was fishing for info.

Ryder shut him down. "Enough. All you need to know is that I have powerful enemies. Men who would relish taking out their revenge on the woman I love instead of me, which means they must never link me to Khloe in any way. Not at today's event. Not in the tabloids. Not ever."

Ryder paused long enough that the sound of her renewed crying filled the quiet of the enclosed space. "Shhh, baby. It's okay."

"It's not okay! It will never be okay!"

He rocked her gently, letting her cry it out until she felt the car coming to a stop. The Marriott was only a few minutes away from

Runway. She needed more time to pull herself together before she could get out.

"Damn, the bloodhounds must have seen me leave and suspected I would be returning with Khloe. I recognize that group over there as some of the aggressive paparazzi that chase after her ruthlessly."

Ryder yelled to the driver through the small half-open partition. "Take us around to the loading dock entrance," before barking at Trevor to call the hotel's head of security to meet them there.

Fifteen minutes later, they had finally made it through the back of house corridors and into the housekeeper's service elevator that would take them to the penthouse suite. The industrial-sized elevator was slow and loud, yet unfortunately, not loud enough to mask the sound of her stomach growling with hunger.

"I'll order us up some brunch as soon as we get to the suite," Ryder promised.

"Oh goodie," she deadpanned, earning her a quick swat to her bottom.

Trevor did his best to ignore their intimacy as he let them know, "Ricky already has a buffet set up in the kitchenette of the suite for us and the staff. The team was starting to arrive when I was leaving. I'm guessing they'll all have eaten and be waiting for you by now."

They exited the elevator and only had a short distance to walk before they arrived at the double-doors labeled PRESIDENTIAL SUITE in large block letters. Trevor pulled out a packet of keys, handing one electronic card to Ryder.

"Hold up. Before we go in, give me a run down of everyone who you expect to be here today."

"Right now, it's just Cathy, her normal makeup artist, and Randy on hair. You haven't met Ricky yet, but he's trying to keep everyone on task. The dress designer has a crew here and then there are two general assistants who the studio sent over. I've met them before." He paused, before adding, "And, of course, the Kaplans are here. They booked the connecting room to stay close."

"Oh goodie again." This time, she glanced at Ryder, daring him to swat her ass.

He grinned. "I couldn't agree more."

Unfortunately, before Trevor could finish his listing, the booming voice of Dean Reynolds greeted them through the door.

Trevor's face contorted with anger. "And then Reynolds showed up as a surprise guest."

As they opened the door, the annoying voice of her ex could be heard as he chastised Ricky for ordering only flat water instead of sparkling.

Despite the tension in the room, Khloe had to fight the urge to laugh at the ridiculousness of Dean's temper tantrum, particularly in light of the heavy shit going down in her life.

The bang of the heavy door slamming closed behind them drew everyone's attention to the new arrivals.

She was glad she'd left her sunglasses on. It gave her the courage to address her ex. "You know, Dean, if you don't like the refreshments in my suite, you are welcome to leave and order whatever you'd like up to your own room."

"There you are, snookems. I was getting worried about you," Dean dared.

Ryder's grip on her hand grew so tight she almost had to gasp.

Trevor moved farther into the room, putting himself between her ex and the angry man glaring at the pretty-faced actor who was too stupid to know he was about to get his mug punched if he didn't stop ogling her.

"Maybe you hadn't heard. This is my room, too," Dean spouted.

"Excuse me?" Ryder growled.

Trevor filled in the blanks. "Yeah. It's a good thing you stayed elsewhere because when I got back here last night, I found the Kaplans had so graciously invited Dean to share the suite. What did you say the reason was again? Oh yes, for appearance's sake," he finished, glaring at Natalie Kaplan.

Khloe couldn't believe her ears. She couldn't have been more clear with her agent and her publicist about her feelings on spending even one single second longer with Dean Reynolds than was necessary. It was her turn to squeeze Ryder's hand so hard that he released his grip, wrapping his arm around her waist instead.

"Who's the new security guy, baby? You better hope the press doesn't find out you've been slumming it with gramps here."

Ryder moved so fast it took her breath away. One second he had his arm around her and the next he had Dean lifted off the ground several inches, his back slammed against the wall so hard several items on the nearby bookshelf rattled.

Everyone in the room stood frozen, looking shocked. Everyone except Trevor, who had a shit-eating grin plastered on his face.

"Everyone out except the Kaplans, McLean and Khloe." When no one started to move, Ryder added a stern, "Now!"

Ricky and the others quickly moved into action, shuffling towards one of the suite's bedrooms. Khloe held her breath, unsure what was about to happen. Only when the door slammed closed did Ryder speak again.

"Listen up, you piece of shit. You gave up your right to breathe the same air as Khloe the day you stuck your dick in Gloria Mining's snatch. If you ever talk to her again with anything other than respect and reverence I'm going to rearrange your face. Got it, *snookems*?" When Dean didn't answer, Ryder continued on. "Within thirty seconds of your feet hitting the floor, I expect your ass to be out of this suite. I don't care where you go, but it won't be here. Khloe will meet you on the carpet later where you'll keep your fucking hands to yourself. This will be your last public appearance with her. *Ever*. Got it?"

When Dean failed to answer, Ryder pulled him away from the

wall a few inches and slammed him back again, this time knocking over several nearby books from the velocity.

"Okay. Okay. I got it," Dean shouted, finally struggling to free himself like a fish hooked on the end of a line.

Khloe had to fight the urge to giggle at the alarmed expression on Natalie's face. She was watching her publicist when Ryder added his final threat. "And Reynolds, God help you if I find out you've had anything to do with this stalker business. I've heard terrible things happen to pretty boys like you in prison."

Dean stopped struggling, his spray-on tan failing to hide how pale he'd turned at Ryder's promise. The sniveling cheater never uttered another word. As instructed, the second his feet hit the carpet, Dean Reynolds was hustling towards the door, never even looking back.

Khloe wanted to clap she'd enjoyed the entertainment so much, but she soon realized the show wasn't over yet. Ryder had turned his attention to the elder couple in the room, stalking towards them with such fervor that Natalie gasped, rushing to put the long kitchenette counter between them before shouting, "Don't you dare come near me, you barbarian! If you so much as touch me, I'll press charges."

Her pulse spiked watching her dominant lover take charge of the situation. He stopped short of the counter effectively trapping the Kaplans in the small kitchen. He crossed his muscular arms, staring her employees down with a glare that took her breath away. In that moment she had no problem visualizing Ryder as the dangerous man he'd assured her he was the night before. The knowledge brought a full body shiver, realizing how lucky she was to have him on her side.

The silent standoff continued for a full minute, until Ryder's clipped sentences directed at Hollywood's power couple revealed to her how close he was to losing his temper.

"Let me be clear. I want you gone. But for some reason, Khloe continues to want you here. She says you're the best at what you do, which I find hard to believe. For now, I'm deferring to her decision, but with the following conditions."

Bernie had stepped up next to his wife, forming a united front against Ryder. "Wait one minute, young man. You're in no position to demand conditions. You're here because I've allowed it."

Khloe could no longer be a spectator. Bernie's words infuriated her. She rushed to stand next to Ryder, as she shouted, "Enough! Ryder is here because I want him here, and I don't give a shit what you and Natalie want, Bernie. I've had enough of you ignoring my wishes. You know damn well I don't want Dean anywhere near me, yet you invite him here. I don't want to turn my stalker problem into a publicity stunt, yet you keep leaking shit to the press, and setting up interviews I don't want and never should have had to do. And the worst thing is, you were supposed to arrange to keep the crowd at bay at the Chinese Theater, yet hundreds of people were within touching distance of me."

Natalie's sour voice cautioned her. "Don't be naive, Khloe. Fame is fickle. You'll only get one chance at this. Our email box is full of up and coming artists, desperate for us to make them a star like we've done for you."

Ryder approached the counter separating them, forcing Natalie to step back with alarm. "I know your type. Throwing in digs. Trying to make her doubt herself. But, Khloe is the real deal and you know it. She has brains, looks, and talent. The whole package. And she's just getting started. Losing her as a client would be a huge blow to your reputation. So knock off the threats. Hangers-on like you are a dime-a-dozen in Hollywood, so straighten up and remember... You work for Khloe and not the other way around. If you don't, you're out of here."

"Why I never!"

The muffled ring of Ryder's cell phone in his pocket interrupted the fireworks. He dug the cell out and answered it with a gruff, "Axe?"

She couldn't hear the other end of the conversation, but she knew his friend was sharing upsetting news by the angry frown on his face.

"Hold on a sec." He pulled the phone away from his ear long enough to dismiss the Kaplans. "We aren't through here. I'm watching you."

His face softened as he turned towards her. "I need to take this call, and then I'll be back to eat with you."

"But..."

"No, buts. We'll eat first and then you can get ready."

"Ryder..."

"Khloe." It was his forceful Dom voice. "You don't get to pick and choose when you want me here. You'll eat."

"Yes, sir." She hadn't meant to add the 'sir.' It just sort of slipped out, but the feral look that leapt into his eyes at the sound of it made her glad she'd tacked it on.

The lovers lost themselves in their visual connection until Trevor cleared his throat behind her. "Well then. I'll go let the gang back in. We need to keep moving. It's getting late."

Ryder gave her one last predatory grin before he put the phone back to his ear, walking away as he added, "Talk to me, Axe."

# CHAPTER 23

The sound of gunfire filled the darkened theater. Even seeing the smoking weapon on the mammoth screen didn't calm Ryder's racing heart completely. His brain knew that the loud crack had not been the work of the Volkovs, but instead, the effort of a good sound technician working on the movie, *Dirty Business*. Standing in the back, out of the way to be sure he wouldn't be connected to the star of the show, he'd allowed himself to get lost in the spectacular drama playing for the full house of movie critics, press agents and other bigwig VIPs.

He'd seen many of Khloe's movies even before he'd met her. But he'd made sure to take in those he'd missed in their time apart, using the films as a small way to feel closer to her, if even for a few minutes. Yet he was angry that today, when he should be paying attention to everything but the film, he'd allowed himself to be drawn into the suspenseful story on the big screen.

Her performance was magnificent. He was no industry expert, but he had a unique way of judging her skills as an actress and that was that despite being madly in love with Khloe Monroe, her performance was so realistic that even he had forgotten for long moments that the gritty heroine who'd just shot her husband's killer wasn't really Stella Wade, widow, but Khloe Monroe, talented actress.

He'd never felt such pride as the entire theater jumped to their feet to give Khloe and the rest of the cast a standing ovation as the credits started scrolling. As the lights came up, he panicked when he lost sight of her. She remained humbly seated, surrounded by the cheering accolades of her peers. When she finally stood, he could see the adorable blush on her face, reminding him of how unpretentious she was compared to other leading ladies who'd be milking the limelight for all it was worth.

A throng of well-wishers started crushing around Khloe to congratulate her on the film's success. A pang of jealousy sliced through his heart as Jaxson and Chase flanked her closely, keeping the crowd from crushing the star of the moment.

*That should be me. I should be protecting her right now.*

The enormity of their impossible situation was starting to sink in as he watched the woman he loved being hugged and kissed by dozens of people uninhibited by the dangerous baggage he would drag around with him like an iron anchor every day of his life until either he or the Volkov brothers were dead.

When he caught sight of the pimpled coffee boy from the studio trying to press to the front of the throng surrounding Khloe, Ryder used the small two-way radio to alert McLean.

"Peter's moving closer. You have eyes on him?"

Trevor's voice was clear in his left ear, courtesy of the tiny speaker he'd had sent over from Langley.

"Yeah, I've got him. He's holding something that's wrapped up. I'm moving in closer."

"Roger that."

Knowing McLean was there to take close protection of Khloe, Ryder scanned the crowd for other threats, still uncertain who was at the heart of the stalking activities. Axel had uncovered several hot leads, though. Like uncovering that the errand-boy wasn't actually a relative of any movie executives as Khloe had been assured. It was certainly very curious how a kid working part-time for less than minimum wage somehow had the money to travel across the country to attend every opening. Someone was paying for those trips and Axe was working on getting to the bottom of the money trail.

And while that was suspicious, and it was true the young man seemed obsessed with the actress, something felt fishy about it all. His gut told him there was no way the kid had the intelligence or means to pull off the threats against Khloe Monroe, which meant he was a dead end, or worse, a distraction. Until he could ferret out the truth, they'd have to keep a close eye on him.

Ryder scanned the room until he locked gaze with a staring Natalie Kaplan who was leveling him with a glare from the edge of the room where he'd arranged for her and her husband to be seated far from their client. He grinned at her just to piss her off.

By the time he glanced back at Khloe, she was watching him intently, waiting for him to see her. Despite the hundreds of people crowded into the room, within seconds they renewed their tenuous connection. He was struck with an almost uncontrollable urge to go to her... to hold her... to kiss her. Not being able to do any of those things made him physically ache as if he were coming down with a bug.

Khloe finally broke their visual connection to chat with the next wave of well-wishers pressing forward to her location, presumably offering up their congratulations. He watched as Peter got outwardly agitated at being continuously pushed farther away from the actress he was not so patiently trying to talk with. When he rudely elbowed an older woman in a formal gown, pressing to get physically closer to Khloe, Ryder moved into action, skirting around the edge of the room to get closer in case he needed to intervene.

Trevor, who wasn't bogged down with the same anonymity concerns, moved to stand directly behind Khloe, leaning in to talk into the ear of the only man in the room as tall as him, Jaxson, who listened and then nodded.

It took another five minutes for Peter to make it to Khloe. Knowing Ryder would want to hear, Trevor turned on the two-way communication between them so he could listen in from across the room.

"Hello Peter. I'm surprised to see you in Washington." He could hear the edge of anxiety in her voice as she addressed a possible suspect in her stalker case.

"I will follow you everywhere, Khloe. I am your biggest fan." Before she could respond, he reached into the pocket of his jacket and Trevor and Ryder both moved into action simultaneously. Trevor, being much closer, got to him first, stepping between Peter and Khloe and pushing the kid until his back crashed into Ryder's chest.

The two men sandwiched Peter between them as Ryder spoke softly in his ear. "I'd like to speak with you in private, Mr. Martinez. Come with me quietly and don't make a scene."

He clamped down, holding Peter's elbow in a firm grip as he started pulling him away from Khloe and towards one of the side exits to the theater.

Unfortunately, the kid wanted to do things the hard way and started flailing and shouting, "Let go of me. I need to talk to Khloe! I need to give her my gift!"

His shouting was drawing attention and that was the last thing Ryder needed in a room full of photographers and reporters. He hustled them faster, almost dragging the suspect along behind him as Peter stumbled to keep up. Trevor grabbed his other arm and together, they wrangled him through the side exit and into the back hallway of the theater.

Ryder had done a thorough security sweep before the movie had begun. He recognized their location and knew they weren't far from the security office. They headed in that direction as Peter put up a half-ass attempt to free himself from their grasp, uttering nonsensical sounds as they went.

Only once they had Peter in the security office did Ryder bark at Trevor. "Go back to Khloe. I'll handle this."

McLean looked like he might argue to stay, but then thought better of it. One of the two uniformed guards sitting in front of the wall of security cameras stood and took Trevor's spot helping to subdue the flailing young man and letting Ryder know, "I called my boss. He's on his way."

"That's good. Thanks."

Ryder pushed Peter into the hard-backed wooden chair next to the small table in the back of the room. When the kid tried to stand to leave, Ryder pressed his palm against his chest, forcibly detaining him.

"You aren't going anywhere until we have a little chat."

"I don't want to talk. I need to give my gift to Khloe!" The kid's voice was high-pitched and panicked. He was reaching for his pocket, but Ryder swatted his hand away, not letting him reach a possible hidden weapon.

"Put your hands on the table where I can see them."

The suspect's eyes widened, suddenly taking note of his surroundings and looking frightened. Ryder would turn the fear to his advantage.

He made a show of sitting next to him at the table as if they were going to sit down for a friendly cup of coffee together. He then offered, "I can get your gift to her, but you need to help me first."

"Help you how?" Peter's voice quavered, matching the nervous twitch of his left eye.

Ryder slipped into interrogation mode, although he was normally interviewing hardened criminals, not mentally challenged coffee-runners. He forced himself to take a softer approach with his suspect.

"Chat with me for a bit. Tell me how you got to know Khloe so well." He watched Peter's face carefully as he added, "She talks about you all the time. It's clear she cares about you."

The lopsided grin on Peter's face betrayed how innocent and naive the kid was. "I love Khloe. I want to marry her."

*In your dreams, kid.*

"You do realize most men around the globe would love to marry her, right?"

That doused the smile. "Yes, but they don't love her like I do. They only know the actress, but she is my friend. She is nice to me."

"I can see that. Is that why you traveled to New York and now D.C. to attend her release parties? How is it you got invited to the studio galas?"

"I'm not supposed to talk about it, but Khloe invited me herself."

Knowing that was false, Ryder pressed him. "She did? When did she do that?"

He looked conflicted, but eventually leaned in to talk softly as if he didn't want anyone else to hear. "I'm not supposed to tell anyone, but she sent me plane tickets and money. All she wanted was for me to bring her sweets in exchange."

Either the kid was truly delusional or someone had paid for him to fly across the country multiple times which made no sense. Trusting his gut, Ryder asked, "You wouldn't have one of the tickets by chance, would you?" When Peter seemed uncertain, Ryder added, "I sure would love to touch something that Khloe had touched."

His comment placated Peter who reached into his coat pocket and pulled out an envelope full of papers. The block handwriting on the front caught Ryder's attention. It looked suspiciously like the same writing in one of the threatening letters left behind in Khloe's trailer at the studio.

"I like your handwriting." He fished. Peter was confused so Ryder pointed at the front of the envelope.

"That's not my handwriting. That's Khloe's."

Any idiot would know that the unsightly block letters were not the script of the elegant and feminine Khloe Monroe. Still, he used it to his advantage, holding the edges of the envelope in a way to preserve any fingerprints that might be found. So far, the police forensics hadn't discovered any new clues using fingerprints found on the messages, but that only meant that the stalker had never been arrested or didn't have a job where their fingerprints were on file with authorities.

Ryder had been collecting and sending fingerprint samples of all of the people close to Khloe to Axel and the private forensics team he'd hired to work outside of the police limitations. One of Cathy's makeup brushes. A bottle of Randy's hair product. He'd even nabbed an empty soda can from the director on the set, and various other odds and ends for as many of the people who regularly interacted with Khloe as he could.

So far, the tests had turned up nothing of interest, but he was waiting on a call back from Axel with results from the latest evaluation on the samples of Ricky, the Kaplans, and Dean Reynolds that he'd collected at the Marriott and transmitted over images of earlier that day.

Being careful not to touch anything but the edge, Ryder pulled out the packet of papers in the envelope, laying it out carefully on the table.

"Be careful. I don't want you to hurt anything that Khloe gave me," Peter pressed nervously.

Ryder didn't bother looking up, but responded. "Kid, I wouldn't dream of it."

At first, the pile didn't make a lot of sense to Ryder. It was an odd collection of old plane tickets from the past mixed with cards with simple words like 'ECLAIR,' 'FUDGE' and 'CHOCOLATE BROWNIE,' scrolled in the same block writing. Mingled in were candid photos of Khloe in private moments, unaware she'd been photographed.

Ryder's blood boiled that someone had been spying on her. He held up a vaguely familiar photo of a jogging Khloe on the boardwalk at the beach.

"When did you take this photo?" he pressed Peter for answers.

The kid looked confused. "I didn't take it."

"Then who did?" Ryder snapped.

"I don't know. I do know Khloe wanted me to have it. It came with the plane ticket to New York City."

Ryder forced his voice to stay calm. "What else came with that delivery?"

When Peter sat silently, he added a stern, "Show me."

Peter fumbled with the materials in front of him. Ryder hated that any fingerprints other than the kid's might be getting ruined, but since he suspected Peter had handled them dozens of times already, it probably didn't matter.

He pulled out several more photos from the packet. The card with the word ECLAIR on it. A photo of Khloe's Chelsea apartment, the address clearly displayed. A snapshot outside of the Lincoln Square Theater where Peter had shown up.

Ryder held up the photo of her apartment. "Did you go here? Is this how you knew where she lived?"

"What? No. I didn't go to her apartment. I went to the theater." He seemed genuinely flustered.

Ryder looked down at the spread out pile of materials on the table and the glint of metal caught his eye. Infuriated, he reached out and picked up a keyring with two keys on it.

"Is that why you have the keys to Khloe's apartment right here?"

Peter shrunk back, throwing his hands up as if to shield himself from Ryder's forceful interrogation. The kid melted into a pool of nervous tears. "The keys came in the same package, but I didn't know what they were for!"

As he reviewed the materials, Ryder remembered where he'd seen the photo before.

He pounded his fist on the table, making Peter jump. "You expect me to believe that? You just happened to have keys to the very apartment that was broken into while she was away? The very apartment where a copy of this same photo was found hanging on the mirror in her house?"

He shoved the picture into Peter's face, forcing him to look at it. It was one of those in the shrine that had been set up in Khloe's bathroom––the break-in that had scared the woman he loved half to death.

Peter had dissolved into a full-blown panic attack, rocking nervously as he covered his ears with his hands as if he could block out Ryder's questions.

That was the minute he knew without a shadow of a doubt that Peter Martinez was not the stalker. He wasn't mentally capable of planning and pulling off the break-ins and threats. The coffee-runner was a patsy at best, setup to deflect any suspicion from the real stalker. A victim. Maybe not in the same way Khloe had been, but a victim nonetheless.

The head of security chose that time to make his entrance, raising his eyebrow as if to question what was going on. Ryder stood and gave him instructions.

"Call the police in..."

At the sound of Ryder's instruction, Peter howled, afraid he was in more trouble. Ryder sat back down to speak to Peter again.

"Hey, that's enough. How would you like to help Khloe?"

Peter's crying reduced, proving he was listening so Ryder continued on.

"You want to help her, don't you?"

"Yes." His reply was pitiful.

"Okay then. We're going to have the police come in and look through the packet of information that you say Khloe sent to you. We need to check for fingerprints and clues because, Peter, Khloe didn't send this. Someone who is trying to hurt her sent it."

"But why would anyone want to hurt Khloe?" He was so fucking naive.

"I don't know the answer to that, but I sure as hell am going to keep digging until I find out. And that's where you can help. There are clues in this that we need to evaluate."

"You won't take any of it away, will you?"

"I don't know. Maybe, but I'll talk to Khloe and make sure she can replace anything that is missing, okay? Can you help?"

"I guess."

Ryder pushed to his feet again, as his phone started ringing in his pocket. It was the call he'd been waiting for from Axel. He was about to answer when Peter called out to him.

"Wait!"

He turned back, unsure until Peter picked up the small package wrapped in wrapping paper as if it were a gift. Ryder tried to make sense of it all.

"Please take this brownie to Khloe. She loves chocolate."

Ryder reached out to take the small package from Peter's outstretched hand. He didn't want to tell the kid that the chances of Khloe Monroe eating the calories in the huge dessert were slim to none, but he didn't dash the kid's hopes.

"Sure kid. I'll see she gets it." After he took the sweet treat from Peter, he turned to head towards the door, pressing ANSWER on his phone.

"Helms here."

# CHAPTER 24

"So, Khloe. I think you need to tell your fans who the mystery man was last week in Hollywood. You know. The hunk who rode up on the Harley and whisked you away on the back of his bike, beaded evening gown and all. It was so romantic." The reporter shoved her microphone in front of Khloe expectantly.

Khloe's feet were killing her as she stepped into the last of the dozen media booths set up in the grand lobby of the Landmark Theater. She'd been answering entertainment reporters' questions for over an hour now and she was done. Every ounce of patience was gone, and she desperately needed to sit somewhere quiet and regroup. Instead, she had to answer the hard questions.

"Sorry, Paula. There is no mystery. Things were getting a bit rowdy and my security detail arranged to have me whisked out of the fray. It's all rather boring, actually."

Khloe had had to put her acting skills to good use on the red carpet tonight. Hiding her breakup with Dean had been hard enough after they'd sat apart at the screening, but concealing the fact that she was being stalked and now denying she had any feelings for the mystery man who had swept her off her feet in Hollywood made for a tiring trifecta of deceit. Only time would tell how acceptable a job she was doing at fooling the press.

Ricky and Trevor were waiting for her as she extricated herself from the figurative grip of the last invasive reporter.

"I can no longer feel my feet," she grumbled under her breath as she leaned on her security guard's offered arm for support.

"You should have worn flats. No one can even see your feet in that gown anyway."

"Men. Everyone knows you don't wear flats to a gala event."

"Women. Everyone knows they care more about appearances than comfort."

Ricky piped in to support her. "I'm a man and even I'm not wearing flats."

Trevor bantered back. "Yeah, well you bat for the other team so..."

"Guys. Really?" Khloe scolded.

The men at least had the decency to look sheepish. Khloe would love to debate with them, but she was too damn tired. Lack of sleep, the stress of the stalker, much too little food and most importantly, Ryder's pending departure, were adding up to her feeling woozy on her feet.

"Where are Bernie and Natalie? They were supposed to be with me as I did the interviews today to help run interference with the press."

When Trevor didn't answer, she looked up the several inches until their eyes met. She didn't know how to interpret the anger she saw in his gaze.

"Seems they took off early for the hotel."

"Let me get this straight. My agent and my publicist left the D.C. opening of my newest movie without even being seen with me?"

Trevor added, "Pretty much. I think they were peeved at being seated on the sidelines."

"Actually, I think Ryder scared them away. They really don't like him," Ricky added.

When Khloe stumbled on her long dress, Trevor caught her, stopping her from falling flat on her face.

"I want to leave," she begged through clenched teeth, a forced smile on her face.

"But..." Ricky started to argue, but Trevor gratefully agreed.

"It's fine. You've completed everything on the agenda. I texted to have your limo brought around. Let's move towards the door and say our goodbyes."

She asked softly, "Where is Ryder?"

"He got some new information and is talking with the police." Trevor looked nervous as he added, "He'll meet us later."

"I don't want to leave without him," Khloe argued.

Trevor reassured her, "He said you'd say that. He also told me to tell you he'll keep his promise. Not sure what that means, but he said you'd know."

Ryder was reminding her of his promise not to disappear without saying goodbye, but in the end what would it matter? He would still be leaving. Still be saying goodbye and taking her heart with him.

Unwanted tears pricked at her eyes, and she fought to keep from letting it turn into a full-blown bawling session. Not this close to the press corps still interviewing other key players from *Dirty Business*.

*I have to at least make it to the car before I lose it.*

By the time the limo pulled up fifteen minutes later, Khloe was ready to drop. She needed to start working out again. She'd been too busy, and she hated feeling fragile. She pushed down the nagging inner voice telling her she'd feel stronger if only she ate better.

Trevor had been texting the entire fifteen minutes as they made their way to the exit. Even now, he waited to open the door until he'd sent another reply, which was mildly annoying for a woman desperate to get off her feet.

Khloe let Ricky get in first before following, allowing herself to sink into the middle of the plush leather back seat of the limousine. Only once Trevor was seated and the door slammed closed did she realize that the Kaplans were already seated on the bench seat across from her, facing the back of the car.

"There you are. I was looking for you inside. You were supposed to help run interference for my interviews."

"Oh, so now you want us nearby, yet you couldn't be bothered to save us seats next to you for the premier," Natalie groused.

Khloe tried to keep a straight face as she replied, "I'm not sure what the mix up was." She paused, pinning her publicist with a glare before adding, "Perhaps it was the same mix up that had Dean invited to the New York premier."

Bernie attacked Khloe with his now familiar negative lecture. "Don't get cute with us, young lady. You know damn well everything we've done for you has been with one thing in mind-- your success. It's bad enough that you refuse to acknowledge how much we've helped your career, but now you and that hoodlum of yours attack our good name and reputation. I have half a mind to drop you as a client."

A few months ago, the threat of losing the backing of Hollywood's oldest powerhouse duo would have been one of the worst-case scenarios Khloe could have come up with. It was a testament to how much had recently changed for her when her first thought of never seeing the Kaplans again was of relief. Still, she couldn't afford to be reckless. She'd start looking for their replacement, but until then, she'd have to play nice.

"Don't be dramatic, Bernie. You need me, like I need you. You're in the middle of negotiations on that script the studio sent over a few weeks ago."

She watched as the older man puffed out his chest in an exaggerated show of arrogance that made her want to laugh.

"I am about to get you a three-hundred percent pay raise, young lady and don't forget it."

Trevor flinched next to her as he uncharacteristically jumped in to defend her. "Every additional penny Khloe gets for her next film is the result of her hard work and talent and nothing else. You're getting rich off her. In fact, I have it on good authority the initial package offered had a higher base pay for Khloe, until someone negotiated a bigger commission percentage off the top with the studio."

Bernie's double chin shook as he nodded like some bobble-head figure stuck to a dashboard. She'd never seen his face turn that shade of reddish-purple before.

"How dare you even insinuate such a thing? Why are you even speaking anyway? Bodyguards are meant to be seen and not heard."

Trevor broke into an angry grin. "Seems you're a bit paranoid there, Bernie. I didn't name any names."

Impossibly, the elder Kaplan's face grew a shade darker. It looked like he might spectacularly pop like an overinflated balloon.

Natalie patted her husband's knee softly as if to calm him as she rebutted. "You don't know what you're talking about."

Khloe had never seen Trevor so aggressive with anyone, let alone the Kaplans before.

He didn't let up. "I trust my sources. They've brought me some good intel recently."

"And what sources would that be?" Natalie did the talking for the duo.

"The private detectives we hired to get to the bottom of Khloe's stalker case. They've dug up a number of interesting tidbits."

Where Bernie's face remained the ugly purple, Khloe couldn't help but notice Natalie's complexion turning chalky white in the limo's interior lighting. Her sixth sense was piqued as Trevor's hand fell on her leg, squeezing her gently through her gown.

Natalie stammered, "We didn't authorize any private detectives."

"And why is that, exactly? I mean, not that we needed your permission, but I would have thought it would be the first thing you'd do to protect your paycheck." Trevor's grip on her thigh tightened as Khloe internalized what he'd said.

Khloe confronted her agent. "Wait a minute. Bernie, you told me that the studio was going to hire private detectives to work the case to keep it on the down-low from the press."

It was Trevor who responded, not the older man sitting across from her. "The studio did authorize it. They even cut a twenty-five thousand dollar retainer check they were told was needed to secure the very best security firm in L.A."

Khloe relaxed slightly. She'd panicked, surely misunderstanding Trevor's words. For a second there, she'd thought the Kaplans had lied to her. Then she replayed Trevor's words again in her head, and the uneasy flutter in her tummy turned to a full-blown churn.

"So if the studio paid for an investigation, why did you say you didn't authorize it? And what exactly have they dug up?" Khloe pinned Natalie with her glare, recognizing Bernie had gone mute.

The older woman across from her went on the attack. "Investigations like this take time. Unlike your nosy bodyguard here and that heathen of a man you've been degrading yourself with, Missy, we don't interfere and try to tell the professionals how to do their job. I trust that they'll call me as soon as they have a lead or other important information they need to share."

Trevor leaned forward so far that Natalie shrunk back, leaning against her husband as she listened to the bodyguard's response.

"I've been pressing you for updates for days. Until today, I was annoyed by your apathy, but things are falling into place. It's a good thing I wasn't holding my breath waiting for an update since it will never come, will it, Natalie?"

"How dare you! You're an employee. I'm Mrs. Kaplan."

Trevor's bark of a laugh filled the otherwise quiet car. "That's rich. I think you have your priorities a little out of whack there, lady. You have a few bigger things to worry about than what I call you. The only reason I haven't gone to the police with what I know already is that, as you've pointed out, I'm much more than a bodyguard to Khloe. First and foremost, I think of her as my friend, which is why I'm confronting you here, in the privacy of the limo."

"Trevor, why does it feel like I'm the only one here who doesn't have a fucking clue what you guys are talking about?"

Ricky spoke under his breath. "You aren't the only one who's clueless."

Trevor pressed on, addressing the Kaplans. "Are you going to tell her, or am I?"

Bernie finally found his voice again as he growled. "I don't know what the hell you're talking about, but you're fired. When we get to the Marriott, you have ten minutes to get your things from the suite and then you're gone."

Khloe's heart raced. She hated conflict, which was just one of the many unique qualities that set her apart from most of her Hollywood peers who thrived on stirring up trouble and demanding things of the people around them. There was no way she was going to sit on the sidelines of this battle, though.

"Trevor is my employee, not yours. He isn't going anywhere except where I go." She paused, feeling the clamp of her friend's grip on her thigh before confronting the older couple. "You have exactly thirty seconds to start telling me whatever the hell secret it is that you've been keeping from me or it will be you who has ten minutes to clear your things out of our suite when we get back to the Marriott."

Natalie shouted, "You little bitch. After all we've done for you.

The risks we've taken to get you the publicity you need to move into the highest echelon of celebrity."

"What risks? I'm the one getting the threats! I'm the one whose life has been turned upside down by one of the kooks your publicity stunts has fleshed out. Don't think I don't know that you've been planting tidbits about the stalker case with your press contacts. Almost every single interviewer today asked me about it, and they all seemed to have information that I know we didn't release to the wider press corps. You know I didn't want any part of using the criminal case to get negative publicity."

"You are so naive. There is no such thing as negative publicity. Do you have any idea how hard it is these days to compete with the glut of information online? How impossible it is to get a story trending on Twitter and Facebook? I apologize for nothing I've done in the name of doing my job of promoting you."

"I never asked for an apology. I'll settle for the truth."

"You don't want the truth. You want the impossible. You want to just magically wake up and be America's Sweetheart."

"You don't know the first thing about me, Natalie. Do I want to make it big? Sure. I'll give you that. But I don't want to be known for wearing the most exclusive gown or making the biggest splash when I enter a room. Those may be nice perks, but what's always been most important to me is that I get quality roles. That I continue to hone my craft and become a sought-after actress. And not because I'll make more money, but because producers and directors want my talent."

Bernie found his voice. "Wake up, Khloe. Hollywood and New York City are full of talented artists, just like you. You know what most of them are doing? Waiting tables. It takes a lot more than talent to make it in show business and you know it. If you'd get your head out of your ass, you'd see how good Natalie and I are at making superstars."

Trevor cut her off as she opened her mouth to reply. "I'd like to ask a few questions about just how low you would stoop to make those so-called superstars? Let's start with Robby Goldberg. Care to share how you got that asshole into the limelight? I mean it's not like he has an ounce of the talent that Khloe does."

It was Natalie's chest that puffed out proudly this time. "Exactly, and yet we were responsible for his being nominated for a People's Choice award last year. The fans love him."

Trevor scoffed. "The fans don't love him. They pity him. They feel sorry for him."

"Whatever. The only thing that matters is he's getting more offers now than he can possibly handle. He's a household name."

Khloe's brain raced to remember as much as she could about the low-talent, highly-sought-after actor who'd come out of nowhere in the last few years. The only thing she could remember about him was that his son was sick with some terminal disease.

"Whatever happened to his young son? Did he pull through? What was his illness again?" The questions spilled from her mouth as they popped into her head.

They should be easy questions for the actor's agent and publicist to answer, yet the Kaplans sat silently, each refusing to look her in the eye. Her uneasy tummy churned again with an odd sense of dread that she didn't understand.

It was Trevor who answered her. "It was supposedly leukemia, wasn't it? The last press release was that he had been miraculously cured. I remember seeing Robby making all of the morning news programs to talk about the miracle of how God had cured his baby, shedding his crocodile tears. I have to hand it to him. He did at least put on a believable performance there, if not on the big screen."

She was missing something. Why would Trevor be so angry that a young child was cured? She replayed his words. *Supposedly. Crocodile tears.*

Khloe's uneasy feeling escalated. She hated the thought that had popped into her brain. Before she could ask a question, Trevor barged forward with what she could clearly now see was less of a conversation and more of an interrogation of the older couple sitting across from them.

"If you don't want to talk about Robby, then maybe you'll share your overwhelming success with launching Justin Lange's career after he suffered the loss of his wife in that horrific car accident in the Hollywood Hills. It was so unfortunate that she was killed in that single car accident, and yet Justin was able to walk away unscathed. You have to hand it to him. I'm not sure how he was able to pull it all together to make the rounds with every entertainment news program to talk about his terrible loss. Then again, I rewatched some of his interviews recently. I was amazed by his ability to overcome his grief and talk about his upcoming movie projects instead."

The Kaplans and Trevor were in a visual showdown as they sat silently glaring at each other.

"What are you trying to say, Trevor?" Khloe prodded her friend for answers that it felt like he was withholding from her.

Trevor never took his eyes off the Kaplans as he replied. "I don't need to say anything. Justin's *dead* wife has been doing all of the talking with the Mexican authorities after she was tracked down by the insurance agency's private investigator. Seems they got an anonymous tip that she might still be alive. Looks like she'd been blackmailing Justin for more cash to keep the secret that her accident had been a publicity stunt."

Natalie Kaplan's eyes widened so far it looked like they might fall out of her head. In contrast, Bernie slumped to the side, leaning against the interior of the limo as he closed his eyes and clutched at his chest.

Khloe's brain struggled to put the pieces of the puzzle together. She turned their words around, trying to make sense of it all. Trying to come up with something... anything that wasn't as incriminating as the accusations being leveled.

She shook her head as she pressed for answers. "I don't understand. You manufactured a child's illness? Why would anyone do that? And the accident?" Khloe turned the facts around, examining them from every angle before pressing forward. "You faked a woman's death without a care to how it would affect her family? I mean what kind of people would..." Her voice stopped abruptly as her brain pieced the final puzzle pieces together. The answer came out in a whisper. "My God... you did this to me."

Trevor confirmed her worst nightmare. "It was all a hoax. We know you're Khloe's stalker."

His words were like a knife to her heart. Surely if she looked down, she would find blood flowing onto her expensive gown.

Natalie incredibly boasted. "We're in the entertainment business. We feed the media what it needs, that's all. We've learned how to give them what they want, and in exchange, our clients get what they want. Exposure. Fame."

"Jail time," Trevor deadpanned.

Natalie's high-pitched laugh made her sound insane. "Don't be ridiculous. No lines have been crossed. This is show-business."

"See, that's where you're wrong. You knowingly helped Justin Lange defraud his insurance company. You helped arrange for his estranged wife to receive her payoff and even helped book a charter plane for her flight to Mexico. And don't even get me started with the questions surrounding exactly whose body it was that burned up in Justin's car that night, although I'm pretty sure the police are going to want to ask you a few questions about that."

Bernie let out a low groan as he continued to clutch at his chest.

Trevor ruthlessly continued with his verbal assault. "And the charity foundation that collected all of the donations for Robby Goldberg's son's recovery fund was very interested to hear that the young boy had actually never been diagnosed with so much as a common cold, let alone leukemia. It didn't sound like they were too happy about being used as a patsy to collect funds for a group of liars. I'd be expecting a call from their lawyers, too, if I were you."

"You sonofabitch. I don't know where the hell you're getting your information, but you have no clue what you're talking about."

"All we had to do was follow the money. The money trail never lies."

It was Ryder's voice that filled the car. Khloe had been so enthralled listening as Trevor painted the tragic picture of how unethical the Kaplans were that she hadn't seen the smoky glass partition separating the passengers from the front seat of the moving limo slide open. Her heart thumped hard as their eyes locked.

Natalie let out a shriek as she cowered away from the opening in the glass.

Ryder started adding missing details. "Axel and I have been digging into this for the last few days. We have some grave concerns about the actions of your publicist and agent, Princess. We've confirmed they had access to every location threats were left, including keys to your New York apartment. They were stupid enough to send the threatening emails from their personal laptop, allowing us to trace the accounts to their IP address. They were even cocky enough to deposit the $25,000 check the studio gave them into their personal account."

In a few brief seconds, she got answers to questions she hadn't even asked yet. Ryder and his friend Axel had dug into the case, and within a few days, had uncovered the ugly truth about people she'd trusted to help her career. More answers started clicking into place for her. How they'd pushed to use the stalker details for fodder with the press to gain Khloe additional airtime.

But why? They were so successful. Why would they stoop to illegal activities at this stage in their career? She had to know.

"Why did you do it?"

"Do what?" Natalie spat.

"Any of it. All of it. Fake her death. Fake a kid's illness. Fake my stalker."

"Like I said, don't be naive, Khloe. This is how publicity and fame work. You've been around long enough to know I'm right. You don't get to benefit from all we've done for you and your career and then complain about how we did it. I'd rather you just say thank you."

"Thank you? Are you fucking nuts? You scared the shit out of me. I thought I was going to be kidnapped. Raped."

"Well, if you weren't such a goodie-two-shoes, we would have let you in on the plan. You could have taken a nice two week vacation down to some out-of-the-way island and then come back and made the rounds with all of the media outlets to tell your story of your harrowing escape."

"You're certifiable."

"No. We're professionals. The best at what we do. I can see our talent was wasted on you, though. Effectively immediately, you are no longer our client."

Khloe's manic laughter filled the small space. "Are you kidding me? As if I'd allow you to represent me knowing what I know now."

Ryder's voice filled the interior of the luxury car again. "I'm afraid they won't be taking on any new clients. Not if I have anything to say about it."

Natalie had finally recognized her husband was in distress and had turned in her seat to help him loosen his tie, ignoring Ryder's comment. "Hang on, Bernie. We're almost to the Marriott. You can take a blood pressure pill and lay down for a bit until you feel better."

Ryder continued on, "I'm afraid that nap is gonna have to wait. I don't think where you're going has the same accommodations as the Marriott."

As he finished his sentence, the limo pulled into the parking lot of a stately brick building with a steep set of stairs leading up to a pair of extra-tall doors. As they approached the building, Khloe could make out the words above the entrance, carved into the granite; *Police Department - 10ᵗʰ District*. At the bottom of the stairs, a half dozen news crews with cameras and microphones at the ready waited alongside three uniformed police officers.

"What is the meaning of this? I demand you return us to the Marriott."

Trevor chuckled. "I'm afraid your demanding days are over, Natalie. But some good news. You're about to become the biggest story on the evening news. I know how much you love to manipulate the news cycle."

"You little shit. You think you're so funny. There's no way they'll dig up anything on us. We made sure our trail is clean."

Ryder reached through the glass to hold out a small electronic device just as Trevor removed the tie clip from his tie.

"I hate to be the bearer of more bad news, but we've already handed over all of the evidence we've uncovered. It was substantial. But to be on the safe side, we've been transmitting every word since you got into the limo to the detectives working the case. They got to hear the details of all three cases from your own mouth." Ryder grinned. "They had just planned to ask you how your fingerprints were found on the package you sent to Khloe's parents in the Bronx, but thanks to your little tirade, I'm guessing they'll have a few more questions to ask now."

Natalie pulled away from her husband to lunge at Ryder's face poking through the glass window. It was easy enough for him to pull away, leaving her to crash against the glass just before she started pounding with her fists in an angry attack. "You asshole! I knew you were trouble the minute I met you. I should have dropped Khloe then and there."

The door next to Trevor opened and one of the policemen leaned in, addressing her bodyguard, "We'll take it from here. We may have some questions for you and Ms. Monroe, but I won't make you get out into this media circus. Please don't leave town.

If we need anything else, we'll stop by the Marriott." The officer reached out to hand Trevor a business card before turning to the Kaplans.

"I need you to step out of the car now, Mr. & Mrs. Kaplan."

"I will not! There are too many cameras and reporters out there. If you have questions for us, you can come back to the Marriott for us as well."

"I'm afraid that won't be possible."

"And why not?"

"Because you're under arrest. You have the right to remain silent. Anything you say..."

The moment was surreal for Khloe as she listened to her agent and her publicist being read their rights as Trevor and the officer helped Bernie from the car before turning towards a defiant Natalie.

"I won't go. You can't make me." The elderly woman shrunk back to the far side of the car, trying to avoid the clutches of the police officer when his partner opened the door right next to her. She literally fell into the officer's arms. She flailed in an attempt to break free, but she was no match for the muscular lawman as she screamed, "You can't do this to me! Not here. Not in front of the cameras!"

When Natalie was almost out of the car, Ryder called out to her. "Don't worry! Like you said, there's no such thing as negative publicity. I'm sure you'll enjoy having your life ripped apart by the media as much as Khloe did."

They would never know if Natalie answered him because the roar of the reporters shouting the Kaplans' names, crushing forward in hopes of getting a statement and a close-up picture, drowned out any conversation. Only when Trevor got back in and he and Ricky closed the car doors did the shouting get muffled.

She should be happy that the stalker nightmare was over. It was sinking in that she'd never really been in any real danger in the first place, but that knowledge filled her with anger, not relief.

A fury like she'd never felt before was burning in her empty gut. Rage at the Kaplans for duping her and so many others. Annoyance with herself for not seeing through their underhanded tactics. Irritation with Trevor and Ryder for collaborating behind her back to interrogate the Kaplans without filling her in ahead of time.

But overriding all of those feelings was the strongest emotion of them all. Dread. Now that her stalker case looked like it would be closed, Ryder would no longer feel he needed to be there to protect her. In light of the scrutiny that was sure to come their way as the world found out about the Kaplans' lack of scruples, she knew that Ryder would be disappearing into the darker crevasses of the globe.

Just as her tears started to fall, the limo came to a stop on a residential street not far from police station. The door next to Trevor opened and Ryder motioned for her bodyguard and friend to move to the seat recently vacated by the Kaplans. Ricky followed suit, leaving the back seat for Ryder to slide in and close the door before scooping a crying Khloe into his lap.

She'd been trying to hold back her tears, but as soon as his arms enveloped her, Khloe clung to him with all of her might, letting the cocktail of emotions overcome her as she realized the case was solved.

"Shhh. It's all over now, baby," Ryder comforted.

The pent up sob she'd been holding back wailed from her as she agonized, "That's exactly what I'm worried about!"

# CHAPTER 25

*K*hloe squirmed in his arms. They were both restless. That happened when you've been holed-up in the same room for three days.

"Why are you such a wiggle-butt?" Ryder pulled her against his chest, letting her crawl on top of him as their sticky, naked bodies melded together.

Khloe giggled. "I was lying in another wet spot. We seriously need to change these sheets. I'll be mortified if Jaxson, Chase and Emma see how many cum stains there are. We may need to buy them replacements."

Ryder agreed. They'd put the round bed in their friends' loft through its paces. Three days and nights of nearly non-stop sex does that. The only other activities they'd allowed to breach their self-imposed fortress was sleeping, eating and talking into the wee hours of the night.

"Can't we stay here forever?"

She'd asked that question a half-dozen times already. He was losing his patience. Ryder was too practical to entertain such fairytale ideas.

"Khloe..." he warned, using his best Dom voice that had her burrowing into his neck.

She persisted, "But why not?"

"You know why not. We've discussed it. The only way for us to really be together the way we want to is to make sure my enemies are neutralized."

He'd had plenty of downtime to berate himself over his stupidity of leaving the Volkov fortress without putting a bullet into the head of every Volkov man. He was a realist. He didn't often waste valuable thinking time on regret, but there was no other way to describe his present state of mind.

He regretted leaving the Volkov brothers breathing. How different his life would be if only he'd ended their lives before rescuing the Marshalls. He knew there was no knowing if he'd have been successful at escaping had he alerted the guards with gunfire, but he'd wasted enough time thinking about it. He needed to start focusing on how he'd get back inside long enough to do the deed.

Khloe hugged him tighter, objecting to his next mission. "But that sounds too dangerous. I can't let you put yourself in jeopardy again."

She didn't understand. It was what he'd been trained to do. Neutralizing threats against the United States of America was his life's work. Extinguishing anything that might threaten her safety, his new mission.

He tried to change the subject. "Anyway, we're both getting a little bit stir-crazy. Next time we get together I'll be sure to find us a hideout where we can get outside some. Maybe a little beach cabana away from civilization?"

The closer they got to saying their good-byes, the more he tried to talk about the next time they'd see each other. He told himself it was to keep Khloe calm, but he knew it was for himself, too. The thought of saying good-bye to her the next morning when she needed to fly out to the London release party for *Dirty*

*Business* left him feeling empty. He dreaded the moment when he'd have to hand her security back over to McLean and walk away. He was grateful they had a trusted bodyguard to protect her, but it was nearly impossible to push down the anger and jealousy he felt at not being able to be the one to watch over the woman he loved.

Khloe's left hand traced light circles around his exposed nipple, playfully stroking him as she giggled. "Honestly, I do think my who-ha could use a bit of a break."

He chuckled, teasing her back. "Aw, poor baby. Are you getting sore?"

She lifted her hand to slap him playfully. "Having wild, crazy, monkey sex for three days straight will do that to a girl."

Ryder pounced, rolling them quickly to the middle of the bed, pinning his princess beneath him as he used his body weight to press her into the plush mattress.

"I know how to solve this problem." He grinned. "I clearly haven't been using your other body parts sufficiently if your who-ha is too sore. I think it's time to spread the soreness to that puckered ass of yours. Then I can face fuck you to make sure you have a sore-throat to remember me by tomorrow on your flight."

He watched her pupils dilate with a dash of desire and a touch of fear at his dirty promise.

"Don't worry. Those body parts are already sufficiently achy." Was it possible that she was blushing? After all of the kinky shit they'd done together, it amazed him that the woman responsible for his three-day hard-on could still come off as an innocent.

"I'm making sure you'll have something to remember me by while you're walking the red carpet in London. I wouldn't want you to forget me."

"Like that could happen." Tears sprung into her expressive eyes. He'd let her cry it out several times already. It was time for her to start gathering her strength for their coming separation.

"Enough tears. No wallowing. If you want to cry, we're going to need to go downstairs to Black Light where I can give you something to cry about."

He loved the way her eyes widened with surprise at his words. He could tell she was tempted.

"I don't want to share you with anyone," she objected quietly.

"You know we're gonna have to leave here sometime. Life goes on. You have awards to receive. Movies to make."

"I'd give it all up to stay here with you."

Ryder was frustrated. "I thought you said you were happy with the plan to sneak away and spend a few days together every few months."

"Happy isn't the right word. Am I relieved that you're not gonna walk out of my life, never to be seen again? Sure. But I'll never be happy about having to hide what we have together. About having to settle for just a few stolen days every few months."

"Baby, it's the best I can offer right now. I'm going to work night and day to eliminate the threat against us so we can be together the way we both want to be. But until my enemies are dead, this is the best I can promise."

"Why can't we talk on the phone? Or Skype? Even text."

"Those aren't secure channels. I'm having an encrypted device brought over from Langley tomorrow morning before you leave. We can't use it for daily chitchat, but you will be able to use it to contact me. To leave me a message that I'll get and return as soon as I can safely communicate. And don't forget, we can both route messages through Davidson and Cartwright. They've offered to help."

"I'm not going to pass love-notes through Jaxson and Chase. It all feels so high schoolish."

"I'm not crazy about it either. I mean it's not like I can pass along the message of how much I love you and miss fucking you until your who-ha gets sore."

A sad smile crinkled the tiny wrinkles at the corners of her gorgeous eyes.

He pressed her again. "Listen. The club is open tonight. Let's go down and play."

She hugged him tighter, wrapping her legs around his back as he pressed his growing cock against her sore snatch. "I want to stay here and keep you to myself."

"And I want to string you up and flog you until you're on fire for me."

"Sadist," she accused with a grin.

"Guilty as charged."

She wiggled beneath him, making his shaft easily slide through her wetness. "We don't need to go downstairs for me to be on fire for you."

A pang of sheer adoration squeezed at his heart as he looked down into the playful eyes of the woman he loved. He pushed down his own sadness at the thought of having to go months before they'd be together again.

He needed to get control. For both of them.

He barked his order as he rolled off Khloe, pulling her along until he could slap her on the ass as he instructed her, "To the shower. We're going downstairs to play."

Khloe scrambled to her feet, giggling as she got away from his pinching fingers. Her "Yes, sir," went straight to his cock.

*Christ, how the hell am I going to walk away from her tomorrow?*

IT WAS STILL EARLY by club standards, but Ryder was restless to get downstairs. You'd think a man who was used to being penned up for days on undercover surveillance missions wouldn't be going stir crazy, particularly considering he'd had Khloe's perfect body to keep him company for the last three days. But he knew the truth. The sooner he left, the sooner

Vladimir, Oleg and especially Artel Volkov would meet their maker. Only then, would the weight of knowing he was putting the woman he loved in danger by being in her presence be lifted.

*Maybe then I'll be able to turn on my car without wondering if that was the day I'd go boom.*

He knew Khloe was against going downstairs. She'd extended their joint shower by slipping to her knees and sucking his rod down her throat like a Goddamn pro. He both loved and hated how she had the power to weaken his resolve. The second the tip of his shaft jammed against the back of her throat, he'd lost all willpower to slow things down and save it for Black Light.

Even now, she was still in the bathroom primping, applying her dozens of creams to the hairline wrinkles around her eyes.

As if to prove to himself that he could control his own emotions, he reached for his encrypted phone, turning it on for the first time in two days. He'd allowed the police to come and ask them questions that first twenty-four hours, but then they'd both gone dark, shutting the rest of the world out as they'd hidden in Davidson's safe house.

His tension level grew with each ding of his phone, announcing he had over a half-dozen voicemail messages. Then the texts started arriving. He forced himself to read and listen to them all.

There were updates from Axel. Requests for more meeting time from the D.C. police. But the majority were escalating messages from his boss, Webster. They'd started arriving two days ago with:

*Call me right away. Have classified info you'll want.*

YEAH, well unless it's that the Volkovs are dead, Ryder highly doubted that. The next one was even more demanding.

*Dammit Helms, Chip Marshall has been trying to speak with you since you landed back on American soil. He's getting pissed at your absence. Call in.*

HADN'T he done enough for the Marshall family? Why the fuck should he waste even a minute of his limited time with Khloe talking to a guy who probably wanted to say thank you for doing his job.

He then listened to a voicemail his boss had left a few hours before.

*I know I told you to take some time off, but you've never gone dark on me. Trust me when I say that you'll want to check-in ASAP. That's an order, soldier.*

THE MESSAGE WAS out of character for Brandon Webster. A CIA lifer, he knew his boss had honed his normally calm demeanor by living through some pretty fucked up missions before taking his desk job. Ryder had always appreciated the unemotional evenness his superior displayed, even in the most stressful situations. Hearing the frustration in Brandon's voice put Ryder on edge.

He was about to ring the older man when Khloe emerged from the bathroom looking stunning in skimpy black baby-doll lingerie with a matching see-through pair of panties that barely covered her pussy and left her ass cheeks completely exposed. All thoughts of calling Webster flew out of his head. Work could fucking wait until Khloe left the next day.

Ryder's mouth went dry as he was temporarily stunned into silence, watching as she gracefully sashayed across the room towards him. The closer she got, the wider the sexy smile spread on her gorgeous face. When she was close enough to touch him, she had the audacity to reach out, lifting her finger to his chin. Only as she pressed up did he realize he'd been gawking at her with his mouth gaping open.

"See something you like?" she teased.

He had to clear his throat. "Em... fuck... You're perfect."

Her smile doused a bit. "Hardly. I weighed myself. I hope you're happy. I've gained four damn pounds."

"Hell yes, I'm happy." He pulled her into his arms, loving every single inch of her still too-thin body. "That's still six pounds too few. Remember what I told you. If you aren't at least six pounds heavier the next time I see you, you aren't going to be able to sit on this lovely ass of yours for weeks." She tried to wiggle away from him, but he held her tight, thrusting his left hand into her long damp hair and yanking her head back. He towered over her until their faces were only inches apart.

"I'm not joking, Princess. You are going to eat right and start getting plenty of sleep. I'm going to have McLean keep a log for me so I can check up on your progress."

"That's not fair! He works for me, not you. And why does he get to communicate with you and I don't?" Her pout was adorable, but he sure as hell wouldn't tell her that.

"McLean works for *us*. I'm giving him a way to get in touch with me for emergencies only. So imagine how much trouble you'll be in if he has to relay that you're losing weight again."

She opened her mouth as if to argue, but closed it again, wisely reconsidering. Ryder went in to capture those pouting lips in an open mouth kiss that had his woman melting like a candle in his arms. He kissed her rebellion right out of her, leaving a contrite submissive in his arms when he pulled out of their lip-lock.

Ryder reached into the pocket of his slacks to pull out the same thin black choker she'd worn to Black Light the week before. He loved how her eyes softened as he wrapped the heavy jewelry around her neck. The submissive bow of her head fed his dominance, flaming his need for her.

He leaned down to grab the plush terrycloth robe he'd thrown over the back of the nearby loveseat. He held it out for her to press her arms into as he warned, "We need to get the hell out of here or I'm not going to be able to stop myself from ripping that tiny scrap of fabric off your body and fucking you from behind as I splay you out across the back of this chair."

Her giggle only made his already hard cock turn to stone. Anyone watching would never know they'd had sex over a dozen times in the last two days. He put his arm around her thin waist and pulled her against his body as he moved them towards the foyer. Ryder used the electronic keycard Davidson had programed for him to call the elevator.

The trip downstairs was uneventful. The Wednesday night crowd at Runway was thin and the dance music was playing much lower than on a weekend. There was no line waiting to check in with Danny in the locker room, assuring them that Black Light's attendance was down as well. After stuffing her robe in their locker, Ryder attached the jeweled chain to her collar.

He stopped to tweak her nipple through the sheer material. "Be a good girl now."

"Yes, sir," she purred, falling into her submissive role with ease.

A smattering of members was dispersed throughout the dimly lit club. Having been holed up for several days, Ryder pulled Khloe along behind him using the jeweled chain as a leash as he headed towards the neon-lit bar. He could use a stiff drink and looked forward to consuming his two-drink limit. He hoped it would dull the growing unease of their coming farewell.

His friend and former military buddy, Spencer Cook, sat at the bar talking to his own submissive, Klara, who also happened to be the head bartender at Black Light. Klara faced the room and greeted them as they approached the bar.

"I was wondering if we'd get to see you two tonight." She smiled a warm welcome. "Would you like your usual, Mr. Helms?"

"Yep, and make it a double out of the gate. I'll take a fruit juice for Khloe."

"Yes, sir." She turned to collect the gold label Irish Whiskey from the glass shelf.

He was aware that Doms often had their submissives kneel at their feet while at the bar, but Ryder didn't want to waste a single minute of touching Khloe while she was within his grasp. When she moved to kneel behind him, he motioned for her to instead squeeze in between his bar stool and the bar.

"Sit your ass on the foot rail, baby. My cock could use a little attention while I have a drink with Spencer."

Khloe Monroe had just finished sucking him off in the shower less than an hour before, which made her blushing embarrassment at being asked to give him a blowjob while he visited with his old buddy that much more adorable. After she was tucked away, her back against the bar and her head slightly bowed to keep from banging her head, Ryder spread his legs to give her the access she'd need.

Tentative fingers worked his belt buckle before unbuttoning his slacks and lowering his zipper. His hard shaft sprang out, anxious to be free of its fabric confines. Instead of swallowing him as she'd done in the shower, the little minx stuck her tongue out instead, lightly licking only the tip as if she were enjoying a lollipop. Ryder closed his eyes, enjoying the slow seduction of his submissive with a tortured groan.

"Holy shit, you have it bad, buddy."

Ryder forced his eyes open to throw his old pal a dirty glare. "Shut the fuck up. You're just jealous." Still, he couldn't stop himself from stroking Khloe's silky hair as she continued her tentative exploration under the bar.

"What the hell do I have to be jealous of? I can get it time I want," his friend bragged.

Spencer's assertion coincided with Klara's return. She placed a Black Light cocktail napkin on the glassy surface in front of Ryder before setting down his drink.

Only after she'd delivered the cocktail to her customer did she pin her boyfriend and Dom with a sassy glare. "Feeling a little overconfident there, sport, aren't you?"

"Excuse me? Are you aching to have your ass whipped tonight, little girl?" the dungeon master threatened.

Klara grinned confidently. "Promises, promises. You know we don't play while I'm working. Strictly professional. Boss and employee and all that."

"It's a quiet night. I think we're overstaffed."

"Had Adele shown up, maybe, but she called in sick. I'm working solo tonight."

Spencer grumbled, "Lucky for you then. You get a few hours reprieve, but your ass is mine the second you're off the clock."

Klara leaned across the bar to flame the fire with her Dom. "You mean like every other night? I'll look forward to it."

A loud disturbance near the entrance interrupted the dungeon master's flirtation. Spencer downed the last swallow of his own cocktail before pushing to his feet and addressing Ryder. "I'll leave you here to enjoy your drink and suck off while I go see what the commotion is about. Try not to shoot cum on the bar. It's a bitch to get off when it dries."

Ryder didn't bother replying. He was too busy enjoying Khloe's intensifying attention. She had a talented tongue and was presently putting it to very good use. He closed his eyes, loving how his submissive bobbed her head up and down, taking a bit more of his thick dick into her throat with each thrust. She'd wrapped her hand around the base of his cock, acting like a constricting cock-ring. While the pressure was nice, feeling the end of his erection slamming into the back of her throat would be even better.

"Hands behind your back. Use your tongue and throat only."

Khloe obeyed, releasing his cock to fling her arms back as he gripped her hair, yanking her forward, and stuffing his thick shaft deep down her throat until she gagged. The gurgling sound was an aphrodisiac to the dominant.

Ryder lost himself to the glorious sensations, tuning out the sounds of the club around them until it was only him and his submissive, connected in the most intimate of ways.

He was so zoned out, he almost missed Jaxson's voice talking behind him. "I thought they might be wrapping this up soon, but it looks like the old man is having some problems getting off."

It took a minute to register that the club owner was talking about him. Ryder was so close, he didn't want to break his concentration. He could tell his submissive was tiring as he needed to stop to allow her to gasp in air frequently. He opened his eyes, looking down on his princess. His heart swelled with affection as he took in her watering eyes, the excessive drool that seeped from her mouth, stretched wide to accommodate his flesh.

*She's never looked more beautiful.*

The visual perfection pushed him into his climax. The sadist in him loved watching his sub struggle to swallow his spurting jizz. When she pulled away to gasp for a breath, his last squirt shot hot spunk onto her heaving cleavage.

He adored the proud smirk that played on her face as she licked her lips clean. Ryder couldn't resist reaching out to scoop the glob of cum onto his finger, raising it to her mouth and demanding, "Open up, baby. You haven't finished yet."

She was in the process of sucking his finger clean when McLean's voice totally broke the mood.

"So this explains a lot."

Ryder hated the embarrassment that filled his lover's eyes as she leaned into him again, this time to bury her face in his lap, not to suck his cock, but to simply avoid looking at her bodyguard and friend.

He stroked her hair, trying to calm Khloe while getting to the bottom of exactly why a non-member was currently standing at the bar of Black Light. As he looked up into the mirrored wall supporting the shelves of liquors, he saw that Trevor was not alone. He was flanked by Davidson, Cartwright and their sub, Emma.

"I didn't know we were going to have a party here tonight. We'd have waited to get started if we'd known you were coming."

Jaxson stepped up next to him, leaning in to talk softly. "It seems your boss has been trying desperately to get ahold of you."

Ryder's tension level skyrocketed. How the hell would Davidson know that?

"I'm on paid leave. I'll call him tomorrow after Khloe's departure."

Trevor stepped up close on his other side. "I really think you should take the call now."

Ryder turned to take a better look at Khloe's bodyguard. "How did you get in here? You're not a member."

"I called Jaxson and told him it was an emergency."

"What's the emergency? There's no fucking way my boss called you."

"No, he didn't." Trevor hesitated before adding softly, "But he did call Axe."

Now that, Ryder believed. Webster knew Axe's history. He'd authorized contractor's access for Axel to the intel they'd needed to investigate not only the stalker case, but more importantly, the few leads he'd gotten over the years on Mia's disappearance.

Before Ryder could ask another question, McLean reached into the pocket of his jeans and pulled out the encrypted phone Ryder had given him to communicate during the stalker investigation. He shoved the phone at Ryder. "Webster is waiting for your call."

"Now? It's ten o'clock at night. He can wait..."

"For Christ's sake. I didn't go to all this trouble to come down here and watch my boss give you a blowjob. Fucking make the call."

Khloe had wrapped her arms around his waist and was hugging him with all her might. He made out what sounded like a distressed sob as her body started to vibrate against his.

Ryder pushed the phone out of the way to pull on her shoulders. "Hey, that's enough crying down there. I'm sure everything is fine. Come on up here."

He could barely make out her mumbled, "No,"

"Khloe. Now."

The second she was on her feet Ryder scooped her up into his arms and headed to a nearby open couch. As he passed Davidson, he grumbled. "Since when do you allow phones in Black Light, anyway?"

Jaxson pinned him with a serious glare. "Since it seems there is a matter of national security on the line."

Ryder sank into the leather, pulling Khloe into his lap before reaching out to snatch the phone that McLean was holding out to him. He didn't mind her burrowing into the crook of his neck to avoid making eye contact with her friend and bodyguard. Her scent helped calm his own racing heart.

Something big had to be going down to get this kind of attention from Brandon Webster.

He knew the number by heart. It was a requirement of his job to memorize certain phone numbers in case he had to destroy a phone that had been compromised. He often had to move to a new burner cell when things got intense.

Brandon Webster answered on the first ring. "You sonofabitch. Do you have any idea how much time I've wasted tracking you down?"

"Nice to hear your voice too, sir." Ryder forced a calmness into his tone that he didn't feel.

"Don't you dare hang up on me until I'm finished briefing you. Chip Marshall has turned into a major pain in my ass. Almost as big of a pain as you're turning out to be."

"Excuse me? I don't know why the hell we're even talking about Marshall. He's a civilian. I did my job. What the fuck does he have to do with anything?"

"You haven't done any research on him, have you?" The way his boss asked the question made Ryder feel like a dumbass for not having thought to do so himself.

"I've been a bit busy. Why don't you fill me in on the millionaire?"

"Chip Marshall is no millionaire. He is a fucking billionaire. He made his first millions in oil, but his biggest income these days comes from manufacturing."

"This is all very riveting, but..."

"Weapons manufacturing. Cutting-edge, experimental, secretive weapons to be more precise."

That shut Ryder up.

"Where do you think all of the shipments of the SVK semiautomatics suddenly appeared from when you needed them in a hurry?"

Webster paused. Ryder got the impression his boss was choosing his words carefully as he continued the briefing. "Marshall is a friend of our family, if you know what I mean. To say that he was furious to have his wife and young daughters put into danger would be a massive understatement. I can't even begin to express to you the depths of his gratitude towards you for risking your life and years of undercover work to save his family."

Ryder turned Brandon's words around in his brain, listening for the unspoken message his boss was relaying between the lines.

"Are you saying he's a man of action?" Ryder probed cautiously, trying not to let the inkling of hope in his gut lay down roots just yet.

"That's exactly what I'm saying. He has many influential business partners and those *partners* were able to finish the job that you started."

Ryder's heart hammered so hard, he felt his pulse pounding against his eardrums. Could it be true?

"I don't believe it. Are you telling me it was a sanctioned mission?"

"Hell no. I'm telling you that Marshall is a big enough fish that he doesn't give shit about being sanctioned or not. He went off the reservation on this one."

"So why are you the one telling me?"

"Because you won't get your head out of your ass and answer his fucking phone calls. You've turned me into a God-damned message boy and I don't like it."

Ryder didn't give a shit about his boss's aggravation. He was too busy trying to contain his sprouting hope that he was interpreting the message correctly.

"Have you seen visual proof?"

"Only photos."

"Any insider corroboration?"

"Police scanner transcripts. Funeral home hearse arrival/departures. State news reports. So far everything validates Marshall's claims."

Ryder refused to get his hopes up. There was too much at stake to get it wrong.

"And he's sure the count was three? Anything less than that is meaningless."

"I was able to get someone into the church for the joint funerals. There were three caskets."

"Open or Closed."

"Closed."

"Next of kin?"

"Three grieving widows and one grieving mother."

Ryder thought of Irena Volkov, dressed in black playing the part of the wife in mourning. He suspected she'd be relieved in private that the days of being beaten by her husband were now over.

Could he possibly believe his most dangerous enemies were dead?

His boss proved how well he knew Ryder by parroting his very thoughts. "I know you won't believe it until you're able to verify the job is done on your own."

"Yeah, and don't get me wrong. I'm grateful for you tracking me down to get the news to me, but why exactly couldn't this have waited until I came into the office in a few days?"

Webster's sardonic laughter filled the line. "Because Marshall or his aides call me three times a day, badgering me about why he hasn't connected with you yet. He's driving me fucking nuts."

"Why does he have such a hard-on to talk with me?"

"That's the best part. The asshole wants to offer you a job. Can you believe that shit? Seems he's looking to invest in other *business partners* who have your rather unique set of language and organizational skills, if you get my drift."

"So he asked my current boss to pass along the word that he's trying to poach me from active duty?"

"Can you believe the set of balls on the asshole?"

Ryder chuckled. "Actually, I can. It's the size of your balls I'm questioning. Pussy-whipped?"

"Fuck you. We both know Nicolai Romanovski is done in Russia and you're not the 'sit at a desk' kinda guy. So maybe I see an opportunity for a bit of a win-win-win here. Marshall wants you to consider being one of his new *business partners*. You have your next career move lined up that will put your unique skill set to work while allowing you to live your life in the open. Not to mention, I'm guessing he'll pay top dollar, unlike Uncle Sam."

The idea of being able to be seen in public with Khloe terrified him. What if their sources in Russia had been bought out? What if the stories of the Volkov men's demise had been a fabrication?

But what if it wasn't? Could he and Khloe really be free to live their lives together? Could the house in Malibu with the proverbial white picket fence be within his grasp?

"You said win-win-win. What's in this for you, Webster?"

"Nothing specific. I admit, it'll be nice to have a billionaire owe me a big favor. And I like the idea of having friends like you, with the right skills, available to me when I need to take an investigation off the grid, if you get my drift."

Ryder got his drift perfectly. Chip Marshall wouldn't be the only one who would owe Brandon Webster a big favor. If Ryder resigned to work for Marshall, his boss would be expecting to collect something in return at some point in the future. That was how these things worked.

The two men let a long silence fall between them as Webster gave Ryder the time he needed to think through all he'd learned.

"I'm not sure I can walk away yet. I'm gonna need to see the evidence collected so far first, but I will take Marshall's phone number. After all, talk is cheap, right?"

"I expected you'd say that. The bodyguard has a sealed envelope. It should have everything you'll be looking for. I had Hansen deliver it himself to the Marriott."

Ryder hadn't asked how his old handler was doing, but was happy to hear he was well enough to be up and on his feet.

He'd almost forgotten he was surrounded by some of their good friends. As Ryder looked up at Trevor who was standing a few feet away, he caught the bodyguard staring at an intense discipline scene taking place on one of the nearby platforms with great interest.

"Good enough. I'll be in touch then." He was about to end the call, but decided to add a final word at the last minute. "Thanks for tracking me down."

"No problem. Take care."

The call dropped, but Ryder wasn't ready to talk about all he'd heard. Not yet. He kept the phone to his ear for another full minute, using the time to think back through all he'd learned and make some decisions on what it all meant.

He wanted to believe that the Volkov men were all dead more than anything else in the world, but it all felt a bit too sensational. Knowing the crime family the way he did, he found it hard to believe they'd let their guard down long enough to get themselves dead, particularly all of them at the same time. Still, he knew they were often together and that they would have certainly all attended their father's funeral. Had he been on the ground with Marshall's business partners—AKA hitmen—that's where he would have made his move.

"Ryder?" Khloe's shaky voice penetrated his thoughts.

He gave up the ruse of listening, letting the phone drop onto the couch beside him as he hugged his woman hard against his chest. He let hope take seed, spreading through his body like a cool breeze on a hot day.

"Baby."

"Who was that?" she asked tentatively.

"My boss."

"What did he say?" Her question was almost a whisper against his ear.

He'd cut his right hand off to keep from knowingly hurting her. Could he get her hopes up only to dash them later?

Just as he prepared to lie to her for her own good, a flash of their goodbye back in February came to his mind. He'd lied to her that night. No matter that it had been to protect her, he couldn't bear the thought of hurting her again. Not now. Not if he didn't need to.

This was a hell of a time to take a leap of faith, but as he pulled her out of their embrace far enough so he could look into her watery eyes, a sense of calm he'd never felt before settled into his gut. It was unlike anything he'd ever experienced and yet, it felt oddly like he was finally coming home.

Home was where Khloe was.

"He said..." Ryder paused, unsure himself what words would come out of his mouth next. She was patient, waiting for him to clear his throat and announce the conversation to her and their friends. "He said that London is beautiful this time of year."

Khloe's mouth gaped open, almost as wide as she'd need to open to take in his erection. It was his turn to put his finger under her chin to lift up. "See something you like, baby?"

"Does this mean what I think it means?"

"Well if you think it means that I'm going to be there to watch what you eat every day and spank your ass before bed every night that you start to lose weight, then yes... it means what you think it means."

Her squeal of delight went straight to his privates. Despite having emptied his load less than thirty minutes before, his rod decided to rise to the occasion yet again.

Khloe was so excited she was pelting him with sweet kisses all over his face and neck. Their audience of friends had obviously heard the good news because he could hear Emma crying tears of joy behind him while her famous Doms took advantage of her obvious excitement.

Ryder was about to pull his cock out and try to make Khloe's who-ha even more sore when he realized Trevor was standing near the end of the couch looking like a fifth wheel.

Trevor chose then to announce to no one in particular. "Well, my work here is done. I guess I'll be going now." Ryder didn't miss the sadness in the bodyguard's tone. He got the impression Trevor was saying goodbye for more than just the night.

As the taller man moved in the direction of the entrance to the club, Ryder watched him weave his way through the kinky scenes of unknown club members, doing his best not to gawk at the X-rated medical examination in progress.

Like the rest of his decisions over the last hour, Ryder followed his gut. He pulled out of his embrace with Khloe to stand, sitting her on the couch and instructing her to "Stay." He took off after Trevor, having to almost jog to catch up to him just before he disappeared through the door that would lead him back through to Danny in the locker room.

"McLean. Wait up!"

Trevor stopped, but didn't turn around. "I need to leave. I don't belong here."

"Maybe. Maybe not."

"There is no maybe not. This is your world. Yours and Khloe's."

"You're wrong. This isn't our world. This is our playground."

The taller man turned around to pin him with a glare. "What difference does it make? She doesn't need me anymore. She has you now."

Ryder tamped down the pang of jealousy he felt at recognizing Trevor's clear affection for Khloe. He'd always known it was there. In fact, he'd counted on it.

"Listen, I'm not stupid. I know you have feelings for her, too." He paused, noticing her bodyguard didn't bother denying his accusation. "Here's the thing. I won't be able to be with her twenty-four seven. I don't know what this job offer is going to turn into, and I know that I need to help Axe find his missing daughter, even if it is to just bring her body home. He needs closure."

Ryder hadn't had nearly enough time to think through the options he would have in a world without the Volkovs. He would need a lot more time to know what path he would take. But he didn't need any time at all to know one thing.

"I love her, and it scares the shit out of me. This time the stalker threat was bogus, but what about the next time? We both know how truly talented she is. She'll only become a bigger celebrity--a bigger target--with every movie she releases. Every award she wins."

To his credit, McLean didn't interrupt him and he was grateful. It wasn't often Ryder had to give emotional speeches like the one he was presently delivering. "She needs you... I need you. I don't trust easy and since she is now the most important thing on the planet to me, it's important to me to surround her with people I trust."

A sly smile played at the taller man's mouth. "So you actually trust me then." It was a statement, not a question.

"To protect her with your life, sure." Ryder grinned as he added, "You just better keep your dick away from her. I don't share."

Trevor had the audacity to chuckle. "You don't say. I'd never guess that about you."

"Smart ass."

McLean's gaze locked on something behind him as Khloe rushed between the two men. She glanced back and forth between them as if she were prepared to break up a fight. If McLean didn't take his eyes off her skimpy outfit, she might have to.

"There you are, Princess," he said as he reached out to pull her against his side, wrapping his arm around her waist. She melted against him, exactly where she belonged. "McLean and I were discussing the plan for tomorrow's flight to London, weren't we?"

Trevor took one last look at Khloe and then locked his gaze with Ryder. "Yep. I'll have Ricky make the flight arrangements for you to join us. I'll be at the entrance to the Psychic Shop with the limo at eleven, that is unless you'd like me to come up and act like your bellboy again."

Ryder grinned. "Naw, I think I can manage."

"That's good, because my bellboy days are over. Got it?"

"Fair enough."

"Now, if you'll excuse me, I'm gonna head up to Runway and throw back a few beers. I'll see you two kids in the morning."

For a second, it looked like he might lean in to kiss Khloe, but then he thought better of it. Once the door slammed closed behind him, Khloe looked up at Ryder, tears in her eyes.

"What just happened there?"

Ryder pulled her tighter against him. "Nothing you need to worry about, Princess. McLean and I had a few details to iron out."

"Like what?"

He scooped her into his arms and turned to carry her towards the dungeon room where he had the sudden desire to recreate one of their scenes from Valentine's night. "You don't need to worry about it, baby. In fact, I think you'd better start worrying about all of the devious things I'm planning on doing to this gorgeous body of yours."

As he pushed into the expansive medieval inspired space, he was happy to see they had the dimly lit room to themselves.

Only after he scaled the steps to the stage did he put Khloe's feet on the floor. She craned her neck to look around the space, taking in the pointed wooden horse, St. Andrew's cross and dozens of punishment implements on display.

"I was so afraid of you the last time we were here together. It feels like a lifetime ago."

Ryder understood completely, yet her words bothered him. "So are you still afraid of me, Princess?"

Her smile could light a full-city block. "The only thing that still scares me is you leaving."

Ryder unbuttoned the buttons at the cuff of his left sleeve and then began rolling up the fabric. As he rolled up his right cuff, he took a step closer to Khloe. Their eyes locked as he moved to unbuckle his leather belt. He purposefully let the leather snap as he quickly pulled it free of his belt loops.

Khloe's eyes widened as she realized he was stalking towards her. The sadist in him fed on the lick of fear he saw jump into her gaze as he cracked the belt against the empty wooden pony. They were going to have so much fun playing out every single deprived kink his dirty mind could think of, but not until he did one thing first.

He stopped his advance on his submissive to ask. "Princess, what's your safeword tonight?"

And just like that, the fear in her gaze was replaced with a love that he wouldn't trade for the world.

Khloe grinned her most mischievous smile before answering, "Roulette."

"Perfection."

# EPILOGUE

*A*lexi Ivanov pulled the collar up on his jacket to keep the early May chill at bay. Had he known when he left the house that morning that he'd be sitting on a bench in the cold for almost an hour, he would have made different choices in wardrobe.

He took his final cigarette out, wadding up the now empty wrapper and throwing it into the last remnants of a dirty, melting pile of snow already polluted with a garbage can's worth of trash. Not for the first time, he considered leaving.

He replayed the details of the anonymous phone call he'd received on his personal cell phone hours before. The phone that no one but his Volkov brothers had the number to. The mysterious voice on the other end had been brief, but had dangled a carrot he couldn't resist; information on enemy number one.

Only the promise of getting a lead on tracking the traitor Nicolai Romanovski kept him waiting in the chill.

Alexi may not share the Volkov last name, but he was more aware than ever before that he shared their blood. Now that his cousins had been murdered like their father before them, the remaining members of the Bratva were looking to him for leadership.

To say he was in over his head was an understatement.

All his life, he'd been a second-class member of the family at best. Unlike his cousins, his mother had shielded him from the harsher realities of growing up a Volkov, making sure he enjoyed the freedoms of attending university and traveling abroad. He hadn't been groomed for leadership since he was a kid like his cousins Artel, Vladimir and Oleg had been, and it was already showing.

He didn't know the first thing about setting up arms deals with the dangerous underground criminals of the world or smuggling drugs or flesh across the Russian boarders. He'd been a simple soldier. A mule.

Muscles who took orders.

With his cousin's sons all under the age of ten, the remaining Volkov Bratva henchmen now looked to Alexi as the heir apparent to the Volkov kingdom. He was to give the orders now instead of take them. He had dived in, determined to learn as fast as he could. So far the hardest part of the job had been figuring out exactly who he could trust.

While there were many things he was still unsure of, there was one mission he knew he needed to carry out with great clarity. His Uncle Viktor would never rest easy in his grave until Nicolai Romanovski was hunted, tortured and killed. That he and Nicolai had been good friends only angered Alexi that much more. He had trusted the arms dealer and he'd been duped; made to look like an idiot and he didn't like it.

It was dark, almost nine, when a nondescript sedan pulled up to the sidewalk in front of the bench he'd been perched on. The back passenger door sprung open, but no one exited the vehicle. After a few long seconds, Alexi rose on his stiff legs and slowly approached the vehicle. The windows were tinted so dark, he couldn't see anything or anyone inside.

"Please join me, Mr. Ivanov."

That voice. It was so familiar, yet he couldn't place it. Desperate for information, Alexi took a leap of faith and took a seat in the back of the black car. There were no interior lights to see by, so the passenger in the seat next to him remained a shadow. The eyes of the driver met his in the rearview mirror as they passed under an overhead street lamp. He was relieved to see it was George, his uncle's chauffeur.

"It wasn't wise to get into the car without knowing who was picking you up."

His fellow passenger choose to lecture him, which Alexi found ironic.

"Considering you refused to identify yourself to me on the phone, I'm not sure what option you left me."

"Considering the men in your family have been hunted like prey, I'd think you'd be a bit more careful."

Alexi tried not to get defensive, but failed. He needed to know who the fuck dared to talk to him with such superiority. He pulled his cell phone from his jacket pocket and turned on the flashlight app, shining it directly into the face of his fellow passenger.

"Yurdin. Why didn't you tell me you wanted to talk with me? I would have driven out."

Relief to find his uncle's longtime butler sitting next to him was quickly replaced with confusion.

"It wasn't safe to make contact until I knew you weren't being followed."

"And how did you do that?" Alexi inquired.

"I had you followed, of course."

The men rode for several minutes in silence. Alexi's mind raced, trying to understand why the longtime Volkov household servant had contacted him.

He took a guess. "Is this about uncle's will?"

Yurdin growled. "No, although it is about his legacy."

Weren't they the same thing?

After ten minutes of driving through the back streets of Moscow, Alexi recognized they were on the way out to the mansion in Barvikha. He hadn't been there since the night Nicolai had shot and killed Viktor.

The night everything had changed forever.

The drive took much longer with George at the wheel of the sedan than Alexi in his beloved Ferrari. If Nicolai had done nothing but steal and crash his prized possession, it would have been enough to want to hunt him down and make him hurt. But Nicolai had done oh so much more. That night had been the beginning of the end of the Volkov Bratva as he'd known it the entirety of his life.

The driver pulled the car to a stop at the entrance to the estate. The guards at the gate had changed. Gone was the carefree banter of his last visit. Tonight's security sweep was all business. The visual inspection of the guard holding a bright flashlight on the occupants of the sedan wasn't enough. One by one, each of the three men had to place their palm on the screen of a tablet and wait until their identity was confirmed before the guard finally stepped back, nodding to his counterpart in the guardhouse to open the recently repaired and fortified gate.

No one would be crashing a car through the entrance barricade again and live to tell about it.

It was odd to have Yurdin scaling the tall steps at the front of the house next to him instead of waiting to open the front door as was the custom for the butler. It was even more strange when the portal was opened by an unknown servant who bowed regally to them as they were ushered into the house.

Alexi didn't need to be told where they were going. Tonight's visit was business and all family business took place in the underground fortress. Memories of his last trip down the winding stairs with Nicolai beside him flooded back to him. On his last visit, it had been Irena Volkov who been there to surprise them. Today, it was his Aunt Yana, Viktor's widow, standing at the bottom of the steps, dressed from head to toe in black and looking like she hadn't slept in weeks. She probably hadn't. Losing one's husband and all three sons would do that to a woman.

Alexi was unsure of the protocol for their meeting. On the one hand, this was his aunt. He had fond memories of a woman who'd taught him how to color Easter eggs and swim in the sea as a child.

Yet he knew that tonight's visit was about business. It suddenly dawned on him that he and Yana had something in common. The family was looking to her, like Alexi, for leadership in the vacuum left by the men in her life.

As the awkward meeting extended, Alexi leaned in, placing customary kisses of greeting on first one and then the other cheek of the grieving woman. "Aunt Yana, I am so sorry for your loss."

She surprised him with fiery words. "We have no time for such things," she scolded. She turned to Yurdin to ask, "Did you inform him?"

"No, ma'am. It was not my place and it was not secure."

"Very good. Goodnight, Yurdin."

The stately servant bowed and turned to retrace his steps, having been dismissed.

Alexi watched as the mourning woman reached into the pocket of her black slacks and pulled out a key ring before turning to approach the fortified doors to the Volkov man cave. It was a testament to how much had changed that the lady of the house was leading him into a space he was certain she'd never been before her husband's death. The only women to enter before had been hookers and enemies who'd come there to die.

The space was almost empty. Remnants of their past carefree life remained of course, out of place now with such heaviness. The billiards table sat unused. Card tables had no gamblers. Even the spanking bench where there had always been a woman on display for the men's use was bare.

At least his uncle's blood had been cleaned from the stairs. In fact, the pungent scent of cleaning solution permeated the enclosed space.

His aunt led the way silently to the thick, carved double-doors that marked the entrance to the heart of the Volkov Bratva. The fortress within the fortress.

Not surprisingly, new security features had been installed since his last visit. Two cameras had been installed at the upper corners of the doors. One was currently scanning the room for threats while the second zoomed in on Alexi and his aunt.

A retinal and biometric panel was now a fixture on the wall to the right of the doors, yet his aunt did not move to open the door. Instead she turned towards her nephew to stare up into his eyes. He felt like he was being weighed and measured by her weary, yet experienced gaze. Yana may have married into the Volkovs, but in that moment, he was reminded how strong she was. Those eyes had seen things most women would have shrunk away from, yet here she stood, defiant. A Volkov at her core.

"Alexi, our family has suffered great loss."

"Yes, matriarch."

"I've received reports of your efforts to keep the family's businesses together during this time of uncertainty. Your uncle would be proud and grateful for your efforts."

Conflicting emotions warred inside him. Pride for being recognized for his leadership was overshadowed by the knowledge that he was doing a poor job at best. He was relieved when his aunt did not criticize him.

"Thank you, Yana. Your support means the world to me."

She paused, inspecting him in silence before speaking again. "I suspect that, like me, you are finding it hard to know who to trust in this time of uncertainty."

"It is my biggest concern," he answered truthfully.

"As it is mine." She paused again before adding, "I have decided to trust you, Alexi, with my biggest secret."

His pulse quickened at her words. Secrets were the bread and butter of the crime family, but having lost all those she loved to violence, he knew how hard trust must come to his aunt, particularly now.

"I am honored by your trust. I pledge my undying loyalty to you and the memory of my uncle and cousins."

"This makes me happy, Alexi, at a time when I have had very little to feel happiness about." She paused. Her words did not match her expression. There was no joy as she continued, "There is one favor I must ask of you. Do not take my request lightly, for if you agree to my appeal, much weight will be added to your shoulders."

He didn't doubt her warning, yet there was nothing, short of a bullet to the head, that could stop him from pledging his loyalty to her and what remained of the family.

"It will be my honor to grant you any favor you wish."

"So be it. From this day forward, you will be known as Alexi Volkov. Alexi Ivanov is no more. He was your youth. Alexi Volkov is your future."

There had been a time when he'd have given anything to be asked to change his name. He remembered a recent discussion about it with none other than Nicolai himself. Yet tonight, recognizing that it was open hunting season on the Volkov men, he recognized the gravity of his aunt's request.

They stood silently for several long seconds, each unsure of the proper protocol for the momentous occasion. Acting on instinct, Alexi reached for her wrinkled hand and lifted it to his lips. He first kissed her weathered skin and then the large ruby ring his uncle had put on her finger the day they had married almost forty years before.

"You honor me, babushka."

He used the term of endearment and respect his cousins had used for their mother. It brought tears to her eyes that she swished away impatiently.

"We have no time for weakness. There is much work to

be done."

Her strength awed him as she stood a bit taller and added. "You must not speak of what you are about to see outside of these fortress walls. Your life... the lives of my grandchildren... depend on it."

She turned and placed her palm onto the electronic pad while she leaned forward to let the retinal scanner read her unique eye print. The sound of a pop coincided with a low buzz coming from the thick, double doors in front of them. Yana turned the now unlocked old-world brass knob to gain access to the private Volkov cave.

The room was dark and empty. The long dining table bare. Alexi scanned the space, half expecting to find his uncle or cousins sitting in the lounging area, but it too was empty. The naked serving girl, absent.

The raised platform where the poor Linenkos woman had been tortured on his last visit was now hidden behind a velvet curtain that gave the room the feeling of being at a dinner theater or maybe the ballet. Alexi hoped his aunt never found out about the despicable horrors that had been perpetrated against dozens of women and a more than a few men within these walls.

Alexi was confused. He had been led to believe there was some secret here, yet the room was bare. He turned to look at his aunt who simply nodded towards the velvet curtain.

He moved slowly, walking around the long table with deliberate strides before climbing the three steps that took him to the stage level. He reached out to pull the curtain aside with trembling fingers.

Alexi's heart stopped beating. His lungs stopped breathing. Time froze as he tried to comprehend what he was seeing.

A hospital bed stood exactly where the Linenkos spy had been strung up his last time there. A stately nurse in an all-white uniform stood at the head of the bed, examining the many electronic displays and writing notes on a clipboard. A bag of IV solution hung from a clear bag at the head of the bed.

Movement from the corner of his eye drew his attention. An elderly doctor who looked vaguely familiar sat behind a small desk along the back wall of the stage. The men's eyes locked briefly before the doctor nodded tersely in his direction before returning his attention to the computer monitor in front of him.

But it was the unmoving body in the bed that captured and held his attention for long minutes. He found himself inching forward, taking small steps, trying to get closer to get a better look at the lifeless form hooked to all of the life-saving equipment.

The closer he moved, the more distressed Alexi got. Despite being only a few feet away, it was not possible for him to recognize the man in the bed. White gauze covered most of his skin, but that which was exposed was burned and raw. Round, deep holes were randomly dispersed where fragments of hot explosives had burrowed into the victim's body, burning deep below the skin.

He felt rather than saw his aunt step next to him. They stood silently, each looking down at the shell of a man in front of them. It was difficult to know for sure because the entire left side of his face was burned beyond recognition, but as he stared at the lifeless body, Alexi filled with hope for the first time.

He prompted his aunt. "Vladimir?"

"Yes. My strongest son. Our family's hope."

Unbelievably, at the sound of them talking, the patient's eyes fluttered open, although it seemed to take his cousin a moment to focus through the clear agony of pain he was suffering.

His mother motioned to the nurse, "He needs more morphine for the pain."

It was her son who silenced her. "No. Can't... think..." he gritted out.

Tears blurred Alexi's vision and he hated himself in that

moment for the weakness. If Vlad could survive the bombing and the excruciating pain, he sure as hell would be tough too.

Alexi didn't know what words to say. He finally got out, "Cousin."

Vlad opened his mouth to speak, but his reply was only a whisper. Still, it filled Alexi with pride and courage.

"Alexi... my new brother."

The End

⌒

THANK you for reading **Black Light: Rescued**. I hope you'll look forward to the continuing story of Ryder, Khloe and the Volkovs as we begin the next Black Collar Press suspense series called *Black Sky Ops*. Billionaire, Chip Marshall, will be bankrolling Ryder, Axel and a team of talented mercenaries they assemble to take on the world's most dangerous crime families. Both men will need to make hard choices when it comes to fulfilling their duty to their country while protecting those they love.

BLACK SKY OPS will debut in early 2018.

AND COMING IN FEBRUARY, 2018 will be the next installment of roulette fun, with the release of **Black Light: Roulette Redux**. Like last year, I'll be joined by many talented authors to take our kinky game of roulette to a whole new level.

# ABOUT THE AUTHOR

USA Today bestselling author Livia Grant lives in Chicago with her husband and two sons... one a teenager, the other a furry rescue dog named Max. She is blessed to have traveled extensively and as much as she loves to visit places around the globe, the Midwest and its changing seasons will always be home. Livia started writing when she felt like she finally had the life experience to write a riveting story that she hopes her readers won't be able to put down. Livia's fans appreciate her deep character driven plots, often rooted in an ensemble cast where the friendships are as important as the romance... well, almost. She writes one hell of an erotic romance.

~

*Connect with Livia!*
www.liviagrant.com
lb.grant@yahoo.com

# ALSO BY LIVIA GRANT

**Black Light Series**

Infamous Love, A Black Light Prequel

Black Light: Rocked

Black Light: Valentine Roulette

Black Light: Rescued

Black Light: Roulette Redux

**Passion Series**

Wanting it All

Securing it All

Having it All

Protecting it All

Expecting it All

**Corbin's Bend Series**

Life's Unexpected Gifts

Psychology of Submission

**Red Petticoat Saloon Series**

Melting Silver

## Anthologies and Boxed Sets

Twist

The More the Merrier Two

A Lovely Meal

Sting of Lust

Hero to Obey

Royally Mine


## Stand Alone Books

Blessed Betrayal

Call Sign: Thunder


Don't miss Livia's next book!

Sign-up for Livia's Newsletter

Follow Livia on Amazon

Follow Livia on BookBub

# BLACK COLLAR PRESS

Did you enjoy your visit to Black Light? Have you read the other books in the series?

Infamous Love, A Black Light Prequel by Livia Grant
Black Light: Rocked by Livia Grant
Black Light: Exposed by Jennifer Bene
Black Light: Valentine Roulette by Various Authors
Black Light: Suspended by Maggie Ryan
Black Light: Cuffed by Measha Stone
Black Light: Rescued by Livia Grant
Black Light: Roulette Redux by Various Authors

Black Collar Press is a small publishing house started by authors Livia Grant and Jennifer Bene in late 2016. The purpose was simple - to create a place where the erotic, kinky, and exciting worlds they love to explore could thrive and be joined by other like-minded authors.

If this is something that interests you, please go to the Black Collar Press website and read through the FAQs. If your questions are not answered there, please contact us directly at: blackcollarpress@gmail.com.

WHERE TO FIND BLACK COLLAR PRESS:

- Website: http://www.blackcollarpress.com/
- Facebook: https://www.facebook.com/blackcollarpress/
- Twitter: https://twitter.com/BlackCollarPres

# THANK YOU FROM LIVIA

Like most authors, I love to hear from my readers. The art of writing can be a lonely activity at times. Authors sit alone, pouring our hearts into our stories, hoping readers will connect with our words and fall in love with our characters. It's easy to get discouraged at times.

And that's where you come in.

I'd sure appreciate it if you'd take a few minutes to drop me a line or better yet, leave a review to let me know what you thought of the book you just finished. Reader feedback, good and bad, is what helps me continue to grow stronger as an author.

Happy reading!

*Livia*

Made in the USA
Columbia, SC
18 January 2020